The Shape of Sand

The Shape of Sand

MARJORIE ECCLES

This edition first published in Great Britain in 2005 by
Allison & Busby Limited
Bon Marché Centre
241-251 Ferndale Road
London SW9 8BJ
http://www.allisonandbusby.com

A catalogue record for this book is available from
the British Library.

10 9 8 7 6 5 4 3 2 1

ISBN 0 7490 8399 9

Printed and bound in Great Britain by
Bookmarque Ltd, Croydon, Surrey

Marjorie Eccles was born in Yorkshire and spent much of her childhood there and on the Northumbrian coast. The author of over twenty books, serials and short stories, she is the recipient of the Agatha Christie Short Story Styles Award. Living on the edge of the Black Country, where she taught creative writing, inspired the acclaimed Gil Mayo series. A keen gardener, she now lives with her husband in Hertfordshire.

The screech of metal against metal as the demolition team moved in was excruciating, shattering the peace, setting the teeth on edge, though it was unlikely anyone would complain about it; not when it meant the end of the Anderson shelters which had defaced the sweeping lawns at Charnley House for the last seven years. At last they were surplus to requirements, a wartime necessity that had been accepted without fuss, though in the event not a single bomb had ever fallen within five miles. Unfortunately, a prefabricated module was apparently scheduled to take their place.

Harriet, watching the activity from inside the house, hardly knew whether to laugh or cry at all this, imagining what Hopper and his under-gardeners would have said to the desecration of that smooth green sward they and their fathers had spent their working lives so jealously nurturing and tending. These were the lawns where the croquet hoops had been set up, where she and her siblings had played as children, where they'd rolled down the grass either side of the steps to the terrace, and Daisy, who was a pickle, had got her starched petticoats all green.

"Well, here it all is, Miss Jardine. You're welcome to it."

"Thank you."

Harriet turned away from the window towards the woman who was indicating a couple of mottled grey cardboard box-files sitting on the nearest desk. The files themselves she regarded with some misgivings. She wasn't yet by any means convinced that it would be right to bring into the light of day what they contained, or whether the contents would be better left undisturbed. Indeed, she still hadn't decided whether it had been a good idea to come back to Charnley at all, thirty-seven years after she'd left, swearing never to return. Ladies of a certain age are apt to be resistant to change, however adaptable they might consider themselves. But the papers had been an irresistible carrot, as Guy had known they would be.

Ruth Standish, a brisk, capable person, an ex-ATS lieutenant as she'd informed Harriet over lunch, known to all as the Admin Assistant, was voicing some concern. "I do hope all this won't be too distressing for you."

It could hardly fail to be otherwise, but that was scarcely the point. "I believe I shall cope. It's all history now."

All the same, that treacherous old sorrow suddenly gripped Harriet by the throat, so that, for a moment, she couldn't say any more, even though she'd come here prepared for an emotional battering. It was only occasionally now that she was caught unawares like this, transported back in time by glimpses of something half-remembered: her mother's special rose and lily-of-the-valley scent, warm sunlight on peaches, a snatch of ragtime or a tune from an operetta, the intense blue of someone's eyes.

The lid of the top file was half open, the spring clip inside unable to cope with its overflowing contents. The Admin Assistant extracted a bulky envelope from it, enabling it to be closed, and slid both files towards Harriet. Her expression left Harriet in no doubt as to what she was thinking: almost certainly, she'd decided that this was a lady who wouldn't allow herself to be upset, or not for long – who belonged, after all, to that generation who never gave in to themselves. It was what had got them, and everyone else, through two world wars. Harriet must be at least – what, late fifties? Smart hat and couturier-made classic suit that owed nothing to present day fashion, and still looked marvellous, never mind that it had to be pre-1939. Quality told, and its soft moss green colour suited her brown eyes and dark, silver-threaded hair. She was tall and had kept her figure, and moved gracefully. Well, they were brought up to walk and hold themselves properly, those Edwardian girls, no slouching. Without the need for all that standing stiffly to attention, either, or marching, so inappropriate for women, that had been inflicted on the Admin Assistant herself in her square-bashing days – which was at the same time as Harriet Jardine herself, she believed, had been working for the Government as some sort of boffin. Before the war, she had been a mathematics don. A daunting combination, all in all. She still had that spark in her eye which said she could be pretty daunting herself.

"Not to worry," Harriet was saying briskly. "They won't tell me anything I don't already know."

It gave her some satisfaction that she could speak so calmly about that old scandal which had catapulted Charnley into sensational headlines nearly four decades ago, and was still remembered as one of the unsolved mysteries of the century. But she was feeling more in control now than when she had stepped through the front door earlier that morning, having schooled herself to cope with the painful memories it would evoke, yet half expecting, half dreading, to discover Charnley exactly as she had left it, as if caught in a time warp. She needn't have worried. A few of the rooms remained basically the same, but most of the alterations and renovations – some good, most appalling – had turned the house into a different place altogether from the one she remembered. The spirit of the old Charnley had gone for ever, though the shocking events – or perhaps her own perception of them – had left an indelible stain on the air that saddened and depressed her.

She had been shown around and then given a surprisingly good lunch, created by someone with flair who had cunningly overcome the constraints imposed by post-war rationing and shortages. The new dining hall had been created from the former conservatory, a place once full of green shadows and glancing light, but now made gloomy and unrecognisable, since they had seen fit to put up, against one of the formerly all-glass walls, some sort of temporary extension. In her present hypercritical mood Harriet took a dim view of this excrescence. The meal over, Ruth Standish had brought her here into the library. Which was another matter altogether.

This spacious room had always been a place of sanctuary for Harriet, at the heart of the house, but its former ambience of peace, stability and continuity had gone for ever. It was the absence of the pictures more than anything else, she decided, that so radically altered it: the self-important portraits of Rodhythes, and later ones of Jardines, heavily gold-framed, that had once hung in alcoves and in the lofty spaces above the bookshelves. Yet even apart from that, the big old room seemed ill at ease with itself, as if rejecting its new role. The space once occupied by the heavy mahogany central desk and, in front of the open fireplace, the comfortable leather armchairs and sofas in which one could curl up and lose oneself, was now filled with functional seating and army surplus desks and tables, complete with typewriters and telephones and comptometers. Like some monstrous cash register, a Burroughs calculating machine loomed in the corner, waiting for a home. The Turkey carpet had been replaced by a sort of drugget. Gone were the impressive rows of old leather tomes, in favour of stacks of files and stationery and serried rows of insurance documents. Worst of all, the chimney opening in the fireplace had been filled in with asbestos, painted over. It scarcely mattered, there would be no one now to tend the enormous coal fires the grate had once held, even supposing the fuel were available.

Perhaps in an effort to retain traces of the original spirit of the fine old library amongst all this gracelessness, someone had painted the walls a deep ox-blood tone. Surprisingly, that seemed the least of the incongruities, maybe because the colour was, by chance or design, almost the same rich, dark red as the old damask wallpaper which had covered them for at least a century, quite possibly for a great deal longer. As children, they'd hated that gloomy old wallpaper, but Harriet now regretted the removal of something which must be irreplaceable. Tastes change as one grows older.

She opened her crocodile handbag for her gloves and began to draw them on – soft brown suede, elegantly wrinkled at the wrist – snapped the bag's gold clasp and prepared to go. She'd had enough of this new Charnley, and its owners.

All the same, she was grateful to Ruth Standish for having recognised immediately that what the builders had come across might be of sentimental value to the Jardines, otherwise the papers would have been thrown out as so much useless junk, like everything else, during the process of adapting the house to its newly designated purposes. Charnley had stood empty for several years before the First World War had brought a final end to any hope of it ever becoming the family home again, but during that war it had been adapted temporarily as a convalescent home, where soldiers in hospital blue had been helped to recreate what was left of their shattered lives. Afterwards, it had again lain largely empty and neglected (except for the two or three years when a couple of women had made a brave but unsuccessful attempt to run it as a girls' boarding school) during which time it had gathered its quota of superstition and a reputation as a house of ill luck. In 1940 the army had commandeered it as an officers' billet for the duration.

World War Two and the Blitz might now be only a wretched memory, but post-war austerity ruled while run-down Britain was picking itself up. Life was still bound by restrictions and shortages of nearly everything, including materials for all but essential rebuilding and rehousing schemes. So, despite the house's past, and its long period of disuse and neglect, a large City insurance firm which had been bombed out and since housed in temporary premises, had now acquired Charnley as its head office. Its semi-rural situation in the Home Counties was considered not too far out of London and, after months of work, it was almost ready to open. The reconstruction had been done in haste and was regrettable, but then, Charnley had never been the most beautiful of houses. The work still wasn't entirely complete; they hadn't yet started on what had come to be known to the family as the Jessamy rooms, in the west wing. On her tour round the house, Harriet hadn't seen these rooms. She hadn't wanted to. Everything bad had stemmed from that.

"Don't forget the photos." Ruth Standish picked up the bulging manila envelope, so full indeed that it spilled open and deposited most of its contents on to the floor as she passed it across. "Drat, I should've looked for a bigger envelope."

"No harm done."

The Admin Assistant produced a folded brown paper carrier from her own large tote bag. "Here, better use this." They both knelt to gather the escaped photographs, but while Ruth proceeded to tip the photos in, Harriet's gaze was transfixed by one she'd picked out at random.

"Someone you know on that one?"

"Myself and my sisters."

"Really?" Ruth Standish took a look at it and added, unaware of any irony, "You were lovely, all of you, weren't you?" Harriet smiled a little. The very young – and sometimes even those not quite so young, as in this case – were always astonished to be reminded that their elders once had faces as smooth and unlined as their own.

Here they were, the three Jardine girls, nearly forty years ago, youthful and vulnerable when one contemplated the horror that hung so imminently over them: personal loss and sorrow, and the black cloud of that first, terrible, unimaginable war. Posing here in the summer garden at Charnley in fancy dress. Barefoot, wearing robes that were vaguely Grecian, forming a circle with their arms gracefully lifted and disposed, hands linked, fingers artfully intertwined – oh, how they'd agonised over that pose! The scene looked idyllic now, the sepia tones of the old photograph softening the white garments to a golden tint, with the flower-strewn grass and the trees and the folly behind in soft focus. She and Vita, each with their dark hair done up in a classical knot, Daisy with her cascade of shining pale hair, so like their mother's, rippling down her back. It was still thick, though ashen now, and serviceably short. Daisy led too busy a life to be bothered with such personal vanities.

Harriet put the photo into the bag with the others. "What alterations were they making to the schoolroom when they found all this?"

The administrator's eyes rested curiously on Harriet, who ignored the unspoken question: why, if she'd known the papers were in the schoolroom, hadn't she claimed them before? But Harriet knew it wouldn't make much sense if she were to confess that she had, in some instinctive, sentimental move that was totally unlike her, secreted the papers in that old childhood hidey-hole before she'd left for the last time. Nor would she necessarily be believed if she tried to explain that time, and pain, had suppressed even the memory of that particular act until now.

There were two plans of the house pinned to a large corkboard mounted on the wall: a copy of the original, which had been drawn on oiled silk, and another of the house as it had now been converted, showing most of the spacious, airy rooms made into two, or even three. Using her pen as a pointer, Ruth Standish indicated the turreted gatehouse, a later, and not very felicitous, addition to the main buildings, which stood at the bottom of the drive, where the builders were still working, and therefore, like the Jessamy rooms, hadn't been included in Harriet's tour of inspection. "They're making it into a reception area. The box was under the floorboards. Here, in this room upstairs. And you say it was your old schoolroom?"

"And playroom. Not always very convenient when the weather was bad, but we loved it. They let us use it because we could be as noisy as we liked there."

Harriet looked at the plan again, and followed the orientation of the familiar long view from the gatehouse window towards the point where the Norman tower of the church was just visible above a stretch of woodland, now mature enough to obscure most of the village surrounding it, as well as the housing developments which had later grown up along the valley. Between the house and the trees stretched a Gainsborough landscape. Acres of sweeping parkland, designed by Humphrey Repton to sit within a framework of rolling hills, beech forest and chalk downs. She still had a watercolour of that view, painted by Vita. One of Marcus's friends who had often visited had famously written about it, later, from the trenches: '*And in the half-light of remembered days we see the shadows fall…*' Quickly, Harriet stood up.

She said goodbye to Ruth Standish, clasped her arms around the bulging files, entrusted that last photo with the others to the care of Mr Sainsbury's brown paper carrier, and drove away through the archway, past the shiny new dark green sign with Vigilance Assurance's name writ large upon it above the company's logo of two clasped hands.

The dusk of a cool, early autumn day was just beginning to fall when she arrived at the place she presently called home, the small cottage next to the church in Garvingden, a quiet grey village above the Thames, about thirty miles away.

It was really time she found somewhere else to live, she told herself as she walked up the front path, edged with London Pride and a late flush of sweet-smelling Mrs Sinkins. She was becoming too fond of the place, unwisely so, since it wasn't hers to love. After the war, she had found herself at a loose end, almost at retirement age and, for the short working time left to her, reluctant to return to university teaching. She would find something else to do, she decided. Meanwhile, unused to having time on her hands, she had taken on the admittedly not very interesting but no doubt worthwhile job of marking papers in a correspondence course designed as rehabilitation for demobbed service men and women. But while she had been spending the war years as a decrypter at Bletchley Park, helping to break the enemy's coded messages, London had become a different place from the one she'd known. Physical landmarks had disappeared for ever, but what mattered more was the absence of people she had known who were no longer there, for one reason or another. The little house where her friend Frances had lived had vanished from the face of the earth after being hit fairly and squarely by a flying bomb, killing Frances herself. And that street where for a brief time she had known love, and so much unhappiness, was a heap of rubble and bomb craters. Bittersweet memories were the only things that remained. All desire to live permanently in the battle-scarred capital had left Harriet.

She had taken advantage of Daisy's generous offer to stay with her and her husband, Guy, in their Maida Vale house until she could find some small place in the country, but accommodation was scarce everywhere, and nothing suitable had turned up. She was beginning to feel she must be outstaying her welcome with Daisy when she'd unexpectedly had the chance to take over the lease of his weekend cottage from a university colleague who, with the return to peace, had taken a three-year sabbatical to do anthropological research in a remote part of South America. It was a former workman's cottage of two up, two down – a small kitchen-living room at the back, a minuscule front parlour, one of the two bedrooms now a bathroom – but Harriet didn't complain: the last occupants before Tony Bentham had managed to bring up a family of five children in the house. Furnishings and amenities were basic. Tony wasn't houseproud, but then, neither was Harriet. Yet lately, she'd found herself buying bits and pieces of her own, whatever took her fancy, that she thought might suit the house, and even plants for the tiny garden plots, back and front. She'd had all the rooms repainted. The result was still a long way from Charnley, but it was full of light and colour, comfortable enough and easily managed. She had to keep reminding herself it would be foolish to become too fond of the place.

After that very good lunch at Charnley she wasn't hungry, so she settled for a cup of tea and took it into the front room. She found a place for the box files by removing her correspondence course papers from the table under the window to the floor. Sipping her tea, she looked at them with misgivings, reluctant to open what she was already beginning to think of as Pandora's box. Could they possibly contain anything forgotten that would add to the sum of what was already known about the actual circumstances of those long-ago events? She doubted it. It was tempting to feel that the situation should be left as it was, the files put away, and leave undisturbed the dust that had eventually settled. On the other hand, by sorting through them, some sort of perspective might be found to reduce the ballyhoo that had always surrounded the business. It had remained one of the most colourful of those society scandals of the twentieth century, kept alive in the public consciousness by the rehashings of the events in which an insatiable public seemed to delight. Mention 'The Jardine Affair' to anyone, even now, and they'd soon recall what the papers of the time had said. But there had always been something out of balance about the theories put forward by those who had written about it. It would be enlightening to see how their suppositions and speculations, some of which had been bizarre, would stand up in the light of anything new that might turn up.

In the end, unable to resist it, she tipped the papers out on to the table. The shoeboxes into which she'd originally crammed them had long since disintegrated, and the contents had been transferred higgledy-piggledy into the box files. Lord, this was going to take weeks to sort out! At the time, all of this must have meant something to her, but she was dismayed by how much of the stuff there was. A quick skim through revealed sketch-books and some very pretty water-colours of Vita's, various trinkets of one sort or another, old birthday cards, a Valentine, a lace collar, a scent bottle whose lingering echoes of Floris Geranium made her heart skip, a bulky scrapbook which had belonged to Daisy, a few letters and – oh, how could she have forgotten? – that book, picked up from their mother's bedroom. Elegantly bound in grey suede, the pages gilt-edged, secured with a pretty little brass clasp and a tiny lock that she had never attempted to open. For a few seconds she sat, motionless, reliving that other moment when her younger self, struggling with revulsion, had refused to contemplate what secrets it might contain. In the end, she put the book aside and forced herself to go on, right through to the bundle of yellowed newspaper cuttings and letters, handling them gingerly because they were so friable.

She sat back at last, what she'd suspected confirmed – that it amounted to very little, after all. A few old photos, scraps of this and that. Amongst which it was surely unrealistic to hope she would suddenly find the truth of what had happened in that summer of 1910, when others before her had attempted, people far more qualified than she – the police, reporters, other members of the family who were there at the time – and failed. Old papers could only tell you so much, the rest must be conjecture. Too much water had flowed under the bridge, many of those concerned were dead, and others might well be either untraceable, or too old to be considered as reliable witnesses.

There was more to it than that, of course. If she were honest, she had known from the moment Guy telephoned with the news that the papers had been discovered that she would be faced with this dilemma, whether or not to try and dig out a little more of the truth, all those years after she had hidden this trivia, physically and metaphorically. Whether or not to dive into her subconscious and drag out her own recollections. But memory was, alas, a slippery notion at the best of times, unreliable, coloured by uncertainty...

She pushed away the last of her tea, now cold and bitter. Come on, Harriet! Admit it, you always knew what really happened. No, be more precise – you only *thought* you knew. Simple intuition. And what if you were right? Are you justified in trying to uncover what went on during that hot summer?

So there Harriet was, the following day. Having made up her mind at some time during the night that she'd do it – at least try to make some sense of what had gone on by delving into the ragbag of memory and history, and assembling from its bits and pieces a collage of something that might come near to making a semblance of the true picture.

Still undecided, she'd taken her mother's journal upstairs with her when she went to bed. First, feeling like a criminal, she had prised open with almost ridiculous ease the useless

little lock, an indication of privacy rather than a serious security device. In bed, she'd held the book for a long time, still
having that inexplicable reluctance to probe into what her
mother had obviously not wanted anyone else to see. At
length she did open it. On the flyleaf was written: 'My
Egyptian Journal' in Beatrice's familiar, large and rather flam-
boyant handwriting. She turned the page, and then read the
whole journal right through before switching off her light,
after which she lay staring into the darkness, thinking about
it. Finally, she dropped off into a sort of sleep, having decided
she would telephone Guy the next morning and tell him what
she proposed to do.

She was fairly certain he'd welcome her decision. He was an
acute observer and she knew, without him ever having said it
in so many words, that he would be disappointed if she were
to shrug off any chance, however remote, to throw some
light on the tragedy that had always overshadowed the life of
his wife and her sisters.

Her sleep had been uneasy, and she woke feeling not much
rested. The church clock, whose proximity had driven her
mad when she first came to live here, though it no longer
bothered her, tonight had kept rousing her from bouts of
half-submerged sleep. It seemed to her that she counted
every hour, and at five she got up and made herself tea and
toast. She telephoned Guy before eight, then wondered if it
was too early. "Have I got you out of bed?"

"I'm always awake by six."

Harriet pictured him: elderly, bespectacled, deceptively
mild, sitting at his desk, fountain pen in hand, already having
taken old Phoebe, his smooth-haired fox-terrier bitch, for
her sedate walk along the London streets, and tidied the
breakfast things away, while Daisy set off for Hope House.
She pictured the steadily growing stack of manuscript at his
right hand: a monograph which he was writing on the

psychological traumas suffered by civilians seriously injured during enemy attack. As a doctor, too old for military service, he had kept up his busy practice during the war years to deal with the sort of everyday ailments which did not go away simply because there was a war on, while his nights were occupied during enemy air raids with attending to the wounded and dying. It had not been without cost. His own health had suffered, and now that he'd grown older, he was forced to take things more easily. Guy was not, however, a man to be idle, never mind age or infirmity. And Harriet suspected this writing he was doing was more than a mere labour of love, it was both a personal catharsis for the terrible things he had witnessed, and a memorial to the unrecorded and unsung acts of courage which he'd seen performed daily during the bombings.

As Daisy's husband, he'd volunteered to look after the Jardine family interests when the business of selling Charnley to Vigilance Assurance arose, an offer the sisters had thankfully accepted, so that it was to him Ruth Standish had written when the discovery of the papers had been made. He had never known Charnley in its glory days, but like everyone who had ever heard its history, it exercised a fascination for him. He had tried not to sound overly intrigued about what the cache might reveal when he first spoke to Harriet about it. "What do you think? Worth looking into?" he'd asked casually. "Or not?"

"We won't know that until we see it, will we? I'll go over and pick up whatever it is they've found at once, if you'd like me to," she'd replied.

He listened intently now, without interruption, as she told him what that visit had resulted in, and to her description of the house's altered state.

"Shouldn't come as any surprise, but I'm beginning to be sorry I let you in for this, Harriet."

"Nonsense. I didn't like what they've done, but I think seeing it like that has probably helped to exorcise a few ghosts." She hoped she sounded more convinced than she felt. "It isn't really Charnley any longer."

"Have you examined everything you brought home yet? Is there anything new?"

"I haven't read everything yet, and I'd be surprised if anything actually *new* turned up, but sorted out and read with a fresh eye, it's bound to be...well, I don't know, of course, but something might come of it."

There was pause. "Why not do it, then? Put everything into order and write up some sort of an account? As a counterbalance to all that rubbish that was put out, if nothing else."

Harriet laughed gently. "I'm not the person to do that, Guy. But there is someone, isn't there, who might be?"

"Ah. Well, yes, maybe. Not a bad idea at all, in fact." She heard answering amusement in his voice. They understood each other very well, she and Guy. Bringing Nina into it had, of course, been in his mind right from the start, and Harriet was happy enough to collude with him over that. If Nina would consent, of course, which was problematic.

"I'd like to talk to her at any rate, and see what she thinks."

"As a matter of fact, she's coming for lunch. I managed to wangle a bit of extra pork from the butcher. Why don't you come down and join us?"

"That would be lovely," she said tranquilly, knowing this was no coincidence, either. "I haven't seen her for several weeks. Someone's given me some late French beans, I'll bring them with me. Show her that's one advantage of living in what she will insist on referring to as the country."

"Anywhere ten miles out of London is country to Nina," Guy said.

Nina was his daughter, Daisy's stepdaughter. Harriet knew how worried Guy had been about her lately. It was patently obvious that he was seizing this unexpected happening as a chance to shake her out of – well, self-pity wasn't a word that automatically came to mind in connection with Nina, but might in this case have a smidgeon of truth in it. Nothing distorted the personality more than an unhappy love affair. And Harriet knew what she was talking about there.

"I'd better take the train, my petrol's almost done."

But before Harriet could leave the cottage to join them both for lunch, there was Guy on the telephone again. He sounded shaken. "Harriet. Harriet, my dear, prepare yourself for a shock." He spoke hesitantly, unusually for him. "The builders at Charnley have found – something."

"Something else? What is it?"

"I think you and Daisy will have to go down there. The police need to see you both."

1910

Chapter One

1910. The summer when King Edward died, and the new King George was proclaimed. When – except in Court circles, where everyone wore black – the women's hats were as frivolous and silly as usual, when the sun shone endlessly, or so it seemed in retrospect, and the Jardines and their friends played tennis in long skirts, when one could bear to play at all in the heat. When there was tea every day on the lawn under the cedar, with strawberries, sharp and sweet, dipped in sugar. Charnley's grey stones rising solidly, immutably, against the dark green background of the woods behind. The water playing delicately into the basin of the fountain on the terrace, where the stone Laocoon and his twin sons writhed futilely and everlastingly in the coils of a pair of sea serpents, sent to crush them to death and exact vengeance for the god Apollo.

There hadn't always been Jardines at Charnley. They had arrived there a mere sixty or so years ago, when the Rodhythes, minor aristocracy who had previously owned the house for centuries, having ruined themselves through an incurable inherited addiction to gambling and an indifference to property management, had been forced to sell their ancestral home, since it was in imminent danger of tumbling about their ears. Joseph Jardine, grandfather of the present owner, Amory Jardine, had stepped in and snapped up the house and most of its contents, with new money accumulated through his Scottish and Lancashire textile mills. Thereafter, abandoning his cotton empire, he sank an immense amount of money into repairs and renovations, made some neo-Gothic additions by way of towers and a mock-medieval gatehouse to the original Tudor wings and the later Georgian façade, played with his stocks and shares to recoup his expenses, buried his origins and began to live the life of a country gentleman. Three generations later, it had almost been forgotten that the house had ever been owned by anyone else but Jardines, and there seemed no reason why they should not continue to live there for ever.

So it seemed to Daisy, at any rate, cooling off in the shade of the weeping ash after a hot bicycle ride back from the village, whence she'd been bidden by her mother to take horrid old Mrs Drake a jar of calves' foot jelly. Unmarried as she was determined to remain, she could see herself taking root here at Charnley, in the same way as that ancient old crone, Mrs Drake, with whiskers on her chin and her nature soured, had grown into the very fabric of her tumbledown cottage, refusing stubbornly to move into one of the recently improved almshouses. Silly old besom! thought Daisy. (The old woman had not been suitably grateful for the largesse from the big house, though her daughter-in-law had cried shame on her, and Daisy had ridden home the long way round, to punish herself for expecting Mrs Drake's gratitude, and for being mortified when it hadn't come.) But on arriving home, she'd flung her bicycle down in the stable yard and rushed into the kitchen for a glass of lemonade, by now feeling that her penance had been excessive – though she could never help the guilt feelings induced by comparison of her own comfortable living conditions to those of even the best-off villagers.

"Well, I never, Miss Daisy, bursting in like that, what a turn you gave me!" declared the cook, jumping up in a fluster from an afternoon doze in a chair by the window, her apron over her face. "I'm sorry, but my lemonade's all been taken down to the tennis court, and I've only some barley water I've made for old Nurse. I can squeeze you a lemon into some of that, though," she added, relenting, for Daisy was spoilt by all the staff, who liked her unaffected manners and happy nature.

"Oh, bliss, Mrs Heslop, you're a brick!"

"I can be," returned Mrs Heslop drily, "when it do take me that way."

Daisy had downed the drink, cool from the dark pantry, in unladylike gulps, and then begged another, which she carried outside, into the shade of the ash. Still scarlet-faced, the blood beating under her fair skin, she sat leaning against the trunk, her slippery, unmanageable hair escaping from under her boater and sticking to her forehead in unattractive wisps, like wet straw. She removed the hat and flung it to the ground, wishing she could do the same with the offending hair. Oh, why *couldn't* she have been blessed with hair like Vita's – dark, glossy and wavy, framing her pretty face even more beautifully now that it was up? Or like her mother's pale and shining, supremely elegant coiffures, which stayed in place exactly as she wished them to stay? But then, nothing, not even a stray hair, was allowed to interfere with Beatrice's calm intentions. Things always happened just as she wished, in the recognisable, organised pattern that defined her well-conducted, irreproachable life. Impossible to imagine Beatrice breaking out of the mould, as Daisy so longed to do. She was so effortlessly good.

As for Daisy – nothing seemed right to her, that summer, half adult, half child as she was, lingering in the awkward hiatus between schoolroom and coming out. She had no one to talk to: Vita was too busy with her Bertie and their wedding preparations to have time to amuse a younger sister, and Harriet, as usual, contrived to bury herself in the library as much as possible in order to avoid the tennis- and tea-parties, picnics and other entertainments devised by their mother as a guise for match-making. Beatrice's admirable devotion to the onerous duty of marrying off three daughters was unswerving. But Harriet, Daisy thought, might already have made up her mind where her affections lay. There was a sort of tension between her and Kit whenever he was here, they were already linked in everyone else's eyes, though Harriet hadn't yet given her word to him. Perhaps, knowing him so intimately since childhood, she knew it wasn't wise to give in to him too easily. Or that was what Miss Tempest had shrewdly suggested

Positively the worst thing of all about this summer to Daisy was that her governess, Miss Tempest, had astonished everyone (except Daisy herself) by departing to become a suffragette. Leaving Daisy, without her, to face the awfulness of her approaching season, which would not begin until next year, but already loomed as large in her mind as it did in her mother's. There would be her coming out ball to launch her upon the London social scene, followed by an endless round of events, with her mother or dread Great-aunt Edina acting as chaperone to see that she behaved herself, the sort of events Miss Tempest scornfully dismissed as light-minded: Ascot and Henley Regatta and all the rest of it, dances and balls – house parties, dinner parties, after-theatre suppers, all simply in order to snare a young man like Bertie. Oh, misery, no, *not* like Bertie, please not, harmless though he was! Harmless and amiable – but such a ninny! Rich, however, and well-connected, already supervising the building of a lovely house across the valley where he would take Vita to live after their wedding, where they would have three or four children and live predictably ever after. Whereas what Daisy wanted – no, what she most passionately *desired* in the world at this moment – was to join Athene Tempest in that other London, far removed from the world of parties and dances and frivolities like that, and do great and worthy and wonderfully thrilling things by working for women's suffrage. Distribute leaflets demanding votes for women, sew banners (though alas, they would certainly be crooked if she had anything to do with the making of them!). Break windows and chain oneself to railings, perhaps go to prison for it. Throw bombs, even.

Frustrated, Daisy contemplated the impossibility of running away to do any of these things, finished Nanny Byfield's barley water and sat inelegantly, since no one was around to see, with her black-stockinged knees to her chin, and her skirts above them for coolness, showing her drawers; and trying to keep her thoughts from turning to the dreaded arrival of Miss Jessamy, who was to replace Miss Tempest. It was shady under the weeping ash, and though small insects constantly dropped from the canopy, and the roots made for uncomfortable sitting, she stayed where she was. The sounds of tennis being played drifted across to her, and she was far too hot to want to be drawn into a game. But then, as the clock over the stable struck four, came the agreeable realisation that it was too late for that. There would be tea in a quarter of an hour.

Presently, at precisely quarter past four, she saw Albrighton approaching across the lawn at a stately pace, wheeling the tea trolley, attended by the plump, pretty little parlourmaid, Cheevers.

"Ah, Bayah-tree-chay!"

Beatrice Jardine, presiding over the teacups, drew in a deep, steadying breath at the sound of that once-familiar voice. A faint tinge of colour appeared on her creamy white skin, a teaspoon rattled slightly against a saucer, but then she pushed back her chair, rose and walked, graceful and statuesque, across the lawn towards the speaker, extending a hand. "Valery!"

"So!" the young man exclaimed with satisfaction. "You knew me then!"

"How could I not? No one else has ever pronounced my name in that ridiculous way! And besides, we were expecting you."

He raised her soft, be-ringed hand to within a quarter of an inch of his lips, and they surveyed one another, for a moment not smiling. His eyes assessed the woman before him: Beatrice, on the eve of her forty-fourth birthday, was still a beauty, exquisitely dressed in cream shantung, cool and smelling of lily-of-the-valley, gracious and welcoming, the society hostess personified. She saw Valery Akhmet Iskander as the others must see him: milky-coffee skin and a pair of sharp, light-blue eyes, high cheekbones and tight, dark curls, a sloping profile and a wide, white smile, a handsome though unexpected combination due to his mixed Russian and Egyptian parentage. Unusual but, given the melange of nationalities in Cairo, not unheard of. He had put on a little weight since she last saw him. No one would have guessed how uncomfortably hard her heart was beating as she led him forward. "Welcome to Charnley. Come, let me introduce you to the others. I see you and Kit have already met."

"At the station," said Kit, stepping forward to greet her in his turn, taking her long white hand in both of his, and dropping a light kiss on her scented cheek. "Had we known, we could have travelled down together."

As their hands touched, Beatrice experienced as always the tender rush of emotion for the orphaned small boy Kit had been when first she had seen him and drawn him into the bosom of her family. She almost reached out to smooth the wayward black hair that fell in a comma over his forehead. He raised his intensely blue eyes to her face, eyes of a blue that was very like her own, and with lashes that any girl would have envied, not disguising his obvious admiration for her, and causing a distinct but not unpleasant flutter of pleasure in the region of her breastbone. Rather quickly, her hand was withdrawn from his clasp. She patted his sleeve in a motherly fashion, and turned away. Iskander was led to the tea-table and presented: "Valery Iskander, an eminent

Egyptologist whom I met some years ago while wintering in Egypt."

Smiling, the newcomer bowed his head over the hands of several young ladies in straw boaters and high-necked, long-sleeved muslin blouses with cream serge skirts, shook hands with gentlemen still in tennis whites, who nodded a little stiffly and watched him covertly. It was difficult to say how old he was, though certainly not more than in his mid-thirties, which seemed young to have reached the eminence Beatrice had stated. She was perhaps simply being polite. His dark suit was just a little too impeccable in this gathering, his collar too stiff, his moustache narrow and sleek above the full, sensuous lips. But then he was, after all, a foreigner.

Introductions over, a place was found for him next to his hostess, more tea was ordered, more scones, and, as the conversation resumed its generality, Iskander was given time to study his new acquaintances. The bevy of young women resolved itself into no more than three, all of them Beatrice's daughters: there was Harriet, the eldest, in no way a beauty but striking, tall like her mother, and with a crooked smile and a pair of serious brown eyes under level dark brows: a clever girl, no doubt. Little Vita, the prettiest of the three – endearing pansy face, small white teeth, carnations-and-cream complexion, wearing a large diamond cluster on her engagement finger, indulging in playful asides with her young man, Bertram Rossiter, rosy and rather self-satisfied, who was seated next to her. The other man was a neighbour, a fattish, damp young fellow called Teddy Cranfield, the effect of whose exertions on the tennis court could only be guessed at.

At that moment Cheevers arrived with replenishments, and an urgent question for Beatrice from Mrs Heslop, apparently about the fish for dinner. With a little cluck of annoyance, Beatrice rose and stepped aside to deal with the matter, while the conversation round the tea table continued.

"Mr Iskander, how fortunate that you will be here for Mama's birthday next week! Are you any good at play-acting?" Vita dimpled at him. "I warn you – Harriet will try to rope you in, she's of a managing disposition and we're woefully short of men – men who are willing, that is," she declared in mock reproof at her future husband, and the perspiring Teddy Cranfield.

"An ability to stand still would be more useful than play-acting, since it's a *tableau vivant* we're to do! Barely a week to prepare for it – and we haven't yet decided on a subject!"

That was the youngest daughter, Daisy. An untidy child, her long hair not yet up, her features not fully formed into those of the woman she would become, the only one of the three who had Beatrice's gold silk hair, her pale creamy skin, maybe the only one with the promise of their mother's true beauty, but who could tell? She was as yet an unfolded bud. Her looks did not quite accord with her ways, however, that much was apparent even to a newcomer such as Iskander. Like her elder sister Harriet, a lively intelligence animated her face, and she spoke with a vehemence and conviction that could never have come from Beatrice. There was nothing in the least remote and cool about her.

"But why," he asked in soft, rather sibilant, but excellently English tones, "do you not choose something where no men are needed? Boticelli's 'Three Graces' comes to mind." His smooth smile travelled from one sister to the other.

"Too easy," said Harriet immediately. It had been thought of before, and dismissed, but she was too polite to say so. "The audience is supposed to *guess*, you see, Mr Iskander."

"And three such beauties would immediately give away the answer, of course."

Kit gave a short laugh, but Bertie and Teddy Cranfield were reduced to an embarrassed British silence at this confirmation of what their instincts had already told them about the fellow. Beatrice, returning to her seat, said, "Girls, you're not to plague Mr Iskander when he's only just arrived. He needs a little peace after his train journey from town."

"Oh, bother, yes, that train! Isn't it just too tiresome?" demanded Daisy. "Miss Jessamy should have been on it, too." Her thickly dark-lashed hazel eyes sparkled, so attractive a contrast with that golden hair. "Are you sure you didn't see any mousy person in a governessy grey dress lurking in the shrubbery outside the station, Mr Iskander? Or did you, Kit?"

"*Daisy*!" As a perfect hostess, the word tiresome in connection with guests – or even one soon to become an employee – was not one Beatrice allowed to be on anyone's lips. "I'm certain Miss Jessamy will not be like that in the least. There has simply been some misunderstanding, which will no doubt resolve itself shortly," she added, though Rose Jessamy not being on the train would in fact mean all sorts of complications, not the least of which was that Copley would have to be available to take the motorcar (though perhaps the pony trap would do) down to the station again to meet all likely trains...But how unmannerly of her, she thought privately, if she had been prevented from catching the train she had indicated she would travel on, not to have sent word to let them know when she might be expected! Such a communication would not have been difficult, they were not behind the times here at Charnley. The house, as well as being equipped with electric light, three bathrooms and hot water heating pipes running beneath the floors of the ground floor rooms, boasted a telephone set. Or if, like many people, she was averse to using the instrument, why not send a telegram? Even a letter posted in London that morning would have arrived here by now. "She is not a governess, she is an artist," she said, as if that explained everything about the missing woman.

"I expect she paints pretty little woodland scenes," Daisy said carelessly. "What a pity the bluebells are over!" Beatrice widened her sapphire eyes warningly, but chose to say nothing in front of the others, and turned her attention once more to the teapot. Her youngest child was becoming dangerously sharp-tongued. Miss Tempest's departure had come not a moment too soon.

"Don't vex your mama, Daisy," Kit drawled, accepting a cup of tea from Beatrice and watching her from under his lids. "I can vouch for it you will be very pleasantly surprised when you do meet Miss Jessamy."

"Will I? Oh, do tell! I had no idea you knew her!"

"Well, as to *knowing* ... it was I who first took Marcus along to the Alpha Workshops – that's a kind of artists' commune where she's been painting and selling her work. She's regarded as a very talented and most unusual person."

An artists' commune! Beatrice frowned, but only very slightly. After forty, one could not afford that indulgence. She had not been made aware of any communes, artistic or otherwise and, not for the first time, she wondered if Miss Jessamy was indeed going to be the good idea, the solution to Daisy's companionless state she had seemed to offer at the time. When Miss Tempest had so inconsiderately left, it had hardly seemed worth the trouble of finding a new governess – Daisy was almost seventeen and would be coming out next year, and Beatrice knew only too well the tribulations of finding the right kind of person to guide a young girl, especially one so impressionable as Daisy. Look how Miss Tempest had turned out! Inculcating rebellious, quite unacceptable ideas into the girl's head, a fact which Beatrice had unfortunately only learned after the young woman's abrupt departure. Yet Daisy could not be left to her own devices.

The plan to engage Miss Jessamy as a companion for her had come about as a sudden inspiration, born of one of those

reckless impulses, of which few people suspected Beatrice
was capable, after seeing what this Miss Jessamy had done
when making over the London house of Beatrice's dearest
friend, Millie Glendinning. Charnley, unlike the family's
house in London, could not be considered elegant, however
well-loved it was. And at that moment, its brocatelles and
velvets, antique wallpapers and heirloom furniture, the buhl
and ormolu, walnut and mahogany, the mountains of French
porcelain collected on their grand tours by those Rodhythes
whose heavy, gilded portraits still gazed down from the walls,
suddenly seemed to Beatrice to be static and heavy, and lack-
ing in any vigour or newness of ideas. Millie's daringly new
and original decorations on the other hand, the colour and
texture of her brightly painted walls, exuded a freshness,
lightness and gaiety that was like nothing Beatrice – or
indeed most other people – had ever seen before.

She rarely allowed her emotions to take control of her
common sense, but there were times when she could not help
it, and this had been one of them. She was utterly bowled
over by the riot of exuberant design that evoked such disturbing ideas and stirred something dormant within her,
some longing for change, for distant remembered vistas,
some undisclosed awareness that there must be something
beyond the safe confines and predictabilities of life as mistress of Charnley, wife of Amory, and mother to his children.
Few would have believed that beneath Beatrice Jardine's mar-
ble-cool exterior, there beat this longing for something wild
and free – and even, perhaps, something dangerous, which
was trying to escape. But there it was.

When she was told that the remarkable young woman who
had effected this wonderful modern transformation was
seeking other commissions, she drew in a deep breath and
plunged: it was arranged that Miss Jessamy would undertake
the redecoration of some of the guest rooms in the west wing

at Charnley. Speed was not what was required: she was to take her time, as long as was necessary, and in return for an additional fee, keep Daisy occupied, which should not be difficult. Daisy was easily interested, receptive to new ideas.

At this moment, however, Beatrice wondered uneasily if she had not allowed herself to be carried away by the tide of enthusiasm that had swept over her. Had she not acted too precipitately, in contravention of her normal rules to herself where her girls were concerned, had she enquired insufficiently into Miss Jessamy's credentials as a fit person to be with Daisy? She had not yet even seen the lady in question, but had engaged her through the intermediary of Marcus, who, it had surprisingly transpired, had already encountered Miss Jessamy and her work several times. Beatrice was immediately reassured when she thought of how completely she could rely on her son's judgement, which was rarely at fault. Though not yet five and twenty, Marcus was steady and sober, like his father, Amory. If he thought Miss Jessamy suitable, there was no more to be said.

And now it seemed that Kit, too, already knew Miss Jessamy.

She looked up from her teacup, and at that exact moment, caught an exchange between her eldest daughter and Kit that she did not quite understand, an ironic look on Harriet's part which held a certain challenge, an enigmatic one on Kit's. After a moment, Harriet turned to say something to Teddy Cranfield, and Kit brought his glance to rest on Beatrice herself. Her smile answered his. It was, of course, part of his charm, that warm look he bestowed. He had this trick of making one feel there was no one else, at that moment, who mattered.

Yet, despite his sublime good looks – spoiled only (or perhaps not spoiled, simply lifted out of the Byronic cliché) by a rather large nose and an often moody expression, there was something ever so slightly louche about Kit Sacheverell. Perhaps it was his wide-brimmed hats, his flowing ties, the hair that was just a little over-long. She dismissed such thoughts, not willing to think ill of the boy – well, no, a man of twenty-six, now – though she must think of him as a boy to her almost forty-four years.

"I sometimes wish," she had remarked a short while ago to Amory, "that he were a little – steadier, and as for Harriet…" She had left the rest unsaid. Harriet was at the moment a sore point with her, though it was a state of affairs she was determined not to allow to continue. A fine looking, high-spirited girl such as she was, clever and with all the right connections, should have ended her first season engaged to be married. Vita had managed it. Beatrice herself had been married at eighteen and by the time she was Harriet's age had already produced Marcus, the son and heir, and Harriet herself. Instead, Harriet had, it seemed, fixed on Kit. Oh-so-charming but penniless Kit (though he had high expectations, when that ancient old relative of his shuffled off this mortal coil). Beatrice sighed, with frustration, annoyance – or something deeper.

Amory, she knew, did not altogether share her concern about Harriet. Though he constantly joked that his pocket was not bottomless, he had made generous settlements on his three daughters, he loved them and enjoyed their company and therefore did not see any urgent necessity for finding them husbands. A highly moral and upright man who showed a stern face to the world but was invariably courteous and gentle with his family, he had married his beautiful wife for love as he knew it, had apparently found deep contentment and wanted nothing better for his children. Moreover, he liked Kit, and was more forbearing towards him than he would have been to his own son, had Marcus ever given him cause for worry, which he had not. Kit would sooner or later, he said, make a go of his chosen profession as a civil engineer – haphazard choice as it was, with romantic notions about building bridges, though there was not much evidence of that as yet, and it was high time he decided not to hang around so much on the fringes of the art world. "Oh, I suspect Harriet will be very good for him."

"The point is, rather," she had replied, a little sharply, surprising herself, "will he be good enough for Harriet? Will any man? She has such high standards, rather too high, I think, and men do not like clever – or sharp-tongued – women. As for Kit..."

"Well, you are not suggesting Kit falls short in that direction? You know the boy better than any of us, you get on so well with him, Beatrice," Amory said, smiling and patting her hand.

With slight irritation – sometimes, she wished Amory would show just *some* impatience or disapproval, that he would be less predictable, perhaps (dare she say it?) be a little less *dull* – she had let the conversation lapse, but at the back of her mind lingered something Kit had once said to her. "I should like, above all else," he had declared passionately, "to have no necessity to worry about whether or not I might afford to buy what I admire – you know, paintings and works of art, things like that."

It was a pity for a young man with such ambitious tastes and such a disinclination to put his shoulder to the wheel and *work*, that his father had not left him enough money to indulge them, for the present, at least. The old relative had had one foot in the grave for the last twelve years, and was still inconsiderately hanging on. We must not, she thought, let Kit marry Harriet simply because he would then be rich enough to buy anything he wanted. The thought that this idea could be in his mind was so exceedingly distasteful to her, she tried to dismiss it immediately. Kit was not like that.

He would not marry Harriet because it was expedient. Beatrice very much wanted to believe this, but at the back of her mind, she thought he might. There were unexplained simmerings, impatiences, ironies below the surface of Kit's sometimes cynical outlook that occasionally unsettled her. Gave off the whiff of danger. The thought made her feel a little breathless.

The afternoon sunlight filtered through the spreading branches of the cedar, lighting her face with gold. How beautiful she is, thought Kit. No one else could come anywhere near her, her daughters, no one. He was in danger of losing his admittedly not very stable balance over her.

Amory Jardine and his son rode down from London in a first class compartment of the early train they always took on Fridays, when guests were often expected for the weekend. For a while, they spoke of matters of the day: Mr Asquith, the Prime Minister's problems with trade disputes and strikes; the high words in Parliament over the ever-present question of Home Rule for the Irish; incredulity expressed by certain letter writers to *The Times* that the earth could be thought to have actually passed through the tail of Halley's comet, and the growing menace of the presumptuous, troublesome Suffragists. The opinions of father and son were not entirely in accord over this last, and presently they fell silent. Amory opened his attaché case and took out some papers, but Marcus remained uncharacteristically unoccupied. Stretching out his long legs in front of him, crossing them at the ankles, he stuck his hands in his pockets and looked out of the window as the train belched and clattered through the dirty London suburbs and into greener, ever greener countryside, and thence on to a branch line, while pleasurable, rather daring, thoughts stirred in him.

They were physically somewhat alike, father and son, with

dark hair and eyes, though Marcus overtopped his more stockily-built father by half a head, and he was less outwardly austere in his demeanour. He had an engaging shyness of manner, which caused him to stammer a little, but mostly only when his emotions got the better of him. He had become a lawyer and worked in his father's chambers, with the hope of following in his admirable footsteps in the fullness of time. Amory had built up a successful practice at the Bar, had become a KC and was looking for elevation to the Bench. A knighthood was rumoured to be in the offing.

Marcus's reserve, in fact, came from his father. Though in public, as befitted a lawyer, Amory's flow of words could be undiminished, his innate reticence caused him in private life to be sparing of speech, and disinclined to demonstrate his affections, and at times manifested itself as a certain coldness, at least with those he didn't know well. Even so, no one knew better than Marcus that everyone around Amory must always behave with the utmost probity and circumspection, and he looked at him now with a slight tremor of foreboding. But perhaps he was rushing his fences. Perhaps incurring his father's disapproval was a circumstance that would never arise.

Eventually, the train steamed into the little wooden country station. Marcus lowered the window with the leather strap, thrust out his hand to open the door. The platform was empty as usual, except for the accustomed figure of Joseph Jimson, the young porter, whose sole task, it sometimes appeared, was to await the arrival of the trains which brought and bore away visitors to and from Charnley House – and to deliver to the big house on his bicycle the fresh supplies of fish and meat which were sent direct from Billingsgate and Smithfield. If he were lucky, and he usually was, for he was a handsome and likeable young fellow, Mrs Heslop would give him a cup of tea and a slice of bread and jam, or a piece of cake, and if he were even luckier, he'd have the chance to steal a kiss from Polly Cheevers, his sweetheart, before cycling off again.

He touched his cap to Mr Jardine and Mr Marcus as they alighted and walked towards the exit and the road outside, where Copley waited with their motorcar. He expected them to be the only arrivals, but this afternoon there was another passenger.

"Why, there is M-m-miss Jessamy!" declared Marcus a moment later, striding forward with pleasure towards a distinctly eccentric, plain-looking little figure who was scrambling from the end coach of the train, and distractedly attempting to dump on to the platform her luggage, which seemed to consist of a large number of straw baskets, odd-shaped valises, a large satchel and an easel, as well as sundry other parcels, before it should be carried on to somewhere like Leighton Buzzard or any other uncivilised destination. Jimson, who had already had a similar, earlier encounter with Mr Iskander's equally oddly assorted baggage, was already there, helping her and assuring her he would not let the train go with her bags still on board. She smiled her thanks at him, instantly vanquishing the idea that she was plain, and the smile widened even further when she saw Marcus striding towards her.

Amory watched in disbelief as Marcus and the porter gathered up her belongings. Jimson pocketed a shilling, and shouldered the largest of the boxes to the waiting motorcar. Marcus came forward with the owner of the luggage, a great deal of which was now distributed variously about his own person. So this, thought Amory, was Miss Jessamy, who had been engaged to be his beloved youngest child's companion! Much younger than he had expected. Diminutive but very straight-backed, she wore a bunchy skirt short enough to show her ankles, and a loose blouse with a sailor collar and a floppy tie. Her hair was an unruly fiery red mop, cut level with her ears, underneath which a small, Pekingese face peered somewhat defiantly. She was hatless, though a battered straw, somewhat resembling that worn by donkeys, hung down her back by its ribbon. And gloveless. And, if he were not mistaken, Amory thought, scandalised, stockingless!

Jimson kept his face straight and wondered in a mutter to swarthy-faced Copley, Charnley's chauffeur, groom and occasional handyman, as they heaved the box on to the back of the motorcar, what in hangment Mrs Jardine would say when confronted with this second eccentric guest of the day. "Right one, that, ain't she?"

"One of them Bohemiums," returned Copley with a broad wink, watching the young master hand her into the motor as though she were a right lady. "Reckon Mr Marcus'll be well in there. Free love and all that, bet she's a bit of all right between the sheets."

No one knew, or guessed, how momentous – disastrous might be a better word – the arrival of this small person at Charnley was destined to be.

Not Polly Cheevers, the parlourmaid who was watching from her attic window, where she had been sent to change her apron – another clean apron, meaning a penny docked off her wages, and how was she to do her work without getting it dirty at all? – as the motorcar drew up and Mr Marcus descended, helping down that scrawny little figure.

Nor that cheeky-faced Alf Copley, who was grinning at her in a familiar way and looked like as not to pinch her bottom, as he did with any of the maids when he got the chance.

Nor Clara Hallam, lady's maid to Mrs Jardine. A plain and angular woman for whom the world contained quite enough responsibility, thank you very much, without having to help with the rag-tag luggage of red-haired hussies without hats or stockings, as she'd been ordered to. She was deeply religious and attended the Baptist chapel, and deplored the free and extravagant lifestyle at Charnley. Though it was, after all, precisely this extravagance which permitted her employment here.

As for Beatrice...she wasn't there to greet her new guest. The pleasure of that would come later.

Chapter Two

After all, as Harriet reluctantly had to concede, hustling her sisters into the library after tea, the Three Graces as the subject for the tableau was the most sensible suggestion yet – or at any rate the most attainable at this late stage. It might not keep anyone guessing, but that didn't really matter, since the object of the exercise was more to present a charming picture to the assembled guests, as a birthday tribute to their mother, than to mystify.

"Bertie and Teddy have probably forgotten it was ever mentioned, anyway," said Vita carelessly, "and Mama herself didn't hear what Mr Iskander said; she was busy talking to Cheevers, so she won't be expecting it." She was becoming bored with the subject, and cross with allowing herself to be chivvied unceremoniously into the library by Harriet. She would much rather be occupying herself with colour schemes and styles of decoration for her new drawing room in the modern white house across the valley, which was now very near completion, awaiting decisions as to its interior decoration. All she knew was that she wanted no room in it to look anything like the over-elaborate rooms here at Charnley, but neither did she want the sort of peculiar – almost *primitive-looking* – designs this Miss Jessamy had carried out for Mama's friend, Millie Glendinning, and was now about to begin here in the west wing. (How odd of Mama, of all people, to have made such a choice! thought Vita, momentarily diverted.) She herself was quite enamoured with the idea of spare, sinuous, elegant Art.

Nouveau, cool colours and expensive simplicity. There was that Scottish architect and designer up in Glasgow who was said to be very up to the minute...

"It seems rather feeble, but at least it will be no trouble,"

Harriet continued. She had been thumbing through a heavy volume to find a plate of Botticell's 'Spring', wherein the Three Graces featured, and now she had studied it and considered the possibilities, she had to admit it would solve many problems, in view of the small amount of time left. The only uncertainty seemed to be whether Daisy could stand still long enough to hold the pose, or Vita keep her mind on the subject. "No props will be necessary – we can conceal ourselves beforehand behind a curtain in front of the folly, which can then be drawn – all we need besides is yards and yards of muslin–"

"And something underneath it to preserve decency," added Daisy, with a laugh, looking over Harriet's shoulder at the diaphanous draperies which covered but did not at all conceal either the limbs or any other bodily parts of the dancing goddesses in the picture. "Otherwise, Mama would have a fit."

"Good, then that's settled," said Vita, with evident relief.

It was rather unfair of her to have lost interest so quickly, thought Harriet, drawing paper towards her to make a list of what would be needed, since she had been the one who suggested presenting a tableau in the first place, but really, you never knew with Vita; she never thought of anyone but herself and she was good for nothing sensible these days. The only things which absorbed her attention were her dress for The Day, the wedding presents, a few of which had already begun to arrive, and choosing a name for the new house, most of the suggestions for which were either banal or whimsical, and made Daisy hoot with laughter. She couldn't altogether blame Vita, however, that this tableau as a choice of birthday entertainment lacked originality, and showed no subtlety. It was her own fault, she acknowledged impatiently. She had only agreed to perform the thing at all in a fit of absent mindedness, when she was preoccupied and unsettled by other things – mainly the latest letter from her friend

Frances who was – oh, consummation devoutly to be desired! – studying at St Hilda's College in Oxford. If only, thought Harriet longingly, if only! But her father would entertain no such suggestion. He firmly and honestly believed the highest fulfilment for a woman was that of wife and mother, and that only. And as for Beatrice, she dismissed the idea as just another silly notion being bandied about among young women with advanced opinions and too much time on their hands, nothing more than a passing whim. Without their support, there was nothing Harriet could do. She did not have enough money of her own to make an independent move, only her dress allowance and, generous though that was, it was not enough. Moreover, though strong-minded, she was not made of the stuff to flout parental authority, mainly because she loved her father too much to hurt him. All the same, she despised herself for not having the courage to stand out over this, and tried to tell herself she could make up in other ways. She could – her heart lurched – marry Kit, for instance. Marry him and make something of him, and perhaps something of herself into the bargain. Or thereby ruin herself.

"I say, he's rather dashing, isn't he?" asked Daisy.

Harriet blinked, and woke up to find the other two had not in fact divined the disturbing direction of her thoughts as she at first imagined, but had moved on to another subject. "Who is?"

"Why, Mr Iskander, even though his name is Valery!" All three girls giggled, even Harriet, though dashing would not have been a word she would have used to describe their visitor. Less complimentary adjectives sprang to mind. "I must say," added Daisy, "he seemed rather taken with Mama."

"Who is not?" asked Vita flippantly.

Harriet intervened, rather sharply, "More to the point, what did you think of your new governess, Daisy, now that she's finally arrived?"

"A governess is simply the last thing one would expect her to be – the last thing she wants, too, I should imagine. What do you think – she so perfectly hates the name Rose Jessamy that she prefers to be called RJ! And I can see why," added Daisy sympathetically. Its owner was not in the least the flowery, gentle being the name suggested. "I rather liked her," she finished, deliberately understating the case in anticipation of her elder sisters' reactions – Harriet's scorn and Vita's teasing. In fact, she was already on the way to developing a decided crush on Miss Jessamy...RJ. How splendid to be so independent, to chop off your bothersome hair and wear loose, comfortable clothes. No stockings. No *stays*! Freedom, no matter what anyone thought!

It was entertaining to speculate on how RJ and Mama would get on, and who would win, if it came to a battle of wills.

In fact, they had already encountered one another, though not to say in a spirit of controversy, and not in the matter of stays or stockings, but over the decoration of the rooms, which Miss Jessamy had naturally wanted to see immediately she arrived, since they were, after all, the main reason for her being here at Charnley.

She had walked through each one, admiring their proportions, and then stood looking around the last one without saying anything, deep in thought. "Yes," she said drily at last. "This is exactly the sort of thing I imagined, from what Marcus said."

The little pulse of uneasiness, which had previously only stirred, now awoke properly in Beatrice's breast, her hitherto unshaken faith in Marcus's judgement having already been shattered by the arrival of Miss Jessamy...what *could* her level-headed son have been thinking of, how could he possibly have imagined Daisy could be exposed to the influence of a creature who dressed in such an outrageously controversial fashion? The skirt – the lack of stockings! And that hair! If she cared so little as to present herself to the world in such a way, what on earth were her moral principles?

And another thing – Beatrice, who was never indecisive, had discovered to her alarm that she was now by no means as confident as she had been about the work Miss Jessamy was to do. The young woman had asked for – nay, almost demanded – carte blanche to work on the decorations as she wished. It was not so much the fee, it seemed, as the opportunity to experiment, and express herself as she desired in paint, the provision of free materials and her keep provided, which was of paramount importance.

"My dear, you know I leave all that sort of thing to you," Amory had said when Beatrice had first approached him over the matter of refurbishing the guest accommodation in the west wing. "You have such impeccable taste."

But she was beginning to realise, too late, that even Amory might be somewhat shaken when he saw what might be done to rooms where previously the decorations, if needing to be renewed, had simply followed accepted tradition. She had of course known he would be rather taken aback by the sort of thing she envisaged but had simply decided that she would have to enlist the help of Marcus – and possibly Daisy, who could twist her father round her little finger – to persuade Amory that new was not necessarily bad. Now she realised that she might have more than just that on her plate, belatedly remembering that he regarded the Art Nouveau style Vita had so set her heart on as the acme of decadence.

This would not do! She took herself in hand and mentioned the vibrant wall colours, the decorative door panels and stencilled friezes which she had admired in Millie's house, but Miss Jessamy did not seem to be impressed with her suggestions. "Every place needs different treatment, and Lady Glendinning's house is not at all like this one."

That Millie's modern London residence was not like Charnley was undeniable. "What exactly are you hoping to convey?"

Miss Jessamy, she discovered, had a disconcerting way of looking at one fearlessly without saying anything for a long time, from a very fine pair of eyes, the warm brown that sometimes goes with red hair and white skin. And how glorious that hair could have been had it been allowed to grow as nature intended! "I'd like to keep an open mind for a while, until I get the sense of it," she answered eventually. She was in fact surprisingly pretty when she smiled and forgot her fierceness, Beatrice discovered, despite her turned-up nose. "How do you feel about nudes, odalisques, Sapphic themes?" she asked, with an abrupt return to her direct manner.

Beatrice was on shaky ground here, not really understanding what was meant. She had not received a liberal education. Moreover, such generalisation seemed to leave a good deal to the imagination, and Beatrice was not blessed with too much of that quality. "It's not so much what I feel," she replied cravenly (this fierce little person was beginning to intimidate her, something she was quite unused to) "as to how it will affect the visitors who will be sleeping here."

"Is the naked form unknown to them, then?"

Possibly not, since these rooms, a little distant from the main house, were normally allocated to those gentlemen, young bachelors or perhaps widowers, unaccompanied by a lady. Beatrice, however, decided it was time to terminate this conversation. She lifted the small jewelled watch pinned to her chest. "I think perhaps we had better leave the decisions until tomorrow. I hope you will join us for dinner, this evening at any rate, Miss Jessamy, until you establish a routine," she said, hoping that she was making clear this was not to be regarded as a regular thing. She foresaw a rather awkward situation arising with this young woman, who did not fall easily into the category of either employee or friend of the family. Not like Miss Tempest who, when Daisy was dining with the grown-ups, had always made it quite clear that she preferred to take her meals in an egalitarian way with the domestic staff. "I think you will find your room comfortable – if there is anything you need, don't hesitate to speak."

It was not in the best frame of mind that Beatrice left her, more than slightly put out from this somewhat disturbing first meeting.

Well, well. What was done was done. She would have further conversation with Miss Jessamy tomorrow and if necessary, would see her suitably recompensed and dispense with her services. At this particular moment, a more pressing need was to remove the pins from her hair and allow it fall loose, ring for Hallam to undo her laces, and rest in the cool darkness of her room with eau-de-cologne pads on her eyes before changing for dinner...indeed, a necessity if she was to prevent one of the severe headaches to which she was a martyr, and which was hovering just behind her eyes. She would give orders not to be disturbed. Her room over the library was virtually soundproof, and she would scarcely even be aware of Amory moving about in his own room next door.

"Has Lord Wycombe arrived yet?" she asked Albrighton, encountering him in the hall.

"Not yet, madam."

"Perhaps we could delay dinner for half an hour, then. He is motoring down, and one can never be certain..."

"Quite so, I will inform Mrs Heslop."

"Thank you, Mr Albrighton. Oh, and do you think you could remind Mr Marcus, with my compliments, that not everyone shares his passion for that music he's playing so loudly?" If music it could be called. After hearing this particular piece of ragtime for perhaps the fiftieth time, any willingness Beatrice might have had to regard this sound from across the Atlantic as such was definitely waning. "I know you'll do it tactfully."

Albrighton was quite up to this. "Certainly. I will see to it."

They exchanged an understanding smile and Beatrice went on her way, hoping that at least she had gained herself a little more time for rest.

It was, alas, not to be. Deciding she must slip in to the conservatory on her way upstairs to check on the table decorations for that evening, which were always placed there before being taken into the dining room at the last minute, by an unfortunate chance she met the new arrival, Iskander, though perhaps chance was not precisely the right word. He had obviously been on the lookout for her, since his arms were full of parcels which he proceeded to hand over.

"I have brought presents for you, Bayah-tree-chay. And for your beautiful daughters."

"How kind! But it isn't my birthday until next week, you know."

"Ah, but I have others for then."

She stopped herself from too obviously checking the time once more, suppressed a sigh and accepted the gifts graciously, with a smile of real pleasure for the vase of bluish-green glass, ancient and cloudy, a lesser one for the alabaster jar surmounted by the head of Anubis, the Egyptian jackal god who guided the dead to judgment, though it, too, was beautiful, perhaps a copy, which she sincerely hoped it was. A canopic jar, or urn, she knew it was one of a set of four designed for the purpose of holding the entrails of a mummy, intended to be placed in its tomb, on the sarcophagus. The thought was certainly horrid, to touch the object repelled her; she hoped it had not been intentional. Valery Iskander's sense of humour was unpredictable, but she didn't think he would have chosen to perpetrate a joke in bad taste as a guest in her house – especially in the delicate circumstances under which he was staying. She had not asked him here. He had written and more or less invited himself.

"You have not changed, Bayah-tree-chay." His tone was ironic. She wasn't sure whether she was supposed to take that as a compliment, and took refuge in chiding him once more for the affected way he chose to address her.

"Beatrice," she corrected firmly.

"Very well, if the other displeases you so much – though you did not object to it, once."

"Things change," she answered, as remotely as she felt she could. Carefully, she placed the fragile glass vase – so many memories it brought back, most of which she would rather not recall – on a wrought iron table, and walked over to the window, her heels clicking against the metal grating in the floor, and stood with her back to him. "Why did you come here?" she asked in a low voice.

"I was in London, and I thought it would amuse you for us to meet again."

"Amuse!"

What did he want? With hindsight it was possible to see that there had always been something premeditated about his actions. She had persuaded herself that to ignore his angling for an invitation would have been to court disaster, that, after all this time, no harm could arise from his visit, but having seen him, she could not now rid herself of her original fear that he could be here only with some sinister intent.

"I do not recall," he said softly, his teeth very white against his dusky skin, "that you were so particular when we were in Egypt."

Her stomach plunged. He had not forgotten, then. She had never expected that he would, any more than she herself could – but his uncanny way of knowing what she was thinking unnerved her. She lifted her chin. "I never think about Egypt."

He smiled.

It was true, however...in part. Certainly, since the arrival of his letter she had indeed thought of little else, but up until then she had never consciously permitted herself to recall that time. Only in her uncontrolled dreams did it come back to torment her. She refused to meet his sceptical gaze, and to conceal her emotion busied herself with tweaking off the stem of a fern, which was in no need of tweaking, willing herself not to remember what was past and done with. It was no use, this time her mind would not obey her. His very presence prevented that.

The conservatory floor was damp from the gardeners' recent plant-watering, it smelled heavy, earthy and humid, yet her skin prickled as if with the dry heat of the desert, she felt she was breathing in metallic, dusty air at the end of a long hot day. She stroked the feathery fern while under her fingers she felt the dry brittleness of a palm leaf. Outside, a flight of homegoing starlings transposed themselves into a cloud of white egrets, settling like blossoms among the rushes of the Nile.

A pair of geese flew low across the lake in the gold of the dying afternoon, and all she saw were the wheeling, scavenging kites above the streets in Cairo. Marcus had not yet closed his window, or turned off his gramophone, but at least he had exchanged the raucous ragtime for something more acceptable from Merrie England. A haunting little tune floated down through the skylight, into the conservatory, and ended on a dying fall...'Oh, she's a witch, throw her a bone! Nobody's wife...Jill, all alone.'

The tall shadows of the sequoias fell across the smooth green lawn, as dark and menacing as the silent, terrifying shadows of the Luxor Temple. The memory of what had happened there, what had gone before and especially what had followed beat between her temples. Another time. Upper Egypt, ten, almost eleven, years ago, the garden of the Luxor Hotel, with the road running alongside, and beyond it the wide, majestic flow of the mighty Nile, its dark waters broad and powerful, the lateen-rigged dahabeah they had hired to sail upriver moored further along.

She clenched her fists so hard her nails dug painfully into her palm, bringing her back to an awareness of the present. It was, after all, her own fault that Iskander with his reminders of the past was here. She ought to have made some excuse when he had written to announce his presence in London and his wish to renew their acquaintance, for she had immediately sensed danger. Was she exaggerating its importance? Yes, she had to believe she was. There had been friendship between them, once, though she had forfeited that. Accepting this, she was able to regain mastery of herself, and to speak calmly once more.

"Thank you so much for the presents, Valery, I will see the girls get theirs. Ah, there goes the dressing bell. I'm afraid we must go and change now." She hesitated. "I should perhaps tell you we expect another guest tonight, one you have met before – Myles Randolph – Lord Wycombe – will be with us for dinner."

"Major Randolph?" His light blue eyes, so startling in his brown complexion, flew open wide in astonishment – then were instantly veiled.

"The same – though he became Colonel before he resigned his commission five years ago to live on his estate at Stoke Wycombe."

"I shall look forward to renewing our acquaintance."

Their eyes met. She doubted very much whether the pleasure would be mutual.

Myles Randolph, Lord Wycombe, retired Colonel of the —th Royal Dragoons, was the last house guest to arrive at Charnley that weekend. He came in his new motorcar, which he was driving himself, with his manservant sitting in the back, and drew up with a flourish on the gravel beside the front door. Emerging from the red leather interior, he divested himself of his motoring goggles and his long dust coat with some relief, though the journey from Stoke Wycombe, his own estate some forty miles away, had been accomplished in less than two hours through the miracle of the modern combustion engine.

While his baggage was unstrapped, and his man went away with instructions to summon Amory's driver to see to the garaging of the motorcar, Wycombe stayed beside his pride and joy, gazing out over the gardens and the long view towards the church, with a familiar feeling of coming home. He had first come to Charnley with Amory in the school vacations, and for so many reasons, it was always such a pleasure to be back.

"'Cor! Why, it's a motor and a half sir, this!" declared Copley, whistling with appreciation when he appeared and saw the Daimler Silent-Knight standing on the gravel in gleaming splendour. Its proud owner beamed, and for a while they discussed the superiorities of sleeve-valve engines and cylinders, petrol consumption and horse power. Copley laid his dark gipsy paw softly on the gleaming coachwork. "Beats the owd 'osses into a cocked hat, don't she, Colonel?"

"Oh, I wouldn't go so far as to say that," returned Wycombe, feeling bound to spring to the defence of his old love as well as his new. "This lovely lady needs a great deal more attention than a mere nosebag of hay and a brisk rub down! On the other hand she can go at twenty miles an hour! Both have their uses, both their disadvantages."

"I haven't got nothing against 'osses, as fur as they go – but speed, that's the coming thing, that's what it's all about, ain't it, my lord? Must give you a thrill, sir." He looked longingly at the steering wheel.

Wycombe didn't disappoint him. "Well, well, see she's properly housed, will you? You know how to handle her?"

Copley's face lit up. "That I do!" he declared, grasping the starting handle. "You leave her to me, sir! I'll drive her round the back and see to it she comes to no harm."

"Thank you, Copley. Do that, if you would."

Inside the house, Amory had just emerged from his study where he had been ensconced since his arrival from the station, and was hurrying towards the stairs, pocketing his watch. He spun round when his friend was shown in.

"Myles! How very good to see you!"

The two men greeted each other with great cordiality, like the brothers they'd always regarded themselves. They had been the closest of friends since their schooldays at Harrow, and had continued so, despite long enforced separations due to Wycombe's army postings. He was honorary uncle to the children, and Marcus's godfather. They exchanged news until, after a few minutes, Amory said, "Well, we must hurry up and change. I'll see you down here for a drink before dinner, and we'll chat later about what you propose to do. We shall be quiet this evening, just the family – and Kit, of course – you, and one other house guest, whom I think you may remember." He had entirely forgotten Miss Jessamy.

Wycombe raised his eyebrows.

"Does the name Valery Iskander ring any bells?"

Iskander, by God! thought Wycombe with dismay, as he was tying his bow tie, achieving perfect symmetry the first time, as he invariably did. Neat in all his movements, he was the epitome of the professional soldier, tall and well set up in a military way, athletic and vigorous, keen eyed and with a now inbuilt tan to his skin from serving in foreign lands with his regiment for most of his life. He had been forced to acknowledge that he had made a mistake when, five years ago, he had sent in his papers, meaning to live the life of a landed gentleman from then on. The intention did not coincide well with the reality, which turned out to be something for which he had not bargained, though he knew he ought to have expected it.

His estates had always been admirably managed while he had been a serving officer, and he had failed to consider the fact that his decision to take overall control on his return might be resented by the efficient land agent who had done the job during his absence. However, he managed to avoid confrontation, having very soon come to the admission that estate management was not something to be picked up in a few weeks, or even months. Neither did its slow pace appeal to him. His had been an active and often dangerous life, he was constitutionally unable to be idle and he was restless with the quiet existence he was forced to follow. He had been a leader of men, enjoying the discipline and framework of army life and the variety it offered. He had served in five different parts of the Empire, fought in three wars and distinguished himself in all of them. After that, managing an estate seemed tame. He had decided, without much conscience-searching, that there was no reason why the status quo should be disturbed.

It did not, however, resolve the dilemma of how to occupy himself in his newly acquired freedom. He rode a great deal, and spent time in Town, where all the usual occupations available to an eligible man without ties offered themselves, until he discovered with dismay that he was not cut out for this life, either, which now seemed aimless and vapid. He stayed at his club, and tried to renew old acquaintances, only to find that most of them had settled down to raise a family or else were 'killing time till time killed them', spending their life in the pointless way he had come to despise. He was beginning to worry about what he should do with the rest of his life, for he had no intentions of growing into a crusty, frustrated old man, when he came with surprise upon the thing which was destined to give him the keenest pleasure he had yet experienced.

Wandering around his echoing, empty house, seeing it with different eyes after his long absences, he had discovered that some of the pictures which had surrounded him since birth, and which familiarity had prevented him from ever examining with a critical eye, were in fact of some interest. There was, for example, a Caravaggio in the private chapel; a couple of Poussins hung in the drawing room, and several Reynolds portraits of his mother's ancestors graced the hall. He knew little about art, but the quality of these paintings was at once very apparent to him, and stimulated him to find out more. With his usual energy and decisiveness, he immediately set about a process of self-instruction which included reading as much as he could, visiting museums and art galleries, talking to – and learning from – those who did know about such things. Occasionally, he travelled abroad, to Italy and Greece, in search of works of art and antiquities. He had gradually become something of an expert himself. Indeed, the reason for being here at Charnley for the week before the birthday was to catalogue and assess the value of Amory's pictures. This was causing him no little disquiet. If the purpose was to provide Amory with cash, as seemed probable – and extremely disturbing – Wycombe didn't think he was likely to obtain it from the sale of anything he had ever seen hanging on the walls at Charnley. Mediocre family portraits, dull landscapes...his friend was almost certainly doomed to disappointment However, he would have to see what the next week brought. Meanwhile, he did not intend to restrict his time here to the valuation of pictures.

For as he had become more knowledgeable about works of art, he had realised he was on the way to becoming happy, except for one thing.

He was made painfully aware each time he visited Charnley nowadays that he was the last of his line. He realised, perhaps too late, what he was missing when he saw them together, Amory and the incomparable Beatrice, who had given him a son and heir. Hitherto, despite everything, Myles had never found the absence of a wife any great disadvantage – thirty-odd years of army life and his own nature taught one ways of dealing with that sort of need. As for the lack of an heir – well, one must regard that as the luck of the draw, the way life had turned out for him. Of late, however, he had begun to feel differently. The idea of his line dying out, Stoke Wycombe going to some distant cousin, was insupportable. It was not yet too late, too impossible, surely? He was not yet fifty. He had a large fortune and a title to leave. He was healthy, and fit, and was not, he believed, repulsive to women. But he could not yet bring himself round to the idea.

Maybe this time, though...He would see what the weekend brought.

He patted bay rum into his skin until his face tingled with its aromatic oils and astringents and, picking up his silver hairbrushes, he contemplated what the next few days might mean. Iskander. Good God! He thought he had seen the last of that one in Luxor – he might have known that life is never so unpredictable a tiger as when you think you have it by the tail.

Chapter Three

We were eleven for dinner tonight, including the family, which now automatically means Bertie as well, the besotted fiancé, who spends more time at Charnley than he does at his mother's house at Falconforde. Not that I blame him for that: Lady Rossiter is a querulous widow and Henrietta and Lily, both older than Bertie – the Ugly Sisters as Daisy will insist on calling them – are a living warning to avoid the unmarried state at all costs.

To begin with, the evening seemed perfect. We were in the small dining room tonight, and the silver and the polished wood of the table gleamed in the warm, flickering candle-light, the glass sparkled, the napkins crackled with starch. The flowers were roses, two silver bowls of them, one at each end of the table, mixed pink and red, nestling in asparagus fern, with trails of smilax from one to the other, their rich scent wafting all around the room. As we began, I saw that we were having Mrs Heslop's famous consommé, so clear one might almost read a newspaper through it.

Mama was wearing Attar of Roses, which complemented rather than fought with the perfume of the table decorations, as mine did. The Floris Geranium that Kit had bought me last Christmas, saying enigmatically that its sharp edge had reminded him of me, had been a bad choice to wear, but unlike Mama, I had not known what the flowers were to be tonight. She looked beautiful as usual, serene in gold ribbed silk with champagne lace and her pearls. Vita wore her smart pale green *peau de soie* piped in black. It didn't matter what Daisy and I wore, no one was looking at us.

Daisy is old enough now to come down and join us for dinner, but we were still an unevenly matched eleven at the table, though Mrs Betts, the housekeeper, had ordered the D-ends of the table to be set up, in order to form a rounded oval which made the seating informal and less awkward. Mama had placed herself between Kit and Uncle Myles who was even more than usually quiet tonight. He is always rather grave and reserved, though we are all very fond of him – he never forgot birthdays when we were children and was always extremely generous in bringing back curios for us from his various postings overseas. Mr Iskander was placed next to Miss Jessamy, whom we are now instructed to call RJ, if you please! She has a certain charm, one must admit, despite looking most peculiar in a multicoloured robe of sorts and a scarf tied around her head like a turban, covering that truly awful haircut, indeed, but making her appear as though she'd stepped straight out of The Arabian Nights. She and Mr Iskander carried on an animated conversation about ancient Egypt for most of the meal, which quite dominated the table, despite Mama's efforts to disseminate it. Mr Iskander did attempt several times to ask her opinions – she had, after all, visited Egypt and seen those very things he was talking about – but she was not to be drawn, for some reason.

He sets himself out to please, Mr Iskander, perhaps not meaning to be ingratiating, though that is unfortunately how it appears. He has brought us all presents, very pretty trifles of jewellery made of semi-precious stones and twisted gold wire. Out of politeness, Daisy wore the turquoise beads he had given her, and I my carnelian ring, but Vita had declared she could not think of wearing carved amethyst ear-drops rather than the very modern pendant and earrings Bertie has bought her from Liberty's. They are lovely, silver and green enamel, each with a black pearl drop – and the only possible choice for her ensemble that evening, she insisted.

Iskander was not the only one who seemed intrigued by Miss Jessamy. Papa on her other side, the last person one would have imagined would care for her type, seemed to be finding her amusing, albeit in a despite-himself sort of way. Even Bertie's glances strayed occasionally from Vita towards her – and as for Marcus, sitting across the table – well, if I were Mama, I would keep an eye on this Miss RJ, that's all I can say.

Only Kit, seated on Mama's left, looking devilishly handsome as usual, with his black hair and thick-lashed blue eyes and sulky mouth – more good-looking than any man has a right to be, despite his nose – seemed immune to her charms. Or perhaps it was Mr Iskander he did not like. Tonight he was Kit at his worst, impossible as only he can be, obviously in one of his reckless moods, and kept throwing sardonic glances at the pair of them across the table, but was so uncharacteristically silent that at one point Mama asked him if he were not quite well. "Quite well, thank you," he replied, piling another helping of golden fish soufflé on to his plate. "Perhaps there is a little too much hot air in here tonight."

Mama, the perfect hostess, inclined her head, pretending not to understand, and signalled to Albrighton who murmured to the footman to open the french windows. She is so *controlled.* Papa, however, who allows Kit a good deal of rope but will tolerate neither boorishness nor innuendo from anyone, stayed with a morsel of soufflé momentarily poised on his fork. Since no one else appeared to have noticed anything, however, he resumed eating, and so did Kit. Oh dear, I do wish he were not so – volatile! The trouble is, he does not know what he really wants. Papa is of the opinion that a commission in the Guards would have been the making of him, but Kit had recoiled in horror at the very suggestion. He toyed for a while with the idea of the Foreign Office but then rejected it as being too stuffy, and immediately afterwards, with typical perversity, chose a career expressly the opposite of one suited to his nature. But it scarcely matters if he does not succeed in what he has chosen to do; one day he will be rich – riches, the curse of those without inner motivation – so he does not need to consider practicalities. There is so much to Kit that he will not admit, his character is composed of extremes, veering from downright misbehaviour to incredible sweetness. Wise old Nanny Byfield is surely right when she says he could become a saint or a sinner.

Yes. Kit has always been difficult, but at the moment he is altogether dissatisfied with himself – and that is a very dangerous thing to be, with his temperament. There have been times lately when I have been very afraid for him, of something in him that could turn to self-destruction – or to destruction of others, and that includes myself. I do my best to fight it, but I have a desperate presentiment that one day Kit may break my heart – or I his.

Presently, after Mr Iskander had finished trying to explain inscriptions, temple paintings and hieroglyphs to Daisy – always so eager to know, my little sister, so thirsty for knowledge, and how well I understand that! – he began a further discussion with Miss Jessamy, still on the same subject of ancient Egyptian art. Whether anyone else felt the same impatience as Mama evidently did about this, I couldn't judge, but Miss Jessamy at least found the subject all-absorbing. I listened impatiently as he went on to expound a religious belief which seems to me so incomprehensible, based as it was on the worship of jackal- and crocodile-headed gods and god-kings and who knows what else. I was hoping someone might put in a question of more absorbing interest about the mathematical principles which must have governed the building of those amazing pyramids, but the conversation had turned upon the Pharaohs, whose custom it was, according to Miss Jessamy, to marry their sisters. A shocked, uncomfortable silence followed this announcement. How very bold and brassy of her to say such a thing, especially in such mixed company! Then everyone started talking at once. Marcus flushed to the roots of his hair and looked as though he did not know whether to admire her outspokenness or be ashamed for her, but Miss RJ went on eating her duck with green peas and new potatoes as if she was conscious of saying nothing outrageous or offensive. Yet I had a feeling it had been done purposely to scandalise, to shake us out of what she would no doubt regard as our complacency.

Women like her call themselves free spirits, which seems to me to mean they have no codes of ethics or moral conduct, they require only freedom to do as they please without thought for anyone else. It's very odd how often they are admired for it. Whereas women who demand real freedom as a right for everyone, and are prepared to suffer for their beliefs, are still treated as inferior beings: Frances, for instance, whose scholarly and intellectual mind soars above that of most men, is derisively called a 'blue', and unfeminine, or thought radical and dangerous because she is constantly striving for the principle of recognition at all our universities, not only for the right of women to attend lectures, but also to take a degree on equal terms with men. And only think of Athene Tempest and her suffragettes, who are enduring scorn and indignities beyond belief, and suffer such terrible punishments because they are prepared to stand by their demands for the extension of the franchise to women!

I had better not continue. I am in danger of becoming sour – or worse, a prig – as Mama often warns me I shall, and I face a trying week ahead. Needlework is something I have never quite seen the point of, but when I approached Clara Hallam, Mama's maid, for a little assistance with the Three Graces costumes, she puckered her mouth like a Dorothy bag and said she'd see what she could do, but of course Madam would have first call on her for her own preparations, which means we shall see nothing of her unless we *beg!* How Mama tolerates her, I cannot imagine, but at least she can't pinch our arms or tweak our hair now, as she used to do when we were children. We must enlist the help of old Nanny, who will be infinitely more cooperative and has always had a nimble needle and a good imagination, and is certainly more fun than vinegar-faced Hallam – though who is not? The costumes should not be too difficult to assemble, but even so, since Nanny is finding it increasingly hard to see nowadays, it seems a great deal to ask of her.

After her maid had helped her to undress and brushed her hair, Beatrice dismissed her for the night. "Thank you, Hallam, you can leave my hair as it is."

"Not even a loose plait, ma'am?"

"I'll do it myself, later, if I decide on it."

"Very well." Expressionless, gaunt as a crow in her severe black satin blouse and grey serge skirt, Hallam put away her mistress's evening clothes and hung over her arm the afternoon's cream shantung, which had a grass stain on the hem to be dealt with; while Beatrice, impatient to be alone, wrapped around herself her favourite black Jap-silk kimono, embroidered with chrysanthemums and almond blossom, and tied the sash.

"I shan't be needing anything else tonight, thank you."

"Don't forget to drink your tisane before it goes cold. Goodnight, Mrs Jardine."

"Goodnight, Hallam. Oh, draw the curtains back before you go, if you will. Otherwise, it might become too stuffy."

"It is very warm. Likely we're due for a stormy spell. I hope we get it over with before next weekend."

"Oh, don't even suggest such a thing! I never knew such a Job's comforter!"

Hallam smiled thinly, drew back the curtains and left silently.

Beatrice poured from the silver teapot a cup of the camomile infusion – with perhaps something else in it – that would help her to sleep. She knew it would be made exactly how she liked it. That sort of thing was one of the reasons she kept Hallam on. Such a stiff, unresponsive creature, so determinedly frumpy and virginal – though with that unfortunate figure, tall, angular and raw-boned, how could she be anything else? She was skilful in her duties, however, and prepared to sit up until all hours to attend to her mistress; she did not chatter or gossip below stairs, and she wielded a needle as delicately as a surgeon used a scalpel: a veritable paragon. Her bony fingers, moreover, were surprisingly gentle when massaging Beatrice's scalp. One might not like her, but one really couldn't ask for much more.

The discussions about Egypt at dinner, which Iskander had deliberately kept going, had upset her, and when the door had closed behind Hallam, Beatrice walked across to the open window and stepped out on to the balcony, where she liked to take a breath of air before bed each night. She placed her cup and saucer on the little wrought iron table there, but did not sit on the chair beside it. Instead, she stood with her hands on the balcony rail, listening to the tinkle of the fountain somewhere below, staring out into the warm, delicious evening, full of the scents of summer, which decidedly did not have the feeling of an approaching storm to her. It still held the heat of the day, but it was not at all sultry. The trees sighed gently, the sky was black and clear, with a crescent moon and a following star. A night for lovers. She could not bear that thought, it twisted inside her breast like a knife. For a second, pierced with the inevitability of what she was now sure must come, she could not bear her life, and in one wild and very nearly irresistible moment, heard the impetuous creature within her whispering how easy it would be to plunge deep down into the soft, enveloping darkness, into...nothingness.

The impulse was over in a flash, and she drew back sharply, sinking on to the edge of the iron chair, shaken to her core. Her lips trembled against the fluted rim of the delicate china cup as she sipped the tisane, fought for equilibrium and gazed at those stars.

One scarcely noticed the stars in Cairo. The sunsets, which were spectacular, yes, one could hardly fail to be bowled over by them. But when the swift darkness fell, there was too much happening below to bother about the heavens, at least in that first month's frantic whirl of social activity and gaiety, when Beatrice herself had been full of that new-found energy and sense of well-being that comes with recovery after being ill. Exotic, overcrowded Cairo – dust, heat, colour, noise. She had loved it all.

Daisy, her youngest and, as she had previously thought, her last child, was almost six years old when Beatrice had suffered the severe miscarriage which had almost cost her own life and had left her languid and depressed, still feeling vaguely unwell, uninterested in anything and unable to banish the unbearable weight of sadness she felt at having lost a child.

"My dear!" exclaimed Millie Glendinning one day, wafting in to tea at the London house in clouds of Worth perfume, red faille and a new hat. "How pale you look! There's nothing for it but you must come to Egypt with Glendinning and me! I absolutely insist on it! It's just what you need, to be taken right out of yourself." And she forthwith embarked on such an animated description of the delights of wintering in Egypt that Beatrice, despite everything, found herself becoming quite taken up with the idea. Plans had been made, said Millie, to set sail by P&O from Tilbury to Port Said, via

Marseilles and Naples, a bracing, beneficial journey which would take about twelve days, and thence by train to Cairo. She then regaled Beatrice with a list of the diversions they would find among the smart, cosmopolitan society of that city for the first month that would be spent there, staying at Shepheard's Hotel. After which, a dahabeah was to be hired, a private sailing boat, to travel up the Nile as far as Assuan and the first cataract, visiting the antiquities on the way.

"Oh, Amory, do let us go!" Beatrice begged, when Millie had gone. She held her breath. He had never been adventurous, and had grown even less so in middle age.

For his part, Amory was gladdened to see the return, for the first time in months, of the sparkle which had lately been so woefully absent from his wife's eyes, a touch of colour returned to her pale cheeks. She had been so very ill, and he was forced to admit that if the mere thought of such a holiday could do this to her, then some time actually spent there, in the more equable climate of Egypt, away from reminders of the last sad months, would surely improve her health beyond measure. But four months!

"My dear, I cannot possibly spare four months from my duties at the Bar." (Though they did not weigh so heavily on him then as now.) He had added, seeing the disappointment shadow her face, "But that doesn't mean you cannot go. It's not as though you would be alone – and I suppose I might contrive to join you for a short while, later."

"Oh yes! That's surely the answer! If you are certain you won't mind?"

He certainly would not. A giddy month in fashionable Cairo, before the Nile voyage was embarked upon, sampling the delights of the European society which had established itself there, was not at all the sort of diversion to recommend itself to Amory, and to tell the truth he was a little relieved that since his wife would not be alone, he would have an excuse *not* to endure it. He still had his doubts, however, about the suitability of Millie Glendinning as a companion for her. It was true that she always raised Beatrice's spirits, she was amusing, but too flirtatious and too shallow for Amory's taste – he hesitated to use the word fast. Suffice it to say that a little of her went a very long way with him, and he was not sure how far he could trust her, though in what way, it was difficult to say. Beatrice, however, was very fond of her, and one could excuse many of her faults when one considered what she had to put up with in the man she had married. Glendinning was twenty years older than Millie herself, and undoubtedly a monumental bore, who had little conversation beyond field sports and polo, and invariably fell asleep after the port. On the other hand, he owned several thousand acres of Scottish grouse moor, and provided some of the best shooting in the country, which Amory had often enjoyed.

While still in two minds about the wisdom of the enterprise, and rather beginning to regret his hasty half-promise, Amory had suddenly remembered that Wycombe was presently stationed in Egypt – actually in Cairo as a matter of fact – with his regiment, as part of the British Army of Occupation, a thought which immediately cheered him up and helped him make up his mind. The British military presence was strong in and around the city and ensured all manner of entertainments and social functions – gymkhanas and polo matches, charity bazaars and fancy dress balls; there was no end to it. The women would be suitably entertained while being looked after by good old Myles, whenever he was available to squire them around.

"Oh!" said Beatrice when he had explained. "Oh, yes. Myles."

"Just the ticket! I wonder why I didn't think of it before," replied Amory, heartily enough to convince himself, at least.

The slight reserve between his wife and his closest friend had always been a matter of regret to him. This would, he decided, be the ideal opportunity for them to get to know one another better. Beatrice did not appear exactly dismayed at the prospect, but not overjoyed, either.

Nor was Millie, when she was told. She considered Wycombe an old sobersides. His presence threatened to put a damper on what she had determined would be a month of undiluted enjoyment. On their arrival in Cairo, however, it was immediately apparent that Archie Glendinning was desirous of nothing but to be left to his own pursuits. He was at once elected a temporary member of the exclusive Turf Club and was able to attend polo matches and play golf to his heart's content. Millie in turn decided there could be definite advantages to being seen on the arm of a handsome, attentive army officer like Major Randolph, or one or other of his brother officers, especially when it turned out that Wycombe, desirous of being worthy of the trust put in him by his friend, had determined they should miss nothing. However little he might personally relish it, he was tireless in organising their attendance at dances and supper parties, he accompanied them on visits to the bazaars in the din and dust of the native quarters, and instructed them how to bargain for *mushrabiyeh* work, embroidery, alabaster, silk and leather goods. He took them to where they could see street jugglers, snake-charmers and acrobats, though he adamantly refused expeditions to native cafés where the Ghawazee dancing girls performed, which spectacle ladies were well-advised not to attend. Life was so crowded and so full of amusements that Millie was in her element, and dull visits to ancient monuments seemed likely to go to the wall.

But they could not possibly go home without at least seeing the pyramids, and the Sphinx, Wycombe admonished sternly, while vetoing outright the suggestion of an evening ride there on donkey back, by moonlight. He would make the more prosaic, but infinitely more comfortable arrangement of a native arabeah. By moonlight, if they insisted, but not by donkey. Not even by the electric tram, a horse-drawn carriage it must be.

They looked at each other and Millie whispered behind her hand, "Don't tell him!" Whereupon they giggled like silly young girls keeping a secret – for they had already seen the Great Pyramid. When the major had been occupied with his regimental duties, they had made their own arrangements and, forgetting the responsible matrons they were supposed to be, wobbled out on bicycles to Giza, preceded by a syce walking ahead to clear the way. There was, Beatrice secretly admitted, an added spice to the stolen outing at the thought of what Wycombe – or Amory – would have thought of it. No doubt the ancient monument had not been as romantic as it would be if seen by moonlight, but it was a wonder indeed, a marvel, and Millie had been all for making the attempt to climb it – what a lark! But looking at its stupendous size, seeing the ant-like figures clinging to the face, Beatrice had been overcome by a sudden attack of vertigo. Moreover, foolish as the thought was, it had seemed somehow sacrilegious to climb and scramble over what was, or had been, a sacred monument. It was the first intimation she had of the effect this strange land was to have on her, that she would be seized by the same fascination and awe that had gripped Egyptologists and others for centuries. Fortunately, Millie's enthusiasm had waned when she saw the perspiring state of those who descended and heard from them that getting to the summit was a matter of being literally hauled there by a couple of natives, in return for baksheesh. Too tedious, she declared. The bicycle ride back to Cairo would be tiring enough.

They said nothing to Wycombe of this adventure, however,

and therefore saw the pyramids twice. They also visited the Sphinx and went along with the other cultural activities he planned for them all, whenever he could manage it.

In between, they found other amusements. Beatrice had discovered a French dressmaker and a divine milliner, and Millie had winkled out someone who made perfectly exquisite gloves, not to mention a jeweller who sold better (though consequently more expensive) things than the cheap and showy trinkets offered in the bazaars, which probably came from Birmingham, in any case, said Wycombe. In the afternoons, they sipped mint tea and listened to the military band at the Ghezireh Club and wrote postcards to send home: Cairo was marvellous – colourful, strange, exotic and crowded, but full of flies and exceedingly whiffy. The noise was unbelievable – street cries, the continuous clanging bells of the electric trams. Donkeys and people everywhere. It was still very hot and it never rained. Be good children and I'll bring home the red fez I have bought for you, Marcus, and the stuffed leather camel saddle which might be adapted for your pony, and French dolls for the girls. Mama is feeling much better.

Indeed, by the time they were embarked on the Nile voyage, Beatrice was in finer spirits than she had thought possible when they had started on this trip.

To accompany them on the journey was a young man by the name of Valery Iskander, hired on Wycombe's recommendation as the ideal person to be the organiser of the trip. He was a student of archaeology at the Al Azhar University, and was said to be as extremely knowledgeable about Egyptian history as he was about Nile travel and the local customs. It was a great asset, too, that he was part Egyptian, and thus would be able to hold his own with the notoriously independent reis, the sailing master of the boat, and keep an eye on the crew. He was a penniless, but pleasant and cultivated young man, despite his family's unhappy history. His father had left Russia after falling foul of the Tsar's secret police, and there had never been a moment when it had not been dangerous to try and return. His parents were now both dead, and he lived a pinched and somewhat precarious existence on the fringes of Cairene and European society, often despairing of his situation. But his Egyptian blood would not let him be melancholy for long.

His presence on the boat promised well.

Chapter Four

"So there's no more to be said. Your mother doesn't approve of Egyptian themes for redecorating her guest rooms, and that's that."

Rose Jessamy scuffed the beautifully raked gravel with the toe of her shoe, spoiling its symmetry and raising little puffs of dust, scowling at the writhing stone figures rising above the basin of the fountain as though they were to blame for her being put out of countenance. It was still early and the morning was hazy, but very warm, giving promise of real heat later in the day. The old roses climbing the walls gave off a rich, heavy scent, the sound of the splashing water was a cooling antidote to the massed geraniums blazing in the geometrical flower beds, each with a standard fuchsia sentinel in the middle and a border of royal blue lobelia.

She dipped her fingertips in the fountain and dabbed water impatiently on her wrists. "She sent for me first thing this morning to talk about what I intended to do. And I'm bound to say that I feel she's not willing to open her to mind to original ideas."

"Maybe not," Marcus replied cautiously, unable to escape recollections of that rash, unladylike remark Miss Jessamy had made at dinner the previous evening. One wouldn't be, after that. Not his mother, at any rate. "Though I m-must say, it sounds rather stupendous. She might be persuaded, though I agree that last night she didn't seem at all keen to be reminded of Egypt. I was too young to know anything about it at the time, but that trip of theirs couldn't have been much of a success. That f-fellow Iskander – I'd love to know where they encountered him…"

They began walking towards the wisteria-hung pergola, where it was cooler. Rose, recalling Beatrice an hour ago in a café-au-lait satin bedjacket trimmed with white swansdown, leaning back against frilly white pillows, her pale, shining hair tumbled around her shoulders, drinking her morning tea and nibbling a nearly transparent piece of bread and butter, was still smarting at the rejection of her brilliant ideas. "I had thought of friezes, you know, going round the walls, a sort of Nile panorama, if you see what I mean, gold on black, boats with high prows, kings and queens in those wonderful tall headdresses, those dramatic hairstyles! Ra, the sun-god, on the ceiling, and the wall paintings in ochres and terracotta, reds and greens, with that ravishing blue they used to decorate the temples." Her enthusiasm was making her quite lyrical. "The idea came to me when I was talking with Mr Iskander, over dinner. For a long time, I've been fascinated with the ideas coming out of Egypt – there's such a beautiful simplicity and dignity about those austere figures, and those pure, clear colours! I lay awake half the night, thinking about it. The possibilities seemed endless, but…" She broke off and lifted her shoulders. "Well, there it is."

"Don't be too disappointed. I'll speak to Mama and see if I can bring her round to your way of thinking." Marcus had very little hopes of any success, for he was somewhat out of his depth here. Not being artistic himself, knowing nothing about Egyptian art or archaeology, it seemed to him there was a danger the rooms might end up resembling the insides of tombs, which made him rather sympathetic to his mother, but he smiled encouragingly.

"I don't see her ever agreeing to it. I shall have to compromise."

Glancing at the set, angry little face of the young woman walking beside him, he couldn't imagine she would be very good at that. "Some solution will be found. You mustn't take it to heart, that would never do. And I simply won't allow you to lose any sleep over it, Miss Jessamy."

"Have you forgotten how I detest that name?"

"Oh, sorry – but look here, I c-can't go on calling you RJ! It's ridiculous, and besides, it doesn't suit you at all, you know."

"Neither does Rose!"

"Oh, I don't know about that." Marcus stopped walking, the better to see her, and grinned engagingly. "You have rather a sweet face," he added wickedly, suspecting it would enrage her all the more, but meaning it all the same. "Rosa Perfecta, perhaps – ivory, flushed with pink around the edges in the heat, but with exceedingly sharp thorns."

"I don't believe there's a rose called that!"

"Then there should be. When I retire and take up my inheritance here, I shall breed the perfect rose and name it that."

"Breed roses? You?"

"Why not? I've always had the idea at the back of my mind. They're such jolly flowers, roses. I shall stop making all that filthy lucre at the Bar and come home and listen to Scott Joplin and be a p-perfect nuisance to Hopper and his under-gardeners...meanwhile, I'll find you a beauty to wear at Mama's birthday party."

"What nonsense you talk! I shouldn't really be here at all for your mother's birthday."

"I don't see why not, it was she who asked you to come, after all – impatient for you to get started on those rooms, I dare say."

"And now–"

"Dash it, she'll come round, I'm certain of it! After all, she wanted something different, and agreed to give you carte blanche. Anyway, I for one am glad you came."

He smiled down at her. She had to tilt her head to look up at him. She noticed he was hardly stammering at all. He had beautiful white teeth and a kind face. "Rose, I–" Suddenly, he swung round. "Daisy, what the deuce are you doing lurking about here?"

"I wasn't lurking!" retorted Daisy indignantly, emerging from behind the high brick wall that hid the kitchen garden, carrying a small basket. "I've just been to the hothouses for some peaches for Mama's breakfast. Don't they look luscious? All rosy and downy. I shall decorate them with fern and tuck in a rose. Red, or yellow, what do you think? Tell me, which one shall I ask Hopper for? You know all their names, Marcus."

"Rosa Perfecta," said Marcus, looking at Rose Jessamy. She blushed and her mouth curved upwards and for a moment, forgetting herself, she looked quite pretty.

So he really did know something about roses, she thought. How clever of him to be so very unusual. But no, she didn't think he would ever do anything for effect, as Kit Sacheverell did. She knew he was nearly twenty-five but how young he seemed, in comparison to her! How unworldly. Not in the least like Kit, either, with whom relations had swung to and fro ever since their meeting last year, in ways she didn't always like to think of. There was a thread of darkness running through Kit which it wouldn't do to underestimate or ignore. He was unpredictable, and probably ruthless at times. Perhaps she was a little like that, too, especially where her work was concerned. But Marcus, never. You would always be sure of him, she thought. He would always be the same. She was beginning to regard him with more interest, this young man with a passion for ragtime and roses.

Daisy, clutching her basket of peaches, turned back. "By the way, Marcus, we're going to need you and Kit to help us with this tableau."

Marcus groaned.

"Only to pull back the curtains – and to bring your gramophone and a record. Copley has promised to rig things up in front of the folly, and – oh, help!" she cried as the stable clock struck nine. "Harriet is waiting to pin me into about a hundred yards of muslin. There's *miles* of sewing to be done and she'll be cross with me if I'm late."

"And I had better walk down and see what I'm letting myself in for. It looks as though Copley's already begun." Down by the edge of the lake, by the white Palladian folly in front of the trees, he and one of the footmen could be seen moving around, assembling various props.

"Yes," said Daisy, "he's setting it up now so that we have plenty of time for rehearsals."

"Since Daisy appears to be occupied at the moment, will you come with me, Rose?"

Oh, Rose, is it? thought Daisy, as she left them and hurried back to the house. He was evidently smitten, poor Marcus. It was a thousand pities, because even Daisy knew they'd never let him marry a girl like that. Nevertheless, she was rather pleased.

When she had breakfasted and completed her leisurely toilette, but before she had dressed, Beatrice sat with a pile of unread letters before her, facing the unpalatable fact that she might have been wrong.

A couple of hours earlier, after a disturbed night when images and recollections had been chasing each other around like demons in her brain, Miss Jessamy's suggestions in the matter of the guest rooms had seemed monstrous. She might have known that it had been Valery Iskander's discourses on Egyptian art, last night at dinner, which had put ideas into her head and excited her so much. Well, that made no matter, the young woman could not be allowed to dictate her own preferences, a constant reminder of everything Beatrice had tried for over a decade to forget. She had wasted no time in informing her that under no circumstances did she wish the rooms to be decorated in the Egyptian manner. She would be pleased to consider any other suggestions Miss Jessamy might have to make, providing they were sensible ones. The young woman had had no choice but to accept, but Beatrice had felt resentment seeping from every pore.

However...all that had been said in the aftermath of a bad night. Now that she was bathed, violet-powdered and perfumed, her hair brushed and carefully arranged in its puffs and rolls, she was more in command of herself, and beginning to feel not only that she might have been a trifle hasty, but also rather foolish for letting the matter so upset her. One must admit that the ideas put forward were original – and since there was growing excitement being generated at the moment, as Miss Jessamy had not failed to point out, on account of the number of newly discovered tombs which archaeologists were presently opening and revealing in all their magnificence, Ancient Egyptian themes were set fair to become all the rage. It might, indeed, be amusing to be one of the first in the field. After all, she herself had been left breathless with admiration at the scope and magnificence of the originals when she had first encountered them. This was not rudimentary or primitive art, she had realised, but the mark of a high civilisation. It was merely an unfortunate association of ideas that was preventing her from accepting them here at Charnley – and probably, it suddenly occurred to her, with a suddenness that took her breath away, from exorcising that haunting fear from her mind for ever. After years of not allowing herself to remember, she found that now she could not stop thinking about it, like probing a sore tooth. It kept coming back to her at every odd moment, such as now, when she could do nothing but wait for her maid to reappear with the blouse she was seeing to. She looked at the little gilt clock on the mantelpiece and tapped her foot impatiently. Hallam was taking her time; only a few stitches were needed, for goodness' sake, just a couple of inches of the tiny feather-stitching which had come undone on the finely pin-tucked bodice.

"Another blouse, the cream silk, perhaps?" Hallam had suggested.

"No, I'd like to wear the lavender grosgrain skirt," Beatrice told her firmly, "and there's really nothing else which is as cool, or looks quite so well with it. I'll wait until it's done before I finish dressing."

Holding the lavender blouse to her flat and frumpy chest, Hallam closed the door quietly behind her as she departed without further comment in search of needle and matching silk thread.

Beatrice rummaged among her jewels and set aside the jet brooch to wear at the neck of the blouse when it was returned; then, almost as if it were a sign, at the bottom of the box she saw a golden cross surmounted by a loop, the Egyptian ankh which symbolised life.

The dahabeah *Hathor*, named after she who was the goddess of the sky, joy and love, had been everything even Millie could wish for. As a sailing boat, it was smooth and stable, as a place to live, commodious and convenient, almost a modern hotel in miniature. There were five cabins, besides quarters for the crew, and a saloon that was luxuriously furnished, right down to a piano with a paisley shawl draped over it, and was kept cool by the breeze which blew through its opened ends. Nothing about Egypt was conspicuously clean, but the boat had adequate sanitary arrangements, and was even equipped, amazingly, with that most modern of Western appliances – an ice-box.

Luxor, where they would leave *Hathor* for a few days' stay at the Luxor hotel, before journeying further up-river to Assuan and the great dam being erected across the Nile, seemed improbably distant as they left Cairo behind. There was no necessity to hurry, however, no definition of time, and as the boat began to sail its course up-river a feeling of informality and relaxation descended like a benign presence. The days slid by in a dream; the boat glided swiftly between mud banks, clumps of papyrus, palm groves and lebbek trees, while the khaki-green waters of the Nile lapped against the sides of the boat...the Nile, which at a distance always seemed so slow but was in essence a great, moving, powerful force. One became more and more aware of its power as one drew nearer to its source, and contemplated the mystery of the yearly inundation that flooded the land before the great river emptied its waters into the sea – that miraculous annual flood which brought down rich, alluvial mud to fertilise the banks, and irrigated the crops upon which the health, happiness and wealth of the people of Egypt had depended for thousands of years.

But the delights of living on *Hathor* had soon palled for Millie. She had never envisaged the voyage being as boring as this, with nothing more taxing to do all day than recline under the shade of the awning on deck and doze, or read novels, waiting for cold drinks to be brought, while the endless procession of cargo boats passed by, laden with fodder and sugar cane and water-pots. Listening to the lateen sails cracking in the sprightly wind that invariably sprang up before noon – and all the while a ceaseless background noise from the Arab crew: the endless jabbering and the wailing that passed as singing, accompanied by their weird musical instruments. Worse than the bagpipes at Glendinning's Scottish shooting box! The tedium was relieved a little at night when they all played cards, and she could summon up enough energy to play the piano, and sing for them, but it in the daytime it was too hot – and growing hotter each day as they sailed south – to do anything other than lie prone.

Beatrice was not much fun since they had embarked on this voyage. She seemed to have entirely lost her taste for the gossip and inconsequential chatter Millie lived by. Glendinning was no use at all. He slept and snored on deck while his face and neck grew an alarming shade of brick red. Sometimes he shot water-fowl and wild duck, and once or twice he went off on camping expeditions to do some more shooting. He would acquire the services of a dragoman to conduct him to where he could bag quail and snipe, which were then prepared by the cook for their table. He fished, and sometimes caught some, but not as many as the Arabs with their dragnets. He was happy as a sandboy.

"Cheer up, Millie! Remember how much you wanted to come here," he constantly urged her.

I must have taken leave of my senses, thought Millie. Three months on this boat! "Oh, Glendinning, I never dreamed it would be like this. What I wouldn't give for a decent cup of English tea!"

The unaccustomed food had upset Millie's stomach, the heat gave her migraine, and – utter calamity! – she was without her maid. From the moment the silly woman first set foot in this land, she had done nothing but complain. Her nose was permanently turned up at the suspect foreign food and lack of hygiene. Venturing out into the noisy, smelly, cosmopolitan rabble in the dusty and insalubrious streets had her reaching for her smelling salts and her trusty umbrella to use as a weapon – she wasn't going to end up alongside the dead donkeys in the malodorous Khalig Canal which ran right through the centre of Cairo, if she could help it, food for the wheeling kites which swooped down in front of your eyes for rubbish and carrion! But the last straw had been the cramped quarters she was supposed to inhabit and share with Clara Hallam on the dahabeah – Hallam, forever saying her prayers and taking up so much room with her bony elbows and big peasant feet. She had taken one look, then departed on the next ship home, declaring that nothing would make her stay a day longer in this heathen place.

Millie had thankfully packed her off, but then immediately began to regret it, though Beatrice had said at once, "Don't fret about it, Hallam will maid us both."

It was an offer neither Millie nor Hallam had any choice but to accept. To be sure, both ladies had taken the advice to adopt loosely cut, plain brown holland riding habits with divided skirts as a comfortable alternative to their normal elaborate, constricting attire whenever they went sightseeing, and they wore their hair as simply as possible, but to be without a maid was unthinkable. Hallam's determinedly virtuous performance of her duties nevertheless convinced Millie she would almost have done better without her. She moaned and fanned her face. "No wonder I don't feel at all well!"

"You'd feel better, Millie, if you didn't think about it so much, and took an interest in what there is to see," Beatrice said, somewhat tartly. She herself had never looked or felt better in her life. Despite the broad-brimmed hats she was careful to wear, her thick, pale skin had acquired a golden flush from the sun. More than that, the electric, tonic effect of the desert air seemed to have cleared her mind and sharpened her senses. She was receptive to everything – and since Millie refused to be engaged in sensible talk or discussion, she found herself more and more in the company of the knowledgeable young man who was in charge of their expedition.

Millie shrugged off the advice petulantly. "As far as I can tell, one temple is very much like another." However hard she tried, she could not work up much enthusiasm or awe for the hot, stuffy monuments they visited en route, with their everlasting, unintelligible wall-paintings and inscrutable gods. "One can have too much of a good thing. If I am forced to admire one more statue of Rameses the Second, I shall scream!"

"Well," Beatrice replied shortly, "if you took the trouble to listen to Valery Iskander, and knew the context in which they'd been built, you might be more sympathetic." She was becoming quite sharp these days.

"Oh, *Iskander*!"

"Don't dismiss him so easily. He knows what he's talking about."

Whatever Millie might think of him, Beatrice considered that intense young man to be a find. His extraordinary eyes, pale blue in his dusky face, lit up when he was required to explain the significance of each temple deity, or to decipher the mysterious hieroglyphics, or when he was propounding every last detail of the lost civilisation of the ancients. It was entirely due to him that the Nile journey was given meaning and purpose. Listening to him, her head had become filled with stories of how the pyramids were built by means of circumpolar stars and the dark, still point; with talk of spells and incantations and riddles; of eternity and resurrection, and the Doors of Heaven. He did his best to unravel for her the complexities and mysteries of the ancient religion, but she was bewildered by one based on the fear of self-begotten, self-existent, almighty Ra, the god of all; by the multiplicity of grotesque gods and goddesses, their dual nature and their half human, half animal shape; horrified by human sacrifice and the obsession of the ancients with the world of the dead. But she realised Iskander was in love with his country's past, speaking of Tuts and Ptolemies as though they were but one generation removed, his enthusiasm making them seem still alive. His deep knowledge of his country's history and its culture amounted almost to an obsession.

She understood a little of this passion when she saw for herself how the past was still all around them, often disregarded. The colossal fallen statue of Rameses the Second, lying in the dust at Memphis...mud hut villages built on the rubble of former civilisations, hallowed stones plundered for re-use as native hovels...temples used by gypsies whose fires had blackened the interiors, where sparrows and bats nested above the porticos. Enchanting, black-eyed, filthy children playing among the ruins of a temple and wanting to sell them a kid for a few coins.

But Millie refused to show an interest in any of this. "We might have walked along the Embankment in London and seen as much," she objected petulantly, at gloomy Denderah. "At least there is one of the original obelisks there to see."

"But not in its original context."

Millie's stomach upsets continued, and she could hardly contain her impatience for their arrival at Luxor, where a decent hotel, baths, and soft beds awaited them. Not to mention Major Randolph, who was to join them there and spend his leave with them. He at least managed to make excursions interesting without trying to stuff one's head with incomprehensible facts about a dead civilisation.

The eternal, dun-coloured cliffs beyond the lush valley plain became shoulders of hills covered with golden sand-drifts as they journeyed further up the Nile, into Upper Egypt. Dust-devils spiralled litter, leaves and sand into miniature whirl-winds; then the north wind failed and the khamsin blew for days, making navigation impossible. The hot, suffocating wind from the south drove them all down below decks, while it buffeted anyone unwise enough to venture out, and coated everything in sight with desert sand. Tempers frayed, and even the normally happy, smiling crew became cross and morose.

"It will become hotter still," warned Iskander, smiling imperturbably, "but not as hot as in what they used to call 'the evil days of summer'. The sun is pitiless then."

The choking khamsin at last departed. When they went on

deck, the sandbanks had been blown into new and mysterious shapes, and the sky was quiet and still once more.

"I will tell you a story about the khamsin," said Iskander. "There was once a pharaoh's daughter, whose name I have forgotten, beautiful and young. She went down to the riverbank, walking under a canopy of silk held by her handmaidens, to bathe in the Nile before her marriage to an old man whom her father commanded her to marry, but whom she did not love, for there was a young prince who had already claimed her heart. She lowered herself into the water nine times, and each time wished that she might die before the marriage could take place. The prince she loved, disguised in the form of a crocodile so that she did not recognise him, glided silently up to her. In her despair, wishing for death, she said, 'I give myself to thee.' Now, these were also the words which meant a solemn promise thereafter to be bound to a man as his wife. 'Come with me,' said the crocodile-prince, and they swam away together. Her handmaidens, believing she had been eaten by the crocodile, beat their tambourines and uttered long lamentations of grief. Her father sorrowed for his daughter, while for three days, the khamsin blew. When it ended, the king saw that the wind had carved and shaped in the sand outside his window the form of a crocodile, with his daughter in its jaws. So afraid was he that this was an afreet, an evil spirit come to haunt him, that he publicly expressed his remorse for the wrong done to his daughter, and promised anything their heart should desire to anyone who would kill the crocodile. At this, the princess came forth by day from the darkness, walking towards him with her young prince, radiant with happiness."

"And of course, they all lived happily ever after," said Beatrice with a smile.

Iskander smiled too, his wide, white smile and, as he often did, took her hand in the most natural manner, gently stroking it as he talked, a liberty she permitted without thinking too much about it. She had grown used to it, and to the compliments he paid her, not in the light, social way she was accustomed to, and had always taken as her due, but looking at her with those strange eyes as though he meant every word. The way he pronounced her name made her smile. "Ah, Bayah-tree-chay, the shape of sand, like life, is whatever we wish it to be," he murmured softly.

The boat glided on, and the sunset turned the sky to fiery rose and gold, and its reflection lit the rocks either side of the river so that they, too, were rose and gold, before the sun went swiftly down and they turned black and menacing. A vulture landed on the edge of the rail, then took off. Beatrice looked up, and saw Millie standing at the entrance to the awning, a silk stole in her hand. Her bright eyes went from one to the other, then Iskander, without haste, conveyed Beatrice's hand to his lips, "Goodnight, Bayah-tree-chay." He stood up and lazily walked across the deck. When he came to Millie, he bowed and raised her hand to his lips, too. "Goodnight, Lady Glendinning." The iciness in his voice matched the cold blue stones his eyes had become on seeing Millie.

In the silence after his departure, Millie said, shivering a little, holding out the stole, "Are you not cold out here? Come down below and talk to me. Glendinning is asleep again, and I'm likely to die from terminal ennui with having nothing to do, and no one to chat with."

"As you wish, though I haven't felt the cold." But now, aware of the warmth of the heavy silk as it slid around her shoulders, Beatrice realised how chilly the night, with the onset of its swift darkness, had in fact become.

Millie paused before they went below, and looked her straight in the eye. "A word of warning, my dearest Bea. Amuse yourself all you want...but be careful. Amory is not a man to be trifled with."

Beatrice paled a little under her sun-warmed skin. This was rich, coming from Millie! Whose flirting had always gone somewhat beyond the bounds of circumspection, at weekend house parties, and elsewhere, for that matter. Who had, in fact, changed her original opinion of Wycombe in Cairo, and had set her sights firmly on him. She could scarcely wait until she met him again at Luxor – though her instincts where he was concerned, Beatrice thought wryly, had failed her there. He would never be interested in the likes of Millie.

But how dare she? With difficulty, Beatrice managed to keep her indignation under control. Valery Iskander was, after all, nothing more than an interesting companion. He was a mere twenty-two, a boy. And she was thirty-three. Yes, he had been holding her hand when Millie had arrived on deck. Yes, she had found the experience pleasurable, and perhaps needed to examine her motives in allowing it. But she was not deliberately flirting with him, as she might have done with any young admirer in London, so what did that signify?

The days slid by as they approached Luxor. Like the natives who sat in the sun and did nothing, or took all day to perform the most simple task, Beatrice was happy enough. Unwitting of what lay ahead for her. Waiting. She did not know for what. She had glimpsed something else, some vaguely understood part of her, something of that same inexplicable longing that occasionally assailed her in her decorous life at Charnle, and thought it might be vouchsafed to her.

As soon as Hallam had hooked her into her skirt and the cool lavender-coloured muslin blouse, its pin-tucked bodice now invisibly mended with exquisite, tiny stitches, re-ironed and free from every crease, and she had picked up a matching silk parasol trimmed with black lace, Beatrice, still feeling magnanimous at what she proposed, strolled out into the garden, outwardly purposeless, but intent on seeking out Miss Jessamy without delay.

She found her on the lawn in front of the house, giving Daisy, who had a sketchbook on her knee, advice as to how to proceed with a drawing of Marcus, who lounged on the grass a few feet away. They were all laughing when her shadow fell between them and the sun, causing them to look up. The laughter subsided when she said she had come to see Miss Jessamy about the guest rooms, and a rather horrid little silence ensued, but when she told them of her change of heart, Daisy threw down her sketchbook and jumped up to embrace her. Miss Jessamy went almost as red as that terrible hair. And Marcus just grinned, as if he had known all along that she would change her mind.

Beatrice was mortified, not having thought that her negative decision would have been received so critically by others as well as the young woman herself. Neither had she imagined such rapport would already have been established between Miss Jessamy and Daisy, not to mention Marcus. But at least it appeared that she had not entirely forgotten her role as companion to Daisy.

She left them sitting there, and with these thoughts occupying her mind strolled down towards the lake, and the summerhouse, where she was surprised by Iskander, sitting there as if he had been waiting for her.

"I hope you are being looked after properly, Valery. Is everything to your satisfaction?" she asked, endeavouring to play the polite hostess, while every nerve screamed danger.

"Not everything," he said, with meaning. There followed a long silence.

"What is it you want of me?" she asked at last in a low voice.

"I simply want explanations, an answer and an apology."

"For what?"

"Your conduct towards me in Luxor. I want an answer to the question – why? That is all I have come for, what I want to know. Why?"

"I simply don't understand."

"Oh yes, Bayah-tree-chay, I think you understand very well."

Chapter Five

Beatrice's birthday morning, a week later, dawned bright and clear. Her breakfast had been cleared and she had risen and was sitting at her dressing table when Amory came into her room, clean-shaven and smelling of bay rum, with a smile on his face and in his hands a flat box bearing the name of the Bond Street jeweller he always patronised.

"A very happy birthday, my dear. I didn't come along earlier, not wishing to disturb you. You're going to have a very busy day today."

"Oh, the children have already been to see me," replied Beatrice, smiling and waving to the masses of tissue paper and ribbons still strewing the bed. "Lovely presents, so sweet of them."

"Well, here's another that I hope you'll like."

Resting on white velvet inside the box was a parure, comprising a matching bracelet, necklace, earrings and a crescent-shaped hair ornament that was almost, but not quite, a tiara. They were exquisitely fashioned, thickly studded with amandine garnets set in marcasite, not nearly so splendid as the sapphires he had given her on their twenty-fifth wedding anniversary, or the pearls when Marcus was born, but charming of him, she thought, as he said, oddly embarrassed, it seemed to her: "Mere trifles, of course, but I believe you've expressed a liking for garnets more than once."

"I have – and these are quite delightful!" She had meant to wear the heirloom emeralds tonight, but she was careful not to give any indication of what she'd intended – and in any case, the garnets' setting was more modern, so much lighter than the heavy gold one of the emeralds. She hooked the earrings into her ears and, smiling, held out her wrist for him to fasten the bracelet around it. He pushed it gently up on to her rounded forearm and then walked behind her to slip the necklace around her neck and fasten the clasp at the back. She was pleased with effect of the delicate cascade of gleaming stones against the creamy skin of her throat and as she felt his fingers warm on the nape of her neck, she twisted round in his arms and impulsively offered her lips to be kissed. "You are so good to me, Amory. I don't deserve it."

"Nonsense! No one could have a better wife. A few bits of jewellery are no compensation for the support you give me. I consider myself a fortunate man, to have a wife so accomplished, as well as so good. And now I must leave you. Work awaits me, even today."

"Of course."

When he had gone, she sat on amidst the pretty, frivolous, untidy clutter of her bedroom, curiously deflated. The breeze fluttered the lace curtains between the heavy folds of the ivory silk drapes to either side. The peach-coloured plush upholstery, the Aubusson carpet, the gold-shaded lamps perfectly complemented the prettily papered walls. The cheval mirror reflected the silver and crystal on her dressing table and the glow of the garnets against her flesh.

She removed the jewels, struggling a little with the clasp of the necklace. Leaving them in a little, shining heap on the dressing table for Hallam to put back in the box, she reached for her silver hand mirror and stared critically at her reflection, allowing the light to fall mercilessly on it. Birthdays were a time for assessment, especially after forty. But, thank God, she could see few lines on the smooth skin of her face. If there were grey hairs, the pale gold prevented them from being obvious yet. Even her neck showed no signs of ageing. Doubtless she *was* an asset to Amory, in all the ways he had suggested. They entertained lavishly, both here and at the London house in Mount Street, and she had gained something of a reputation as an accomplished hostess. They went out a great deal into society, and she had long been accustomed to the adulation she received as a notable beauty. Yet she would have exchanged all – or nearly all – the compliments in the world simply...

You must not expect too much of him, she chided herself. God knows, Amory was not an easy man to know, but the one thing she had learned about him was that he was the sort who, once he said he loved you (which he had done when he asked her to be his wife) did not see the necessity for ever saying it again.

Picking up her hairbrush, she caught the scent of the two long-stemmed white lilies which Kit had sent to her, now on her dressing table in a tall Lalique vase of amber glass. Their perfume was almost dizzying. The tiny shadow which had threatened to darken the day melted away. 'Beatrice, I could think of nothing more perfect for you,' said the accompanying note, which he had signed, 'Your Dante'.

Silly! she told herself, smiling. He should have grown out of all that by now. At his age it was rather dangerous to flirt so outrageously with one who was virtually his aunt, indeed had been all but mother to him. She really should discourage him, but she knew no way other than being unkind – and besides, the delicacy of the compliment could not fail to flatter her. The quick warm colour once more flew to her cheeks as she recollected the note. She had been given lovely birthday gifts – exquisite lace handkerchiefs, a gold card-case, scent, a silver bookmarker – all expensive trifles of one sort or another. Iskander had sent along a truly beautiful heavy gold clip, set with lapis-lazuli, as deep and brilliant a blue as her eyes. But of all the gifts – perhaps even including the garnets – the simplicity of the lilies, and the message, pleased her the most.

Thoughtfully, she drew the brush several times through her hair, then left it and pulled a chair up to a small French writing table standing near the window, to write a note of thanks (for he had sent the lilies via Hallam, and not brought them himself). It cost her a great deal of thought before she finally began: 'My dearest boy...' She hesitated about how she should sign it and finally wrote, simply, 'Yours with the greatest love and affection, B,' and enclosed it in an envelope.

Presently, she rang for Hallam to run her bath and help her dress. She gave her the envelope. Her mood had swung again and she was feeling suddenly suffused with happiness for all the world. "Oh, clear up all this mess, will you, while I have my bath – and don't forget to keep those lilies topped up with water. See what the master has given me! I shall wear them tonight with my new gown. They might have been bought with it in mind. Though of course the emeralds would have looked absolutely wonderful," she added as an afterthought. "Clever of him, though, especially since he hasn't seen the dress yet. Are you sure you haven't shown it to him? No, of course you haven't, Clara!" She laughed.

"Indeed not," said Hallam stiffly, scandalised that the master's gift was being treated with such scant regard...Mr Jardine, so kind and considerate as he always was. She, for one, would never hear a word said against him. Nor would she ever forget how he'd agreed to take on Fred as his chauffeur and give him another chance after that spot of bother he'd been in: Fred, that bad, handsome lad who was her youngest step-brother, her favourite because he'd always stuck up for her against her bullying stepfather.

With infinite care she replaced the garnets in their appointed places in the velvet-lined box.

Immediately following Beatrice's agreement that the guest wing should, after all, be decorated in the Egyptian manner, scenes of great activity had ensued, with Rose Jessamy, in smock and breeches like a boy, taking charge and ordering everyone about. The rooms were cleared and stripped, ready for action. Only the bare minimum of furniture for comfort would be retained when they were finished. Beds would have new bed-heads and feet, rather like the profile of a Nile boat. Fireplaces were to be torn out and if necessary replaced with new. Servants were allocated to help her, with Fred Copley, chauffeur/handyman, sent to assist, and proving himself particularly useful – when he wasn't covertly ogling RJ. While Wycombe, with increasing gravity, went around inspecting and assessing the pictures in the rest of the house, the work here had already begun and swift progress made, despite the number of people, Amory included, who constantly appeared and got in the way, widening their eyes at the apparent mess which preceded the actual painting.

"Are you sure that young woman knows what she's doing?" Amory had demanded of Beatrice in some trepidation, after he had looked in to see how the work was progressing the first day, taken one horrified glance and withdrawn hastily. "She's got the plaster off the walls and I don't know what!"

"Oh, I shouldn't worry about it." Beatrice had now decided to be Miss Jessamy's greatest advocate, having been vouchsafed these glimpses of what the finished rooms might look like. One couldn't help but admire her artistry, the sureness of her sweeping brushstrokes, and the speed and concentration with which she worked, ripping off the old plaster and replacing it with new – for each day's work on the frescoes she was painting round the walls, she explained, must be done directly on to fresh, wet plaster. What pleased Beatrice most was her discovery that the trompe l'oeil marble columns and pediments were going to render the spacious rooms even more spacious, with false perspectives that lent distance and enchantment, that the whole thing would be, in fact, far from the unrestrained riot of exuberant images she had feared, but dignified and elegant, exactly like some of the illustrations in the books from the library which had stood on the shelves, unopened, for decades, and which Rose had found and shown her to demonstrate how it would look. And how much kudos all this was going to bring Beatrice amongst her friends!

The birthday celebrations took the form of an evening reception, and the guests were around seventy in number. A thoroughly egalitarian affair it was to be, embracing neighbours as well as close friends, in line with Amory's liberal principles, even to the inclusion of the rector and his wife, though that was perfectly acceptable, for the lady was the daughter of a general. A cabinet minister graced the occasion, and two of Amory's colleagues came with their wives – and in one case a daughter, a lively and charming girl called Coralie, of whom Beatrice had great hopes for Marcus.

Marcus had done the right thing and given Beatrice the names of several of his friends who could be invited to become acquainted with his sisters, and the young folk crowded together and laughed and flirted and some of the young men drank enough to make them noisy, but not overly so. Their elders strolled about the lawns with ladies on their arms, also flirting, though more discreetly, and admiring the roses (though no one saw a *Rosa Perfecta*). The champagne flowed and was excellent – Amory could never be faulted in that direction. And of course the food was plentiful: on the supper-room table the salmon's cucumber scales gleamed under aspic, the beef was red and juicy as the gentlemen preferred it; the bowls of peaches, grapes, nectarines and figs had been brought to a high point of perfection through Hopper's solicitous tending; there were patties and pies, pastries, cakes and jellies, and three splendid ice puddings if you didn't care for strawberries.

Bertie had brought his family – his mother and the two

Ugly Sisters, who sat together without moving, looking down their noses at all this extravagance and doing their best to put a damper on the occasion – but no one took any notice of them, except Marcus, who had excellent manners and brought them strawberries and cream, and the champagne to toast Beatrice, which they mostly left untasted.

"Oh, Jerusalem, what frights they are! Glowering away in corners, making one feel one must apologise for them all the time!" Vita hissed to Harriet. "If I'd known what they were like, I might have had second thoughts about Bertie. Imagine, if one has a daughter like Etta!"

"You know you would have done no such thing," replied Harriet, watching Vita smiling ravishingly at her beloved across the room, for a moment envious of her, being so openly and unashamedly in love – even though it was with Bertie.

"Perhaps you're right. Do look at Millie! Did ever you *see* such feathers and tulle? But at least that headdress is better than the hat she wore for Cousin Kitty's wedding! I'm sure that was a whole duck, not just its wings, sitting on it, and perhaps its nest, too! Maybe it weighed her down permanently, and that's why she's still looking so miserable!"

Millie was indeed looking less vivacious than formerly, under her astonishing headdress, as she talked to Iskander, whom she had of course met before. Beatrice had been in two minds as to whether to invite her, but in the end had decided it would be wiser to do so than not. "She won't come, but she'll be pleased to have been invited," she'd asserted confidently. Having her own particular reasons for not antagonising Millie, Beatrice still received her, unlike many other hostesses, for Millie had very recently been involved in an open scandal, so notorious it had caused even the compliant Glendinning, accustomed to turning a blind eye, to take the ultimate step and sue for divorce. She was still technically

Lady Glendinning, not yet plain Mrs Kaplan, if ever she would be – but, poor Millie, if only she had been discreet for a little longer! If only she could have known that not a month after the *decree nisi*, Glendinning would die of an apoplexy, leaving his vast fortune to a distant cousin! By doing exactly what she wanted all her life, Millie had succeeded in losing what she most desired. Moreover, Mr Kaplan, who was a banker, was said to be rich, but not so rich as Glendinning, though in truth he was almost as boring.

Millie, however, had accepted Beatrice's invitation. It was a mistake on various levels. For one thing, she was being cut by most of the people there, though a few were coldly acknowledging her in deference to their hostess. For another, Millie could not now stand comparison with Beatrice. People who knew them both knew that they were the same age, but unlike Beatrice, who ripened ever more lusciously as she grew older (though her critics said there was a danger that she might at any time become a little overblown, like a rose which has been open too long), Millie was shrivelling. She looked slightly desiccated, and her once-discreet make up had become heavy-handed and careless. Perhaps, too, she had grown short-sighted – one cheek was very much rosier than the other, like an apple that had caught the sun only on one side. Her patchouli perfume could be discerned yards away. Her attempts at youthfulness made her look clownish, and rather sad.

"She ought not to be allowed out in daylight," remarked Daisy, joining them.

"Oh, Daisy!" scolded elder sister Vita, but laughing, unable to hide her amusement. Then, "Ah, there's darling Dolly!"

"In that case please excuse me," Harriet said, rolling her eyes. Dolly Dacres was Vita's dearest friend, who was to be one of her bridesmaids and who was to be married herself, to a rising young man in the Foreign Office, a month after Vita.

"With the two of you together talking weddings, there'll be no getting a word in edgeways."

"I haven't seen you all day, where have you been hiding yourself?" Beatrice asked Kit.

"Oh, I borrowed Wycombe's motor and took myself out for a spin. I couldn't stand all the fuss going on here."

"And he allowed you to? You surprise me."

"Oh, he'll do anything for me," Kit said carelessly. With an odd little smile twisting his lips he glanced to where Wycombe was standing, for the moment alone.

Beatrice conceded, reluctantly, that this was true. She said rather sharply, "Well, it was too bad of you to disappear, on my birthday, but did you get my note about the lilies? Thank you, my dear, a perfectly charming present."

"Not as charming as the recipient," said Kit. "You look like a lily yourself tonight."

Beatrice smiled, deciding to accept the flattery for what it was worth. She knew she was looking her best in the new oyster silk crêpe-de-chine from Paquin, with a black velvet rose tucked in where the deep vee neck met the high, self-embroidered waistband. She had to glide, rather than walk, a gracious white swan, for the skirt of the dress was fashionably narrow at the ankles, with only a kick of short pleats in a triangular godet to one side, a necessity to enable her to move at all. She carried a black silk fan, her sculpted, silver-gilt hair gleamed, and Clara Hallam had skilfully used the new hair ornament to anchor a cluster of black feathers into it to further show it off. The garnets glowed like fire against her voluptuous bosom.

"Should you like some more strawberries?" Kit asked.

"No, thank you. I *should* have liked to have gone with you when you took Wycombe's motorcar out, though. There's been no peace here today."

"I wish I'd known. We could have driven off into the wide blue yonder and never come back," said Kit, fully aware that he had drunk one glass of champagne too many and was perhaps going beyond what was acceptable.

Apparently not. "What fun!" Beatrice laughed. "But Harriet would never have forgiven us."

Suddenly, the banter had vanished. They were skating on the edge of very thin ice indeed. "Where is Harriet?" Beatrice asked abruptly.

"I don't know. She's got her sights on me to help with this entertainment they're getting up. Oh Lord, there she is, I must go." He raised her hand to his lips, blue eyes gazed into blue for a full half-minute. He was not quite sure whether he heard, or imagined, her whisper, "Later," for she had already turned her head.

Halfway through the festivities the daughters of the house disappeared and presently the guests were urged to assemble under the trees whose leaves trembled in the hot, breathless evening, in front of the folly, down by the lake. There, little gilt chairs had been set out in rows before a curtain, looking suspiciously like the one from the old nursery, which had been rigged up between two elms. From behind it issued muttered whispers and smothered laughs, until Marcus started up his gramophone and the curtains parted.

Later, Harriet wrote in her notebook:

We managed to get through the tableau without disaster, despite my fears. Daisy looked fresh as a flower and Vita perfectly lovely, though nothing could make any of us look like a goddess. Vita in particular is too warm and too – well, earthy, and her eyes danced at Bertie all the time we kept up our pose, which we were in fact able to do for several minutes before Marcus started his gramophone and Vivaldi's 'Spring' began. This was the signal for us to come to life, and we danced in a circle, as gracefully as we could manage, until Kit and Marcus drew the curtain on us, to a storm of applause and shouts of "The Three Graces! Bravo!" Gratifying, even though it was mostly out of politeness. Mama was looking so happy, smiling and clapping, with the lovely garnets Papa had given her glittering against that gleaming oyster silk.

And then, as the music continued, Daisy danced off the 'stage', waving her arms about, followed by Vita and me, and we all went quite mad. The guests joined in, even Teddy Cranfield danced with – or rather dragged around – poor, lumpy Selina Horsley, and Miss Jessamy, who had been sitting a little to one side, doing sketches of people, was pulled to her feet by Marcus. She barely comes to his shoulder. I would have loved to see those sketches she'd been doing, but when I asked, she said, quite politely, that they were only for her own amusement. Bertie, of course, danced with Vita, and Daisy danced by herself until one of the Houghton-Vesey boys beat his brother to claiming her after only a moment or two. I wasn't surprised. She looked ravishingly pretty. Mama had better look to her laurels when her youngest daughter is launched into society.

Kit whirled me around for a while and then went off in search of more champagne, though he'd already had enough, and I was very much afraid I was going to be paired off with Mr Iskander. Oh, misery! as Daisy would have said. He was the spectre at the feast tonight, looking bored and sulky, except when I had caught a glimpse of him near the backstairs, deep in conversation with – *Hallam*!

How very odd, I reflected, until I remembered that Hallam had been with Mama on that Egyptian tour they had taken, so they would be acquainted. Perhaps they were talking about Egypt. He is rather a bore on the subject of his own country and its proud civilisation, but it is the only thing which one can find to talk to him about, and the only time he becomes animated. Although I cannot find it in me to like him, he is such a fish out of water that I can't help feeling a little sorry for him – though not when I think of those eyes, which can be so – merciless, is the word that comes immediately to mind. Is that why Mama sometimes seems so uneasy in his presence, and avoids him whenever she can? Possibly he and Hallam were commiserating with each other – he was obviously not enjoying himself, and she had taken umbrage at being detailed to be on hand with smelling salts for any of the ladies who were overcome by the heat, and a needle and thread ready in case of small, necessary repairs.

I escaped and went across to Papa who was standing a little apart, in the dusk, his eyes on the dancers. "You look very solemn, Papa. Why don't you dance with Mama again?"

"Wycombe does it so much better than I. They make a very handsome couple, don't you agree?"

That was true, but neither looked as though they were enjoying themselves. "Won't you dance with me?" I asked, tucking his hand beneath my elbow.

He smiled and began to shake his head. He does not really care for dancing at all, but then he looked at me and I suppose he thought I had asked him because I felt left out – a *wallflower*! "And save me from Mr Iskander," I added, rather quickly.

"That's a fate I would not wish upon anyone," he said, after a moment's pause for thought. Papa does not often make jokes – and when I looked at him I saw he was not smiling. He was in a very strange mood tonight. Then he did smile, and bowed very gallantly and took my hand and escorted me to join the others.

* * *

Lord Wycombe and Beatrice waltzed politely, holding themselves carefully apart, as if they'd be glad when their duty was over. They spoke little, and avoided looking at each other. Perhaps they had nothing to say, or perhaps they were afraid of what they might say if they did speak.

Then suddenly he said, abruptly, "What was Kit saying to you? Was he telling you how he inveigled me into letting him borrow my precious Silent-Knight?"

"Inveigled? Does that mean blackmailed?" She smiled. "But what hold could he possibly have over you?"

He almost missed a step, held her a little tighter until they regained the rhythm. "That was not what I meant," he answered stiffly. "No, he threatened to get in the way and disrupt proceedings if I did not, which you know he's perfectly capable of doing."

"He means no harm. It's just a lot of silly talk because he's not sure of himself."

"Then it's time he was, at his age," His Lordship said sternly, his eyes resting for a moment on Kit, who was leaning against a tree, part of a group, but not joining in. Despite himself, his expression softened, and he sighed. "He's allowed too much rope. A spell in the army would have knocked all that out of him."

"You sound just like Amory!"

"That's hardly surprising. We think alike on most things."

Their glances met. Hers was the first to fall. "Oh, Beatrice!" he exclaimed wearily, under his breath. After that, they danced in silence until she was claimed by someone else.

"Well, Bayah-tree-chay?"

"Well, Valery?"

"I am still awaiting my answer."

This had to stop. One way or another. She knew that it would come to the point where she must bow to the inevitable – but would it end there? Tonight she had been so very happy, and because of it, she found a sudden determination, a strength surging in her that she hadn't known she possessed. She would not allow anything to spoil tonight, nor mar her life by regrets that she hadn't taken the opportunity when it arose. So be it. She let her hand rest on his arm. His other hand closed over hers and at the remembered touch, her breathing quickened. "Very well. Tonight, when everyone has gone."

Chapter Six

The celebrations had been a triumph, and social success always gave Beatrice an unusual animation. She felt vibrant and alive, keyed up, aware that the wine, plus the decision to act, at last, had brought a becoming flush to her cheeks, a sparkle to her eyes. At midnight, when the very last of the guests had gone home, or to their rooms if they were house-guests, her senses still felt as tautly-tuned as violin strings. The night could have gone on for ever, as far as she was concerned. While the servants, some of whom had to be up at five the next morning, hurried to clear away the debris of the party and leave the rooms tidy, aching for their beds after their long, hard day's work, their mistress drifted through the rooms where the aromas of cigar smoke, flowers and women's scent lingered, as if reluctant to let it all go, bending her head to breathe in the scent of a bowl of roses, touching this and that, looking out into the blackness of the now still garden while stroking a velvet curtain, as if drawing its sensuous feel into her fingertips. Staring at the ormolu clock on the drawing room mantelpiece, her shoulders tense, then from the portrait of herself above it, painted by John Singer Sargent, to her actual face in the looking glass, suddenly anxious and sad, as if she didn't really know who this stranger was. At last she made her way to the foot of the stairs – but no, it was only to murmur to Albrighton that she'd decided to take a last turn in the garden. A footman clearing the last of the plates from the supper room dared to roll his eyes at the butler, but Albrighton, always correct, pretended not to see. Waiting to lock up, he swallowed a yawn, stretched his eyelids and wished his shoes weren't so tight.

It wasn't until some time later that Beatrice at last went up to her room and sent for Hallam, who must have been dropping with fatigue but wasn't allowing herself to show any signs of it. When the hair ornament and feathers had been removed and she'd been helped out of her dress and stood only in her shift, her black kimono loosely shrugged on, Hallam stood waiting for her to sit before the mirror.

"Oh, leave my hair!" Beatrice said, suddenly impatient. "I'll see to it myself."

The other woman paused, hairbrush in hand, her eyebrows raised.

"I'm quite capable of taking a few pins out, Hallam!" she said sharply. "You may go."

"Very well." Hallam put the brush down, bent to pick up an armful of the silk underclothes Beatrice had stepped out of, and left.

Almost immediately, the door from Amory's dressing room opened and he came in just as Beatrice was lifting her arms to remove her hairpins. He had discarded his jacket and replaced it with a red silk dressing gown, and he was wearing his soft, morocco leather slippers.

"I have just come to say goodnight, Beatrice."

"Oh, it has been such a lovely birthday!" She went to him, and impulsively wrapped her arms around his neck, resting her cheek against his, moulding her soft body against him. She was almost as tall as he.

He kissed her gently on the forehead and held her at a little distance. "A tiring one, for both of us, I'm afraid, but I'm glad you enjoyed it so much."

"Everyone helped to make it lovely. How clever the girls were with their little tableau – and they looked so charming."

"We have some very beautiful daughters – almost as beautiful as their mother." His eyes rested on her with his wonted admiration, but she felt, as always, that his response was detached, dictated by propriety rather than warmth. When what she wanted, what she desired most of all...

'*Save me,*" she longed to say, '*Save me from myself...*'

"See you get a good night's rest," he finished. "I have a couple of hours' work to do before I go to bed. Goodnight, my dear."

She immediately withdrew herself and turned away so that he should not see her face. Her voice was flat as she said, "It's very late. Must you work tonight?" It was well after midnight, there were dark circles under his eyes and his face looked drawn. He worked much too hard. She had never regarded herself as a clever woman, but it had occurred to her more than once that he drove himself too far, striving perhaps beyond the limits of his own competence.

"I'm afraid I must."

"Goodnight then, Amory."

"Goodnight, my love."

After her bedroom door had clicked behind him, she sat staring at her reflection. All the life and animation had drained from it. Her face was paler than the shift beneath her wrapper.

She still had on her jewels and slowly, she took off the garnet bracelet. It slid like a snake on to the glassy surface of the dressing table. She unhooked the pendant earrings and laid them beside it, then lifted her hands to undo the necklace. Her fingers were not quite steady and she was unable to undo the awkward clasp behind her neck – better to leave it to Hallam's deft fingers, rather than break it. She reached for the bell to call the maid back, but her hand stayed in mid-air. For one horrifying moment, it seemed to her that the necklace encircling the base of her throat was a raw, gaping red wound, and the garnet drops depending from it were gouts of blood.

With a great gasp of despair, she buried her face in her hands. Amory, Amory! Was this, then, the form that retribution, Nemesis, fate, call it what you will, was to take? After all these years?

* * *

Wycombe had joined the party at Luxor, where they had already spent two days in the first class Luxor Hotel, in what seemed like sybaritic splendour after the confines of the dahabeah. It was pleasantly crowded with European society, and Millie had consulted the resident English doctor and been given some medication for her upset stomach. She had availed herself of the laundry facilities and those of the hairdresser, had even found that the hotel served excellent English tea, and was, consequently, much improved in temper by the time Wycombe was due to arrive. She had not yet come down to have breakfast with him and the others, which they were taking in the welcome shade of the hotel's garden, overlooking the Nile. The fierce heat of the sun had already burnt off the sharp coldness of the early morning and was glaring from the sky on the procession of black-robed and veiled women who walked gracefully down to the river-bank, balancing heavy loads on their heads. The Nile boulevard was white and hot and dusty, and onto it, from the buildings at the side, fell deep shadows, sharp and dark.

"How very nice it is to see you again, Beatrice," said Wycombe. He added stiffly, "You are looking very well. The journey has obviously suited you."

She who accepted compliments gracefully, as a matter of course, felt a quick flush warm her cheeks. "Why thank you. I don't believe I've ever felt better in my life."

After so long in the sole company of Egyptians (Glendinning, at the moment devouring a plate of three fried eggs and several slices of extravagantly buttered toast, scarcely counted), Wycombe's very Englishness was at once a shock and a tonic. He had come by rail overnight from Cairo, but after fourteen hours in what was said to be a train de luxe, the definition of which all depended on your standards of comparison, nevertheless managed to arrive trim, clean-shaven and spruce as always, the epitome of the British army officer.

Beatrice slowly ate some sweet, pink-fleshed melon, and watched a now familiar scene, sharp and clear in the hot sunlight: the busy traffic moving up and down the wide river, a felucca crossing to the west bank, leaning to the breeze, its sail like a curved white wing, while on the quayside further down, a host of dragomen, guides and donkey boys in their galabeyas and skullcaps sat on the ground, gossiping, smoking, one eye out for trade. A steamer had just arrived, and a shrill gaggle of eager, barefoot children in their short, vividly striped shifts chased each other around while waiting to beg baksheesh from the Cooks' tourists who would shortly be pouring down the gangway.

"How long are you able to stay, Myles?"

"I've accumulated some leave, so – nearly three weeks. Then I'll return with Amory, by rail, and leave the rest of you to sail back to Cairo. You've heard from him?"

"Yes. He will join us in a few days at Assuan, as planned," murmured Beatrice.

Glendinning clapped his hands loudly for the white-turbaned waiter to bring more coffee.

"At once, effendi."

"Must wait until Jardine arrives before we go to look at the dam, of course," Glendinning said, rubbing his fiery chin. He had developed a bad case of prickly heat and had forgotten to apply the camomile this morning. "Sort of thing he'd appreciate."

The building of the great dam at Assuan was an enormous undertaking, its complex of locks, drains and sluice-gates across the Nile, the greatest engineering work, next to the Suez Canal, ever undertaken in Egypt. When completed, it would hold back an immense reservoir of water which would enable the land to be irrigated throughout the summer, and make it possible for many otherwise waste and barren regions to be brought under cultivation, for cotton and the other crops on which the country's life and prosperity so desperately depended. It was the sort of enterprise which was certain to have Amory's wholehearted approval.

"Pity he wasn't here for the rest – missed some dashed good shooting on the way here," Glendinning added, getting his priorities right.

It was indeed a shame he had missed so many wonderful things, agreed Beatrice, thinking guiltily of the journal she had started, which she had meant to keep religiously every single day, so that Amory could at least read about the marvels he would unfortunately have no opportunity, in his short stay, of seeing for himself. Her intentions, alas, had proved better than the deed – or perhaps it was because, in the end, what she had confided to her little book was purely for her eyes only. However, she had written regularly to him, letters that were posted at the various stopping places near to the railway, as it followed the line of the Nile – that same railway he would be journeying along in a short time. In her mind's eye she had seen him with her letters in his hand, characteristically pulling his long upper lip and smiling slightly as he read what she had written. She had described, with as much detail as she could recall, the awe-inspiring monuments to a lost civilisation they had already seen, yes, but very little of the feelings they inspired in her (all that was too complicated, too involved with hidden meaning and her increasingly complex reaction to everything around her, as they journeyed ever deeper into the heart of the ancient world). Instead, her letters were confined to what she saw of the life lived along the banks of the river, in which people washed their clothes, performed their ablutions and carried from it drinking water in pots on their heads. She had described the water buffaloes tended by small boys, and the shadoufs that raised river water in leather buckets to irrigate the fields. She wrote about glimpses of distant minarets, so clear against the sky, of muezzins singing their queer, wailing call to prayer five times a day, and of Moslems kneeling to obey the calls, wherever they happened to be. Of a solitary camel and its rider, silhouetted against the magnificent sunset on a far distant hill. And often she would think: Oh, Amory! and wish intensely that he were with her. And was, for some reason, very glad that he was not. But soon, now, very soon, he would be here.

Spreading jam on a French croissant and pouring more coffee, Wycombe said, "You're right, Glendinning. The dam construction is something not to be missed, but it's only one of many expeditions we must make from Assuan. I'm told the splendid repairs to the temple at Abu Simbel are well worth the effort of getting there. A tremendous undertaking, carried out by our own Royal Engineers – and under dashed difficult circumstances, I might say."

Millie arrived at that moment, just in time to hear his last remarks. She greeted Wycombe with a coquettish smile, very pleased with herself, quite restored and looking piquantly attractive this morning under a wide-brimmed Leghorn hat, wearing a muslin dress which had been exquisitely laundered and starched, even by her exacting standards. "Just a little fruit, please, waiter," she said, as he drew out her chair. Then, as he left, "What was all that about? More ruins?"

She was still quite determined to be bored with tombs and temples – and also with donkey rides, which had *quite* lost their appeal – and looked deeply uninterested on being told about Abu Simbel, rolling her eyes when Wycombe informed her that the great rock temple, originally carved out of the heart of a vast hillside, was yet another conception of that indefatigable builder, Rameses the Second. Now relieved of the three thousand-year burden of sand which had silted over them, as high as their heads, four colossal statues, over sixty feet high, guarded the entrance, each in Rameses' royal likeness.

"In case anyone should be in doubt as to who the builder was," Beatrice teased her.

"Hmm. That man was vainer than Narcissus – and didn't *he* fall in love with his own reflection and die of unrequited love? You see, I'm not so ignorant as you think, Beatrice! I do remember something from my lessons," said Millie lightly. "But when all's said and done, it's just another old temple."

"Oh come, it's an astonishing experience," Wycombe chided, though mildly enough, and he said it with a smile. He had grown accustomed to, and sometimes was amused by, Millie's outrageous statements when they were in Cairo. "Like nothing you've ever seen before, you may count on that. I think we may change your mind before then. You can't come all the way to Egypt and fail to see one of its greatest wonders. Meanwhile, you had better tell me what you have been doing since you arrived in Luxor, then we may decide how to expend the rest of the time here before we embark for Assuan."

Millie shrugged as she began to peel an orange. "Oh, we've done very little, to be truthful, except to have a delicious rest and do a little shopping."

He nodded approvingly. "That was wise. You'll be quite prepared now for seeing the temples here, and the City of the Dead."

"The City of the Dead!" Millie shuddered theatrically.

Beatrice contemplated the next two, or maybe three, no doubt exhausting days which would be necessary to explore the necropolis of ancient Thebes, covering many square miles of the river plain and its surrounding, rocky cliffs, where in remote and hidden valleys was the astounding collection of rock-tombs and temples of the ancient kings and queens.

"I suggest," said Wycombe, "we make a trip to the west bank tomorrow, then take a day's rest before exploring

Karnak. Not forgetting the temple here, of course."

He waved a hand in the direction of the Luxor Temple, smaller than the stupendous ruins at Karnak a couple of miles away, but equally as impressive, and said to be even more beautiful, standing but a few hundred yards from the hotel, its ancient columns bizarrely situated right in the middle of the modern little town.

Millie was rather unsuccessfully stifling a yawn, while Beatrice herself felt slightly piqued by the military precision with which Wycombe had taken over the organising of their time here. However, he was putting himself out to be gallant and agreeable. He had been here before and therefore knew what was what. And on the whole, it was so much easier simply to put oneself in the hands of someone so capable, even if he was being rather managing.

Millie, who made no secret of the fact that she could summon up little interest in such a trip, was weighing up its disadvantages. Of necessity, it would entail becoming hot, dirty and exhausted, not to mention having to wear that dreadful brown holland get-up, plus heavy boots. On the other hand, one might remain here in the hotel, with ample time to prepare to greet the intrepid explorers on their return – smiling, scented and clean, in a pretty frock and hat.

"Well, perhaps I may be persuaded to visit Abu Simbel," she acknowledged at last. "But for the moment I've had quite enough of sightseeing. I'm told there are bats in some of the temples! Supposing, Beatrice, they got entangled in one's hair!" She shuddered. "No, I mean to stay here in the hotel for a few more days and take advantage of some *modern* civilisation – I have made the acquaintance of some very nice people. The Bellinghams are spending several weeks here, and I dare say I shall pass my time very well with them."

No doubt her decision had been influenced by the fact that the party she was referring to included a young man of effete but handsome appearance and poetic inclinations who affected to have taken a shine to her, but if she had expected to be left to her own devices, she was doomed to disappointment when Glendinning announced that he, too would stay behind. "Give the donkeys a chance, what?" he guffawed, patting his substantial girth, "and we can take the opportunity to look for some antiquities to buy before we leave, eh, Millie? Any tips, Major?"

"The English Consular Agent is the most reliable dealer. You'd be advised to do business with him, otherwise you're likely to be palmed off with shams. I'll go with you when you are ready to buy, if you wish," Wycombe offered, apparently feeling that Glendinning's way of dealing with the natives by shouting loudly at them would be no protection against their natural-born cunning.

Millie sighed, but obviously felt that even her husband's company was less onerous than trekking through barren valleys to inspect inaccessible tombs. So it seemed to Beatrice that she was fated to spend the next few days in the company of Wycombe. She brightened, however, when she thought of Valery Iskander, who would accompany them, and make their visits so much more rewarding by the wealth of detail he was able to give.

But when it came to the point, Wycombe seemed to have unaccountably taken against the young man, and told him he was free to take a break and pursue his own interests. They would hire a guide. "You do not need a guide," Iskander insisted, his pride affronted, "I can tell you all you wish to know."

Beatrice, too, found herself upset at the idea of his being so summarily dismissed, but her protests did not seem to count for much and Wycombe said privately to her, afterwards, "I'm afraid I made an error of judgement when I was persuaded to hire that fellow in Cairo. This combination of the

Egyptian and the Russian temperament – I don't trust him."

"Why ever not? If you knew him better, you'd realise how much he knows, and how much he feels for this country. He looks on it as his own."

"Precisely! I hope he's not one of those Nationalist hot-heads. They are dangerous men, wanting to rule Egypt for themselves when they have no idea how to do it. They should appreciate how much the improvement in their conditions and way of life has been made possible through the services rendered by the British."

Pompous as it was, it was an unusually impassioned speech for Wycombe, and both he and Beatrice fell silent after its stiff deliverance. She felt profoundly that he was wrong, that Valery Iskander was not of this ilk. That gentle, idealistic young man? It was disturbing to think of hot thoughts simmering beneath the surface, but there were things about him, she had to admit, that she didn't understand. Those eyes, for instance, that had turned so cold when they had rested on Millie, that time on the dahabeah. But their acquaintance was short and perhaps, after all, she did not know him as well as she thought. And indeed, she was beginning to feel she would never know Wycombe at all. The focus of her unease with him shifted slightly. She had always thought him basically cold and unresponsive, but now she felt a dangerous frisson of something she could not quite name.

"I don't mean to be unfair," he said. "You must know, Beatrice, that I have only your welfare at heart."

She traced patterns in the dry, gritty sand beneath her feet and remembered the touch of Iskander's brown fingers as he gently stroked her hand in those long talks they'd had as they sailed up the Nile, his smooth young flesh. A flush started at her neck and mounted to her cheeks. But she was grateful for the concern that prompted Wycombe's interference, and said so, laying a hand upon his sleeve, the first time she had ever willingly made a spontaneous gesture towards him It was a rather large, well-shaped hand, browned by the sun despite her precautions. He looked at it for a long time. "Indeed, Beatrice," he said at last, raising his eyes. "But this Iskander – it doesn't do to let the natives forget their place, get too big for their boots, you know."

Natives! Her momentary sympathy with him vanished. He was talking of Iskander – Valery Iskander, who had been part of her life for the last weeks, who had taught her so much and had awakened in her feelings never before experienced. She tried to excuse the unwittingly wounding words but the antagonism was back between them.

Iskander sulked and would hardly speak to her, no matter how prettily she coaxed him, and then went off on his own concerns.

Later, in her journal, she wrote: '*He intrigues me, but sometimes frightens me. A dark, fierce excitement beats in me, when I think what might happen, what I want to happen; then I hear the echo of a still small voice which says this was not precisely the sort of advice that had guided my infant teaching.*'

The visits to the west bank, and even to the great temple at Karnak were, in fact, quite eclipsed by what happened later. She remembered being awed by the Colossi, the funerary temples and the silent, ancient tombs in the Valley of the Kings, but nothing of their detail. With more exactitude, she recalled the debilitating heat, and her vow that whatever happened, she would find some excuse not to re-visit the sites when Amory would be with them. She had marvelled at the immensity of Karnak, its pylons and columns, ten times the height of a man, sat for a while watching the palms reflected in the Sacred Lake. She was hushed into silence, endeavouring to comprehend a dark religion whose temples could accommodate thousands of people to witness, though not to take part in, arcane ceremonies taking place in inner sanctums where only the priests were allowed, in order to perform their secret, mystic rites, for the holiest and most inaccessible shrines were only for the high priests, who were the link between the people and the terrifying dark gods with power to flood the land in the annual deluge and to send drought, pestilence and death.

But then all of it faded to nothing, after the Luxor temple.

Only recently restored, the temple was within a stone's throw of the hotel and could be visited at any time but, as so often happens when this sort of decision is made, it had gradually been pushed to the end of the itinerary. At one time approached from the greater temple of Karnak by a two-mile paved avenue, lined with ram-headed sphinxes, its massive sandstone columns had once supported the roof of a temple dedicated to the god Amon. Over the centuries, it had suffered from earthquake, sacking and burning by Christian iconoclasts who wrecked shrines, smashed statues, disfigured bas-reliefs and then abandoned it. On the years of accumulated rubble, mud-brick houses were built, and its stones were used to keep back the inundations of the Nile. A few years ago excavations had begun, forcing the native population to abandon their houses, much against their will. Misery seemed to have seeped into its stones and even before she entered, it was a gloomy and depressing place to Beatrice, haunted by the past.

The visit had been made too late in the day, when dusk was already beginning to fall. Perhaps she had been too tired to appreciate its remaining splendours, or was sated or overstimulated by the ruins of mighty Karnak, where she'd been made to feel insignificant and slightly lost in the midst of its overpowering magnificence. Why, afterwards, the temple at

Luxor, though small only by comparison with what they had just been exploring, should have affected her so adversely, she felt unable to explain. Whatever it was, it had overwhelmed her. It was true that the sacred building was more beautiful, less obviously awe-inspiring than Karnak, yet she knew that she would never be able to remember it, ruined, empty and dead, without terror. Or maybe it was simply the echoing darkness and the deep, silent shadows which had oppressed her, the weight of memory, old ghosts. What was certain to her at least was the actual thing that had happened there, in that small chamber.

It was reached by a progression through several preceding chambers, each of which became smaller, and the portals lower as one approached the inner shrine. It was necessary to step over a raised threshold in order to enter it – the enclosed birth-chamber of a royal child, son of the god Amon, a future king, said their guide. The light was nearly gone, and voices echoed eerily. A torch was held up for them to see the inscriptions, the rayed suns upon the roof. Complex scenes carved in relief upon its stones told the story of the child's conception and birth, and predicted his royal status. It was all at once too much. Birth was still too closely associated in her mind with death, both had touched her too recently for her to think objectively: feelings on the death of her unborn child, when she had been so ill herself, and had almost died, came back in a rush. Time stood still while she felt herself caught and trapped in an engulfing sense of despair. The walls of the chamber pressed in suffocatingly, she couldn't breathe. Panic set in, then just as quickly receded as she began to have the sense of a presence behind her in the darkness, and felt strong arms enfolding and supporting her from the back. Instead of despair, there came a flooding feeling of peace, a release. Until the hand from behind cupped her breast and gently pressed...a purely human presence. For a while she leaned back, not resisting the flood of sensation that swamped her. Then she knew what had happened, realised that she was allowing something dark to erupt into her world, opening the way, inescapably, to what would transform her life from its soft sweetness by a dark, unclean emotion which at that moment she felt would choke her.

She twisted herself from the arms and turned blindly to go back. Stumbling on the threshold of the chamber, she forgot to bend her head, crashed into the low stone lintel, and felt herself falling...

The next thing she knew, she was in bed, back at the hotel, and Millie and Hallam were fussing around her.

Old terrors, old fears, but never, ever, to be forgotten.

Blindly, she raised her head, for a moment not knowing where she was. Behind her, in the pretty, frivolous bedroom, the little French clock struck two, synchronising exactly with the tinny strike of the clock over the stables: Amory was punctilious about his clocks keeping time. Beatrice blinked, realising he had been gone but fifteen or twenty minutes, while she had lived through another, distant, lifetime, it seemed. In an effort to recover herself, she rose, opened the french doors on to the balcony and stood there, letting her heart resume its normal beat and the night air cool her feverish brow. An owl swooped across the moon, some small creature screamed in its death throes. The trees soughed and the scent of the Madame Alberic Barbier climbing rose lingered on the balcony. The soft, English darkness beyond was as deep as any in the desert, though the stars were not as bright.

It might have been minutes, it might have been hours later when she heard him open her bedroom door again.

"I am out here," she called softly, her heart beating with hope, not turning her head, "I needed some air."

Footsteps sounded behind her, and she turned as he joined her on the balcony. She gave a stifled cry.

"You thought I was Amory!"

"Yes." She had begun to tremble. A thick pulse beat in her throat.

"He has gone into his study. He will be there for hours." He placed his hand on hers as it lay on the balustrade and she did not withdraw it. They came closer, his free hand moved to her white arm, stayed a moment, then moved to her throat, her cheek, and gently rested there. They stood, eye to eye, not speaking, not moving, but then body to body, lip to lip. Until, with one accord, they moved back into her bedroom.

The light went out and after a moment the cigarette of the watcher in the garden was also extinguished.

Chapter Seven

The following day, Vita lay in the hammock under the cedar, trailing one pretty little foot, a soft cushion behind her head, half asleep, her thoughts drifting, listening to the church bells pealing their summons for morning service, pleased with herself for having resisted the pressure to attend. It was too hot to go anywhere, too pleasant to be doing anything other than lazing here, day-dreaming, just feeling perfectly happy. She was going to marry Bertie, and she didn't care a fig that everyone else thought she was doing so simply because she had managed to make a good catch, in her first season – she knew otherwise. Her family liked him well enough – who could fail to like Bertie? – but at the same time it was obviously they thought he was a bit of an ass. Vita, however, though far from being a fool, didn't crave intellectual stimulation. Unlike Harriet and Daisy, she wasn't the clever type, nor had she ever wanted to be. All she had ever asked was to marry and have three – or four – darling children. She was just very lucky to have found the right man so soon...

I, Victoria Edina, take thee, Bertram Granville George...

Her bridesmaids were to be in palest blush pink. Beatrice was of the opinion that they should, all eight of them, be in traditional white, but pink would be kinder to dear Dolly's slightly sallow complexion (Dolly had chosen cream for her own wedding gown, for that very reason). Besides, Vita herself would be wearing white satin, pure and virginal.

She felt the heat run right up from her neck into her face as she remembered last night's fiasco and what might have happened. They had both drunk too much champagne. As soon as was polite, Bertie's mother and sisters had indicated they'd had quite enough of the festivities, and wished to be escorted home. Bertie, half-drunk, had whispered that he would be back, she must wait for him, pretend to go to bed and then come out again to meet him. Greatly daring, she had promised. What a lark! She would have promised him anything. But oh, what machinations she'd had to resort to in order to avoid being seen as she slipped out! In the end, she had managed it, and waited for him, heart beating, ready to slip into his arms. Under his soft, insistent persuasions, she had led him to where she was sure they wouldn't be disturbed, so that they might kiss and embrace as they were never allowed to do in daylight. And goodness knows what it might have led to if they hadn't been so rudely interrupted –

Vita put her hands to her flaming face. Heavens, no! What was she thinking? Nothing like *that* would *ever* have happened! Bertie was too honourable, he would never have let her risk losing her reputation, and besides, he knew she was *not* fast, or immoral...she was not! Hot shame coursed through her, but at the same time, there was a secret inner excitement that told her if Bertie had insisted, she just *might* not have resisted enough...

"Vita!"

"What?" Vita sat up, almost tipping herself out of the hammock, which at least served to cover her confusion and gave her time to collect herself. "Oh, it's you, Daisy. What's wrong?"

"Do wake up! I can't find Mama anywhere."

"She's gone to church, I suppose."

"No, she hasn't. Hallam says not. She's in rather a state, Hallam I mean – she hasn't even gone off to the Baptists this morning, which speaks for itself. She'd rather miss eating for a week than her Bible class! She says Mama didn't go to bed until late last night, but when she took her morning tea in to her – she wasn't there."

"Well, don't ask me! She may have gone for a walk."

They looked at each other and burst out laughing. The unlikelihood of this amounted to an impossibility. Beatrice never walked anywhere if she could avoid it, except perhaps to take a gentle stroll in Hyde Park when in London, or as far as the lake, here.

In any case, she rarely put in an appearance before eleven in the morning. Sometimes it was noon, especially on Sundays, or when they had been entertaining late the previous evening, as had happened yesterday, but she was usually to be found before then in her room, writing and answering letters and invitations, often from her bed, flicking through fashion journals or busily making plans for entertaining guests here or in Mount Street. But as for rising early and going out to take the air...!

"Perhaps she's gone for a spin with Papa."

"He's in the library. With orders not to be disturbed. And Copley's polishing the motorcar in the yard."

"Have you asked anyone else? The servants–"

"Well, I suppose Hallam's asked them, I haven't. Kit's gone back to London, Uncle Myles left for home an hour ago, Harriet's off to church with Marcus – and Mr Iskander doesn't seem to be about, though I don't imagine he's gone to church. What religion is he, do you suppose? I wonder what the rector would say if he turned up there...perhaps he's run off with Mama!"

"Daisy, don't be such a goose! I know, she'll have gone across to Nanny's cottage. That skirt material came from Swan & Edgar's yesterday, and I was supposed to take it across, but I forgot, and Mama was quite cross with me."

"I dare say you might be right. I'll go over and find out. I want to see if Nanny's cough's better, anyway."

"Shouldn't you be helping Miss Jessamy? I thought that was the reason you'd been excused church."

"Oh, I escaped. She's having difficulty with one of the walls and creating such a dust! And since I've been worked to death all week, I felt I deserved a break. She's a real slave driver." Indeed, Rose had driven Daisy, installed like the sorcerer's apprentice, almost as hard as she drove herself and the staff who had been enlisted to help her with the heavy work.

"You do look a sight, darling Daisy," said Vita with a laugh, stretching out a hand to rub at a streak of paint on Daisy's flushed cheek, rolling her eyes at the plaster-spattered breeches and smock which her sister had been allowed to wear for the duration of the work – and for that only – in imitation of the workmanlike garb Rose Jessamy donned to paint in.

"I know," answered Daisy, with satisfaction. "But it's such fun."

"If you say so."

"Wait until you see the finished product."

"Gracious, I have no intentions of doing anything else but wait!"

But not everyone was avoiding all the mess and clutter, Vita knew, especially the men – Wycombe and Papa, as well as Kit and Marcus, who never ceased to marvel at the quick and competent way in which Miss Jessamy wielded a trowel and a heavy hod of wet plaster, leaving the walls smooth as silk and ready to be worked on.

Vita said, rousing herself from her lethargy, "I'll walk across to Nanny's with you and take her last month's *Ladies' Journal.* She loves to look at the fashions." The girls were all very fond of their old nurse. "You'd better change first, though," she added. "If Mama catches you outside the house in that garb, you'll never be allowed to put it on again."

"I suppose I must." Daisy pulled a face, but went off to change.

When she came back she had on a skirt and a fresh cotton blouse, her face was washed and her hair brushed and tied back with a large black bow. They walked the hundred yards or so to Nanny Byfield's cottage in the lane at the edge of the woods, but found her alone, sitting on a chair outside the door in the sun, turning the heel of a sock without even needing to look, the four steel knitting needles flashing in the light. Poor Marcus! Yet another pair of thick, grey woollen socks, which he must pretend to be pleased with, when he'd been wearing silk ever since he left school. But he would never let Nanny know that.

"No, I've seen nothing of your mama this morning. Maybe she got up early and went out into the garden and waited there to join the others when they went to church," Nanny suggested.

"Mama, putting a toe out of bed before she's had her tea? Oh, Nanny, you know better than that!" laughed Vita, though Beatrice quite often did not have any breakfast. "And besides, how could she dress, who'd tighten her laces for her?" Their mother had never been known to leave her room without being properly equipped to face the day, her hair done and her corsets defining her splendid curves.

"Never say never where your mama's concerned, or she'll surprise you in the end! And as for getting up early, well, she was always up and out in the fresh air before everyone else in the family, when she was a girl. 'It's too *shiny* a morning to stay in bed, Nanny,' she used to say, 'I don't want to miss a moment of it!'" Nanny Byfield, who had been Beatrice's nurse, too, had reached the age when she loved to reminisce and never missed the opportunity of taking advantage of a captive audience. "Oh, she was a madam, and no mistake! 'When I grow up, I want to do this, I want to do that!' there was never any end to it. 'Well, then want will be your master, young lady,' I used to tell her, but I don't think she ever listened." She smiled and drew up a further length of thick grey wool to hook between her fingers as she changed needles, having revealed such totally unexpected facets of Beatrice's character that Vita and Daisy, after one glance at each other, were temporarily silenced. "Out she'd run, down to the keeper's cottage, and calling out for Clara Hallam to come and join her."

"*Hallam*?" they chorused, united in astonishment.

"Well, you knew she was the gamekeeper's step-daughter on your grandfather's estate, same age they were…"

"Yes, we knew that – but not that they were *friends*!" Vita said.

"Well, as to friends – it was always Miss Beatrice this, Miss Beatrice that, lady and servant, you see, never mind their ages, and very right and proper, too. But neither of them had anybody else, only a houseful of stepbrothers in Clara's case, young Fred that she ran wild with, until Miss Bea took her up. Miss Bea without even a mother, and as for her father…he'd always wanted a son, and when his wife died giving him a daughter, he'd no interest."

"Poor Mama!" said Daisy.

"Oh, she never seemed to mind that, what she'd never had she didn't miss, I suppose," Nanny said briskly, "and I didn't see any reason then to discourage the friendship with Clara – as long as I kept an eye on it…it taught Miss Bea she might not be the only one in the universe, and Clara learned better manners than she might have, with all those rough brothers, and to speak nicely. Her mother had been sewing maid up at the Hall, and she made sure Clara knew how to sew. For all her gawkiness, she had neat fingers, and she was a quick learner, I'll give her that. So she was all set up for becoming your mama's maid–" She broke off, abruptly and looked down at her gnarled fingers, which had stilled on her knitting. "Well, that's enough of my old maunderings."

When she looked up again, she could see how taken aback they were. "Don't you take too much notice of what I say, my dears, she soon forgot all that when she met your father and learned that a contented marriage and a good husband is worth a peck of wishful thinking. She'll be back from church with the others, you'll see."

But the churchgoers returned without Beatrice, and a small fuss arose, annoyance tinged with a frisson of uneasiness. All kinds of unlikely suppositions were put forward as to where she might be, but mostly it was felt that she must, on a whim, have suddenly gone to call on someone, or accepted an unexpected, off-the-cuff telephone invitation to luncheon – from someone who must, in that case, have sent a conveyance to fetch her. It was the only reasonable explanation, but left too much unexplained. In particular why, if she had decided to do something so astonishingly out of the ordinary, had she not let anyone know?

It was Marcus, on his arrival home from church, who put an end to these speculations. "Mama?" he repeated. "She hasn't b-been seen since last night?" No one else had quite looked at it like that. "Then something's happened – we must look for her immediately. I'll m-muster some of the m-men."

"No," Amory said steadily, his face pale but admirably controlled. "There's no need for that yet. Don't make a to-do over it. There's bound to be some simple explanation."

Marcus seemed about to protest, but Harriet laid a restraining hand on his arm, and after a moment he subsided, though the look of panic remained. He had seen, like Harriet, that their father's unwillingness to instigate such a search just yet might well arise from an uncomfortable feeling that by doing so he would be admitting that something, after all, might be sadly amiss. Which possibility could not, really must not, be considered.

The bell rang for luncheon, and everyone assembled, with the exception of Miss Jessamy, who never ate at midday, just a piece of fruit, it seemed – and nor was Mr Iskander there, either. Enquiries from the housekeeper as to his whereabouts subsequently elicited the information that he had departed

Charnley early that morning, leaving behind a nightshirt in a drawer and a bottle of macassar oil on the dressing table, though fortunately he hadn't forgotten to leave a sizeable tip for the servants. He had asked with such assurance for the pony trap to take him to the station for the first train that Copley had assumed the family were aware of his departure. Gone, bag and baggage, without even a note or a word of thanks to his hosts! Disappeared, like the genie in 'Ali Baba'! This was deplorable, and it was also unexpected. Whatever else, Iskander's manners had always been impeccable.

"He obviously couldn't stand us one more day – he was probably as sick of us as we were of him," said Daisy cheerfully.

"*Daisy!* I will not have you speaking like that, of one who was a guest in this house!"

Daisy stared round-eyed at her father, blushing to the roots of her hair, with difficulty stopping herself from bursting into tears. He had never before reprimanded her outspokenness. She was, after all, known in the family for her irreverent comments, which normally evoked a tolerant smile. "I – I'm sorry, Papa."

His face cleared, he patted her shoulder. "Well, well. But no more of it, hm?"

But Daisy had only been voicing everyone's thoughts. Valery Iskander had not been a man one could be comfortable with. Doubtless he did very well in his own country, but he'd been out of his element here at Charnley. Yet he had stayed on, seemingly unaware of overstaying his welcome. After more than a week, by which time everyone had said all they had to say to him, and conversation was beginning to reach the desperate stage, his going was undoubtedly a relief.

Luncheon was announced. The saddle of mutton with redcurrant jelly, the apricot tart to follow, were got through somehow, a strange affair without Beatrice presiding over the table. No one seemed to want to eat much. Everyone tried to avoid looking at the clock as the hands crawled round, and still Amory deferred the search.

Eventually, telephone calls were made. The Jardines had an intricate web of friends and relations, measured by the thickness and complexity of Beatrice's address book. But to tell the truth, it was impossible – ludicrous! – to go so far as to believe that she would have suddenly taken it into her head to visit any one of them, without prior warning or a word to her family. Nevertheless, Harriet took on the task of calling the likeliest, using more guile as to the reason for her calls, so as not to arouse undue alarm or suspicions, than she had dreamed she possessed. Only when she rang Stoke Wycombe did her flimsy pretexts fall flat.

"What's wrong, Harriet?"

"Oh, Uncle Myles!"

It was such a relief to pour it all out, to have the ear of someone who listened intently, put sensible questions and then, when all the facts had been made known, announced that he was driving over to Charnley immediately, despite the fact that he'd only just arrived back home from there. As she hung up the receiver, Harriet felt better just for knowing he would soon be on the scene, with his gift for organising, and his common sense and indefatigable energy.

"Come, Amory, what are you thinking of? Marcus is right, an immediate search must be made of the house, the grounds," he announced immediately on his arrival, clasping his friend's shoulder. It was now late afternoon, there was not a moment to be lost, he urged.

"Very well." Amory was pale and tense, outwardly controlled but betrayed by the constant tugging at his long upper lip, and by his eyes, which by now were frantic. It was as apparent to him now as to everyone else that he really had no choice but to agree.

A search of the grounds was commenced by all the outdoor staff, supervised by Wycombe, aided by Marcus and two of the footmen. After a while, Amory took himself off to make a personal search of the house, moving methodically through the splendid confusion of rooms, every nook and cranny of which he had known intimately for fifty years, sparing no effort, even to ransacking through its long-forgotten attics and squeezing through the window which gave out on to the leads, from where he'd shot at pigeons as a boy. He searched through chests and trunks and the little corner room off one of the staircases, always known as the priest's hole, though whether it ever had been used as that was a moot point. He omitted nowhere, not even the cellars – but he found nothing. And what had he expected? That Beatrice, of all people, had suddenly lost her mind and had wandered off to one of these farthest reaches of the house and got herself trapped, locked in, perhaps fainted? Well, an accident of some sort was the only possible explanation that was now lodging uneasily in everyone's mind.

No one yet had mentioned dragging the lake.

The searchers returned, without success. It had grown too dark to carry on, but they were prepared to start again in the morning, at first light. A hush gradually settled over the house, servants tiptoed about as if there had been a bereavement, irritation and incomprehension turned to real worry and finally, as the unnatural day dragged on into night, dread. Nothing in the bewildered family's well-regulated lives had prepared them for this feeling that they were all lost in the dark, wandering without any landmarks. They simply had no idea what to do. There was no precedent to follow because nothing like this had ever happened before. People – especially someone as well-conducted and predictable as Beatrice – did not simply disappear into thin air.

Then the certainty that she must turn up, somewhere, that she would be found, ill or injured – even Daisy's wild surmise that she might have been abducted, and some sort of ransom note might be expected – was eventually rudely scotched by Hallam's report that certain of Beatrice's belongings had also disappeared.

"You are sure you are not mistaken?" asked Amory, blankly.

"No, sir. A grey walking costume and a small valise, under-clothes and her silver-backed hairbrush," Hallam recited stiffly, her hand to her flat bosom. "It was only when I noticed her hairbrush missing that I thought to check on her other things."

Of course the woman was not mistaken about this. She knew every item of her mistress's wardrobe intimately. She was a disobliging creature, all too easily disposed to take the huff, but there was no denying she was utterly dedicated to Beatrice and all her concerns and was without doubt blaming herself for not having checked it earlier. It must have cost her a great deal to report on what she had discovered, for there could now no longer be any doubt that Beatrice's disappearance had been a deliberate act.

It was unclear who first made the connection between her disappearance and Valery Iskander's unscheduled departure. Perhaps it was Amory who saw the connection first, from whose lips a shocked exclamation burst. It was followed by a stunned silence. Daisy's eyes filled with tears, horrified that her flippant remark about the two running off together had been nearer the truth than anyone could have realised, and fervently hoping that Vita would not remember it.

Vita, however, was struggling against her own unworthy first thoughts: how could she do this to me? Why did she not at least wait until after the wedding? For she knew now that if the unthinkable should turn out to be true, then Bertie's mother would never allow him to marry her, Vita, the daughter of a fallen woman. Through some oddity of his father's will, Lady Rossiter more or less had control of her son's fortune until he was twenty-five, so Bertie would have no choice. Still, she was ashamed of herself for thinking these thoughts at a time like this and hoped the tears would not fall. She looked at the floor, in case Harriet divined what she was thinking – she was always so quick to latch on to these things.

But Harriet, too, was busy with her own reactions, endeavouring to convince herself that such a thing just wasn't possible. Of course, women before now had caused scandals by eloping or bolting with unsuitable men – look at Millie! – but there had never been a breath of anything scandalous or indecorous connected with Beatrice – a little flirting, perhaps, here and there, but that was the commerce of fashionable society, and with renowned beauties such as Beatrice, it was understandable, and did not count. And, well...*Iskander!*

As for Marcus – his first instinct after the revelations had been to rush upstairs and into the west wing to find Rose Jessamy. Preoccupied with her work, it had barely seemed to register with her when he had told her earlier that his mother was missing, but Marcus knew she would, all the same, have heard and remembered it. She was so sharp and penetrating, so defensive of her position as an artist, it was easy to dismiss her as self-absorbed, yet he'd found that her judgement of people and situations was usually cool, but right. If there had been anything between his mother and this fellow Iskander, Rose would have been the one to notice. He longed for her calm detachment. But he restrained himself, knowing instinctively that she would certainly tell him that his place, at the moment, was here with his family.

"Even if one can begin to contemplate such a thing happening, Father," he said, "Mama would not have failed to leave a note to tell you at least, what she intended. She is *meticulous*–" He broke off, flushing, running a hand through his hair. "That sounds r-ridiculous, in the circumstances, but even so, I'm sure she w-wouldn't…"

Wycombe said, "As a matter of fact I rather agree with you, Marcus. Simply by going away like this at all, your mama hasn't acted in anything like her usual rational way, so leaving without a note of explanation might be difficult to believe, but must be accepted." His thoughts were in turmoil. Good God, this was the very devil! Of all things, he hadn't expected this. "Well, he's capable of it," he said grimly at last, voicing a coda to his own speculations, barely aware that he had spoken this last aloud.

"But – Beatrice?"

"Beatrice too, Amory, I'm afraid. We've all underestimated her. There – there have always been unexplained depths to her–" He broke off abruptly. "I should not have said that, I am overstepping the line." Yet despite his bracing attitude, which was to be expected of one who had confronted and been in charge of worse situations than this, there sounded to be some underlying shock, as if something in him that he was not able to accept had been challenged.

"No, no, Myles," Amory replied. "We must look the truth in the face. But before jumping to conclusions, we must be absolutely certain. All this is speculation. We have no means of knowing if she really has gone with Iskander." He added with an unexpected touch of bitter humour, "But if that is the case, it is to be hoped he's rich. She has taken nothing with her of any consequence, according to Hallam. Except the new garnets – and those," he added bitterly, "are of little value, compared with some of her jewels, and unlikely to bring in enough to keep Beatrice in anything more than gloves and stockings for long."

Marcus said, suddenly, "This is a temporary madness! She

will return, I know she will. *Nothing* would have made her leave us all like this if she were in her right mind!"

There came into the room a sudden ray of hope. Then everyone looked at Amory and the same thought entered every mind: what would Amory do if she *did* return?

Chapter Eight

Yet another day has gone by, and the shock waves have not yet settled, the ripples are still spreading from the dark centre of the pool where the stone was thrown in. We are all restless, unable to settle, and earlier this evening, I wandered up to Mama's bedroom, where I stood looking at the rich elegance spread around. Papa is right about one thing, at least. She will find living without luxury insupportable, not to mention an existence beyond the pale of society, even if she means to live in Egypt for the rest of her life. Ostracised! I simply do not understand how she could willingly have chosen that – when she knows very well what it will mean to her, she who has always lived surrounded by people whose high opinion is paramount to her. Especially not with the example of Millie Glendinning before her. Simply for an *affaire*? Try as I will, I cannot envisage my cool, sophisticated, conventionally worldly Mama suffering some overwhelming passion for anyone – let alone Valery Iskander! – allowing it go so far beyond her control that she has lost sight of all she is forsaking. Yet what other explanation is there for her reckless behaviour? We know nothing of Iskander, or of the circumstances in which they first met. Papa might know more than he is saying (and remembering the unquestioning way he seemed to accept the reason for her abrupt departure, it seems to me he very likely does) but I for one could never pluck up the courage to ask him.

The bedroom curtains had not been drawn together and bright moonlight silvered the room; it bore a strange, abandoned, forlorn aspect, but I was reluctant to light a lamp. Whether I was viewing the scene coloured by the loss we were all experiencing, I had no means of knowing, but the things she had left behind seemed to be invested with a poignant life of their own, reminders that stirred a complex web of emotions in me. Mama and I have not always seen eye to eye, but I have always loved her. Or have I – truthfully? A dutiful affection, yes, I feel that, but true, profound love, such as I have for Papa? I do not know, but even so, I am tormented by the knowledge of how dreadfully unhappy she must have been to reach the point where she could abandon us all. And more than that: why have none of us ever seen it? Feelings of self-blame and guilt are an indulgence we cannot afford, but still I ask myself if my sisters, too, have felt this same faint remoteness between herself and her daughters which I think I have always sensed, without being consciously aware of it. Marcus – well, like most men, I suspect, he adores his beautiful mother.

I wish I could share his unshaken belief that she will return. Sometimes I do indeed believe that one day she will reappear, and everything will return to normal, just as if she had never gone away, but at the same time I live in dread of the consequences if ever that should happen. Papa is such a stickler for correctness, that everyone around him must live their lives honourably; it goes without saying that his wife must be beyond reproach. I cannot even consider the possibility of his overlooking what she has done and taking her back on condition that she behaves herself for the sake of outward appearances. Yet the alternative, divorce, would be equally unthinkable. Divorce puts both parties at the mercy of civilised society. Marital misdemeanours may, and do, occur, but they must not be *seen* to occur. As it is, tongues will begin to wag soon enough, there can be no hiding for long the fact that my mother has gone. It will undoubtedly cause shame to fall on her name, and as for Papa – well, he is bound to suffer more, trying to carry on with his life, knowing that everyone knows she has made a fool of him. He is not a man who can bear to be laughed at.

I could not keep still, and was pacing about the moonlit room while thinking all this. Clara Hallam had tidied it, but had left one or two items lying where they were, a sentimental touch which I would not have suspected the woman capable of. An abandoned white kid glove lay on the arm of a peach velour chair, an extensive array of Mama's cosmetics was lined up on the dressing table. A nightgown of dove-grey silk was lying across the cream satin counterpane, ready for wear, pinched in at the waist by Hallam as though her body were inside it, flung back in a pose of abandon. Hallam, when she told us, said her mistress had taken little else but the grey walking costume, something I found so difficult to believe of Mama – she who changes her clothes several times a day! – that I decided now to check for myself.

But Hallam was right, nothing else appeared to be missing. I even opened the wardrobes where her furs were kept, cedar-lined to keep out the moths, unlikely as she is to need furs in Egypt. There they all were – the sables which my father gave her rippling sleekly under their protective shoulder wraps, and still clinging to them was that distinctive scent she orders to be made up specially for her in Paris, by Worth. Her favourite cloak hung there, a long, exquisite garment of gold tissue, also lined with sable; silver foxes and a soft, thick velvet evening coat of mole colour, trimmed with miniver.

Closing the door, I noticed that same scent lingering on the air in the room itself, yet overlaid by something faintly rotten. Those lilies on the dressing table, that was it! They were over, past their best, already beginning to fester in the tall glass vase. The lilies Kit had given her for her birthday.

Kit. He is going to take it very badly. He admires Mama so tremendously. There has always been an unusual rapport between them, and something being said beneath the surface that for some reason I have never cared to probe. We haven't seen him at Charnley since Mama went. I am disappointed in him, I thought he would have rushed down here immediately to offer his sympathy. I have been waiting, longing to unburden myself, but he has not yet come.

A difficult decision lies ahead for me. It does not need second sight to see that as the eldest daughter, it will be universally accepted that my moral responsibility is now to take over Mama's social duties for my father's sake. Escape, to a worthwhile life of my own, would now seem to be even more out of the question than before, at least until I marry, when I might well simply be exchanging one form of imprisonment for another. Unless, of course, I were to marry Kit.

I believe he, at least, would never expect me to sublimate my own desires and pretend to be a conventional wife. He would respect my need for fulfilment outside the boundaries of running a home and raising children. I should be allowed to follow my own inclinations, to study as I wished...but to marry simply to gain such freedom seems to me the worst form of dishonesty.

Papa, for one, has never been against a match between us nor, I believe, was Mama, though I never fully understood her attitude. On the one hand, she urged me to make up my mind before it was too late, on the other, she constantly warned me of what might be in store if Kit and I were to marry. As if I had not worked that one out for myself!

I am racked by indecision. Do I truly love Kit? That dangerous attraction he has for me somewhat frightens me in its intensity, for I realise it is not necessarily love. But even if it were, marrying him could be a disaster. He could never, for instance, be the rock against which I could lean in times of stress, as my father has been for my mother. Nor, I suspect, does he have that capacity for faithfulness which one might expect from a husband. While I have no desire to possess another human being utterly – I would despise myself if I had –

I do not want to share him with a side of his nature over which he has no control. But – he makes me feel alive. He teases me and makes me laugh, not always an easy task, I admit. I feel *right* with him.

I had had enough of such thoughts. And suddenly I had no wish to be in this room any longer.

I turned to go, and it was then I noticed the grey suede journal on the writing table by the window. I had once or twice seen Mama making entries in this book, but she always put it away when anyone came into the room. It had a tiny brass lock, and I picked it up, though without any intentions of forcing the lock and intruding on private thoughts. She must have overlooked it in her haste to leave, but the thought that someone else – Hallam, perhaps, if she had not already done so – might find a way of opening it and reading it, made me slip it inside my pocket.

The following week was one which, for the rest of her life, Harriet could never contemplate without despair. A week which was an awful anti-climax to those events which had gone before, and was the beginning of the path towards what inexorably followed some time afterwards. A week in which hope died.

The police later went over everything that had happened from the time when Beatrice disappeared to the time of the fatal tragedy, in an effort to find out what had caused it, but not as much as they might have done, had they not previously been told about her leaving. Marcus had refused to give up on his insistence that the police should be informed of her flight, even in the face of his father's indifference and Wycombe's warnings about the publicity which would inevitably ensue.

"What can the police do that we haven't done?" Amory had said heavily. During the space of a week, he had grown older and greyer. He had been brought up not to exhibit his feelings, but the struggle not to do so was clearly almost too much for him. He would pull out of it, he assured his children, but it was difficult to believe. An accidie seemed to have entered his soul, utter despair. "Supposing they trace her, supposing they do find her with this fellow Iskander, are they going to force her to return?"

"I simply won't believe she is so lost to all decency that she has gone off with that man! Dash it, Father, she may have had some sort of brainstorm and be wandering God knows where. She may even b-be–"

"Marcus!" said Wycombe quietly.

Amory, roused out of his own lethargy by his son's evident distress, put a hand on his sleeve. Marcus subsided. "All right, Father. I'm sorry. But if there's any chance at all, shouldn't we take it? We must *n-n-never* give up hope of finding her and p-persuading her to return!"

He was silenced by the look on his father's face, but then Amory said heavily, turning away, "Do as you wish, my boy, do as you wish."

"Perhaps Marcus is right, old friend. Maybe it would, after all, be in everyone's interests to inform the police," said Wycombe, after several moments' deep thought.

So they were called in, though afterwards Marcus said they might have saved themselves the trouble. The two policemen who came were from the local force. Uncomfortable at dealing with the gentry on such highly personal matters, and working under directives from on high, they seemed happy to accept the obvious conclusions, without too many questions. "I'm afraid it seems to be a cut and dried case, sir. Your wife and the Egyptian gentleman disappearing on the same day, as it were," said a sergeant by the name of Maitland, an inexperienced young man with baby-blue eyes who looked as though he wasn't old enough to be told about such things.

They asked the obvious questions, received the expected answers, which Maitland's constable wrote laboriously in his notebook. Then he said, "It's been a week – and you have had no communication whatever from your wife, sir?"

Amory, who had already told them this, merely nodded.

Maitland coughed and said, with as much reproof in his tone as he dared, "It might have made things easier, sir, if you had reported the disappearance at once."

"We believed she would return," Marcus said. He met the baby-blue eyes and saw they were not by any means as guileless as he had at first thought. "As she still might. Or be found, at any rate."

"I shouldn't hold out too much hope of that if I was you, sir. Not much chance of tracing anyone, once they're out of England – and as for Egypt!" Egypt might well have been beyond the stratosphere, as far as he was concerned. He added, speaking once more to Amory, "as I believe the Chief Constable has – er – already indicated, sir."

So someone had had a quiet word in the ear of the Chief Constable, and perhaps the Lord Lieutenant of the county as well. The Home Secretary, even, it was tempting to think. At any rate, it was clear that whatever Maitland himself thought, what he was saying had come first from the lips of higher authority. To Harriet, at least, it was obvious they were just going through the motions.

"Well now," the sergeant went on heartily, "you say you have carried on with your normal life, sir, this week? You and your son went up to your chambers in London just as usual?"

"As to that," said Amory heavily, "things will never be normal again," a sentiment which was later recalled by Sergeant Maitland and his constable.

But it was inevitable that a modicum of normality returned, although the focus of the house had disappeared, its centre fallen apart. No one had realised how Beatrice had managed the smooth running of Charnley, without seemingly raising a finger. It barely existed without her. Mrs Betts carried on the usual housekeeping routine, knowing exactly what had to be done, but it was not the same. They had the identical menu for dinner twice running in one week.

A few days after Beatrice's disappearance, Wycombe departed, there being nothing else he could do, and on the same day Rose Jessamy announced that in view of what had happened, she, too, would be packing her bags and leaving.

"But you can't!" said Marcus. "You can't leave the rooms as they are! Mama would want you to finish them. What will she do if she comes back and finds them half-finished?"

There was a pause. "Marcus, she isn't going to come back," Rose told him gently.

"How can you possibly know that?"

"Women don't get to the stage where they decide to do something as drastic as she has done, and then simply change their minds."

"She will at least write, I know she'll write," Marcus said desperately.

"Marcus…"

"Then will you stay and finish your work – for my sake?"

She felt a sense of panic, as if she were being bound and tied with cords, like Gulliver in Lilliput. She was becoming far too fond of Marcus; the freedom which she cherished above all else was being threatened, while it was obvious in which direction his feelings were directed. "It was your mother who commissioned me to do the rooms, Marcus. I don't think your father will have any interest in paying for them now."

"Let me speak to him – and if he agrees, will you stay and complete the work?"

She looked at his unhappy face – he was taking this so much more badly than the girls. She had come to know that, underneath his reserve, Marcus was a passionate young man, and much of his passion was for Charnley, the family, and the sense of continuity meant by it all. Charnley was at the centre of his being, what gave meaning to his life, more so than it would ever mean to Amory. He had revealed throughout this crisis – though doubtless unaware of the fact – a growing responsibility for the house, and the family, an awareness that this was what he was cut out for. More important to him than his career at the Bar would always be his life here, carrying on the old traditions, keeping the house and family going, growing roses. When he had got himself over this first hurdle, this refusal to accept his mother's betrayal, he would, sooner or later, accept this himself. Where this left her, she preferred not to think too deeply about.

"Very well," she said, more gently than was usual with her, "if he agrees, I will finish what I started."

Amory made no bones about it. "But of course Miss Jessamy must carry on until it's done. She needs the money, and we must fulfil our obligations."

The weeks went by, and Amory withdrew more and more into himself, and Vita lost so much weight that none of her dresses fitted properly. But after Beatrice's portrait had been removed from the drawing room, the John Singer Sargent, in which she wore a deep blue velvet dress that echoed the blue of her eyes and caught the translucency of her skin (and perhaps, it could be discerned now, a certain reticence in her eyes) Amory began to look a little better. August came, but he declined an invitation to shoot grouse in Scotland, and another for a partridge-shoot in September. But when October arrived, he announced that he might as well go along to Stoke Wycombe for the pheasants, and an audible sigh of relief went through the house. He went down to the gun room the evening before his departure to inspect and choose the guns he was to take with him, and was there for some time before the single shot was heard.

An accident, while cleaning the barrel, was the conclusion the police came to. It could not be anything else, for he had made arrangements to leave the following day for his friend Lord Wycombe's shooting party, and he had left no note. He had been in slightly better spirits of late, and had obviously begun to accept the disappearance of his wife. But to anyone who knew Amory, acceptance of Beatrice's defection was not a possibility. As for an accident, it was unthinkable. No one could more rigidly have adhered to the rules of gun-cleaning than he. To play about with a loaded gun was as foreign to his nature as to forget to shave or clean his teeth each morning.

For the next few weeks Marcus, the new heir to Charnley, was closeted with his father's men of affairs: solicitors, bankers, brokers. Finally they went away and he called his three sisters into the library. He, too, had lost weight, and his height made him look gaunt. His face was careworn with responsibility. He wasted no time in coming to the point.

"I have decided to sell Charnley."

No one answered him. Three black-clad mourning figures sat before him, speechless. Three pairs of female eyes gazed at him with blank incomprehension. Amory's marble clock on the mantel struck six, in a tired sort of way. No one had remembered to wind it up this week, and it was running down. The sound died away, and still no one spoke. It was as though the enormity of what Marcus had said had struck them all dumb.

"I have no choice!" he shouted angrily at them, at last. "There is no m-money. Not a penny! Have you any idea what it costs to keep a great place like this going? Even if I were to sell the furniture and keep it empty, it would still eat money – leaking roofs don't repair themselves! Dry rot doesn't simply go away! How much money is needed to pay the staff their wages, do you think? Do you realise we employ forty-five people in all?"

"But they won't have any wages at all, if you sell Charnley," said Daisy at last. "What will they do?"

With an effort, Marcus calmed himself. "I'm sorry, n-none of this is your fault, and it must be as much a shock to you all as it was to m-me."

Harriet said, "Just how much money is there?"

"After death duties, scarcely a penny, apart from your settlements, though they too have been greatly reduced and aren't what one would have expected. Our father's income from the Bar died with him, of course, and I have to tell you that whatever was left of the family fortunes has been going down the drain for years – taxes and so on, not to mention the cost of what I see now was an unbelievably extravagant lifestyle. Keeping two expensive establishments going, entertaining so lavishly – Good God, the cases of wine that were consumed – and Mama's dressmaking bills alone must have been astronomical! More disastrously, it also turns out that Father made some very unwise investments – presumably in an effort to reverse the situation, but which have had exactly the opposite effect."

There was an even deeper silence while they tried to digest this unexpected view of their prudent, circumspect father. Marcus went to the desk, opened the silver cigar box and extracted one. He inspected it for a while, rolling it round in his fingers. "I want you all to go to stay with Great-aunt Edina until I finally decide what to do," he announced at last.

At this, Daisy gave a little shriek. "We can't! Her house is like a mausoleum – I should die if I had to live there! She's a dragon!"

"She's also lonely, and would be glad of your company."

"Oh, Marcus!" wailed Daisy.

Harriet rose and poked the fire. A log split in two and fell with a crash into the embers, sending a shower of sparks up the chimney. "I'm sorry, Marcus," she said, turning round, "I know you're being faced with a difficult situation, but I will make my own decisions. My sisters may stay with the great-aunt in London, but I shall be going to study – in Oxford, if possible."

"Harriet? I had thought – you and Kit…"

"No, not Kit. I have made my choice. I shall go up to Oxford, as soon as may be."

"Then I," said Daisy with a defiant sniff, "shall write to Athene Tempest and ask her if I may join her in London."

Marcus ran his hands through his hair. He hadn't expected rebellion. "That I cannot allow, Daisy! Athene Tempest is a dangerous woman – or rather she puts herself in dangerous situations with this Women's Suffrage business. I am responsible for you now, and I won't let you do that."

"You can't stop me!" Daisy cried passionately. "I shall run away!"

"Let her go, Marcus. Miss Tempest won't let her come to any harm," Vita said quietly.

Marcus looked uncertain, rather taken aback by having what he had regarded as almost insoluble problems solved before his very eyes. These were snap decisions his sisters were making, which he never trusted but perhaps, all things considered, they might work out for the best.

But of course, there was still Vita. What was going to happen to poor, heartbroken Vita? As if with one accord, they all turned to look at her. She said calmly, "I will stay with Great-aunt Edina. She is my godmother, and she'll probably be quite nice to me."

"You can't! Think of the food – and that hateful little dog!"

"Perhaps I can persuade her to change the food, Daisy. And I really don't object to Floy."

Marcus touched her shoulder. Of his three sisters, he was most concerned about Vita. Perhaps she was speaking the truth and really didn't mind the prospect of the great-aunt's strictness, the gloomy old house, the terrible food one was always served up with there. She didn't mind *anything*, these days, it was as though there was an invisible barrier between her and the rest of the world. She had given that great ass, Bertie Rossiter, his ring back – before he could break their engagement himself. He had accepted her decision, while swearing that if she would wait for him another two years, until he was twenty-five, had control of his own money and could do as he wished, he would still marry her, despite everything. Marcus would believe that when he saw it, and privately thought she was better off without him. Yet losing him had almost extinguished their fun-loving Vita.

He felt guilty, condemning her to a future with the joyless great-aunt, the prospect of which was horrible for anyone, but he could not believe it would be for long. There were several eligible young bachelors in the offing who would be prepared, as he did not think Bertie's mother would ever be, to overlook the stain on the Jardine family in return for pretty Vita, though perhaps not so many as there might have been when it became common knowledge that her inheritance was almost negligible. All the same, he was sure Vita would soon find herself consoled by some other young man.

"And you, Marcus," said Harriet, "what do you intend to do?"

"Me?" For a moment, he looked rather embarrassed. "Oh, when everything is wound up, I intend to go to Egypt. I am going to try and find Iskander…"

And, hanging in the air, was the unspoken but very clear intention that he was going there to find their mother."

Chapter Nine

The demolition gangs had gone. The Anderson shelters were no more than a memory. After two world wars, Charnley was almost back to its former self, the builders ready to move in to begin the last phase of the remedial work on the fabric in the west wing, containing the guest rooms which had come to be known as the Jessamy rooms.

Although the windows had been flung open for weeks, to allow through draughts to dry off the walls, Rose Jessamy's paintings were in a woeful condition, for the most part peeling off the walls and now beyond hope of saving. The English climate was at the best of times unkind to frescoes, which need dry, airy conditions to survive, and in this case the walls had been running with damp for many years. Thankfully, dry rot hadn't made its slimy-fingered encroachment, and though mice had nibbled away at the wainscotting, and bats and birds had occasionally found their way in through missing window panes, the structure itself had suffered hardly at all, maybe because the wing was the only bit left of the original Elizabethan building, a manor house built in the days when solidity was more important than style.

It was just before the builders' break for elevenses that a discovery was made which halted proceedings and put several of the husky labourers right off their tea and Spam sandwiches, and a few of them off their lunch as well.

The foreman plasterer, arriving to size up the job, pushed back his cap and was scratching his head and staring at the vestigial paintings of crocodile gods, cow-headed goddesses, frogs and jackal gods, a winged sun and a symbolic eye "Blimey!" His eye unerringly picked out an almost hidden but graphically explicit fertility symbol surviving among all this abundance. "Cop an eyeful of this lot, Sid – but don't let young Mick see. We don't want him excited."

Young Mick, however, who was twenty-three, strong as an ox but believed to be only ninepence in the shilling, was more engrossed in the bony remains of a bat he had just picked up; a pipistrelle, minuscule, perfectly-formed. He gazed at the tiny creature's skeleton as it lay on the palm of his hand, its claws no more than an eighth of an inch long, its teeth, and even the fragile structures supporting its wing membranes still intact. Ah, the beauty of it! "I've seen worse when we were serving in Italy, I have so," he answered, barely giving the wall painting a glance.

"Oh you have, have you?" Ernest the foreman gave him a sardonic glance and pulled his steel rule from where it was wedged between his cap and his ear. "Well, ne'er mind, eh? More to the point – this whole flippin' place's going to need replastering! Look at this chimney breast, for a start." He gave an experimental poke to a sphinx. It disintegrated and fell in damp, loose flakes around his feet, releasing the distinctive, dirty smell that comes only from old plaster. "What did I tell you? Perished right through! Here, move over and let's have a proper shufti." He leaned his hand on the wall and a great deal more plaster came away, revealing crumbling brickwork. Another prod, and several of the bricks fell with a soft thud into a cavity behind. "Would you credit that, not a bit of mortar? No wonder it's fell down! OK, get cracking, Mick – get them bricks out and piled up."

Removing the bricks was easy, since they had simply been laid on top of one another, without any attempt to cement them together, with only a skim of plaster in front. As they were moved, there appeared the gaping hole where the fireplace aperture had formerly been. When they were finally cleared and the cloud of choking dust had subsided, the hole was seen to be blocked with a little mountain of twigs and ancient jackdaw nests that had fallen down the tall chimney, together with a mound of soot and all that was left of the nests' unfortunate occupants. A few hundred skeletons, a pile of fragile bones, beaks and feathers. The smell was appalling.

Ernest and Sid moved on to the other walls, knocking and prodding, while Mick desultorily began to stir aside the debris in the fireplace with a broom. After a moment he leaped back "What's up, mate?" asked Sid.

Mick crossed himself. "Jasus! I think you'd better come and take a look."

Daisy Tempest – who had been Daisy Jardine – threw down her pencil and abandoned the hopeless task of trying to make the week's rations for fifteen women and girls into a passably interesting menu. She stared glumly out of the window overlooking the Whitechapel Road, nibbling the end of her pencil. Can't do it, she thought, and it wasn't the food coupons and the availability of liver to eke out the meat ration she was thinking about. Can't just send the girl away to support herself – and her child. How would she ever manage? Barely seventeen, a child herself, but her respectable middle class parents in Ruislip wouldn't even consider taking her back, not with the shame of an illegitimate baby. Yet Lorna was adamant that she wasn't going to give up her child for adoption: the result of a few so-called romantic nights with a young man her parents knew nothing about, who'd persuaded her to 'go all the way' because they were going to be married anyway, weren't they? A circumstance which had turned out not to be on his agenda when he found out she was pregnant. She was a soft, pliant girl who had shown herself to be biddable and willing during the weeks she'd been at Hope House, but in the matter of giving away her child, she had a core as hard as steel. "I'll kill both of us first!" she'd announced dramatically. Their charges, here at Hope House, were often graceless and ungrateful, hiding their shock and despair with bravado or bad behaviour. One poor girl had come to them only last week after being fished out of the Thames, just in time. Looking at Lorna's pale, obstinate little face, her declaration wasn't something Daisy was prepared to put to the test.

"Why don't they just take the kids away at birth without the mums seeing them? Better all round, in my opinion," declared Athene Tempest.

"You don't really think that." Daisy knew that her former governess liked to see herself as plain-spoken and no sentiment. Blunt yes, she might be, but underneath, she was like one of those pre-war Charbonnel et Walker liqueur chocolates, with an easily melted shell and a heart-warming centre.

"Well, what else do you suggest, then?" Athene asked now. "Soft talk isn't going to persuade Lorna."

Daisy shook her head. She hadn't a clue. It could be a dispiriting business altogether, this caring for unmarried mothers. She did try to be more like Athene, who never let it get her down, but Athene was helped by her dim view of men in general, and in particular the ones who, in her own words, got these girls up the spout and then buggered off.

"Well, nor is emotional blackmail." Easy enough for Athene to point out the benefits of having the child adopted, but dismissing the mental anguish such a situation could cause was beyond Daisy. We're getting too old for this sort of thing, both of us, she thought, though at fifty-three, she didn't feel old, not in any sense. All right, she'd put on weight, taking after her generously proportioned mother, and she didn't have Beatrice's outstanding looks. She couldn't be bothered to do anything more than scrape back her faded blonde hair back from her face with a slide, and she knew, really, that she ought not to wear those heavy woollens and tweed skirts that were not kind to her hips. But they were so serviceable. Like me, she sometimes thought, one of that unsung band of splendid women who voluntarily gave their time to public service and were capable, unflappable, hard-working and unfailingly good humoured. Which did feel rather dispiriting.

Athene was rubbing a hand across her face and saying, "I don't know, I really don't! Why do we carry on?" It was a rhetorical question, one that Daisy had heard her ask so often that it didn't need an answer. In any case, they both knew that this settlement in the East End was both Athene's passion and her *raison d'être*.

In 1920, the Great War over and the fight for women's suffrage won, Athene had been looking round for something else to occupy her formidable energies, with Daisy not far behind her. Daisy had wanted nothing more than to put the anguished years of that first war right out of her head: too much meaningless suffering, too many dead. She and Athene had been directly involved, driving ambulances in France, to and from the field hospitals behind the front lines, while men and boys they had known were being picked off like flies. Like Peter Houghton-Vesey, who had danced with Daisy on the night of her mother's birthday, and to whom she'd almost become engaged a few years later, who had been blinded and burned by mustard gas, and died before they could marry.

He wasn't the only casualty from that lost world of Charnley. Men went away and many never returned, or returned maimed for life. There was Teddy Cranfield, amazing everyone with a posthumous VC. Dolly Dacres, Vita's friend, left a young widow with two children. Copley, Hallam's cheeky half-brother, with his saucy grin and the broad wink at you when he thought no one was looking – he'd inveigled himself into driving one of the London omnibuses shipped to France to convey troops to the front line, had been blown up and lost an arm and thereafter lurched around with the empty sleeve tucked into his jacket pocket – until later, ruined, he had died of drink. While Joe Jimson, the handsome, cheerful young porter at the railway station, had come home severely shell-shocked, unable to speak a word, and finally hanged himself in the outside privy. After that, Polly Cheevers, the parlourmaid at Charnley, who had gone to work in a munitions factory where the picric acid dyed her hair and skin yellow, had left Charnley forever, to learn typewriting in London and live in a YWCA hostel.

And Marcus. Daisy kept the last photograph she had of him on her desk. Taken in uniform, in 1915, just before he died, one of the hundred-thousand killed or missing in the appalling fiasco of the Gallipoli landings – The Glorious Failure – a young army captain leading his men into certain death. The photograph showed a face, still young but serious and responsible; the eyes giving nothing away of those unspeakable experiences he'd already gone through. But her brother had become unknowable before then, parts of his life after Charnley had been a closed book to the rest of the family. That long ago tragedy had affected Marcus perhaps most of all of them.

"Well?" Athene broke into her reverie, putting her teacup down in a businesslike way and standing up, ready for the next thing awaiting her. "*Something's* got to be done about that child. No ideas at all?"

"I'll see if I can't find her a room somewhere, get her a job and someone to mind the baby while she does it. Not ideal, but what is? I've tried all the usual things, telling her what she faces, that her baby will have a better life with parents who can provide for him, but she doesn't believe it."

Truth to tell, Daisy sometimes wondered if she believed that herself. Certainly the child would be better provided for, materially. For how could even that sort of undemanding, unstinting love Lorna had now for her baby withstand the constant strains of a life with all the odds stacked against both of them? Daisy recognised the terrible choice, even though it had never been one she'd had to make. She'd never been alone, and friendless. She'd never had a child of her own.

She'd been over forty, already too late for that, though she hadn't known it, when she married Guy Tempest. But she'd still have married him, even if she had known.

She'd first met Athene's brother several years before. He had married late, his first wife, Cécile, being a Frenchwoman from Epinard, with whom he'd fallen in love while serving in the Royal Army Medical Corps. She had died suddenly when their child, Nina, was eight, and Guy had seemed permanently set in the role of grieving widower. It had taken Daisy some time to realise that when he had finally asked her to marry him, it had been for her own sake, not simply as a replacement mother for his by-then thirteen-year-old daughter; for after Peter Houghton-Vesey had been killed she had, like so many women of her generation, accepted that she was doomed to spinsterhood. Other things had taken the place of marriage in her life – she'd slaved with Athene to set up Hope House, she'd poured all her considerable energies into battling with authority, striving to overcome the stigma of her own privileged origins and spending her spare time and enthusiasm closely affiliating herself with the Labour Party and lobbying for better conditions for the working class. She'd even been persuaded to think of standing for Parliament, right up to the point where she'd allowed her name to be put forward as a candidate when a constituency in the north east became vacant. Her forthrightness, integrity, sympathy for the underprivileged – and not least her easy camaraderie – had made her possible selection almost certain. Her prospective coal-mining constituents loved her, she loved them. She had walked with them on the Jarrow hunger march to London. And then, Guy had proposed to her.

Daisy saw no contest between marrying Guy and becoming a career politician. She'd immediately withdrawn her candidacy. It was the one thing over which she and Athene, strongly supported by Harriet, had ever radically disagreed. She didn't need either of them to point out – though Athene did, often and vociferously – that Guy had enough respect for her intelligence to support her pursuit of a career, and would loyally back her up – she knew that, but...well, there had still been a chance that she might have a child of her own.

Time slipped by and that never happened, but she wouldn't acknowledge that she might have made a mistake about her career. Instead, she buried her dreams and kept on working with her unmarried girls, her committees and societies. The next war, and the continual passing through London of servicemen on leave, desperate for the comfort of women, made the hostel busier than ever. She was always occupied, could never spend as much time at home as she wanted, and was thankful Guy took it all in his stride.

The telephone rang. "Daisy?"

It was Guy, as if she had conjured him up just by thinking about him. The heavy black bakelite receiver grew even heavier in her hand as she heard him out, her face ashen. "Oh, God," she said, and then, "Yes, yes, of course I will. I'll come home immediately."

"What is it?" Athene asked, as the receiver rattled into its cradle.

Suddenly, even young Lorna's problems seemed to recede. "Guy's just heard. The builders at Charnley...Oh, Athene! They've found a – a body! The police want me and Harriet to go down and identify–"

Athene, who had seen as many dead bodies, and parts of bodies, come to that, as Daisy had in France, was nevertheless equally horrified at the prospect.

Daisy pushed her chair back with a great effort. "Must go

home. We're going to collect Harriet at her cottage and go on to Charnley from there."

"You're not driving?" Athene's alarm was evident. Her brother had given up driving some time ago, when his eyesight had become troublesome, but she obviously thought Daisy was in shock, and in no condition to be in charge of a motorcar. In her opinion Daisy was an erratic driver in any state.

"No, Nina's already on her way over to have lunch with Guy. He's sure she'll drive us on to Harriet's. Harriet was coming down for lunch, too, but he caught her before she left home."

Athene seemed relieved to hear this. Her niece was a capable young woman and would drive safely. "Cup of tea first."

"Don't have time."

But Athene, who knew the effects of shock when she saw it, insisted. If the body's been there all that time, it's not going to go away now, she thought, but had the sense not to say.

Nina Tempest had set out early for her lunch with her father, in order to pick up some small items of shopping on the way – some of Guy's favourite tobacco, a bunch of flowers for Daisy, and a call at the library to pick up a new book or two for herself. Walking at a brisk clip, the high heels of her new shoes tapping, skirt swinging, hair bobbing on her shoulders, she was unaware of the admiring, speculative glances that followed her – pretty young woman looking forward to meeting her lover, perhaps? They couldn't have been more wrong.

During the past couple of weeks, she had at last begun to feel more at one with herself, and today, she was suddenly fuelled by optimism and energy, firing on all cylinders. She dared to hope that at last she was regaining her sense of humour and that natural capacity for getting the most out of life which had made even her conscription into the WAAF something of a lark, rather than simply an experience to be endured. On this glorious early autumn day, when the plane trees were already beginning to shed their leaves in a golden carpet on the shabby, war-scarred suburban streets of North London, she felt it was time to get on with her life again – her life, as opposed to the work in which she'd absorbed herself for the last fifteen months. The end of a long, hard slog. Too long, perhaps. Sooner or later she had to find some answers, admit that burying her head in the sand was getting her nowhere. Stop using her work as an excuse, and come to terms with her future, look at things in a clearer, and more honest, light. Face the truth. Or whatever other tired, worn-out cliché you cared to employ.

The truth was not exactly elevating. She'd spent nearly five years as the lover of another woman's husband, a man named Matthew Maran, snatching hurried meetings as and when they could throughout the war, worrying about his safety as a senior army officer in various war zones, waiting for the war to end, the children of his marriage to grow up, or the marriage itself to disintegrate. Then, when all these things had at last come about almost simultaneously, her lover found he'd changed his mind about spending the rest of his life at her side. He'd seen no reason why their relationship shouldn't carry on exactly as before, however, which she'd interpreted rightly, the scales falling at last from her eyes, to mean that he regarded their long, passionate affair, and what she had believed was love, as nothing more than a convenience. She was shaken to the core. And guilty, too, morbidly obsessed by that legacy from her French, Catholic mother, the nuns at her convent school: the feeling that her misery was some sort of punishment for what they would have seen as lying and adultery.

She hadn't been prepared to accept the new situation on

Matthew's terms, and in the end, she'd summoned up enough courage to walk away. She blamed herself for the naivety that had envisaged a future which could never have been more than make-believe. On her release from the WAAF, financial necessity dictated that she had to resume her previous, mind-numbingly dull position working in a bank, but she'd also taken the plunge, and committed herself and every moment of her spare time to writing That Book. Nothing heavy, nothing more than a light historical romance, something she'd always meant to try. Without distractions, writing far into the night and wearing a determined pair of blinkers (on her emotions as well as on the outside world) it was done, speedily and more easily than she'd even dreamed of, and to her delight was accepted for a modest sum and published. Her second would soon be at the proof stage and the publishers were wanting another. But having driven herself so mercilessly, she'd found she was temporarily written out, in a kind of limbo.

The fact that she was without a creative idea in her head was beginning to nibble rather ferociously at the edges of her conscience. Two books were no guarantee of financial security and she could not afford to give up her job at the bank, but today, with a couple of days off due to her, she felt almost light-hearted as she made her way across London via tube and then bus towards the rambling, untidy terrace house in Maida Vale which had been home until she'd been called up, and thereafter a place to stay when she was on leave. After which, she had found her own bed-sit, having discovered independence, too precious ever to relinquish completely again. Besides, she had been aware that without her, Daisy and her father had somehow developed an easier way of acknowledging the separateness of their working lives while still retaining the respect and affection that held their marriage together.

Nina loved her stepmother – it was impossible not to love warm-hearted Daisy, who gave so generously of her time and energies to other people, often making tactless remarks and blunders which nobody took amiss because it was obvious she meant so well – but at the same time, Nina knew she hadn't been an ideal substitute mother, being too often wrapped up in her own busy life, too preoccupied with injustices in general to have much time or insight to spare for recognising individual problems nearer to home. On the other hand, within her own lights, she had been good for Nina – never intruding into the dead Cécile's territory, acting more as a good chum than a mother figure.

But with Daisy had come Harriet, and Harriet was a different proposition.

Never mind the difference in their ages – from the start, they were on an equal footing. It wasn't only that they were on the same wavelength about books and music, and laughed at the same things, they were somewhat alike in character – determined, impatient, perhaps, unwilling to accept fools gladly. A little intense about relationships. If there were reservations between them – and there were a few – it was simply because each respected the other's innate need for privacy. It was a rare, strong friendship, treasured by both women, though not overtly expressed.

Guy had telephoned before Nina left home to tell her that Harriet was expected for lunch, too. They hadn't met for some time and she looked forward to it with anticipation.

Chapter Ten

The sun glancing on its many windows did nothing to lessen the elegiac sombreness of the grey pile that was Charnley. Perhaps it was the absence of sound – no clanking of metal sheets being thrown into lorries, as when Harriet had visited it the day previously, no sound of grinding machinery dismantling the air raid shelters. Only silence, so profound it was hard to believe that the tranquillity of the house had ever been disrupted – by family tragedy, by two world wars, or even by the discovery of a body that might well have remained undiscovered until the house fell down.

Daisy alighted from the car and looked around. The restoration work now being within an ace of completion, on the outside, at least, the great old house had regained some of its former self-respect, now that roof tiles had been replaced, its tall chimneys repointed, broken windows reglazed and the lead flashings that had been stolen put back.

"It's hardly changed at all!"

"Wait until you see the inside," replied Harriet.

She was relieved to see that her sister had pulled herself together somewhat. Daisy had been uncharacteristically silent and withdrawn on the way there, sitting in the back seat next to Guy, occasionally dabbing her eyes, obviously shaken to the core by the news of what the builders had uncovered. It was so unlike her to go to pieces in this way that Harriet, rather than advising her sharply to pull herself together as she might otherwise have done, had tried instead to prepare her for the changes she would see inside the house. She doubted Daisy, absorbed in her misery, had taken much interest.

"Go ahead," Nina was saying now to the other three, "I'll wander around the gardens while you go in. Unless, of course…"

She threw an enquiring glance at Daisy, but Daisy had dried her eyes, blown her nose and answered quite firmly, "No need for you to come inside, darling – really. You go and have a little look around – I don't expect we shall be long."

She gave Nina's arm a squeeze, then determinedly followed the others. A young uniformed constable stationed by the door came forward to conduct them through the hall – which now held a reception desk, presently unmanned – towards what had once been their father's study. The Holy of Holies. The room which now, according to the wooden label lettered in white and screwed to the door, belonged to Mr E.G.Aiken, whoever he might be. The policeman knocked on the door, poked his head around it and said something to the occupants, and a middle-aged man came out. He introduced himself as McLellan, the Home Office pathologist, and took Guy to one side, leaving the others to join the sizeable knot of people already in the room.

Harriet and Daisy were given chairs in the bay window, overlooking the fountain on the lower terrace, where the stone figures of Laocoon and his sons remained intact, still struggling in the coils of the sea serpents, though the basin was dry and cracked. Harriet hoped someone would eventually get the fountain to work again. Its derelict state seemed almost more of a sacrilege to her than the name-plate defacing the study door, the disappearance of her father's mahogany desk, and his books. She wondered what Daisy was making of it all. She was gazing out of the window, as if refusing to face the once familiar room and acknowledge the changes which had taken place in it. Although she was by now obviously making an effort to regain her normal air of cheerful solidity and good-natured competence, she wasn't being too successful. Unnervingly, she had that look she'd had sometimes when she was a child, lost and bewildered at the unexpected unfairness of life: little Daisy, in the grip of some childish grief – usually over some deceased pet or a doll with a broken arm, a sisterly squabble, or perhaps because of a small punishment for a misdemeanour. There had never been much more cause than that: Charnley had been a civilised home where people were kind to each other, and good humoured; where real anger rarely surfaced, where there was indeed little need for it because people had been well brought up; it was not done to show feelings...and therein, maybe, had lain the fault. Perhaps there had been too much bottling up of destructive emotions.

The body which had been found was that of a woman, they had been told.

Harriet had believed that both she and her sister had long ago gone beyond the point of shedding tears for their mother, but she was discovering that this new and terrible revelation was no less painful now than it would have been forty years ago. She had always, at the back of her mind, been convinced that Beatrice must be dead – and that their father must have thought this too, and it was that which had contributed to him taking his own life. But to have it confirmed, after all these years, and in this macabre way, was breathtakingly cruel. This would change everything...

'This' being what had just been uncovered, and what they were required to identify...the mouldering rags of what was still recognisable, though only just, as a black silk kimono embroidered with chrysanthemums and a dragon motif on the back, and a fine necklace of garnets: all that remained to indicate that the body had once been that of Beatrice Jardine. They lay on a couple of utility desks pushed together into the centre of the room to form a makeshift table, together with a small leather valise which had gone mouldy, containing a silver hairbrush, a walking costume, and delicate, rotting, embroidered silk underclothing.

"Yes," Harriet said, and Daisy too nodded. They both

turned away.

It was obscene, a nightmare. Their mother's body, lying so near, all the time they had been searching for her. And afterwards, too, when they had gone on with the business of living at Charnley. The implications of where she'd been found – behind one of the walls Rose Jessamy had painted – were horrible beyond the bounds of credibility.

The pathologist, McLellan, a bony Presbyterian Scot who did not believe in shuffling around the truth, had faced many horrifying deaths but this discovery was shocking, even to him, and was the reason he'd taken Guy aside and left the others to go ahead into the room where the articles to be identified were waiting. "You're a doctor, you'll understand what I'm about to tell you. The deceased was murdered, strangled by ligature. With her own necklace – you realise what I'm saying?"

Guy wasn't actually quite sure what the pathologist was getting at. He knew that after nearly forty years there would be nothing left but a skeleton, nothing left to identify except a bundle of bones. It would certainly be possible to tell whether she had been strangled, if the delicate hyoid bone in the larynx had been fractured – and if the necklace was still in place around her neck, it would be assumed that had been the ligature. "But–"

"Hear me out, please, Tempest," McLellan intervened. "She was found in a chimney. Where draughts could circulate freely. To be blunt, the body was mummified, covered in dust and cobwebs. The necklace was still embedded in the flesh. Not very pretty."

Guy was temporarily bereft of words. Eventually, he found his voice. "Mummified? A chimney? Good God! How the devil– ?"

"How and why she got there is none of my business, or

even who she is. All I can say is how she died. If it turns out the body *is* that of their mother, the ladies are going to find this added circumstance difficult to accept, so it will probably come better from you. That's why I wanted to tell you first."

"Yes, indeed. Very thoughtful. I appreciate that."

But grateful as he was for the delicacy that had prompted the pathologist to give this warning, Guy thought he would rather do practically anything else he could think of than have to face his wife and Harriet with this.

When the others had gone into the house, Nina was left looking dubiously at the gravel paths surrounding the bare beds and borders. Ruinous to high heels. On the other hand, she couldn't walk on the sharp little stones in her stockinged feet, and she was curious to see more of this Charnley she'd heard so much about but never seen before. Besides, her father's ancient Sunbeam hadn't improved since the days when Guy had first taught her to drive it, and she'd be glad to get out and ease her cramped limbs and the tension in her shoulders. Reluctantly, she slipped back into her shoes, kicked off as unsuitable for driving, and walked gingerly along the front of the house, intending to take the mossy steps to the garden and the old fountain below. It wasn't long before she was cursing those dratted heels afresh. She should have had the forethought to borrow a more sensible pair from Daisy, or Harriet, though she'd have had to stuff the toes somehow, since they both took a larger size than she did. Actually, her whole outfit – a cherry red two-piece, made last week to cheer herself up, the blouse with a frilly jabot – felt ludicrously frivolous for such an occasion. Nothing to be done about it now; she'd left home not knowing how grimly the afternoon would turn out. She turned a corner and there, unexpectedly, was a further wing set back from the main body of the house, a much older part. Tudor? Workmen's tools, several skips and ladders stood outside, and a heavy, dark oak door with iron studs and door furniture was wide open.

It was tempting. She stepped inside and found herself in a long corridor.

"Oi! Sorry miss, can't come in here! Admin's through the front door and turn left."

"I do apologise, but I wasn't looking for Admin." Turning back to make as dignified an exit as possible, she was confronted by a man in the uniform of a security guard.

"That's all right, miss. Lots of folks get lost around here. Where is it you want to be, then? Personnel office? You'll be lucky, though – I hear most of the new staff's been taken on, now we're nearly ready to open proper."

"I'm not looking for a job, I'm just curious." The admission caused the friendly look to be replaced by one of suspicion. "My people used to live here," she smiled, stretching the truth somewhat, "but I've never seen the place before."

"Oh, I see." He eyed her with a little more favour. "All the same...sorry, but nobody can come in here just now, on account of the police..."

"It's all right, Simmons, I'll deal with this."

Nina turned to see a self-consciously elegant, fair-haired young man in a smart, double-breasted pale grey suit. She immediately recognised the glamour-boy, God's gift to females smile, and gave him a cool glance. Ex-RAF, fighter-pilot, she guessed, his long upper lip looking as though it ought to be still sporting a handlebar moustache. "I *am* the police, actually," he drawled. "Detective Sergeant Fairchild." He held out a hand, appraising her with rather more interest than a police scrutiny warranted. Her hackles rose further. "And you are –?"

"Nina Tempest."

"Ah. Then you're with the lady who–"

"Yes."

"Bad show, all this."

She acknowledged that with a nod and made to continue her way outside, but he stopped her, saying, "I suppose you were wanting to see where the body was found?"

He'd marked her down as some sort of ghoul. She threw him a look shot with dislike, but he seemed to be the sort with whom that didn't register. She said coldly, "No, I wasn't. It was the Jessamy rooms I wanted to see – just to look at those wonderful wall paintings I've heard so much about."

"Not much wonderful about them, now! That's where they were working when they came across the body, behind a chimney-breast." He sounded slightly bored.

"Oh."

He eyed her, weighing up options. "If that's all you want, I don't suppose it'd really matter–"

"No thanks, I don't think so, not now."

But there was no denying she was intrigued – actually, a bit more than that. She knew from Daisy something of the events here at Charnley that had disrupted for ever the Jardines' pleasant and protected life, though her stepmother had never dwelt on particulars, in fact she'd been inclined to gloss over details whenever the subject of the old days came up. So Nina only knew what she suspected was a highly edited version of the old scandal. But her writer's instinct told her that here was a story waiting to be uncovered, something which was almost certainly going to reveal the answer to the riddle of a woman who'd been missing for nearly forty years. A body had been found, and though she knew no more than that yet, it seemed that to her that it must almost certainly be that of Beatrice Jardine. And those wall paintings, and how they came to be executed, were part of the story. All the same...

"No, I couldn't, really. I wouldn't want to get you into trouble."

The policeman looked at her. Nina's smile was one that had disarmed better men than he. He hesitated only for only a moment longer. "OK, I dare say I could stretch a point," he said, anxious to disabuse her of the idea that he might have no authority in the matter, "if you really wanted to have a quick dekko, seeing as you're part of the family. As long as you don't go past the tape on the other end…"

"I promise I don't want to see anything other than those murals."

"Won't get much out of 'em, I'll tell you that. They're a dead loss, in rotten condition, damp and all that. The – er – the one room's – strictly off-limits, right?"

She looked along the corridor and saw again the tape stretched across. "I certainly wouldn't want to see that one, anyway."

"Good show. I'll come with you, then."

She'd walked into that one, but she saw that there was no other way she was going to see what she wanted. He escorted her along the corridor and opened the door of a room just before the police tape began and where a wooden-faced constable stood on guard. "Sorry, no further than this, but the next room's very similar."

She hadn't been expecting much from what he'd said, but the large room she was looking into was at first glance a disappointment, all the same. Here and there a whole section survived – in particular, part of a border of lotus and papyrus still fresh and brilliant as it had been the day it was painted, but for the most part, flaking plaster showed only patches of what must once have been vibrant colour, the only indications that once queens and pharaohs, gods and goddesses had marched around it in a glorious panoply of colour, the greens and lapis blues and the shine of gold against their brown-red skin, the white of their kilts and black hair. The tall white crowns of Upper and the reds of Lower Egypt.

And yet. It could all have been an artistic muddle, she thought, but it wasn't. What she hadn't expected was to find that the rooms must have captured so much of the flavour of the glory and elegance that once was ancient Egypt. The room she was looking into was much, much larger than she had expected – or was it? Wasn't it just that it had been given an illusion of added length, and perhaps dignity, by a clever use of perspective – *trompe l'oeil* columns and architraves –

"Not much to look at now, is it?"

"Not much." But even in this condition, her imagination providing what had once been there, it took Nina's breath away. It was evident that Rose Jessamy must have been inspired when she painted these walls.

Detective Inspector Linus Grigsby from Scotland Yard was in charge of the case, a big man with a Cockney accent, wearing an ill-fitting suit of some thick brown material (demob suit – sizes small, medium and large, guessed Harriet) which he filled to capacity. He had a battered face and looked like a prize fighter, an impression reinforced by his habit of rocking lightly on the balls of his feet when making a point. Not prepossessing, but at least he was demonstrating tact and sympathy. He had cleared the room, previously overcrowded with several members of the police, the pathologist and his pretty young secretary, there with him to take notes. He had asked for tea to be sent in and when Guy returned, had left them alone while Guy squared his shoulders and did his best to prepare them for something more macabre than they could possibly have envisaged.

Mummified. Strangled with her own necklace. Left in that chimney. That was grotesque enough to have to cope with by any standards, but it did at least put paid to those ghastly imaginings about her not being dead before the chimney had been bricked up – though that had been the first appalled thought in both their minds, in their faces as they'd looked at each other, when they had learned where their mother's remains had been found. All those horror stories, heard and shivered over with frightened delight as children: stories about the west wing being haunted by the ghost of the Roman Catholic priest who had been hidden in the priest's hole, the door sealed to prevent his being found, and who'd died before he could be rescued. Other tales of mediaeval nuns being punished for their sins by being walled up alive and left to die...

Guy soon put an end to that sort of speculation before it could be voiced. "I'm afraid there's no doubt she was murdered, the necklace proves that. Her body must have been put where it was to conceal the fact."

Daisy said suddenly, into the seemingly endless silence that followed, "Who's going to tell Vita?"

Vita. Oh, yes.

"I suppose it's up to me," said Harriet, after a moment.

Daisy pushed a stray hair behind her ears. "Actually, I don't mind. This is going to knock her sideways."

And of course, Vita must be handled with kid gloves. And I, naturally, thought Harriet, am not to be trusted to do that. Probably rightly. Vita had always resented being told what to do by her elder sister. She'd never listened, had gone her own way, even when it meant ruining her life.

All the sparkle and vivacity had gone out of Vita from the moment she'd given Bertie Rossiter his ring back. He had taken it, promising to put it on her finger again when he had control of his own fortune, yet within the year he had succumbed to his mother's bullying and married the lumpy Horsley girl. Even worse, with incredible insensitivity, he had taken his new bride to live in the house where he and Vita had hoped to start their marriage.

Within a few weeks of hearing that, Vita had become engaged to Lord Wycombe.

What? Wycombe?

None of her siblings could, at first, absorb the idea, still less believe that Vita could possibly be serious about accepting his proposal, and was not going to be moved by their arguments. He was *old* – as old as their father had been! He was their Uncle Myles! The very idea was almost – incestuous. If Vita would only give it time, she would certainly find a younger man.

But no one on earth could be more stubborn than Vita when she wanted to be. Or, as Harriet knew, more secretive in her thoughts. And in the end, after making the supreme effort to forget he had ever dandled them on his knee, it became just possible to acknowledge she might have known what she was doing. Wycombe was, after all, handsome, athletic, cultivated, titled – and rich. Rich enough to make it possible for Charnley to be kept in the family – had that been her idea? If so, Marcus would very quickly have disabused her of it. He would accept that sort of sacrifice from no one, least of all his sister. But many a girl other than Vita would willingly have married a man nearly thirty years older than she was for the advantages such a marriage brought. As Lady Wycombe, she continued to live the life she had been brought up to expect. She gave her husband his heirs – two sons, the love of his – and her – life. She was an accomplished hostess, her social calendar was full, she was popular, free to do pretty much as she wanted. But was she happy? Seemingly, yes, at least on the surface – until that terrible tragedy which had come to her later. After which, it was hard to get anywhere near Vita. Though she'd come through, after a fashion. Been psycho-analysed and emerged at the end of it a different woman.

All the same...her stability was still fragile, there was always the sense of her being on the edge.

"I dare say you're right, Daisy," Harriet said more circumspectly. "She'll take it better from you."

"I won't telephone – I'll go and see her tonight. Guy?"

"We'll call on our way home." He patted Daisy's hand. The way in which she'd received the news had been disconcerting, coming from Daisy, who always coped so sensibly with everything, but perhaps the tears had been necessary. He was not worried about her, or not in the long term. She would suffer and grieve over this, but already he could see her recovering, reverting to being splendidly capable again. Thinking of other people, as always, in the same way she worked herself to death over those girls of hers. Harriet worried him far more. Outwardly, she seemed her usual self – shocked, of course, though still astringent, ironic, self-contained. And yet beneath it, he sensed what he could only feel was a barely concealed panic. Had she, he wondered uneasily, found rather more among those papers she'd gone through yesterday than she was admitting to? Or was it something else? You couldn't always tell with Harriet.

Grigsby had given them twenty minutes alone, but now he was back, followed almost immediately by a younger, handsomely self-satisfied looking detective, accompanied by Nina, rather white-faced.

"Oh, Nina," said Daisy, her eyes filling again, "there's something rather awful–"

"I know, darling. Sergeant Fairchild has just told me." She went and stood in front of the two older women, taking a hand of each.

Grigsby said, "Thank you, Fairchild," with the sort of look that implied later retribution.

Who the hell had given him permission to blab to that young woman? He wasn't the sergeant Grigsby would have

picked to work with him on this job if he'd had any choice.
Bright enough, if his interest was caught, but too cocky by
half, couldn't forget he'd been an RAF officer and flown a
Spitfire, one of the Brylcreem boys in their handsome blue
uniforms, while Grigsby himself had never risen above the
rank of army sergeant in the Military Police. Fairchild had his
eye on promotion and didn't take kindly to Grigsby being his
boss – Grigsby, who'd come up from the ranks, who'd
learned what he knew on the beat, in the same streets where
both he and the villains he caught came from. He had a reputation for toughness and thoroughness. He was a bulldog –
when he got his teeth into a case, they'd have to be prised
open with an iron bar before he'd let go.

But truth to tell, this was far from his usual sort of investigation and he felt like a fish out of water, though Fairchild
thought it was going to be a piece of cake – and maybe that's
how it would turn out, in its own way – meaning that nothing in the way of evidence would emerge after all this time
and the enquiry would die a slow, natural death. His sharp
antennae told him he'd need to keep his wits about him here,
all the same. Both women had taken the gruesome news better than he expected, but neither, even the younger, would
easily be fobbed off, or be likely to wilt under interrogation.

"You'll appreciate that in the very unusual circumstances–"
he began, then cleared his throat and went straight into it: he
would need to question them in detail, he said, about events
around the time when their mother had disappeared. He
remembered to soften it by adding that he realised he was
asking a lot after such a time lapse, but added that it was
essential he should have as complete a picture as possible.

"You must have records," Harriet Jardine returned sharply.
"Or did the man in charge of the investigation not make any?
Sergeant Maitland, wasn't it?"

The chief inspector was not one to be overawed by an

imperious woman, however impressed he was by her memory. He sensed in Harriet Jardine a tendency to be hostile. Charitably, he put it down to shock. He wasn't feeling all that chipper himself, come to that; it was the first time in his career he had ever had to deal with a forty-year-old mummified corpse, and having seen it he hoped it would be his last. Forty years – or very nearly! The odds on solving a murder that long after it had happened weren't ones he'd have laid money on. He was tempted to wonder if it even mattered now – but only briefly. Justice always mattered, to somebody. He doubted, all the same, whether he'd be given the go-ahead to spend much time or resources on what was probably an insoluble mystery, with not a cat in hell's chance of bringing the perpetrator to book. The victim herself, had she lived, would've been – what? Over eighty. And the murderer most likely dead and buried by now. He tried not to let his thoughts show. He said stiffly, "Sergeant Maitland is no longer with us." Which sounded like a euphemism for Maitland being dead. Whether he was or not, Grigsby hadn't a clue. He'd simply meant that he'd retired, donkey's years ago, and maybe that was lucky for him.

While being driven down here from the Yard by Fairchild, Grigsby had familiarised himself with Maitland's old notes about Beatrice Jardine's disappearance and her husband's subsequent suicide, and had got a distinct whiff of Billingsgate. With the facility he had of reading between the lines, he sensed that the case had been bodged – or more likely, facts and situations had been turned up which were unacceptable, and had then been brushed under the carpet. The family had been local gentry, after all, in with the Chief Constable and God knows who else, and that had mattered in those days. The war had altered that sort of social hierarchy. The sort of thing that couldn't happen today. Could it?

"This new evidence that's turned up has thrown a different

light on the case, as you'll appreciate. There'll be questions now that never needed to be asked at that time. I shall need your help, both of you, if we're ever going to find out who killed your mother, and why."

Harriet sensed, rather than heard, a hint of coercion and her hackles rose. "We might have known that at the time, if more effort had been made to trace Valery Iskander."

Grigsby might have pointed out that this was most likely due to pressure being put on poor old Maitland *not* to trace the Egyptian, but he held his tongue. "Miss Jardine, Mr Iskander leaving suddenly isn't evidence of his having committed this murder, if that's what you're implying."

She was silent for a long time, and then gave a slight smile, an attractive, crooked smile that made her look quite different, more approachable. "Forgive me, you have your job to do. But you must admit it looks suspicious."

"What I'm more interested in is the fact of the body being found where it was. The room was in the process of being decorated with those Egyptian murals, right? Was Mr Iskander concerned with that?"

"Only in so far as he put the idea into her head. Miss Jessamy's head, I mean. Rose Jessamy. She was the woman who was doing the decorating."

Grigsby was less insensitive than Harriet imagined him. His small, sharp eyes regarded her shrewdly. The bitter irony of finding a mummy in rooms decorated with Egyptian temples and pyramids and sphinxes hadn't escaped him. He hadn't yet quite grasped just why it had been decided to paint those rooms like that, unless it was something to do with that Nile trip the victim had apparently taken years before. But the implications, in regard to the murder, were clear. "That wall was certainly plastered and decorated after the body was put in the chimney – so the person who was painting the walls is someone we shall need to talk to."

"Rose Jessamy? You think *she* killed my mother and put her there?" Harriet Jardine laughed shortly. "Well, unless she was actually killed in that room, I should think you can rule out the possibility. She was a slight little thing and Mama was not small."

Grigsby had seen photographs of Beatrice Jardine that were with the case notes. What his mother used to call 'a fine figure of a woman'. Like a younger Queen Mary, Mrs Jardine had been a stately lady, full-fleshed, a bit haughty looking – though if the camera wasn't lying, she'd also been an absolute stunner, a real Edwardian belle. Lillie Langtry, Alice Keppel and Mrs Patrick Campbell rolled into one.

Mrs Tempest, the younger sister, suddenly said, "I think I can help you there." Up until now, Grigsby had assumed her silence had meant she was too upset to speak, but it seemed she might just have been deep in thought. "She – Rose, I mean – would chip off the old plaster in the evening, ready for plastering it up the next day, so that she could paint directly on to it with watercolours."

"Chip it off and then replaster it? Sounds a mite cock-eyed!"

"Not so much as you might think. You have to do that with frescoes. Paint on to the wet plaster, to make it more durable."

Grigsby gave her a sharp look. "She did it herself? Then she couldn't have been any weakling."

"Well, I don't think she was, if it comes to that, even though she was only little. Artists have to be quite strong, you know, if they're doing that kind of work. But she'd only to plaster a bit at a time. You draw the whole design on the wall first. Then you chip away the bit you want to work on, re-plaster it and paint it while the plaster's still wet. That's what makes it last so long – provided conditions are right. But there was talk of maybe putting another fireplace surround in that room, which would fit in better with the new decorations than the old-fashioned thing they'd just pulled out, so she agreed with my mother that she'd do a temporary job. Paint on to the dry plaster on the chimney breast – that's a technique called *fresco secco* – and redo it later if necessary."

"You're very knowledgeable, Mrs Tempest. You an artist, too?" She didn't look like his conception of what an artist should be like. With her comfortably plump figure and her warm, hazel eyes, Daisy Tempest looked more like his sensible, trustworthy Aunt Nellie – though a good deal sharper than that old dear.

"Heavens, no, I just used to help her. I was very young, thought it was all so glamorous and different. And it was certainly great fun. But something I do remember...that morning, the day Mama couldn't be found, Rose was having difficulty with that fireplace wall. She'd plastered it up the night before, hoping it would be dry and smooth enough to paint the next morning, but in actual fact she was very surprised that it was neither. She seemed to think she hadn't been careful enough the day before."

"So it's possible someone else re-plastered the chimney breast during the night?"

Daisy said slowly, "Yes, that *was* what I was thinking."

"Have you any idea where we can get in touch with Miss Jessamy?"

The sisters exchanged a look. "No one's heard of her for years," Harriet said. "Not since she left Charnley." And then she added, "Inspector, where are the other garnets?"

Grigsby regarded her. "What others, Miss Jardine?"

"It was a matching set – what's known as a parure – there was a bracelet and earrings and a sort of comb to fix in the hair, as well as the necklace. My father had given them to my mother for her birthday. She was wearing the whole set that night – and none of them were found among her things afterwards."

"You can be sure of that?"

"Oh, yes. My father made some remark about them being the only jewellery she'd taken with her."

"I can tell you they weren't in the valise. There was only what you saw – spare underclothing, hairbrush and so on."

Grigsby thought: garnets, a bracelet and earrings, missing. Jewellery of relatively little intrinsic value, not worth killing for – especially when other jewellery – several rings, one of them an engagement ring with a cluster of what looked to Grigsby like very fine diamonds – had been left on the body. But worth thinking about, although the circumstances of the murder suggested more than killing for what could be snatched. Daisy Tempest had voiced this when she'd protested, "What on earth could anyone have wanted to murder Mama for? She never had a wrong word with anyone!" Grigsby had heard what she said. It was what most people felt when their loved ones were killed, not understanding that there didn't always have to be a recognisable or sensible reason. He'd known a throat cut for the price of a packet of fags, or a face smashed in with a broken bottle for a pint of red biddy. Or a person knifed because some mad devil just didn't like the look of their face.

After questioning them for some little time more, making sure that Fairchild had noted down all the relevant details, he said that was all for the present and let them go.

Fifteen minutes later, having seen the car containing the family off the premises, Fairchild returned.

"Well, what do you think?"

"Obvious, isn't it?" the sergeant said. "Their mother and this Iskander they said she'd met in Egypt had had an affair there, then when he pops up on the scene all those years later, she doesn't want anything more to do with him. He's browned off, kills her and scarpers."

"Or her husband finds out, kills 'em both, and then later remorse – or else fear of being found out – causes him to top himself."

"In which case," responded Fairchild brightly, "there's another body somewhere here at Charnley."

"Walled up as well?" Grigsby rubbed his nose. "I'm full of good ideas, me, but pulling the whole bloody place down just on the offchance of that isn't one of 'em. Actually, I'm not sure anything is that obvious about this case. Except that when a good looker like she was is strangled, you can bet your life there's sex lurking in the background. The murder of a man's wife, followed by his suicide, generally means only one thing. You've got that list the Jardine ladies left?"

Fairchild flourished it. "The ones I've starred are the family, and those guests who stayed overnight. The ones who are still with us, that is. And most of them are, it seems. Apart from the son who was killed in 1915, and this woman Rose Jessamy–"

"Let's have a butcher's."

Fairchild passed the list over. Grigsby shifted to take it, and his chair creaked ominously. His little eyes screwed up even more narrowly as he read, running his finger down the names: "The three Jardine daughters. The son, Marcus. The Egyptian – and who's this Sacheverell?"

"Long time friend of the family. Almost like a son, I gather."

"Talk to him. And what about the servants?"

"There was the lady's maid, Mrs Jardine's maid, that is, but she left soon after her mistress disappeared and no one's heard of her since. Housekeeper and butler long dead, ditto chauffeur. I'll see if I can dredge up any more. Oh, and there was this Lord Wycombe staying as a house guest as well. Apparently, he's quite famous, some sort of art historian or such-like, must be knocking ninety by now but he's still alive and kicking. Rum do, that – he married the middle Jardine girl, old enough to be her father. I've also starred a Mrs Millie Kaplan – Lady Glendinning as she was at that time – who wasn't an overnight guest."

"Why her in particular?"

"Apparently she was a great friend of the deceased – and she was with her on that Nile cruise when they met Iskander."

Grigsby tapped his teeth with his pencil. Harriet Jardine had told him there was some sort of diary written by her mother when she'd been in Egypt, at least a decade before her murder. She'd seemed to think the diary, and some note-books of her own – doubtless full of some schoolgirlish out-pourings – could give some sort of clue as to why Beatrice had been murdered. Grigsby had been quick to nip her idea of the Egyptian as murderer in the bud. It might come to that – his convenient disappearance the morning after the murder was suspicious and would need accounting for – but if he had murdered her, was it feasible he could have hidden the body where it was found? The Gladstone bag found with the dead woman, containing her missing clothing, suggested to Grigsby that someone had set up the idea they had run off together. He always preferred to go the simplest route first in any investigation – and this time he had a gut feeling that the culprit would be found nearer home. On the other hand, he was by no means convinced that Harriet Jardine would let go of the idea that these diaries meant something – and the last thing he wanted was her conducting enquiries on her own account, so maybe he'd better let Fairchild take a look at that journal of her mother's. But not until they'd exhausted other lines of enquiry.

Chapter Eleven

The year was beginning to creep towards autumn, with a sharp nip to the nights, and back in her cottage at Garvingden, Harriet knelt to put a match to the paper and logs in the grate. Spicy apple logs from a tree in the garden which had blown down in the March gales.

Nina sniffed appreciatively as they caught hold. "Mmm, lovely!"

"They won't last out the winter," Harriet said, "but I've managed to get a couple of hundredweight of coal delivered as well. Tom Stretton – he's the verger – sawed the tree up for me. That's another advantage of living here – where in London would you find someone to do things like that?"

Harriet's new enthusiasm for burying herself out here, away from everything, was something Nina couldn't share with her, apple logs and other country delights notwithstanding. She murmured, "Where in London would you need to, with electric fires and all? The country might have its charms, but–" She'd been going to add that whoever said it was 'a kind of healthy grave' had her on his side, but in the circumstances, she felt that anything to do with graves was better not mentioned.

The rural life wasn't for her, but all the same, she'd been determined not to leave Harriet alone that night after their return from Charnley. Guy had seconded the idea, feeling less nervous of being driven home by Daisy, now that she was showing every sign of having got over the initial effects of shock. They had already left, on their way to break the news to Vita.

"I'll go back by train tomorrow," Nina had said. "You can find me a toothbrush, I suppose, Harriet?"

"I'm sure I can, but I warn you it'll mean a bed on the sofa, and you'll have to get up early to catch the bus into Oxford for the train – there isn't another bus until noon. I'm nearly out of my petrol ration, so I can't drive you."

"I believe I might just be able to do that small thing."

Harriet gave in and squeezed her hand. "It'll be good to have you here."

They ate a makeshift bread and cheese supper, for which neither had much appetite, skirting round the events of the day. The ice was still too thin over those dark waters to venture on it. Nina did her best to lighten the heavy mood the day had brought by keeping off the subject and trying to make Harriet smile with stories of the other inhabitants of the house where she had her bed-sit, minimising its shortcomings and its location, making it sound attractively unconventional. Harriet, who had visited her there, knew that it was not. But she admired the spirit that had prompted the attempt. She watched her step-niece affectionately as she sat casually relaxed, feet tucked under her on the sofa. Narrow, high-cheekboned face, quick, fleeting smile, her dark eyes and her intrinsic elegance an unmistakably Gallic inheritance from her mother. Her hair was loose, a dark tangle where she'd run her fingers through it, and she was thinner than Harriet thought she should be, but having said that, she looked better than she had for some time. She was making an effort with her clothes again, and evidently getting over that disastrous affair, never a match designed in heaven. In a moment of shared intimacy, when the break-up with her lover had finally occurred, Nina had confided in Harriet, and Harriet, who had for a long time suspected something of the sort, had refrained from offering the usual anodyne remarks: time heals, it will pass, knowing from experience such platitudes were hateful just because they were true. She'd listened, and let her cry, and then, when Nina had dried her eyes, she'd opened a bottle of carefully hoarded wine.

Which seemed like a good idea now, tonight.

And, true enough, after the first glass, in front of the fire, with the curtains snugly drawn, Charnley didn't seem such a dangerous topic. "I'm glad I've seen the house," Nina said, thinking how different Harriet's life here must be in this small cottage, cosy in the leaping firelight, from where she'd started life – that grey, rather forbidding pile of Charnley, with its endless corridors and hotchpotch of rooms. "Though it wasn't at all as I imagined it to be."

"Which was – ?"

"Larger than it actually is, for one thing. And I must admit I thought it would be – more gracious. You know, all white and Palladian, everything in proportion."

Harriet smiled wryly. "It was never that. Bits have always been added on here and there over the years, just as the fancy took the owners. And I can't see they're doing anything to improve matters now. All the same, it was a comfortable house, happy…" The sap in one of the logs boiled and spluttered. A spark flew out on to the rug and she stamped it out with her foot. "Would it bore you to look at some old photos?"

"Just the opposite. Now I've seen the place, I'd love to see everyone who lived there"

Harriet produced an album of faded burgundy leather, and the grey cardboard box file which still held the other photographs that she'd brought home with her the previous day, and came to sit next to Nina on the sofa.

The pictures had all been taken in that golden era before the First World War – golden at least for the privileged people featured in them. Nina was entranced by the hour-glass figures of willowy ladies in long dresses with sweeping trains and enormous, elaborately-trimmed hats perched on their equally complicated coiffures; by the gentlemen in light-coloured Homburg hats and wing collars; young men in blazers, flannels and boaters or with their hair flattened like patent leather to their skulls with pomade – all taken against a background of smooth lawns and terraces and country houses: Charnley and others like it. At social events, when they were always at their ease – chatting, smiling, simply passing time in a life devoted to the undiluted pursuit of pleasure – barely forty years ago, but light years away from the present. It had taken two world wars, Nina reflected, to bring women of that generation and upbringing to the stage where they could do something worthwhile with their lives, and actually earn their own living. Daisy working in the East End with her unmarried mothers, and Harriet, a teacher of mathematics at a university – who would have thought it, looking at those pictures?

"Didn't anyone ever do any work in those days?"

"My father did. He was an extremely busy lawyer – and Marcus, too."

Here was Marcus, with his parents. Among crowds of people, racehorses in the background, Ascot maybe. He was very tall, overtopping his father by half a head, bending to his beautiful mother. An exquisite work of art was Beatrice Jardine, leaning on her frilly parasol, as artificial as a china doll in lace and a pearl choker, her figure corseted into a fashionable Grecian bend, her hat a crown of roses and a sweeping brim, from which an edge of perfect profile showed. As they looked at the picture, both women felt an overwhelming sense of something they could not name. A fleeting sadness, perhaps, for something lost for ever.

But here was the Three Graces photograph. "Well, look at this!" said Nina. "You and Daisy, I can see that – but who is this? Vita? It can't be!"

Hardly surprising that she hadn't at first recognised the pretty, animated girl with the rounded limbs, laughing eyes and the roguish smile as the smart and brittle Vita of the present day, or as the strange, silent woman Nina remembered seeing when she'd been taken down to Stoke Wycombe once, by Daisy. The visit had not been a great success. She'd been fourteen or fifteen, overawed by its grandeur and rather in awe of Lord Wycombe, too, a reserved man who only became animated when he showed them around his art collection, which included some incomprehensible modern paintings from Europe that he called 'expressionist', at that time being condemned as decadent by the Nazi regime in Germany, but which he said would be collectors' items in a few years' time.

They were, however, given a splendid tea, at which Vita joined them, though she scarcely seemed to acknowledge the fact that they were there. Daisy later told Nina that the Wycombes had suffered a terrible tragedy, when both their children, two boys aged twelve and fourteen, had died at the same time, in a diphtheria epidemic at their school. After that, Vita had for a long time lost interest in the outside world, and even in her looks, and spent her days sketching and making paintings, the merits of which no one could judge, because they were, like Vita herself, never allowed to see the light of day.

"Yes, it is Vita. It was taken when we were performing a sort of tableau at Mama's birthday party." Harriet put the picture down rather abruptly, picked up another, and laughed. "Millie Glendinning, good heavens, at Cousin Kitty's wedding! That unfortunate hat – who could have forgotten it?" Unfortunate was the kindest thing one could say about it, thought Nina. Excessively large, and with a bird of equally monstrous proportions nesting on it, it dwarfed the small woman beneath it. "She was Mama's greatest friend, but what we used to call rather fast, I'm afraid." Harriet sobered as she added, "There was a scandal, and a divorce. Papa never really liked her. Poor Millie. I think the birthday was the last time I ever saw her."

There were still more photos. "I'd forgotten how many

pictures were taken that evening. And Rose Jessamy was there capturing everyone in her sketchbook, too, though I never saw anything she'd done, and as far as I know she never showed them to anyone – except perhaps Marcus. Poor Marcus, he was rather bowled over by her, I think. But it wasn't suitable, it could only have ended in tears, even if things hadn't turned out as they did."

The logs settled in the grate, the evening outside grew darker as Harriet leafed through the album. So many people, once alive and confident, so many now dead.

There were dozens of photographs of Beatrice, eminently photogenic as she had been. That charming smile, that tilt of the chin. And, caught off-guard, that ironic look she had handed down to Harriet, which made Nina think she could never have been a woman easy to understand. Pictures of her alone, and with other people. In one, she was chatting with a man who stuck out a mile among that homogenous crowd of white, upper class males. A dusky skin, a sloping forehead, crinkly dark hair, light eyes and a white, un-English smile. A soft, plumpish man. This, then, was Valery Iskander, the man who had disappeared the next day, seemingly with Beatrice Jardine. Until her body had been found. Not, on that showing, the face of a murderer. But who could tell? *'One may smile and smile, and be a villain.'*

Harriet passed over it without comment and presently came to a rather blurred impression of a small person in a long flowing gown of indeterminate style. "Oh look, here she is...Rose Jessamy – R.J, as she wanted to be called. I think she rather fancied herself as one of the avant-garde, a would-be Bloomsburyite. I've often wondered what happened to her – perhaps the police will trace her now – she never became famous, as we were all convinced she would."

Those painted rooms, never to be used, scarcely seen, even, after they were finished. Those doomed aspirations that survived only as flakes of colour and crumbling plaster. How short and transitory their life! How ironic and sad that only such a tragic discovery had brought them to notice, too late. Harriet turned the pages and Nina saw Rose Jessamy there again, still blurred. "Who's this good-looking man she's with? I haven't seen him in any of the other photos."

She felt Harriet grow very still beside her. "Oh, that? I'd forgotten he was in here. That's Kit."

Nina waited. It was quite evident, from her tone of voice, that Kit was someone of importance to Harriet, but she merely said, in a dismissive voice, "He was a very distant cousin. He came to live with us when he was orphaned as a small boy."

"Like another brother?"

"No, Kit was never like a brother."

There was a sense of hatches being battened down. Harriet closed the album. The subject was obviously off-limits and Nina felt she had been tactless. Once, she had asked Guy why Harriet had never married. "There weren't the young men to go round, you know, Nina – so many superfluous women in her generation," had been the answer. Perhaps Kit, like Marcus, had been yet another one of the thousands of young men who lay forever in the mud of Flanders' fields. But if he had once been close to the family, lived with them, wasn't it odd that she had never heard any mention of him from either Harriet or from Daisy?

"On the way here, Dad said there were papers as well as photos, and you were thinking of putting them all together." Perhaps, thought Nina, there would be some mention of Kit there.

"Did he also tell you I'd planned to rope you in to give me a hand?"

"No – but of course I will – were you thinking of a sort of family history?"

"If I was, yesterday changed that." Harriet took a sip of wine and put the glass down carefully, and then said abruptly, "There's a journal my mother wrote when she was in Egypt." She hesitated momentarily. It was unlike Harriet to be undecided. "I think you could help, first by reading it, then telling me what you think. I believe it might – just – have some bearing on why she was killed. Have a look at it and try to read between the lines, if you will – isn't that what historical novelists call interpretation?"

Nina smiled faintly. "You're not afraid you might have to curb my imagination?"

"It can't be any more imaginative than some of the constructions that have already been made on the subject! But you don't have to make your mind up immediately."

"No, I'd really like to be in on this. So where is it, this journal?"

"In a minute."

Harriet remained silent, evidently sorting her thoughts, while sounds one never heard – or noticed – in London came into the room – a branch creaking in the wind that had got up, a sudden spat of rain against the window like a handful of flung gravel, a little hiss on the hot fire as rain found its way down the chimney, the deep reverberations of the church clock. Harriet twisted her glass round and round, and the dregs of wine in the bottom looked like blood reflected in the light of the flames. "You might think you remember everything, but memory's an unreliable commodity," she said at last. "Things never discussed, pushed away over the years, until you begin to wonder whether they actually happened or whether you only imagined they did. There were accounts at the time, of course, newspapers and so on, the usual mass of speculation from uninformed sources. No one ever came within a mile of the truth. Not even those of us who were close to her. But now–" Nina was amazed to hear a kind of dread in her voice.

"At least you know what happened to her now," she reminded her gently. "There's still the question of who killed her, of course – but that'll be up to the police to find out, won't it?"

"And you think they're going to?" Harriet raised her eyebrows. "Nina, that police inspector. He's a different kettle of fish from the other one who looked into things after my father died, I'll admit – but he's working with a forty year handicap and my natural scepticism makes me wonder – "

"Wonder what?"

"How much time and money Scotland Yard will devote to this. Looking at it from their viewpoint, the odds on solving the case aren't hopeful. They've practically nothing to work on. Whoever did it could conceivably be dead by now and in any case, they don't seem to have much enthusiasm for following a trail as cold as that. I told the inspector about my mother's journal, and about some notebooks of mine that I wrote at the time, and asked if he thought they'd be any use He gave me a very old-fashioned look, as if I thought it was all some sort of detective story."

Wondering how to answer, Nina came across and knelt on the hearthrug, held out her slender hands to the blaze, then reached out for Harriet's. The flames reflected in her eyes the concern she was feeling. Harriet was usually so much in control. But the events of the day hadn't been without cost, she was pale and drawn, as if she was in for one of her migraines, the paralysing, pain-shot headaches inherited from her mother, which occasionally prostrated her. She'd just lit another cigarette, which wasn't going to help. "Darling," Nina said, "you're not really thinking of trying to find out who did this all on your own?"

The answer was oblique. "It isn't likely the police are going to tell us everything they may discover – I don't suppose, in fact, they're obliged to tell us anything at all if they don't choose to. But I *have* to know for certain what happened that night. I must." She drew fiercely on her cigarette. "Now that we know at last how it ended. Somebody must have known things at the time that never came out into the open. I for one was aware of much that I never spoke about…"

"You?" Of all people, Nina could scarcely envisage Harriet keeping quiet in such a situation. "Then why didn't you speak?"

"There was nothing I could put my finger on. I didn't *know*. And I believed at the time that what I suspected could only have hurt everyone even more." Nina waited for Harriet to say what those suspicions had been, but nothing was forthcoming, though it was clear she was keeping something back. If it had been anyone else but Harriet, Nina might have thought she was afraid. Was there someone she was hoping to protect?

"There might be a lot of things cropping up now that will be hurtful," she said quietly

"Nina, I *know* there will be. But it's too late for those sort of regrets, now. And what could be worse than what they've just found? I'm not fooling myself, I know it's possible we may never make any sense out of it – but someone has to try."

For a moment there Harriet had looked as though she were treading barefoot on broken glass, not knowing where to step next, but the expression was soon replaced by a more habitual certainty and determination. She would never, Nina saw, really admit to the possibility of failure. In Harriet's numerate, logical world, problems were always capable of solution. If A equalled B, then C must equal X. Or something.

"Grigsby wouldn't admit it this afternoon, but I think the same thing could easily happen now that happened before. Swept under the carpet – though then it was for fear of the scandal. I know that wasn't entirely the fault of the police – it was tacitly understood that there was to be no real effort to trace Mama, you know. If not too much was made of it, the gossip might be stopped. And then, when my father took his own life, and there was no concealing there was something wrong any more, everyone was left to assume that she'd run off with the Egyptian and my father had shot himself because he couldn't bear the thought of living without her. Which naturally," she added drily, "made a bigger scandal than ever."

"It must have seemed a reasonable enough explanation at the time, though," Nina said slowly, thinking there might be another one, which would surely not have escaped Harriet. "But now you think this Iskander might have killed her before he disappeared?"

"I said as much to the Inspector, didn't I?"

Abruptly, Harriet picked up from the table a slim book covered in limp grey suede, with gilt edges to the pages and a pretty little brass clasp fastening it. "The journal." She sat down again, still holding on to the book, and stared into the heart of the glowing logs, her gaze turned inwards.

"What is it, an account of their trip to Egypt?"

"In a way, but it's rather more than just a record of what she saw. Reading between the lines...no one else has ever seen this – I only read it myself for the first time last night. It was amongst the things I brought home yesterday, and I'd forgotten it existed until then, although I actually found it just after my mother had gone. But somehow, reading it then would have seemed like an intrusion...we all, you know, hoped she'd return, though I think we must have known she never would. And then, when we left Charnley for the last time...I simply bundled it up with all those other things when I hid them. What on earth makes one do something like that?"

"Superstition, I suppose. Maybe leaving something behind ensures you'll return. You know what they say."

Harriet thrust the little book at last into Nina's hands, and then suddenly stood up and fetched three rather dog-eared exercise books with marbled covers from a drawer. "Here are those notebooks of mine, as well. You can get some idea from them what went on at Charnley just before Mama disappeared. You might see some connection with the time in Egypt that I've missed. You needn't read them just yet, or even right through, just the relevant passages that I've flagged." After a moment's reflection, she said abruptly, "Forget I said that, read the lot, if you're so inclined. You might as well know the worst. And in any case – well, just read everything."

"If it's private–"

"Privacy," said Harriet said, sounding more like herself, "is a luxury none of us can afford in all this." She yawned and stretched. "I'm for bed. I'm not used to wine these days and it's made me sleepy. I'll bring you a cup of cocoa and some blankets before I go up."

"I'll make the cocoa while you get the blankets."

Later, left to herself, Nina undressed before the dying fire and snuggled the blankets around her on the sofa, the rain now beating in earnest on the window-panes, the hot drink on a table by her side. She wasn't at all sleepy and the light of the single lamp falling on the pages of Beatrice's elegant little book was inviting, even more so when she saw the inscription on the flyleaf: 'My Egyptian Journal'. While in the WAAF, Nina herself had served for a short time in Egypt – in Alexandria, and in a transit camp in the Canal Zone. That had been modern, wartime Egypt, of course, but on one of her leaves, she and a fellow Waaf had made an expedition to Upper Egypt, visited the great temples at Luxor, crossed to the Valley of the Kings. It would be interesting, if nothing else, to compare Beatrice's impressions with her own.

She read fast, but the fire had burnt out by the time she had reached the point where Beatrice and her party had arrived at Luxor and were preparing to visit the places Nina herself remembered.

Wycombe, who had joined them there, had – though it was not explained why – apparently been dead against the young Egyptian, Iskander, accompanying them on their excursions, and though Beatrice seemed to have made some attempt to insist that he should, she had seemingly given in to Wycombe's wishes in the end. No reason was given for this, either.

The entry recording all that finished somewhat abruptly at that point, except that below it, in a different coloured ink, as if written later, as an afterthought, were the words: *'He intrigues, but sometimes frightens me. A fierce excitement beats in me, tinged with shame, when I think what might happen, what I want to happen; then I hear the echo of a still small voice which says this was not precisely the sort of advice that had guided my infant teaching.'*

There was no explanation for this enigmatic utterance, and Nina quickly turned the page, hoping to find, in the account of the expedition which followed, not only descriptions to stir her own memories, but also some hint as to who the 'he' might be. But she was disappointed on both counts. The expedition to the west bank did not seem to have been an unqualified success. Millie had clearly been right not to go with them, Beatrice commented briefly, the experience had been debilitating and exhausting. So exhausting, it seemed, that it had left little energy left for recording her impressions of what she had seen. She wrote only flat, brief descriptions of the Colossi, the funerary temples and the Valley of the Kings, quite unlike her almost lyrical descriptions of other, lesser wonders previously encountered. It was the same with the equally lacklustre account of the subsequent visit to Karnak on the following day, this time with Millie accompanying them, and whose marvels were faithfully described, but without enthusiasm. This, Nina felt, was intriguing. Perhaps Beatrice had not been feeling well, had succumbed to the heat or one of the minor indispositions the food and climate of Egypt induced. Or maybe it was Millie's refusal to participate, or her unwilling presence in the latter visit, that had cast a gloom over the events. Whatever it was, none of the awe-inspiring ruins, some of the greatest wonders of the world, apparently aroused any strong feelings in her.

But then had come the visit to the Luxor Temple, a totally different matter.

This had obviously been so traumatic an experience that the words had poured out on to the paper with a vehemence that caused the pen to splutter and made difficulties in deciphering parts of what she had written. The luridness of the account, her reactions to the guide's flickering torch throwing grotesque shadows on the walls, the emotions the experience had aroused in her, the terror that had made her spin round to escape, the bang she'd received on her head, made it tempting to believe that she had been suffering from some temporary madness, brought on by an overdose of culture, or too much exposure to the sun.

Indeed, the entry finished on a note of bathos, with Beatrice simply saying how she remembered nothing after the accident until she had found herself in bed, back at the hotel, with Millie and Hallam fussing around her.

And that was virtually the end of the journal, except for one final brief entry:

Luxor, Monday, 19th April.

"It has not taken much to persuade Millie and Glendinning to cut short the Nile trip and to abandon the plan to sail back to Cairo on *Hathor*. The dahabeah will be taken back to

Cairo by the sailing master, while we will all return there by train with Amory and Wycombe. In fourteen hours we should be in Cairo – in as many days again I shall be back home with my children at Charnley, safe in my own settled existence, Egypt behind me. Had I but known!"

But what it was that Beatrice had not known remained unwritten. Nina sat for a while, the book in her hand, speculating on what this could be. She turned back the pages and it was only then that she noticed a looseness between the cover and the last pages, a space, in fact, where a section of the journal must have been removed.

Thoughtfully, she put the journal down, and picked up and flicked through the notebooks with the marbled covers, without any intentions of reading them at this late hour. Like her mother, Harriet had obviously been a compulsive recorder of her own feelings, for although, as she'd said, the notebooks didn't contain day-by-day accounts, they were fat, and the pages well-filled with her forceful italic script. But as a phrase here and there caught her eye, Nina's attention was held. She went back to the beginning and once started, found she couldn't put them down, her mind inevitably searching for connections with what Harriet had written and the events she'd just read about that had happened in Egypt, eleven years previously.

Chapter Twelve

Nina had agreed to Harriet's suggestion that it was best for her to stay at the cottage for the time being, if they were to work together. There should be no difficulty about time off from the bank, since she'd been taking her holiday entitlements in dribs and drabs in order to leave the school holiday period free for those people with families, and she was still due to at least two weeks. After a hurried cup of coffee the next morning, she set out in pouring rain, wearing Harriet's mac and a borrowed umbrella, and took the first bus from the village to catch an early train into London, leaving Harriet to get on with some of her correspondence papers, which she vowed absolutely must be marked. There might be a subtext there: wrestling with the corrections of such imponderables as quadrilateral equations or the square on the hypotenuse, felt Nina, to whom anything above the ten-times table lurked in the unplumbed depths of uncharted seas, must surely concentrate the mind wonderfully, leaving it free to work subliminally behind the scenes on personal problems. Maybe that wasn't so far off the mark. Nina couldn't get over the feeling that Harriet's insistence on the Egyptian connection with her mother's murder masked a fear that the real truth was to be found nearer home – within the family, even. And that – possibly – she'd seized upon this chance to rout it because, in truth, she didn't have enough to occupy her mind. There was very little stimulus to be found in the country.

The train was already almost full when it arrived, but she managed to get the last seat in the compartment which drew up beside her on the platform, after which it was standing room only for the City-bound office workers cramming in like sardines. The windows steamed up. Everybody smoked. Leaning her head back against the seat, she closed her eyes and wondered how many nights it would take to become accustomed to the church clock, punctuating the silence with its regular booms, on the hour and the half hour, each time just as she was about to drop off to sleep. She'd spent what was left of the night, after finishing Harriet's notebooks, in a restless, half-comatose state. But it wasn't only the clock: she knew that the events of the day, and what she'd afterwards read, so far into the night, had been so much in her mind that she clearly hadn't been sufficiently composed for sleep before turning out the light.

As the train lurched towards London, and strap-hanging commuters banged against her knees and their wet umbrellas decanted water into her shoes, the events of the previous day still passed cinematographically behind her closed eyes, mixed in with the images of Egypt: the grey stones of Charnley and the now flawed splendour of its painted rooms mingling with visions of hot sand, burning skies, pyramids, temples and ruins.

She was already so fascinated by what she'd read that she felt she might easily become obsessed with unravelling the mystery of Beatrice Jardine's life and her appalling death. A forty-year-old murder should by now have lost its horror for someone who had never known the victim. Had the body been nothing but a pile of bleached bones, perhaps Nina could have regarded it more objectively, but knowing that the outstandingly beautiful woman she had seen in those photographs last night had ended up so macabrely dead, as a mummified corpse behind a disused chimney wall, strangled by her own jewelled necklace, only increased the surreal sense of horror. By this morning, she knew she was as committed as Harriet to finding out as much as possible about the events that had led up to the murder.

It was still all so much in her mind that she thought she must be hallucinating when, just as the train was drawing into the London terminus, she opened her eyes and saw in front of her the headline on the newspaper of the bowler-hatted businessman opposite. The news had already broken. Well, it had been inevitable that the press would sooner or later get hold of it – and there it was, on the front page of one of the national dailies: 'MUMMY FOUND IN COUNTRY HOUSE'.

She was able to read no more, the train was drawing to a halt, and the man was folding up his paper and putting it into his briefcase, but the headlines had to concern Charnley. How many other mummified corpses could have turned up yesterday, for goodness' sake?

She bought the paper for herself as soon as she left the train and, sinking on to a seat, she read the brief report. The headline was in heavy type, but with only a few column inches on the subject beneath it. There had, after all, scarcely been time to gather a host of gory details, and the police had evidently not yet given out the identity of the body. She was initially relieved to find that it merely said, with an understatement this particular paper was not noted for, that a mummified corpse had been found during restoration work being carried out at Charnley House. But it ended by referring to an inside feature. Turning to that, she found Charnley described, with the paper's usual hyperbole, as 'a former stately home, ancestral residence of one of London's former top lawyers, once noted for its glittering house parties.' Inevitably, it went on to recall the circumstances nearly half a century ago which had led to the 'dramatic suicide of Amory Jardine, tipped for a knighthood in the next honours list, following the mysterious disappearances of his wife Beatrice, a notable Edwardian beauty and society hostess of the day, and of one of their guests – an Egyptian gentleman...' There followed a brief outline of Charnley's subsequent fortunes until the time it was bought by Vigilance Assurance. The article was, on the whole, more restrained than she'd expected, though the inferences were obvious, given the item on the front page. No doubt they were saving their big guns for when the identity of the corpse was officially identified as that of Beatrice Jardine, and the confirmation that she had been murdered, and how, in all its grisly detail.

The rain had diminished to a murky drizzle by the time she emerged from the station, no less unpleasant, and the skies still pressed down like a lid. Nina took the crowded tube and then walked from the station to her bed-sit to pick up what she would need by way of sensible clothes and shoes for the country, ration book and other necessities, including her old Remington typewriter – allegedly portable, but weighing a ton – and told her landlady she would be away for a couple of weeks. She rang the bank and spoke to her manager. He was not pleased when she asked permission to take the two weeks' leave owing to her, at such short notice. She knew he had been hoping she would forego the rest of her holiday entitlement, now that it was getting so late into the year, but she stopped herself from feeling guilty. She'd hitherto done her best to be accommodating on the subject. She didn't exactly occupy a key position at the bank, and a rescheduling of duties would be all that was needed to take care of her absence – if indeed, they noticed it at all, she thought cynically.

Guy telephoned her while she was packing up her things, but their conversation was unsatisfactory. She didn't feel she could say what she wanted to say when the telephone was in the hall, with the dining room door ajar and Mrs Prior inside, one ear cocked, but he didn't seem to want to chat anyway. He'd spoken to Harriet and knew of the arrangement for Nina to stay at Garvingden. Apart from the Lamb & Flag, the shop, the vicarage and the district nurse, Harriet was the only other in the village with a telephone (the rest considered it an unnecessary expense), but it had proved its worth over the last few days. Now Guy was asking, "Can you leave your belongings in the left luggage at the station, and slip over here before you go back to the cottage? Take a taxi – Daisy's at home and she wants to talk to you."

"What is it? Have you seen the papers?"

"Yes, darling, we have, but you'll know what it's all about when you get here."

Nina normally found that sort of exchange irritating, and tried not to sigh. It was one of her father's little foibles: he rather enjoyed keeping one hanging on, wondering what he had in store. From the tone of his voice, which sounded excited rather than gloomy, she thought it was unlikely there would be more unpleasant revelations, but by the time the taxi drove up outside the tall narrow house and Guy had hurried out to pay the driver, her mind had turned over all sorts of possibilities.

"Sorry it's taken me so long, Dad," she said, kissing him as the taxi disappeared. "It took me ages to find a cab. I thought for a while I was going to have to go and queue for a bus, so I was glad you'd suggested leaving my case and things in the left luggage, but then one came along…"

"Listen, Nina," Guy broke in. "There's someone here Daisy wants you to meet. We're in the back."

"Who is it?"

But he wouldn't say.

In the comfortably shabby room overlooking the long-by-narrow garden, they were drinking coffee, and its aroma mingled with the rich, lingering smell of the tobacco smoke which her father's pipe had wreathed around. Nina's entrance into the room caused an immediate uproar: Guy's fat old fox-terrier skidded across the polished floor to greet her, ruckling the rugs and leaping around her in a frenzy of ecstatic joy, trying to reach Nina's face to lick it. Nina laughed and bent forward to pat the old dog, incautiously stepping on the displaced rug, which slipped from under her feet. She would have fallen if she hadn't been caught by the man who had risen awkwardly as she came into the room.

"Down Phoebe!" Guy commanded above all the hubbub. The dog froze, then simply keeled over on to her side, beat her tail, and immediately went to sleep. In the resulting silence, they all laughed, and Nina turned to look at her rescuer.

"Phoebe obviously knows who her friends are," he said, holding out his hand. "You must be Nina."

He was a big, athletic-looking man with a craggy face, wearing the uniform of a commander in the Fleet Air Arm. His movements were somewhat awkward; he walked with a slight limp, and it seemed to her that the turn of his head was deliberate, so that she was immediately made aware of the disfigurement of one side of his face: a puckered seam of shiny new skin that ran down from his temple and disappeared under his collar. Someone saying this is what I am, take me or leave me.

"This is Tom Verrier, Nina." Daisy didn't offer any further explanation. Something – the arrival of this man? – seemed to have flustered her. Odd. But then Daisy, who coped with difficult situations every day of the week at Hope House without turning a hair, when faced with them in her own life frequently didn't quite know what to do. She sought refuge now in insisting that Nina needed a sandwich and took herself off to make it, bringing it back with fresh coffee.

The sandwich was typical of Daisy's attitude to food, made with scraps of cold mutton left over from Sunday. Nothing could help the greyish Government-decreed bread, which was dry, or the taste of margarine predominating over the dabs of mint sauce with which she'd mistakenly tried to enliven it. Still, as always with Daisy, the gesture had been well meant, and Nina, not having had any breakfast and brainwashed by warnings not to waste food, managed to get most of it down, with the help of the coffee, and only then did she find out who this stranger was and why he was here.

Almost the first thing she learned about Tom Verrier was that he was Rose Jessamy's son.

Harriet, amongst her other telephoning, had called Vita first thing that morning, and as soon as she rang off, Vita picked up the phone again and began to dial a well-remembered sequence of numbers. Her hand shook so much she had to make several attempts before she eventually succeeded and heard the ringing tone at the other end. It rang, and rang, and she thought despairingly: He's not there. But wait! Maybe, in her fumbling haste, she'd dialled the wrong number. Try again. Still no answer. She had the receiver halfway back towards its rest when she heard his voice. "Dr Schulman here."

"Oscar! It's me!"

"Vita, my dear! What is wrong?" She registered that he could obviously tell that she was upset, simply from the tone of her voice. She made an effort of will to steady it.

"You don't know, then?"

"Not unless you tell me."

There was a measurable pause. "Oscar, I must talk to you. Something's happened. You must come round immediately."

"Of course I will come, if you need me, you know that. But – immediately?" The Middle European accent was barely noticeable, except when he was speaking on the telephone, but his beautifully modulated voice, calculated to soothe the most nervous of patients, did little to reduce her sense of panic. "I have several appointments, and business to do before that. I can come to you this afternoon, perhaps–"

"I really do need you here, now. I simply c-can't explain over the telephone, and–" Her voice broke on a sob, and she couldn't go on.

He was silent for the space of a second then, evidently sensing that this was more urgent than her usual plea for his attention, he said, "Vita, make yourself a cup of tea – *tea*, I say – and lie down. No gin. And *no pills*. Do you hear? I will be with you as soon as I can. Ten minutes?"

"Darling Oscar" – a shake of relief in her voice – "I knew I could rely on you."

Oscar Schulman had arrived in England in the spring of 1938, after the Anschluss, the annexation of his homeland, Austria, by Adolf Hitler. No Jew would be safe in Vienna after that. He was thirty-eight at the time, a childless widower. The son of wealthy doctors, he was already a distinguished and prosperous doctor in his own right. Since he had no dependents, and was possessed of the necessary money and influence, he experienced little difficulty in obtaining the requisite exit and entry visas which would allow him to come to England.

After qualifying, he had specialised in psychiatric medicine, still in its infancy in England and regarded with a certain amount of suspicion, although, as in America, personal analysis was becoming increasingly the thing amongst those who could afford it. He'd been lucky enough to find somewhere almost immediately where he could carry on with his work, at a fashionable London clinic that was rapidly gaining a name for itself. It was here that he met Vita Randolph, Lady Wycombe, when he inherited most of the patients of the colleague he replaced. She had a history of depression which had, in fact, led to a botched attempt at suicide, and had resulted in her eventually being persuaded to attend the clinic for treatment. Her reluctance to do so was matched only by her husband's scepticism of such mumbo-jumbo, but after a few months in Schulman's hands her condition improved, though whether the sessions she spent with him had been entirely successful was something he continually asked himself. Be that as it may, she had at last emerged back into the world. Determined, it seemed, to make up for the years she'd missed, incarcerated in self-imposed exile at Stoke Wycombe, by making a complete volte-face in her life, she'd ventured for a brief period into the society of those who had pretensions to literature and art. She spent much of her time, when she wasn't reclining on a sofa, wearing frocks of a vaguely arty nature, eating chocolates and reading the latest literary offerings of her new acquaintances, in attending their exhibitions at small galleries off Bond Street, joining in their evenings of endless intellectual discussion, conducted in an ambience of wine fumes and cigarette smoke. But the affectations soon palled, and besides, she wasn't clever, or able to pretend she was, and she felt they rather despised her. After that, for the brief period left before the war, she took up with a set she had known in her youth who were smart, modern, fashionable, joining in the frenetic activity all that implied – the social whirl of cocktail parties, weekend house parties, holidays on the Riviera. Spoiled and indulged in the matter of money and freedom by her elderly husband, who did not seem to mind what sort of life she led, as long as it suited her and did not demand his continued presence, she spent more and more of her time at their London house while Wycombe seemed content to remain as often as not in the country.

The war soon put an end to all that. Wycombe's age had precluded any direct involvement in the hostilities, but Vita was ostensibly employed in some sort of secretarial capacity with the Admiralty Board. What it was she did there, Schulman had never quite been able to imagine, Vita and any kind of discipline not being synonymous, but whatever it was, it had sat lightly on her shoulders, and had never interfered in any way with her social life.

Schulman himself, arbitrarily classed as an enemy alien, had been interned on the Isle of Man for over a year, but doctors were urgently needed, especially doctors of his sort, and he had been released to work with some of the psychologically damaged young men and women who had been in the worst of the fighting. It was not without a certain amount of trepidation that he'd returned to London, and the problem of Vita.

Schulman had a great charm of manner as well as undoubted expertise in his chosen profession. He couldn't fail to be aware that this neurotic, attractive woman, young still, and with a husband now well into old age, had been more than half in love with him, but this was an occupational hazard in his profession, and he was too sensible of the impropriety of the doctor-patient relationship, as well as of his delicate position as a refugee emigré, to allow anything other than friendship to develop between them, though he was often sorely tempted, even now. There had in fact been a brief time when he had almost thrown caution to the winds, but he had not allowed himself the indulgence. He had managed to extricate himself with his usual grace and without damaging her self-esteem, by appealing to her sense of the romantic, suspecting that the angst of what she regarded as their impossible love would not be entirely unwelcome. On his release from internment, he saw that had been the right line to take. Her attachment to him had become less intense, and now, several years later, though still inclined to cling too much to him for support, she had gradually come to look on him more in the light of a trusted, reliable friend on whom she could always fall back, he hoped, rather than as an unattainable lover. He regretted this a little, but it was safer.

The rain had stopped. He found a cab that took him to Embury Crescent, through the muggy, overhung morning where the clouds were struggling to break through.

The burnt-out shells of several adjoining houses in the

crescent, caused by an incendiary which had effectively demolished one and spread to its neighbours, loomed through the murk. God knew how the Wycombes had managed it, but their house, which had in fact escaped serious damage, had already been restored to its pre-war smartness. He ran up the steps and lifted the polished brass knocker on the glossily painted black door, which Vita opened herself, with a speed that told him she had not heeded his advice to lie down.

"Vita, my dear." He embraced her and then, holding her at a distance, scanned her face. He could detect no smell of gin on her breath. "What can have happened?"

"I'll tell you, in a moment." She held out her hands for his outdoor things. He divested himself of his overcoat and his hat, ran his hands through his curly, iron grey hair, still thick, if receding at the temples, and squared his shoulders. But further scrutiny, as she led him into her drawing room, told him that this was going to be more than one of her minor *crises des nerfs*. She was carefully made up, and dressed as usual in a chic, expensive outfit, midnight blue this time, with long sleeves and a diagonal front fastening, trimmed and piped with matching velvet. Her hair was still thick and dark, perhaps helped by her hairdresser, and she had taken recently to wearing her curls lifted and gathered back behind her ears, revealing the finely sculpted contours of her face. She looked elegant, pin-thin, fine-drawn. But her brown eyes looked huge, and the extent of her pallor, accentuated by the fashionable fuchsia-pink lipstick, alarmed him.

"Have you seen the papers, Oscar?"

"Not this morning." Unusually, he had abandoned his normal practice of scanning the morning papers in favour of a new textbook which he had begun reading the night before, and which was absorbing him so much with its new ideas that he could not put it down.

Vita indicated a copy of *The Times* on a table, folded to show an article whose headline he could not read from where he stood. "I think you had better see what that says, and then you can tell me what to do."

"First, we must make ourselves comfortable. Some coffee, perhaps?"

"Oh yes, of course, I must have interrupted your breakfast. I – I'm sorry." She looked distracted.

"No matter." He gave her a quick glance. "But I think it better we take things slowly, hmm? You make some of your good coffee, while I read this." She would be better occupied doing some mundane task – and he knew the coffee would be excellent. She who had been waited on hand and foot all her life had, during the last six years, been forced by circumstances to manage this not inconsiderable house very capably with only the help of daily women, and, if it suited her, could be surprisingly competent at many household tasks. "By the way, where is your husband?"

"At Stoke Wycombe, where else?"

Her high heels clicked on the parquet as she walked with her usual swift, impatient pace to the kitchen, where he soon heard the rush of water, the welcome clatter of crockery. He did not function well without breakfast, and his Viennese soul was yearning after his abandoned coffee and rolls.

He was left alone in the restful room, its décor the modish style of ten years ago, unmarred by any wartime austerity. Black-out blinds had now been taken down, and the crisscrossed brown paper reinforcing strips across the window panes removed. All was cool, neutral colours with touches of black, furniture with clean Modernist lines, the vivid geometric pattern of the curtains at the tall windows the only splash of colour, apart from the pictures. Another painting, he noticed, had been reinstated. Chagall? he wondered, as he sat down with the newspaper, companion for the Kokoschka, the Kandinsky, the other vibrant examples of modern art hanging on the walls, which Wycombe had acquired pre-1939. In his old age, he had become a connoisseur and passionate collector of all things modern in the world of art – even to the extent of selling other, less recent acquisitions, to buy them, in the confident certainty that they would accrue in value. The Randolph fortunes, though by no means negligible even yet were, like so many others – albeit in a nation that had won the war – victims of a shattered economy. Most of his art treasures had been safely stored away for the duration, but were now being brought back into the light of day and, under his supervision, hung once more where they belonged. Undoubtedly that was what was occupying him in the country at this precise moment.

Schulman picked up the paper and instantly saw the reason for Vita's agitation as the headline, and the name Jardine, sprang out at him. He read what followed and then folded the paper neatly once more and sat waiting, thinking what to do. When he could smell the coffee, he went into the kitchen to bring the tray in for her. It was as good as he'd imagined it would be, though he sighed a little, regretting the absence of even a biscuit to go with it. It was unlikely there was such a thing in the house. Food was not a priority with Vita. He debated whether to ask for some toast, but in the circumstances, decided against it.

She extracted a Balkan Sobranie cigarette from the silver box on the mantelpiece for herself, knowing he didn't smoke, and flicked an enamelled table lighter before coming to sit next to him on the sofa. Her fingers were still not quite steady.

"When did you hear of this?" he asked.

"Last night. Daisy and Guy came to tell me. She and Harriet had been to Charnley to –" Her voice faltered.

"Last night? And only now do you let me know? Oh Vita,

Vita!"

"I needed to think it over on my own – don't you see that? Oh, they wanted me to go back with them, or for them to stay with me, but I couldn't have borne it. All the talk, all those memories!" She tapped out some ash into the onyx ashtray. Her fingers were thin, her polished fuchsia finger-nails immaculate. "Well, now you've read the article, what do you think?"

"I think it is a very terrible thing to have happened, very hard for you, and your sisters, to accept. But when you can do so, it will be better. It will establish a conclusion, bring an end to many years of uncertainty. You will at last be able to mourn your mother properly."

"Do you think so? Do you really think that's all there is to it, Oscar? What about finding the person who killed her?"

"The police–" he began, then stopped, finding himself more afraid for her than he had thought possible. He resumed, carefully, "You will have to prepare yourself for a great deal of intrusion into your private life, both past and present."

"It's already started. I've had Harriet on the phone this morning, warning me that the police will be coming to see me. I'm afraid she's annoyed with me because I won't do what she wants." She gave a brittle laugh.

"And what is it that she want you to do?"

"She's acquired some of the family papers, and it's given her some crazy idea about reconstructing everything that went on at that time..."

"Would that be such a bad thing?"

"I can't do that, Oscar! I can't, and you know why." She looked away, but not before he thought he saw the glint of tears flickering on her lashes.

He said, firmly and quietly, turning her round and holding her gaze, "No, I do not know why, not fully. Do I?"

There was little he hadn't learned about her insecurities, her image of herself, her relations with her family, after those long sessions spent with her, letting her talk, patiently listening. But gradually, even as the layers stripped away, he had been bound to admit that they had never reached the very centre, the root of what it was that had ultimately ended in her breakdown. Somehow, even in deep therapy, she had not let go, had managed to keep something back. There was something she wouldn't let herself acknowledge, that she was hiding from, afraid to face. Always, no matter how gently he had led her, she had withdrawn at the crucial point. And there he'd had to leave it, only to approach it obliquely, the next time. Sensing her need to cooperate, he'd been prepared to wait until she did. But each time, when she had almost reached the point, was in fact teetering on the brink, she'd abruptly wrenched herself back. There came a time when she'd refused any more treatment.

He knew that any further approach had to come from her, that she must ask to be released from the burden she carried. Was this, now, the time? Was this dramatic discovery of her mother's body to be the catalyst, the shock she needed? How could he suggest it to her? He began to say, gently, "Don't you think it is time you let yourself remember–"

"No, No! You mustn't ask me!" She screwed the cigarette butt angrily into the ashtray, looked up and, with an abrupt swing of mood, said in a trembling voice, "Of course, Oscar, you're right, as usual. I do have to tell you, I can see that. But it's not a case of allowing myself to remember. I don't think I've ever – *really* – forgotten – it's just that it seemed too shameful a thing to suspect, or that I was putting the wrong construction on it."

He gave her time to get herself together, not revealing his exultation. At last!

"After my boys died," she went on eventually, her voice not

quite under control, "well, you know how that affected me, losing both of them, at once. But I'd been obsessed by thoughts of death long before that – everyone dear to me seemed to die and leave me – Marcus – my father. And my mother...my mother, most of all. I became tormented by thoughts of whether she was actually dead or not, where she might be...and then, quite suddenly, when I heard she'd been found, something I'd seen the night she died came back to me, and I put two and two together and made the connection–" She stopped, overcome.

"Can you tell me about it – if it is not too painful?" These moments of eidetic memory could be unbearable. He held her hands to stop their trembling.

"I think – I think I must, now."

Later, into the silence that followed the outpouring of all she had previously held back, Vita said in a choked voice, "Dear Oscar, I shouldn't have transferred my burden to you."

"But you see. You feel better, hmm?"

And she did, a little.

"I should have guessed what it meant, shouldn't I? But I didn't, until it was too late. I was married to him by then."

"You were not to know. You had led a sheltered life. And you were very young." And, he wanted to ask her, but did not, are you sure?

"Yes, I was, wasn't I? Young and so naive."

Abruptly, she rose and left the room, returning with a few old, faded sepia photographs. "There you are, that's what I was like when I was young." One by one she passed across pictures of a plump, vivacious, exceedingly pretty girl. "Me, dressed for the hunt. And me again when I was a child, with Marcus, and Harriet holding Daisy, the new baby. And here's one with Dolly Dacres, my dearest friend. I was to be her bridesmaid, until... Look, here's this, actually taken on the night – the night Mama died." Finally she fell silent as he took this last picture from her, one where she was dancing, barefoot, with her sisters, clad in filmy garments of a vaguely classical nature. He looked from the laughing girl with the sparkling eyes and rounded limbs to Vita as she now was. She had begun to weep; big, silent tears which poured down her cheeks, tears he knew were a necessity, and he was filled with a tenderness he had never known before. He took her in his arms and laid her head on his shoulder. Presently she was able to speak again, though her words came disjointedly. "You see how it has been for me? I knew I was cowardly not to ask him about it, but I owed it to him to keep my part of the bargain. He'd married me, and kept me, and he's always been so kind to me – that's what I thought, don't you see? But now, now that she's been found – oh God!"

Yes, indeed, he saw how it had been for her, and at what cost? Even he could find nothing to say for the moment, he could only shelter her in his arms. They stayed like that for several minutes, while he gently stroked her cheek.

"I smelled coffee as I came in so I've brought myself a cup. One to spare?"

They froze. How long had he been standing there? Just how long? The master of the house himself, standing at the half-open double doors to the room, smiling and holding a cup and saucer. Perhaps he'd been there some time, surveying the tableau in front of him. His wife, obviously overwrought, her beautiful make up smeared, being held by the man sitting on the sofa next to her. The air vibrating with emotion. She turned as if in slow motion towards him and for a moment didn't seem to register who he was. Then her gaze refocused. "Myles!" She blinked and threw a hurried glance at Schulman, and received an almost imperceptible nod. Her voice was husky with tears, but controlled, when she spoke. "I didn't hear you come in. You should have let me know you'd be coming."

He walked towards her with his upright, military carriage and bent stiffly to kiss her, still holding the cup and saucer. In a seemingly involuntary movement, she turned her head, and the kiss landed somewhere in the region of her ear. "It was an impulse," he answered, "after Harriet telephoned me with the news. I knew what a shock it would be for you. No time to telephone you if I was to catch the train down – you all right, my dear?"

Vita said, "How can any of us be all right?"

"Well. Well." He seemed at a loss as to what else to say. "Schulman, how are you?"

"I am well, thank you. There is no need to ask how you are!"

It was difficult to believe Wycombe was the age he was, an unbelievable eighty-six. His hair was white, and time had etched lines on his face, but he still had the soldierly bearing and physique that many a man twenty years younger would have envied, the same austere, direct look that told of the drive and initiative to carry through any course of action he intended. Seeing his pictures restored to their proper places seemed to have released a new source of energy in him. They were the only things in life he cared passionately about now. Perhaps once, he and Vita...but he had always been a man difficult to read, seemingly stiffly inculcated with military attitudes. And yet, deep within him had existed that love of beauty, and a capacity for deep affection, such as he'd had for his sons. And possibly other areas of his life that no one, least of all Vita, could ever have suspected. It was understandable why Wycombe had married a beautiful young woman thirty years his junior – he had wanted an heir, and a hostess – but it was difficult for even Schulman, practised at reading motivations as he was, to accept the reasons why Vita had married him. Theirs was a strained relationship now, whatever it had once been, but he had supported her throughout her break-down, and that had not been easy, God knew. Rigid in his attitudes, he had always done the right thing, an officer and a gentleman to the last.

At that juncture, Wycombe's eyes registered the old photographs on the table and he stiffened.

"How long are you here for?" Vita asked as she poured his coffee, unaware of his glance.

"What? Oh, a day or two. Must get back. The packers, you know…"

It was difficult to say what might have transpired then, had the police not arrived.

Harriet had finished marking her stack of papers by eleven, made herself a cup of coffee and lit a cigarette. She'd tried to spin the job out but she'd known it wouldn't take her all that long. The day stretched before her. An idea entered her mind, so unexpected it took her breath away for a moment. Almost without making a conscious decision, she squashed out her cigarette and picked up the phone – she would make a couple of quick calls, and if by doing so she could arrange a meeting, she would just have time to change into clothes suitable for Town before the next bus at twelve. She'd already told Nina to take the front door key. "In case I'm not in when you get back. We're nearly out of bread and I may be down at the shop. I'll use the back door."

Recalling this little exchange now, it occurred to her that maybe the idea was not so unexpected after all, that she'd known what she was going to do all along. Yesterday, the world had shifted on its axis and it was imperative that she must do something to restore the balance of her life. Best get this over with. It would, after all, sooner or later become inevitable.

Chapter Thirteen

His latest skin graft had taken well, and his plastic surgeon had assured him he'd soon be able to get back home, to Egypt. The treatment had been lengthy, and during the last year, endeavouring to come to terms with his new face, Tom Verrier had sometimes questioned his own motives in volunteering to join up on the outbreak of hostilities. It was a question to which he'd never actually found the answer, apart from the fact that he'd felt a strong compulsion to do his bit in this European war in which the different homelands of both his parents were involved – an unnecessarily quixotic compulsion, in his father's opinion, but then Egypt had, in effect, become Michel Verrier's adopted country and his native France a distant memory. He was a precise, ironic man, still working on the various important digs on which he and Tom's mother, Rose, had worked, he as an archaeologist, she on the restoration of wall paintings. When Tom had talked of volunteering, Michel, pragmatic Frenchman that he was, had suggested that some sort of job could have been found for him in Egypt, perhaps working in a civilian capacity with an army intelligence unit based there, but he didn't bring any emotional pressure to bear, though he wasn't getting any younger, and must have been aware that the chances of their ever meeting again could be uncertain. But he'd known Tom well enough to realise that the restless itch he had in his blood, that damned uncomfortable penchant for adventurous travel to remote places of the earth, couldn't be contained by some desk-bound position while a war to end all wars was being fought on the other side of the world.

The Declaration had come at a time when Tom had actually been at home, having just returned from Peru, where he'd been gathering information on the Inca civilisation. He realised his next project would have to remain on hold for the duration, but his in-built restlessness would need some other outlet. He'd picked the Fleet Air Arm for no better reasons than it obviated the necessity for choosing between the Air Force and the Navy, and that they were prepared to accept him, which he felt was as good a reason as any.

He'd flown Swordfish aircraft from the battleship *Warspite* and his luck had held out until the day he'd been catapulted off in the Mediterranean to attack a German U-boat, when he'd been hit by enemy fire and spiralled into the sea in flames. He was damn lucky not to have been either drowned, like the rest of his crew, or fried to a crisp. As it was, he was pretty badly burned and knocked up in other ways, and was sent first to the burns unit in the naval hospital at Basingstoke, then transferred for special treatment when things went wrong to East Grinstead as a patient of Dr Archibald MacIndoe, a breezy but temperamental New Zealander who was pioneering plastic surgery on young airmen, who cut through red tape like a hot knife through butter and wouldn't take no for an answer. Months of skin grafts followed, with interminable hanging about in between. Going home between his treatments wasn't an option, home being the flat in Heliopolis he shared with his father, largely unoccupied because Michel was usually away working on some dig or other and Tom exploring in the Andes, the Himalayas or some other far-flung part of the globe. He could have wangled a lift on some RAF plane or other had he been so inclined, but what was the point, simply to stay in the empty flat?

By now, MacIndoe was saying, give it another few weeks, another slight operation, and Tom could be looking towards being discharged, demobilised and on his way home. Meanwhile, he'd bought himself an old Riley Nine, ten years old and still full of guts, and when he could scrounge petrol, he spent his time tootling around, looking at old churches and villages that were there before the Norman conquest, castles and cities with ancient streets, crooked little houses and cathedrals that took his breath away with their calm beauty. He'd fallen in love with England – even its weather, which gave it its green, lush countryside, so different from the arid landscapes of his own homeland – and with nearly everything else about it, its air of genteel shabbiness, battered London theatres, village pubs. He had a feeling his next book, rather than being set in the remote stretches of the Hindu Kush, as planned, might be centred upon little old England.

At present, he was spending some time in London, delighted to find there were still historic sites and ancient, tucked-away churches which had survived not only the Blitz, but the Fire of London four centuries earlier. Yesterday, he'd visited St Paul's and seen the damage done when a bomb had crashed through the roof into the choir, bringing several tons of the fabric with it. He'd stood gazing at it, trying and failing as usual to comprehend the futile destruction and misery of war, then he'd left, putting several pounds more than he could afford into the collecting box for the repair fund which had already been started. And then, this morning, over breakfast in the small hotel on the Gloucester Road where he was staying, he'd picked up the newspaper...

Charnley House. The name had leaped out at him. Good God! Who ever said there were no coincidences? Charnley had been a must on the list of places he'd intended to visit before he finally left England. He'd had no notion who owned the house now, whether he'd even be allowed inside, or if the frescoes his mother had painted would still be extant (though she'd always stoutly averred they would last for centuries, given the right conditions), but he'd been determined to find out. Then he read the rest of the report in the newspaper and discovered that the police were anxious to trace a woman named Rose Jessamy, who had once been employed to do some wall paintings at Charnley. His stomach did a roll. Not much liking the ominous sound of that – a body being found behind a wall that his mother had been working on – he nevertheless immediately went to the police. They were as cagey as he'd anticipated. They asked him a lot of questions and parried more of his own. He suspected that they'd very little to go on. They had, however, been willing to tell him how he could get in touch with the Jardine family. A telephone call, and here he was.

Nina struggled on with the horrible sandwich. She began to feed bits surreptitiously to the old dog, and the bits got bigger. When it was finished, she reached out to pour herself more coffee (which was, to tell the truth, not much better) and saw her stepmother's eyes on her. "Sorry, Daisy, not terribly hungry," she murmured apologetically.

"That's all right. Never been partial to mutton myself since Mrs Heslop sent up a roast saddle for lunch, that day–" She broke off abruptly. "Well, we have to be grateful for what we can get, nowadays. And what is Rose doing now?" she asked, turning to Tom. "Is she still working in Egypt?"

"My mother? No, she died when I was just a boy."

Daisy was sorry, remembering her first impressions of that small, vital person with her unconventional clothes and behaviour. In the short time they'd known her, how she'd *electrified* them all! Shaken them out of their complacent lifestyle, awakened them to other possibilities. Even Mama, who'd astonished Daisy when she'd suddenly agreed to the bizarre notion of using an Egyptian theme when decorating the guest rooms. (Though perhaps it hadn't been so bizarre, after all. Later, after the first war, when more tombs were being excavated, the style had become all the rage.) And as for poor Marcus…

"Forgive me. I didn't mean–"

Tom waved away any possible embarrassment. "That's all right," he said easily, "it was a long time ago. She was killed in a rock fall in a newly discovered tomb she was working on, when I was very young – too young to remember all that much about her. Except the way she used to talk about those paintings she did at Charnley, I've never forgotten that. Working on them was apparently what first inspired her to go to Egypt, and once there, she'd no desire ever to return to England. She vowed, according to my father, that she'd found her spiritual home."

Daisy gave him a sharp look. "Hmm. So that's what she said? She said that was why she went to Egypt?"

It must have been something in her tone that brought a wariness into Tom's voice. "Well, I gather it wasn't the main object of her visit, but it was why she stayed. As you probably know, she originally went there with your brother, Marcus, in search of Valery Iskander."

Daisy had not known until that moment that Rose had accompanied Marcus on his abortive trip to Egypt, none of the family had, and her quick flush betrayed this, but she merely nodded. He went on carefully, "I suppose there must have been some compelling reason why they went all that way to search him out, but I never learned why – until today. My mother never talked much about her previous life, apart from various aspects of her work, and my father taught me to respect that need, as he did. Perhaps that was why they had such a successful marriage. A partnership in every sense of the word."

Had he said something he shouldn't? Daisy was looking resolutely at her sensibly clad feet. He couldn't have known that in a sudden piercing shaft of memory, she was recalling a hot, bright June morning in the rose garden at Charnley, when she had come round the corner from the hothouse with a basket of peaches, and Marcus had been standing looking down at Rose, holding her hands, smiling and talking nonsense about '*Rosa Perfecta*'. It wouldn't do, she'd known it even then, at that young age. Looking outside one's own circle – for a wife, at least – was social disaster. Evidently, Rose had been of the same mind. Poor Marcus, whose intentions had been nothing if not honourable.

"They worked and lived together, you see, my parents," Tom was going on gamely, "hardly ever spent a day apart in the whole of the rest of her life. She adored him, and my father...he isn't a demonstrative man, but he was devastated when she was killed."

There was a short British silence after this, while Tom, sensing undertones and deciding not to say what he'd come to say, after all, picked up his cup of weak grey coffee and found only the dregs, for which he was immensely thankful. It had apparently been made with some extract out of a bottle and boiling milk, so that a skin had formed on top almost immediately, and had been served with some rather pointless biscuits which were called 'rich tea', for what reason he could not fathom.

Wondering how to continue, he stared through the window. The rain had begun again and he could just see to the end of the garden, a broken down fence and the back of what had once been the garden of the house in the next street, now given over to willow-herb and a tribe of feral cats, the scourge of the dog Phoebe's life, he'd been told. The house itself was no longer there, it had left a gap like a missing tooth. Few houses around here could have escaped, entirely. Here, in this very room, was a crack in the wall, running diagonally from floor to ceiling. He thought perhaps they didn't notice it any more. It seemed to have been subsumed into the unremarkable, shabby comfort of the room, along with the threadbare rugs on the scuffed, polished boards, the faded watercolours against wallpaper weathered to the colour of wheaten biscuits, and the worn covers on the chairs with their washed-out roses and frilly skirts, against which the old terrier bitch was now snoring at her master's feet.

He saw Nina looking at him, got a glimpse of that sweet, fleeting smile. He made a conscious effort to keep his hand from straying to his facial scar, which itched unbearably at times as it healed.

He was nonchalant about his wound, in the best tradition of war heroes; and had never asked himself how much he really minded. He hadn't been any oil painting to begin with, and since his face had never frightened the horses or put the girls off, he reckoned he'd be all right again, given time. What did worry him was other folks. The shrinking from his scars (or even worse, the bright, determined acceptance of his damaged face, the tendency to smile at him more often than was necessary). He'd developed a tendency to judge people by how they reacted and all three here had stood up to the litmus test well. Equanimity was to be expected of the old man – he was a doctor, after all – but not necessarily of Daisy Tempest or, more surprisingly, of Nina. By now, he'd come to expect an initial shrinking away by most attractive young women, but she'd neither pretended not to notice, nor had her eyes been drawn back to his face again and again. Nice brown eyes, a sense of fun behind them Mouth that curved up, even when she wasn't smiling.

The old man, tamping down tobacco in his pipe, suddenly said, "So in what way can we help you, Commander Verrier?"

"Oh, Tom, please." More suited to directness than tact, he had to think carefully before answering the question. "Not quite certain. I'm sorry to have intruded, at a time like this, but I have to say this, though it's not something any of us want to think about, I imagine – I can't believe that my mother could in any way have been mixed up with your mother's death, Mrs Tempest. But whether she was or not, I intend to find out. If there's anything you can tell me about her at that time, it would help. I guess she wasn't perhaps an easy person, in many ways, but there was no one quite like her." His eyes crinkled with amusement. "Even allowing for the fact that I'm prejudiced."

"I knew her for only a short time," Daisy said drily, "but I was convinced she was unique."

Glancing at Guy as she finished speaking, she bit her lip. Tom, however, chose not to see this as a two-edged remark, since he didn't think she'd meant it to come out like that. He guessed, from the half-amused looks on the faces of the other two, that Daisy Tempest might be given to saying the wrong things at the wrong time. He could understand that. Tactfulness wasn't something he'd been born with, either.

"Of course I'll tell you what little I can remember about Rose," she was saying now, more gently. "But first, tell me something: have you any idea why they – my brother Marcus and your mother – went to Egypt and sought out Iskander?"

Tom did know now, from his earlier meeting with the police, but he was reluctant to put it into words.

"Well, I'll tell you. They went to find my mother," said Daisy bluntly. "It was generally thought, when she disappeared and couldn't be found, that she'd absconded, possibly to Egypt, with Iskander. But as it turns out, that couldn't have been the case, the body they've just found at Charnley being hers."

"Yes. The police inspector told me that. I'm so very sorry."

"Ah," said Guy. "Inspector Grigsby. What did you think of him?"

"He's OK, I guess. For a policeman."

They'd met that morning at New Scotland Yard. Direct by nature, Grigsby was not one to shilly-shally. But despite the man's stated intention to find the solution to such a bizarre and interesting case, he gave the distinct impression that he didn't intend it to feature largely in his schedule. Tom hadn't initially been able to prevent the feeling that at higher levels it was not being regarded with the utmost urgency. Grigsby was obviously hard-pressed with other concerns, doing his best to keep several balls in the air at once. He'd spared time to see Tom, and reluctantly made him privy to the few facts which he thought it necessary for him to know, but the constant interruptions about more immediate matters, the telephone calls, people popping in to remind Grigsby of this and that, all seemed to indicate pretty conclusively that this particular case was unlikely to receive his undivided attention. He suspected the discovery of the body was an embarrassment rather than a task demanding instant action, and that the police would doubtless go through the motions, and that would be that. From the sergeant, too, had emanated a sense of boredom – boredom and impatience at being landed with a case whose origins were so far back that he'd decided it hadn't the remotest chance of success. Tom had begun to feel he was wasting their time. Despite this, there was one pressing question to which he needed an answer: were the police regarding his mother as a likely suspect for the murder? The response had been equivocal. No motive for the murder had yet turned up. On the other hand, they were bound to say that there had been a certain disagreement between Rose Jessamy and the murdered woman over the form the decorations of the guest rooms were to take.

"A slight disagreement? And you suggest that's a motive for murder?"

The inspector lifted his big shoulders. He had small, intelligent eyes, very shrewd. "Mrs Jardine was reportedly delighted with the way the work was turning out – so we have to assume they'd reached some sort of amicable conclusion. However..."

Tom was trying to keep on an even keel, not showing how this business had shaken him. Here he was, on a simple visit to London, intending to visit Charnley merely to see something of his mother's work – and then he'd walked into this! The idea that his mother – his mother – had murdered this woman, scarcely known to her, was just plain bloody silly. It would be convenient for them to pin it on her – someone now dead. But he was damned if he'd wear that, he thought with one of those rare, incandescent flashes of rage that sometimes beset his otherwise moderate nature. Yet someone had committed that murder, and what was more, someone competent enough, and with enough knowledge of the nature of his mother's work, to have plastered up the wall afterwards.

"We have to hold all the options open, you know, though to be frank with you – which maybe I shouldn't be, but I will – at this point your mother seems an unlikely suspect," Grigsby said, relenting. "Don't mean, though, that murder isn't done, more times than you'd think, for motives that you and me wouldn't waste a minute's thought on."

He held Tom's gaze with his own. You didn't have to be long in his presence to sense that underneath the casual exterior, there lay a fierce energy, and an exceedingly sharp mind. A pity he wasn't going to apply it to this case. Grigsby had said 'at this point' with a barely discernible emphasis, and it stung Tom into an immediate decision. "Well," he said shortly, "forgive me if I'm not too sanguine about that. I give you warning that I for one don't intend to let the matter rest."

The sergeant cut in, before he could be stopped, "I shouldn't worry too much about your mother's part in it. It's really fairly cut and dried." He ignored his inspector, who looked as though he could swat him like a fly on the wall with one of his enormous hands, and would doubtless do so once they were alone. "Amory Jardine discovered his wife was having an affair with the wo – the Egyptian." (He had been going to say wog, Tom knew it, and if he had he might have got more than he bargained for, and not from Grigsby. Lucky for him, he managed to bite it off in time.) "Jardine killed his wife, and most likely the – gentleman, too."

"Professor Iskander, you mean? That's unlikely," Tom said shortly, "since he's alive and well and living in Cairo."

That made Grigsby sit up, and took the heat off the sergeant. "Tell me more, Mr Verrier."

So Tom had told them what he knew of Iskander, that he was now a respected academic, an eminent Egyptologist. "And you're wasting your time if you think he could commit murder – he's the gentlest soul imaginable – and he's certainly not capable of bricking up and plastering a wall! You should hear my father on the subject of his 'help' on one or two digs!"

Grigsby said, "That's as maybe, Mr Verrier, but what you've told us is a very helpful piece of information. We need to confirm the story of his being taken to the station in the trap, and in the event of not being able to trace any servants of the time...well, we may have to get the police in Cairo to talk to him. Just to corroborate, you understand." Tom didn't think he was going to get much more out of them and there hadn't seemed to be any point in wasting their time further, so he'd made his departure, with a final pessimistic word from Grigsby: "I promise we'll do what we can, Mr Verrier – but don't expect miracles."

That had been this morning. It seemed a long time since. He saw now that Nina was looking at her watch, standing up. "I must be making tracks."

"I'll see if I can get you a taxi," her father said doubtfully.

Tom asked, "Where are you bound?"

"Paddington station, to pick up my things, and then to

Garvingden, my aunt's cottage."

They all knew it was easier to get a sack of sugar off-ration than a London cab. "I know all about trying to get taxis in London. Let me drive you to the station," he offered. "Better still, while we're at it, why don't I drive you right down to – where did you say? Garvingden? How far is it? Thirty miles, thirty five?"

"Twenty-three. But what about your petrol?"

"Let me worry about where that comes from."

She had the sort of face you could read easily. He could see her trying to suppress guilt feelings at the suspicion of black market petrol, and weighing that up with having to try her luck with a taxi. If he would simply be kind enough to drive her to Paddington, she said, it would only be a matter then of catching the main line train to Oxford, and afterwards getting herself across town for the bus to Garvingden. It wouldn't take long, and it had stopped raining.

"With all that baggage?" He jerked head towards the open door into the hall, where he could see a pile of cases and bags. "It wouldn't be any trouble." He was determined not to let her go. He was already far gone.

"Well, if you're sure, it would be kind."

"On the contrary, it would be a pleasure," said Tom, his eyes lingering on that smile.

Some hours later, just before supper, Daisy sat with her feet up, knitting one of her shapeless jerseys from another which had been unravelled, while Guy occupied himself with *The Times* crossword. Nowadays he did most of the cooking, now that he didn't have a practice to look after, and he'd become skilled at eking out the rations. The last of the mutton had been rescued from the fate of ending up as one of Daisy's sandwiches by being minced with onions, carrots and celery and would presently appear as a very acceptable shepherd's pie. A fragrant smell issued from the kitchen. Guy's pipe was going well. The lamps were lit.

Daisy was glad enough to sit quietly, even though she hadn't been into Hope House today, since Athene had threatened to send her straight back home if she appeared. She was still unsettled by that visit to Vita the night before, which had upset her so much she hadn't slept properly, an unheard of occurrence with Daisy. Vita, after listening to what Daisy had gently told her, had insisted on being left alone, though one knew it was the worst possible thing, remembering what had happened...once before. But Vita was well again now, wasn't she? And even this couldn't be as terrible a shock as that awful, tragic misfortune she'd suffered. And it *had* been a misfortune, an act of God that no one could have prevented, though Vita had always held herself responsible for it, which was ridiculous. The boys had been at school when the epidemic started – but she'd blamed herself for sending them there, though what else she could she have done? Boys went away to school, and that was that. But the way mothers reasoned was something unaccountable, as Daisy knew, suddenly recalling Lorna and her baby.

It wasn't right, though, leaving Vita alone. It had worried Daisy, and she'd felt no better after ringing her again this morning, when she wouldn't even talk about the subject any more. "I've already been lectured by Harriet, so please, not you as well, Daisy. I'll be all right. I'll cope with this in my own way," she'd insisted.

Which was what Daisy was afraid of.

"She has Schulman," Guy said now, comfortably, when she mentioned it. "He's a good chap, even though he's a German, won't let her do anything silly."

"Austrian."

"Same thing," said Guy. "Nearly."

"Guy!" But yes, Vita had her doctor friend, though Daisy

couldn't help wishing it was she, who was so well-equipped for helping women and girls through crises, on whom Vita was prepared to lean.

"Come on, don't let this business get you down, old girl," said Guy. That silly expression – old girl, indeed! – had always irritated Daisy. She was not old, she was fifty-three, and neither was she a girl. But she'd never told him how she hated it. Dear Guy, he meant so well. "And nor must you let Harriet upset you," he added.

"I've no intentions of letting either of them do that!" She was more than glad to get her thoughts off the subject of Vita. "But I might as well say it as think it, I'm not happy about Harriet deciding to play Miss Marple." Daisy was a great reader of detective stories and had a collection of Agatha Christie's books, which she kept by her bedside and read and re-read, because, she was wont to say ambiguously, they helped to send her off to sleep. "Don't mind doing my bit to help, but it was all so long ago. Let the police get on with it, I say. To tell the truth, it's my opinion we might all sleep easier in our beds if we never *do* find out who did that fearful thing to Mama."

There! She'd said it, the notion that had been nagging at her, the thing she could never have said to anyone but Guy. She added fearfully, "What if it should turn out to be some-one we *know?*"

He stopped her with a touch on her arm. "It's out of our hands now."

"Yes, but Harriet doesn't trust the police to find out. She always thinks she can do things better. And I do wish she wasn't involving Nina in it."

"Nina will be in her element. It'll take her out of herself. Besides, I rather think that young man isn't going to let the matter rest in the hands of the police, either, so I doubt they'll be on their own," Guy said. Tom Verrier had struck him as being impatient with authority and quite prepared to circumvent it where necessary. "Very taken with Nina he was, did you notice?"

"Well, Guy darling, who wouldn't be? And a good thing for her if he is. I've never said anything to you before about this, thought it better not to worry you, but you know, she hasn't been very happy over the last few years. Began to suspect it when she broke that soup tureen that belonged to your mother. I think she's been having an affair."

Guy, who was quite used to following his wife's non-sequiturs, merely said, "My dear, I've known that for years."

"Oh, you have, have you? Did she tell you?" she demanded, taken aback. He shook his head. "Then how did you find out?"

"In the same way as you did, I suspect," Guy said drily, "I saw the letters addressed to her when she came home on leave, and since she used to go all colours when she saw them and put them straight into her pocket, and since she never spoke to us of anyone, and there were times when she looked quite ill with misery – and broke tureens – I put two and two together."

"Oh, Guy, and you never said!"

"There wasn't anything we could do if she didn't want to talk to us – and you have quite enough on your plate with those naughty girls of yours."

They understood each other very well. They had a very comfortable relationship, given a little relish by the occasional sparring over mildly controversial matters, never serious. He was sometimes sorry, and always humble, to think that she had never fulfilled her potential, that she had blown out her own brief moment of glory like a candle flame, without any hesitation, just to marry him. She had never for one moment showed that she might have regretted that, despite the fact that the desire to have his child had never been fulfilled. Well, well, all that was water under the bridge – and he didn't think either of them had ever wished undone the decision to take the other as their partner in life.

He said suddenly, "I think there are just about two glasses of sherry left in that bottle in the cupboard. Shall we indulge?"

Putting the small crystal wine-glass, pre-war, very fine and very precious, to her lips, Daisy mused, "It must have been a very unhappy affair, I think."

"But one that's over, I'm certain. I think she's finding her feet again."

"And he did offer to drive her all that way home," said Daisy, with a satisfied little smile.

Chapter Fourteen

For the last half hour Sergeant Fairchild, his elegant jacket removed, had been bashing away with two fingers and commendable application at the old Imperial on the corner desk. The last sheet of paper ripped out, he heaved a sigh, put on his jacket and left the room.

Grigsby looked up as he went, remembered that he had been going to tear him off a strip on the subject of how Egyptians should be referred to, and decided it would be a waste of time. Wogs, after all, was what everybody called 'em in the forces, same as French frogs, Italian wops, Irish micks and German krauts. No worse than Yanks or Limeys. But they weren't in the forces now, and if the sergeant wanted to go where he thought he was headed, it was time he learned to watch his step and not give offence.

Fairchild returned, placed a large mug of tea on Grigsby's desk, took a chair opposite, with a cup and saucer for himself. "No biscuits, sorry. The canteen's run out."

Grigsby grunted. He liked nothing better than a ginger nut to dunk in his tea. He reached out and stirred a generous, glutinous spoonful of sweetened, condensed milk into the mug of steaming black liquid, screwed down the lid of the jar into which his long-suffering wife had decanted the milk from a tin, and put the jar back into a drawer. He licked the spoon and swigged down a big gulp of the tea, now thick as soup. Fairchild, sipping milkless, sugarless tea delicately from his own teacup, averted his eyes. When he looked again, he saw that Grigsby was watching him. "Finished typing your notes up from this morning, Sergeant?"

Fairchild shuffled together and handed over the notes he'd been transcribing since their return from Embury Crescent and their visit to Lady Wycombe, which had followed immediately on the departure of Tom Verrier from the office –

simply because there was an unexpected hour unspoken for, and Grigsby, like nature, abhorred a vacuum. Fairchild hoped his somewhat shaky shorthand had stood up to it, though he knew Grisgby didn't really need the notes – he had a memory like an elephant and Fairchild thought this could conceivably be some sort of test. He'd guessed the inspector wasn't best pleased with him for some reason, hadn't wanted to be saddled with him in the first place. Well, hard cheese. But better to keep a cautious eye on him, all the same.

"Hmm." Grigsby put the sheaf of papers back on the desk, shoved his hands into his pockets and got up to walk about the room. He was a restless man and could never sit still for long at his desk. Talk, talk, talk, that's what this case was going to mean. Turning over ancient alibis and the dry facts of what was now history – and where would the actual proof be, at the end of it? He only ever felt really at home with action out on the streets, here in the smoke, knowing his patch like the back of his hand, working all hours God sent, if need be, on the go. Though that didn't mean he couldn't function anywhere, even in the snooty surroundings of the house in Embury Crescent.

A stroke of luck, that had been, catching the old cove, Lord Wycombe, there as well, since he apparently preferred to live for the most part on his estate in the country and his visits to his wife at their London house were few and far between. Grigsby could understand that. He thought him a cold fish, and couldn't see his sophisticated wife being content to bury herself in the country with him – he recognised her type, smart, nervy and neurotic, a Londoner by choice. The interview had taken place in the presence of a third person, a Doctor Schulman. A psychiatrist – a head shrinker. Grigsby had looked at him distrustfully, but husband and wife had both assured him the doctor was a trusted friend and they wished him to remain. Grigsby had gone along with it, since he'd seen immediately that he'd caught them all at a moment of tension. Lady Wycombe had obviously been crying her eyes out, but she'd excused herself when her husband had shown them in, and returned several minutes later, ravages repaired, and apparently in complete command of herself.

There'd been a pile of old photos on the low table in front of the sofa to which he and Fairchild were directed, the topmost one showing three young girls dancing barefoot in the open air, dolled up in some sort of flimsy costumes. He had no difficulty in recognising the other two Jardine sisters, Harriet and Daisy, but it was mainly because of the family connection that he'd identified the third as the woman now in front of him. The similarities between that girl and her mature self were there, when you looked, but she'd changed a lot. Still an eyeful, but a million miles from that young, smiling, happy girl. Underneath that self-possessed veneer she had now, she was jumpy as a flea on a hot tin plate.

All Grigsby could hope for was that this investigation would be short and sharp, with a conclusion that was acceptable, if not categorical. He wanted it off his back, but he could be very patient when necessary, and patience was what he needed when it came to sorting out what this lady remembered of the night of the murder. Her story tallied in every way with those of her sisters – except when it came to the end of the evening. At that point she became oblique and evasive for a reason that soon made itself manifest: the party over, farewells had been said, the guests had bowled off in their motor cars or carriages, the family and those guests who were staying overnight had gone to their various rooms to sleep the sleep of the just. Except – and here it came! – for the young Vita.

After some reluctant skirmishing, she'd at last admitted that this was on account of the young fellow she was at that time engaged to, name of Bertie Rossiter, who had lived only a few miles away. After escorting his mother and sisters home in his motor car, he had returned for a pre-arranged assignation with Vita, who had been waiting for him in the garden. They'd then found themselves an empty room in the guest wing, temporarily being used as storage space for furniture from the other rooms while they were being decorated. "Sofas and things, you know," she'd said with an airy nonchalance that didn't quite conceal a blush. She cast a quick, rather defiant look at her husband. But he was sitting rigidly upright, staring fixedly at his shoes, as if trying to see his face mirrored in their highly polished toecaps. "I'd forgotten about it until – until yesterday," she said.

Grigsby found that hard to believe. "Go on, please."

It seemed that matters had not gone very far when they were disturbed by noises, apparently coming from the next room.

"And you now think they could have been the sounds of someone bricking up that chimney?"

"I suppose it might have been the sort of noise you'd expect from something like that – but it couldn't have been."

"No? Why not?"

"Because my mother was still alive long after that." This time, after an encouraging nod from Schulman, the rest came out in a rush. "You see, much later, when I was tiptoeing back up to my room, hoping not to be noticed, you know, her maid was just coming out of Mama's bedroom, saying something to her."

Grigsby's eyes sharpened. "What time was this?"

"Probably about two, or quarter past, I can't remember exactly. It gave me a terrible fright, and I muttered something about the bathroom, hoping she wouldn't notice that I was still fully dressed. But she didn't say anything and I couldn't help noticing how tired she looked. I felt how thoughtless it was of Mama to have kept her up so late. She looked positively wrung out."

"Can you recall the exact words the maid used to your mother?"

"I suppose she said 'Goodnight, Mrs Jardine,' – or something like that. I can't really remember. Why? Is it important?"

"Only in getting the facts straight. Was it usual to keep her maid up so late?"

"On occasions. She did tend to keep late hours, my mother."

"And you – you were in that guest room with your young man all that time?"

No, it seemed not. Rattled by that noise from the next room, the young lovers had fled out into the garden and thence into the folly by the lake. They'd only stayed there for about twenty minutes, she admitted lamely. Probably true, thought Grigsby. They seemed to have been an inept pair of conspirators, and the interruption had likely been a timely deterrent, pouring cold water over the young man's passions, and Vita's own daring having deserted her by that time. Even Grigsby realised it *had* been daring for a well-brought up young lady of the pre-1914 years to go even as far as she had.

"You can check with Bertie if you need to. He'll remember, but I warn you, he'll probably wriggle out of admitting that he does." She added drily, "He's in Parliament now and very much in the public eye."

"So if you don't think someone was in that room breaking open – or bricking up – that fireplace, how do you account for the noises you heard?"

"We thought it might have been Miss Jessamy, coming down to do some work on her murals–"

"That time of night? Dear me, she must have been conscientious!"

"I know it sounds quite ridiculous, but it was just the sort of thing she would do. Odd, yes, but so was she. She was quite obsessive and often worked at very peculiar times. Anyway, whatever it was, I panicked, and so did Bertie."

"There were other people sleeping in that wing. Did they not hear anything?"

"Well, I didn't ask them! In any case, they were right at the other end of the corridor – a couple of Marcus's friends, if I remember – and Kit. The noise could have been them larking about, I suppose, but it didn't sound like that."

Fairchild wrote down the name of Marcus's friend, John Townshend, now a stockbroker. The other had been killed at Ypres. "And 'Kit'?" asked Grigsby. "That would be Mr Sacheverell?" On receiving a nod, he asked, "You know where he can be contacted?"

She hesitated. "My sister Daisy can probably let you have his address."

Grigsby resumed his questioning. "You didn't think to mention the noise you heard, later? When the search was on for your mother?"

"Why should I? Who'd have imagined it had anything to do with her disappearance?"

No one, at that time, Grigsby allowed. And if they had, it wouldn't have saved her life, though it might have saved a good deal of trial and tribulation. "What did you think of this Mr Iskander?" he asked suddenly.

He had caught her off-guard, which was what he had meant to do. "Oh, Iskander! He was really rather awful – he used *scent*, you know. You've no idea what he was like, always touching, getting too close, I don't know why Mama ever invited him to Charnley, no one could understand it. Daisy thinks we might all have been rather beastly to him. All of us except Papa, who was always courteous with everyone."

"He was a particular friend of your mother's, I gather?"

She returned coldly, "If you mean was she having an affair

with him, well, that's outrageous. I know it was suggested at the time – but if you'd known my mother, you'd realise she would *never* have allowed anyone like Iskander...and anyway, it doesn't seem now as though he was much of a friend, does it? Isn't it obvious he killed her?"

The Jardine family, it seemed, were united in seeing Iskander as a convenient scapegoat. "He was invited to Charnley as a guest, though, wasn't he?"

Wycombe, hitherto silent, put in austerely, "As I understood it, he more or less ingratiated himself into being invited. One of those who take advantage of a holiday acquaintance. In actual fact, he was simply one of the crew on the houseboat hired for sailing up the Nile. Or perhaps," he added fairly, "a little more than that, more of a guide, though he was only a student. He appealed to Beatrice because he was, I must admit, extremely knowledgeable and very passionate about his country's affairs."

"You were there, sir, on that trip?"

"Not on the Nile. I joined them in Luxor for a while, but I met Iskander. I wondered at the time if he wasn't perhaps one of those hot-headed Nationalists."

And therefore quite capable of murder? "He's now a professor at the university in Cairo," said Grigsby.

All very interesting, he remarked to Fairchild as they made their way back to the station, but it hadn't got them very far. He'd noted that Wycombe, throughout his wife's story, had said scarcely a word, that whenever she'd needed encouragement to go on, her eyes had sought Schulman's. So that's the way of it, he'd thought. As it always had been, a young wife and an elderly husband, May and December. But he was inclined to think it wasn't as simple as that. There was more going on there than met the eye – for one thing, the lady had only told them half a story. Nothing new in that, either –

witnesses as often as not believed that if they told the police everything they might find themselves as suspects – but Grigsby was alerted. Something had set alarm bells ringing in his mind. Why, he couldn't yet see, but he'd worry at it until he found out.

After doing what she'd come to London for, Harriet found herself with time to spare before the next train back that would make a connection in Oxford with the Garvingden bus. She'd been lucky enough to find a cab, but on impulse she'd paid it off at Green Park, weighing up the advantages of half an hour spent there rather than one in the racket of Paddington station. The weather had confounded predictions and after its early morning gloom had steadily improved throughout the day. Now, mid-afternoon, the sun touched the falling leaves of the plane trees with gold, its light flashed from the windows of red London buses as they trundled down Piccadilly. She drank in the warmth and sunlight like someone who has been deprived of either for months. A couple of hours ago, she had thought she might never be warm again.

A young woman passed, wheeling a Silver Cross perambulator, with a reluctant five-year-old beside her, dragging his feet and struggling with a yo-yo he hadn't yet got the hang of. The little boy wore a smart school uniform, maroon cap and a blazer with a very new badge; his grey flannel shorts were well-pressed, and his socks straight. The pram was shiny, high-sprung and expensive, and something about the young woman, though she wasn't in uniform, made Harriet think she might be one of that lost, but possibly returning breed – a nanny. Oh yes, London was very slowly but definitely licking its wounds and coming back to normality. There were signs of rejuvenation all over the West End: boarded-up windows being replaced, paintwork smartened up, bombsites being cleared, the War Damage Commission doing a wonderful job. In the end nothing, she reminded herself, stayed unbearable forever. For the first time since she'd left the city, she found herself unexpectedly happy to be back there, in her natural environment.

Restoration, however, hadn't yet reached the dusty square she'd recently walked away from, set in the midst of a run-down area comprising working-class terraced housing alongside homes which had once been for the well-to-do. St Peter's Square itself, with the church in the middle of one side, towering over all like a grim watchdog, standing next to its dilapidated vicarage, was a mixture of styles and periods, sooty Victorian London brick predominating. Occasionally, peeling Georgian stucco made its appearance. Most of the houses still bore their wartime legacy, a slightly desperate, backs-to-the-wall look, though nearly all seemed to have survived more or less intact, except for what might have been a couple of houses in the corner, victims of a direct hit. Someone had recently broken through the boarding erected to shield the resulting crater and its rubble-strewn surroundings, thereby opening up a convenient short cut to the main road beyond. It hadn't been mended, and through the gap could be glimpsed a busy stream of passing traffic, and a street market in full swing.

He had said he would wait for her in the church, where they were less likely to be disturbed. The vicarage, he informed her, was like Clapham Junction, what with the phone constantly ringing, and all the comings and goings of the various homeless people the diocese saw fit to foist upon an unmarried parson with empty rooms in his vicarage. At least there were no telephones in the church – nor, he'd added with some irony, would they be likely to disturb many worshippers.

The inside of the church proved to be as bleak, draughty

and as uncared for as Harriet had expected from Daisy's description of it, redolent with the smell of varnished pitch pine, old dirt and a faint underlying whiff of what might possibly be incense. Some sort of scaffolding and building materials were piled around the entrance to the Lady Chapel, blocking the light. Here by the west door however, the interior was curiously light, where some fine stained glass windows remained, but where others, presumably shattered by blast, had been replaced by clear panes. Towards the altar it grew dim but even at this distance it was impossible not to remark on the difference, as if a line of demarcation had been drawn. A red sanctuary lamp winked above polished candlesticks and an elaborate silver cross on a spotless, lace-trimmed altar cloth. There were flowers. Votive candles flickered to one side. The smell she'd detected earlier was almost certainly incense. It came as no surprise. Apparently, he preferred to be called Father Christopher.

"Harriet, here you are."

"Kit."

She swung round to face him. He hesitated slightly before kissing her lightly on the cheek. "How good to see you. And looking as smart as ever."

"Thank you." It was a stilted sort of greeting after all this time. She acknowledged it with a slight smile but eyed him warily, though perhaps there'd been no irony meant. She'd taken care to look her best, after all. The old green suit had turned up trumps, as usual, and a hat had seemed to be appropriate to wear for a meeting in church, but compliments were not what she was here for. And she was quite thankful there were to be no preliminaries, no small talk, no how are *you*?

Silently, they regarded each other across the space of twenty-eight years. And she still felt as she always had in Kit's presence – no match for him, even now: lean and slightly gaunt, but striking, tall as a Mannerist painting in his dark cassock and cloak, which could romanticise even the most commonplace clergyman. His nose, always large, had become beaky, but there was no slackness in his face and the years had hollowed and sculpted his cheeks, giving him an ascetic look. His dark hair, though streaked with grey, was more disciplined, cut shorter, and the wayward, boyish lock had been brushed into temporary submission, a concession to his priesthood. It would soon fall forward again. His eyes still drew one. As blue as ever, and now with a lustrous sort of burning look to them. A saint or a sinner, Nanny Byfield had said, a long time ago – which? Probably neither, just the same old charm at work. His lady parishioners were probably falling over themselves to knit him scarves and pullovers – very likely the same small, select band of followers who cleaned the brasses and silver, starched the altar cloths, put out fresh flowers and ran jumble sales.

It was hard, even yet, to accept the idea of Kit as a priest.

"So what's all this I've been reading in the papers? All this nonsense about a body being found at Charnley?"

"Kit, it's far from nonsense. I'm afraid it's all too true."

She thought he blanched a little, but his look remained steady. "It *was* – your mother, then? My paper didn't go into details."

Deciding that to try and spare him might be thought a condescension, she said that yes, it was Beatrice. She described the condition in which her mother's body had been found. He closed his eyes briefly and crossed himself. He had always had a sense of the theatrical. And yet, his response seemed spontaneous and genuine. He had subtly changed, in ways she found difficult to define, as yet. She added abruptly, "You see what this means, don't you? We shall all have to face questioning as to what we were doing that night."

"Decidedly unpleasant, for those who were there. Fortunately, it won't affect me, since I wasn't."

"Of course you were!" she reminded him sharply, "it was the night of the birthday, you must remember that!"

She, at least, had never forgotten that night. Kit, a young Kit, looking wild and dangerous, a little drunk. Devouring Beatrice with his eyes, risking *une petite scandale*, should anyone notice. But if anyone else had, it had never been remarked upon.

"Well, yes, I was there for the supper, of course. And for your delightful entertainment. But I went back to London later, if you recall. The Lansburys offered me a lift in their motor, and I took it."

No, that was a recollection which had escaped her, nor could the Lansburys confirm it, seeing as they were both dead, an old, autocratic couple who had refused to run for shelter during an air raid and were killed when their house received a direct hit. Certainly she hadn't seen Kit the day after the birthday celebrations, nor for very much later – and how she'd longed for him then! – but she'd been under the impression that he, like Iskander, had left by an early train the following morning. In the mood he'd been in the previous night, it would not have been out of character for him to leave abruptly, perhaps saying only a casual goodbye and a thank you to one or other of her parents before legging it out to the station. She couldn't actually swear that he'd stayed the night, though she'd always assumed he had. The years had blurred many memories.

If what he'd said was true, he could not have had any part in Beatrice's murder, and though there was no way of proving it, part of the heavy weight of suspicion she'd carried around for so long lifted. Previously, she'd always known when he was lying, or trying to get himself out of trouble, but now, she couldn't tell whether she had lost that facility, if it was he who had got better at lying or if he was actually telling the truth.

"Thank you for coming to tell me about this, Harriet. It was a kind thought."

Kindness wasn't what had brought her here. She had come determined, once and for all, to get to the heart of the matter, but even yet she balked at asking outright the question to which she so desperately needed an explanation.

How was it they had never before talked about her mother's disappearance, except in the most superficial way, without any real discussion? There had been opportunity enough later, God knows. Looking at Kit now, she knew that the answer was because they had, both of them, always been too afraid of the truth.

They were still standing awkwardly in the aisle where they had met. "It's not very warm by the door, but it's such a mess further in, I think we'd better sit here," he said suddenly. "Incendiary through the roof, no money for repairs yet." He gestured towards the muddle of planks and supports around the Lady Chapel, and then led her to a dusty pew near to where they stood. He didn't appear to notice the dirt, or to see the dangerously worn places in the strip of matting down the centre of the aisle, the mouldy pile of tattered hymn books and the Mothers' Union banner leaning drunkenly on its pole in one corner. Or the kneelers at their feet which were losing their stuffing at the edges. All of it a startling contrast with that so immaculately kept sanctuary. Yet the church might once have been one of some distinction, she thought, her eye taken for a moment by a beautifully carved marble memorial wall tablet which still remained intact, dedicated to some eminent worthy of the parish, his virtues and his benevolence.

She came back to hear him saying, "And what else, Harriet?" and with an effort went on with her story. When it came to the point where she and Daisy had had to identify the black silk kimono, Kit put his head in his hands. She kept silent. He might have been praying. At last he raised a ravaged face, and when he spoke she was completely taken aback. "Why did you leave me, Harriet? We might have had a good life together. You could have saved me."

Whatever he might have said, that was the last thing she expected to hear from him. Had he forgotten the misery of that time, and the violence of their final disagreement? And had he not, after all, found his own salvation?

Their short life together – what had it been?

1918. Rooms in a grey house, in a grey, north London street, a few weeks before the Armistice. Kit home from France on leave, for the moment safe, though with a wound stripe on his sleeve and his nerves shot to pieces.

The wound had not been life-threatening and his body healed quickly, though it took long enough to save him from being sent back to France. She too had been sent home from working behind the lines as a VAD, her constitution weakened after a bad bout of 'flu. When Kit, nearly a decade after Beatrice's disappearance, had suddenly reappeared in her life, she'd given in to what she'd formerly resisted, and agreed to live with him. He had seemed so pitifully in need of her, and she'd told herself there was no one she cared enough about who would be shocked over that impropriety. Neither of them mentioned marriage. Which was just as well, since their relationship turned out to be every bit as unsatisfactory as she had feared it would be, all those years ago. But how could she have left him? Never – not when those dark and dangerous forces, which she'd always sensed in him, had turned, frighteningly, to threats of self-destruction. Not with the memory of her father's self-inflicted death. Nor even when she was asked to leave the post she'd obtained as deputy head of a women's teacher training college. She had left Oxford with the highest qualifications, the training college was lucky to get her, but they had rules: lady teachers were forbidden to keep on their positions when they married, and as for *cohabitation*! Harriet had kept her private life a closed book from her colleagues at the school, which had inevitably fuelled the rumours, a mistake she saw too late. She was asked, very politely, to resign.

Fortunately, Kit had enough money for this at least not to matter, and anyway, it was of little account compared to the continual worry about his state of mind. From their flat high above the street, he stared out day after day at the area railings three storeys below. He had talked wildly of shooting himself. She had been forced to take charge of his pills and sleeping draughts. He had terrible nightmares, and she never knew how much he remembered of what he had revealed to her during his ramblings. He disliked talking of the time before the war, at Charnley, and he never spoke of Beatrice or Amory, if he could help it, except in his sleep. He saw doctors and psychiatrists, to no avail.

And then, deliverance had come in the form of a chance meeting with an old army friend, a young padre named Rupert Fleetwood, who had himself served in France, who understood, in a way Harriet was only partly able to do, the crisis Kit was going through, the terrors that had caused it, and the horrors of trench life, which he had shared. He was patient, and listened. He and Kit had long discussions, deep into the night, and gradually, the wild dreams abated, and the threats of suicide were no more. But instead, a general apathy and aimlessness took their place. He took offence and sulked when Harriet tried to persuade him to do anything constructive, pointing out that he didn't try to run *her* life for her, which was true, but enraged her. Reluctantly, from time to time, he agreed to try various occupations, none of which, unfortunately, lasted...he did not *have* to stick to anything which turned out to be uncongenial, he did not *have* to work in order to earn his living. It was what she'd always feared –

that the fortune left to him by his rich relative would be a millstone around his neck. The fact that she was right was no comfort to either of them. She had to face the fact that they were tearing each other to bits, and the passion she had always felt in herself was slowly dying.

Until, out of the blue, had come the announcement that he was going to enter the Church. A decision not only incredible, unbelievable, unconvincing, unnecessary, but stupid, and totally *wrong*, Harriet raged. He had chosen to do this in exactly the same mad, impulsively thoughtless way he had chosen the equally unsuitable profession of civil engineer – and look where that had got him: the idea rejected and thrown away when he finally admitted he would never be successful – or have the necessary application to enable him to make himself so.

She had appealed to Rupert Fleetwood.

"I can't help, Harriet. This decision is none of my doing. I can't help because I don't know what it is that's troubling him."

"Surely...what he's just been through – in the trenches?"

"No," he said, "it's not that. Not entirely." But what it was had never been vouchsafed. And she was now oppressed by the thought of what the answer might be.

She realised Kit was still waiting for her to reply. '*Why did you leave me?*' he'd asked, which was unanswerable now, all these years later. The urge to spare them both further embarrassment almost made her say lightly that she hadn't been able to see herself in the role of parson's wife, but innate honesty rejected such flippancy. She said quietly, over his bowed head, almost to herself, not knowing whether he would hear: "We weren't any good for each other, you and I. We never were." They had always travelled along parallel lines which would not meet at infinity or elsewhere. His decision to enter the Church had been the last straw: she'd been able to take no more and had walked away, albeit leaving a piece of her heart with him, gone to live with her friend Frances, and begun to concentrate in earnest on her career. She had, to her shame, believed more in her own rightness than in him.

For it seemed she'd been wrong. Here Kit still was, nearly thirty years later, still in holy orders. That he worked hard and unstintingly among his mainly poor parishioners, that he thought little of himself and was even loved, she knew from Daisy, the only one who had resolutely kept in touch. She might even come to believe that, thinking of the over-crowded vicarage he'd mentioned, noticing that his cassock was shabby, green and shiny with age and frayed a little around the cuffs and hem.

Reaching out, he took hold of her unresisting hand, holding it with a firm, dry clasp.

"What did go wrong between us, Harriet?"

This time, she couldn't look away from his compelling eyes, she couldn't pretend not to understand. She had resolutely refused to see him from the day they had last parted, knowing he could still persuade her to return to him, but unable to face the whole merry-go-round of emotions starting up again It was a path she didn't want to go down now but she knew she must if she was to know what she dreaded, yet had to hear.

She forced herself to speak, to be honest. "It was my mother, always between us, wasn't it?"

He froze. "I don't understand."

She looked at him, long and hard, searching for a better answer than that in those blue eyes. "It's no good," she said forcefully, "I must know, Kit. The truth."

He was taken aback by her look, for a moment unable to think of an acceptable answer. "I've been punished," he said at last, obliquely, "but I've made my peace with God and allowed myself to be forgiven. Can't you forgive me, too?"

He hadn't, after all, changed as much as she'd hoped. He was still capable of avoiding issues. About Kit's conversion there had always hovered the question: why? She had eventually settled for guilt that needed to be absolved. But guilt related to what? A near-incestuous relationship with Beatrice? Or worse? "You might at least do me the honour of answering me honestly now," she said. Then, when he didn't speak, taking a deep breath, she asked, "Kit, were you having an affair with my mother?"

He stiffened but met her challenge steadily. "No."

She still didn't know whether to believe him or not, but it was no use, she wasn't going to get any further admission from him, that much at least she did know. A lifetime lay between them – of love and misunderstandings, of hope kindled, and hope unfulfilled, but the shutters had come down between them as, eventually, they always had.

Defeated, she had left to return home, her doubts still not satisfactorily quelled, but another one at last understood: after she'd severed her relationship with Kit there had, later, been another man, who hadn't been free to marry her, but with whom she'd been happy for over fifteen years, until he had died. A good, kind and loving man with a wonderful sense of humour. She had been grateful for what he'd given her. It was more than many women had. But she had always, at the bottom of her heart, believed that no matter what, it would always be Kit. The one and only. And that whatever he had done it could, ultimately, make no difference.

But now, at last, she knew she had been chasing shadows.

Chapter Fifteen

The note propped against a jug of bronze chrysanthemums on the mantelpiece said that Harriet had gone up to London. Nina frowned, asking herself what could have prompted this sudden decision, when Harriet had allegedly been up to her eyebrows in work. The note went on to say she should be home by late afternoon but in fact, barely had there been time to read it before she followed close on their heels. Looking very elegant in her moss green suit and a smart hat, she came in, saying, "Good thing I gave you a key, Nina," before registering the presence of a visitor, the explanation for the unusual occurrence of the car parked in the lane outside.

"Rose Jessamy's son? Good heavens!" she repeated, taking the large hand of the battle-scarred young man Nina had brought back with her. Could it be possible? But of course! Scanning his face with a shock of recognition and understanding, she realised there was no mistaking that smile. And though he appeared loose and relaxed, underlying it was a sense of controlled energy and determination, no doubt inherited from his mother. No one who'd known Rose Jessamy and seen her work could doubt that she had been possessed of a great sense of life force. "Well," she said, taking off her hat, shaken despite herself, "since I don't believe in coincidences, tell me how you came to find us. Did the police send you?"

"No. But it was through them I found Mrs Tempest, your sister."

"Daisy? She must have been so pleased to meet you. She was very taken with your mother."

Harriet didn't as a rule warm quickly to new people. Instant rapport with strangers always seemed slightly suspect to her, but she was very conscious that this often made her appear distant at the beginning of an acquaintance. Tom Verrier, however, didn't seem intimidated by her, as people often were, mistaking her reserve for coldness, and she soon felt her wariness dissolve and, as he talked about his mother, she relaxed. "We only knew Rose briefly," she commented, noting *en passant* how his eyes followed Nina as she went into the kitchen to put the kettle on. "But I'm sorry to learn she died so young. She became a restorer, you say? I hope she kept on with her own work as well, it'd be a great pity if not. Those frescoes at Charnley–"

"Yes, she left a lot of paintings and stuff, and that's one of the things I was hoping to do in London...to try and arrange some sort of retrospective, and perhaps one later in France as well. She was beginning to make quite a name for herself over there before she died. Maybe it'll have to wait until the art world gets back on to a normal footing, but I'd like to put out a few feelers. It seems the least I can do for her."

It was warm in the room, with the late afternoon sunlight slanting in through the windows, lighting up the copper jug of glowing, bronzy-gold garden chrysanthemums on the mantelpiece, filling the room with their bitter-sweet tang, the essence of autumn. They were almost exactly the colour of Rose Jessamy's hair, something she hadn't passed on to her son. Any legacy from her seemed to be in the readiness for action Harriet sensed in him, pleasing her, coinciding as it did with her own inclinations. "That's a splendid idea," she said. "My sister Vita's husband may be able to help you there – he's quite famous, knows all the right people in the art world."

"I'd be glad of an introduction to him. Have I heard of him?"

It seemed that he had, and was very impressed when Harriet explained who he was. At the same time, she wondered, if Rose had been making something of an impression

with her work in France, why Wycombe, with his ency-
clopaedic knowledge of all things in the art world, had never
heard of her. Perhaps he had, but had chosen to say nothing.
With his rigid sense of propriety, she didn't doubt he might
well have felt it was inappropriate to mention the name of
one so closely associated with a time of tragedy for the family.

When Nina returned with the tea, Tom got up from his chair
with only a slightly awkward movement of his left leg, hardly
even a limp by now, due to some excellent physiotherapy.
Moving aside the magazines on the coffee table to make
room for the tea things, his hand brushed against hers as he
took the tray from her. He felt her awareness of it, but she
didn't look up, busying herself with the cups and saucers, her
movements neat and economical, just the slight flush on her
cheeks betraying her. He waved away the milk as she held up
the jug, glad that the tea seemed stronger than Daisy's coffee.

"Hope these biscuits are all right, Harriet," she remarked
doubtfully, "they were the only ones I could find."

"Heavens, they're as old as Adam! They were slipped into
my basket as a favour so I couldn't bring myself to refuse
them, though biscuits aren't my thing."

Nor mine, either, thought Tom, observing with resignation
that they were rich tea again, but he took one and pretended
there was nothing wrong with it, though it tasted like a
mouthful of soft chalk.

She sampled one herself and pulled a face. "Eat them at
your peril, Tom. Good thing we have some hungry sparrows
around here."

As they drank their tea, he was amused to feel both women
watching him, Harriet especially. He felt her summing up
this person, this Tom Verrier who'd been catapulted into

their lives, possibly trying to absorb him as she would a new mathematical concept. On the way here, Nina had told him about this formidable aunt, who had been a don at London University, her subject mathematics, who'd worked during the war as a boffin on some highly secret work that she was forbidden to talk about, even yet. He'd expected a frumpish intellectual and was relieved to meet a mature woman, attractive and smart, and with a sense of humour, whom he immediately liked.

He was at ease with her from the word go, in pretty much the same way as he'd been at ease with Nina. When they'd set out from her father's house, Nina hadn't seemed to feel the need to keep up a stream of endless chatter, unlike most young women he'd known, and since he'd needed to concentrate on finding his way out of the city, that had suited him pretty well. He'd no intentions of letting the silence continue, however – but in fact it was she who had put the first question, as soon as they were clear of the city and driving through the grimy, run-down suburbs that reflected a war-weariness more apparent there than in the reawakening city centre. When she'd seen he was free to give his attention, she'd begun by asking him what he did for a living in civvy street. "Are you an Egyptologist, too – or a painter like your mother?"

"God, no, I can't draw a straight line! And as for Egypt and all that – too familiar, I guess."

"All that? Too familiar? Egypt! Dear me." He grinned, pleased that she could tease him, which boded well. "I spent some time there when I was in the WAAF," she offered, quickly adding that it hadn't been for long, only a brief tour of duty. It soon became obvious that she really preferred him to do the talking. He noticed she slid away from personal issues and felt that perhaps he was not the only one with scars; only hers might be emotional ones. It had made him feel surprisingly tender towards her.

"Egypt has a lot to offer," he'd said, "maybe too much for me – perhaps that's why I set my horizons further." And then, he was telling her about his journeys of exploration and how he financed them by writing travel books. "Is that so funny?"

"Not at all, it's just that–" Rather diffidently, smiling, she mentioned that she, too, wrote books. "Nothing much, just a couple of light historical romances."

"Now isn't that amazing?" He beamed. "As if it had been meant. And more amazing that we've never heard of each other before."

"Well, I haven't exactly made it to the bestseller lists!"

"Nor me. One day, though." Was he sounding brashly over-confident? He hadn't meant to, but if determination was all that was needed to turn the possibility into a certainty he'd do it, and hopefully in the not too distant future.

Once started, conversation was easy: Egypt, and his childhood there; thumbnail sketches of the remote places which he'd explored before the war and talk of those countries even more distant where he hoped to go in the future. She was a sympathetic listener and he was aware, with a perception that didn't always characterise his dealings with the opposite sex, of an underlying depth to her. She wasn't as young as he'd first thought. He'd had a notion, curious to him who'd always regarded himself as self-sufficient, that one might lean on her in a crisis.

"More tea?" asked Harriet now.

"Please." Maybe it would take away the taste of the stale biscuit, and the three, possibly four more, he'd eaten without realising what he was doing.

"You'll stay for supper, I hope?"

Lord, did he seem that hungry? "Thanks, but I've already stayed too long. I must get back."

"Nonsense, after bringing Nina all this way."

Nina added her persuasions. "We can have a pie. I've brought this tin of meat with me that my landlady got for me – it's a sort of Spam, but it has a thick layer of fat at the bottom of the tin that you can make pastry with."

This had to be British sense of humour. He said hastily, "No, no, I can't expect you to provide for unexpected guests, taking your rations."

"It's very tasty." Her eyes danced. She *was* making fun of him.

"I believe you. So why not save it for a treat? Tell you what – isn't there somewhere around here where I can take you two ladies out to eat? Or even buy some fish and chips? I've become positively addicted to them."

Nina laughed. Heavens, they're more than half in love already, Harriet thought. He couldn't take his eyes off her, and though she wasn't actually blushing, she looked warmed, as if she was lit from within. It made Harriet feel old, and for a moment, the memories the afternoon had brought back choked her. She too had felt that once, that lightning bolt, that certainty. Which reminded her that she'd have to find a suitable moment to say why she'd rushed up to London like that. After reading those notebooks of hers, Nina must be bursting with curiosity about Kit. It would be an exercise of the imagination, finding an explanation as to why she'd broken the non-communication of years.

Tom was disappointed to hear that Garvingden didn't run to a fish and chip shop.

"There's always the Lamb, I suppose," Harriet said. "They'll find us something, if the landlord's in a good mood – not by any means certain – but it might even be something nice if his wife has anything to do with it."

"She's a wizard cook," Nina said. "Shall I ring up and see if they can do anything?"

Love is a winged chariot, and sped her to the telephone and back in a moment with the news that Mrs Binns could accommodate them at seven thirty.

In Tom's opinion, the Lamb & Flag provided every attraction anyone looking for a quaint English pub could wish for. Low pantiled roofs, ivy-wreathed walls, and an interior like a stage set: roaring fire, smelly old dog snoring in front of it, shining horse brasses, spittoons, old codgers in the inglenook, ceiling pickled in tobacco smoke. It also boasted a new-fangled juke-box, which Binns had acquired from a now-defunct American air base.

"Seeing as it's you, Miss Jardine," said Mrs Binns in a stage whisper, "I've found you a bit of something tasty. Have to have it in the back, though. Gets noisy in here later on."

Eating in the Binns' private parlour would be a positive advantage in view of the joke-box, as the landlady insisted on calling it. It might draw in the younger element, as Binns claimed, but its repertoire consisted of all the newest, rowdy records from America and she never tired of pointing out how many village regulars were dropping off...if it was one of the amusement arcades folk wanted, why, they could take theirselves off to the seaside, not look for it in the Lamb! The odds on Mrs Binns winning the argument were long in the village, but at the moment, the jokebox remained.

After the warmth of the snug, where they'd waited for their meal to be prepared, the parlour felt cold. The fire had only just been lit, and smoked. The room was stuffed with old fashioned furniture and kept ferociously clean, though it was used only on high days and holidays. But Mrs Binns had spread her best crotcheted tablecloth on the highly polished Victorian table, and presently there appeared large, hot, plates of home-cured ham and sizzling eggs, accompanied by succulent field mushrooms, as well as home-baked bread and a large pot of tea, to murmurs of pleasure and appreciation all round.

The chimney belched more smoke, whereupon the landlady knelt and gave the coals a vigorous poke. "Drat this old fire! It's not been lit since we had Grandpa's funeral tea in here, six months gone, but it'll be all right, directly, when it gets a blaze on."

"Never mind the fire – this is a feast," Tom said, tackling the ham and eggs.

"Get it down you and don't ask no questions. And mum's the word. I'll have 'em here from all round the Wrekin, else, though it's all from my own pig and my own hens. There you are, what did I say? It's going nicely now." Mrs Binns nodded encouragingly and left them to it.

Wine was as unheard of in the Lamb & Flag as champagne at a teetotal wedding, but the local beer was good, and conducive to conversation. By the time the ham and eggs had been disposed of and the rhubarb pie was but a memory on the tongue, Harriet felt able at last to broach the subject that was uppermost in her mind. "I don't know what the police have said to you, Tom, but at least I hope they've abandoned the ridiculous idea that your mother may have been responsible for my mother's death."

"They haven't ruled out the possibility."

"Then they're bigger fools than I thought."

"I have to say they didn't impress me overmuch," he agreed, laconically enough, but not fooling Harriet. So he had a capacity for anger, beneath that easy manner. Kept under control, directed properly, she'd never thought that was a bad thing in anyone.

Nina, who'd held back her impatience long enough, broke in, before she'd time to weigh up whether or not she'd been indiscreet, "I hope I haven't talked out of turn, Harriet, but I've told Tom about the boxes of papers found at Charnley, and your mother's Egyptian journal. And would you believe – he knows Professor Iskander."

"Do you really, Tom? *Professor* Iskander, you say?"

Tom explained how Iskander had first been an outstanding pupil of his father's when Michel had lectured in Egyptology, had later assumed his mentor's profession, and how their acquaintance had developed into an old and valued friendship. Harriet supposed, recalling the passages in the journals where Beatrice had talked of the young Egyptian's enthusiasm for his country's history and traditions, its ancient civilisation, that it was almost inevitable he should have chosen the subject as his life's work.

"Since you mention the police–" began Tom, "I've only a week or two before I go back to East Grinstead for my last treatment. After that, it's back home. I thought events moved slowly in Egypt, but this lethargy…"

"It's not lethargy," said Harriet, "it's British gamesmanship. Keep things off the boil long enough and they'll go away."

"Not gamesmanship, either, it's inertia. If they've discovered what Tutankhamun ate for breakfast, surely to God–?"

Harriet laughed. "Inspector Grigsby–"

"The hell with Grigsby! Excuse me, but I'm not prepared to sit back and let justice take its own course – not if it's going to take another thirty-seven years! That was the impression they gave me – it's already waited nearly forty years, so what's another few weeks? Or years? Makes me want to light a squib under them. Time's a commodity in short supply with me at the moment, but at least I have the next few weeks to see what I can come up with, and I'm damned if I'm going to leave without at least trying to clear my mother's name." He eyed them speculatively. "Trouble is, this isn't my line of country – and on top of that, I'm coming to it cold, without any prior knowledge, so–"

"You want us to help," said Nina.

"I can't even begin without you."

Harriet's eyebrows rose. "Your grasp of essentials does you credit."

"Yes, well, I do have a sort of vested interest in sorting this thing out. And not only because of my mother." He hesitated, looking from one to the other. "I guess I ought to have told you sooner, but you'll have to know who I am, sooner or later."

Harriet said, "I already know who you are, Tom. I knew from the moment I walked in through the door that you were Marcus's son."

They looked at each other. The same identical crooked smile lit both their faces.

"Yes," he said, "I rather thought you did."

"Fill me in on the background," said Tom, "First tell me what happened to everyone, after you left Charnley, during the war?"

Nina said, "Daisy and Athene – you haven't met my Aunt Athene, Dad's sister, yet, that's a treat in store! – went to France and drove ambulances."

"So they did," said Harriet. "Being suffragettes had made them very intrepid. I was in France, too, but only behind the lines, nursing the wounded. I'd enrolled as a VAD, which was a salutary experience. I don't believe I'd ever so much as held a duster previously, let alone scrubbed floors, but I ended up doing far worse jobs than that. Vita did some nursing, too, when Stoke Wycombe was used as a convalescent home, but she didn't last long. They told her, quite nicely, that 'she wasn't born to it', so she just went back to being the chatelaine."

Tom was amused, "And – Marcus?"

Harriet noticed that. Marcus, not 'my father'. Well, how could a man he had never known be a real father to him? His adoptive father, Michel, though not his biological parent, was the one who had nurtured and loved him all his life, and there was obviously a great deal of affection between them. Physically, apart from his height, Tom bore no definite resemblance to Marcus, though she kept getting fleeting, disconcerting glimpses of that elusive, hard to pin down family look, and that smile which had first told her without question who he was. She thought he might be like her brother in other ways, though.

"Oh, Marcus had already abandoned the Law and joined the army before the war – not the Guards, where he might have kept up the same sort of social life he'd had before, but the Royal Engineers, of all things. Something seemed to have come over him after we left Charnley. He'd changed. We hardly saw him and when we did, he just wasn't the same any more. He'd always been so – well, such a contented, settled sort of person. He loved Charnley – not just its way of life, but the whole idea of it as a continuing cycle – more than any of us, I think. Then afterwards, when he came home from Egypt, he joined the army. It was as if he wanted to cut free completely and put his old life, his old friends, even his family, quite behind him.

"Perhaps because my mother apparently refused to marry him, even when she found she was pregnant. She was a fiercely independent person, I gather, and she couldn't wholly commit herself to him – and besides, she knew she wanted to stay in Egypt for the rest of her life, while he could never leave England permanently. It seems as though, from what you say, he might have had hopes of getting Charnley back one day.

"Yes," said Harriet quietly, "for Marcus, Charnley was everything."

Another silence fell over the table as they contemplated a life, like so many more, cut tragically short before its promise could be fulfilled, until Nina broke it by asking, "Did he ever know – about you, Tom?"

"No. She never told him. She married Dad soon after I was born."

"I'm sorry he died never knowing that he had a son. It would have meant a lot to him." Harriet wondered if it had yet occurred to Tom that he was the last of the Jardines, if on the wrong side of the blanket, that Beatrice had been his grandmother, Amory his grandfather. "Perhaps Rose was right, either way he'd have been unhappy – marrying her knowing she didn't love him, or having a son he couldn't keep by his side."

Drinking Mrs Binns' regrettable coffee – one day, thought Tom optimistically, this nation might learn to make coffee as well as they made their tea – he decided he'd learned as much about the situation as they could tell him, and what should be done about it was beginning to move on its own trajectory, at least in his mind.

"I've been thinking," he said. "It seems to me it'd benefit us all if we operated from the same place. I could stay here. I needn't go back tonight, in fact."

"Here? At the Lamb? Tonight?" Harriet's face was a study. "I don't think they take visitors. And the privy's out at the back."

He grinned. "I can only ask." He left the room, and returned within a few minutes. "Yes, I can stay. If I agree to have Grandpa's old room. I think he might have died there of hypothermia, but Mrs B's going to light a fire, put a bottle in the bed and give me another eiderdown." He looked about to say more, considered them both and then changed his mind. "I'll just hop back to London tomorrow, pick up my belongings and check out at the hotel, and see to one or two other things. Should be back in the afternoon."

Harriet raised an eyebrow. "He has a way with him, Nina,

this Tom Verrier."

There was no such sophistication in Garvingden as street lamps, but as Nina and Harriet left the Lamb to make their way back to her cottage the moon was hard and bright, sailing high in a clear sky, and light spilled from cottage windows. Everyone seemed reluctant to draw their curtains, now that blackout restrictions were a thing of the past, and glimpses of cosy interiors could be seen from the footpath as they walked along, the glow illuminating stiff clumps of michaelmas daisies, and dahlias as yet untouched by frost. From old Tatchell's garden emanated the sharp scent of his prize chrysanthemums, Brussels sprouts and a ripe compost heap. The intimacy of the half-lit shadows seemed to provide the cover Harriet apparently needed for broaching the subject of her excursion to London that afternoon – or as much, Nina guessed, as she felt she was meant to know. As she began, it was with an unaccustomed hesitancy, seeming to find the subject difficult and sounding surprised and rather annoyed that it was.

Nina listened in what she hoped was a sympathetic silence after Kit's name occurred. Having seen those notebooks of Harriet's, she was in a position to know a little more about him, and his relationship with Harriet, which hadn't actually ever seemed to make Harriet very happy. She'd been intrigued to know whether the problems between them had ever been sorted out, and had felt that Harriet, in allowing her access to those notebooks, had opened the door to questions, but now here Harriet was, talking about Kit and herself before the opportunity to ask arose.

Daisy had once or twice hinted at some relationship not to be mentioned in her elder sister's dim and distant past, but had refused to be drawn as to its exact nature, and Nina had automatically assumed this to mean the usual story of a young man killed in France, leaving an irreconcilable Harriet as one of the spinster generation, unloved, unfulfilled. It was an image that had never really fitted Harriet. Much easier to see her kicking over the traces as she had done – and how brave of her that had been, in those days! – defying convention and living 'in sin' with Kit. Even today, when divorce was not quite the stigma it had been, illicit liaisons such as theirs would be frowned upon. At that time, it would have been very shocking. And yet, it had all gone for nothing. The affair had ended disastrously, though perhaps in a way no one could have predicted.

And Harriet had picked herself up and started again and had seemingly led a full and happy life without Kit. There were gaps in the story, probably things Harriet felt were too painful to repeat. Perhaps it was better so. Nina didn't much like what she'd heard of this Kit, holy orders or no holy orders.

Chapter Sixteen

The following morning, Nina took Harriet's old bicycle and rode down to the shop to buy fresh bread for breakfast, using the back road – thereby missing Tom, who was supposed to be on his way to London by then. She'd barely left when the Riley Nine roared into the lane and he breezed into the cottage.

"Can you be ready tomorrow to go away for a few days, Harriet?"

"What? Where to?"

"Egypt."

"Egypt?" She lifted an eyebrow. "May one ask how that's possible?"

"One may. I've been commandeering Mrs Binns' telephone for the last hour and I've managed to hitch lifts for us on an RAF York that's flying out tomorrow," he'd replied, as though this were the most natural thing in the world. "Oppo of mine in the RAF wangled it for me. I shot him a line about...well, anyway. Stop overnight at Malta, then on to Fayed. From there we can easily get to Cairo, stay at the flat in Heliopolis and come back by the return flight later in the week." He made the operation sound as simple as getting a bus from Marble Arch to Oxford Circus. It was probably illegal. Certainly risky.

She recalled his casual remark of the previous night: "There must have been a reason for Iskander to have left so suddenly like that," he'd said. "And there's only one way to find that out – by talking to the old boy himself." He'd rubbed his nose, looking very thoughtful. She hadn't taken much notice. It was, after all, a barely feasible proposition for anyone to think of taking ship and actually going out to confront Iskander, not with the restrictions on foreign travel and the permission needed to leave the country and all the other red tape to be dealt with, not to mention getting into Egypt. She'd evidently seriously underestimated him.

"Come on!" he urged. "It won't be first class travel, but it's a great chance. Are you game?"

Harriet said, after a moment's reflection, "If you mean to do what I think you do, certainly not."

"You disappoint me, Aunt Harriet. I thought you were a gutsy lady."

"Guts, as you so elegantly put it, have nothing to do with it." She busied herself with lighting a cigarette. "I just don't particularly want to meet Valery Iskander again."

"Ah." He eyed her speculatively. "As a matter of fact, I had a hunch you might say that – though I think you might be pleasantly surprised if you did meet him. Does this mean I've expended my considerable charm and powers of persuasion for nothing? There's not much point in my going to see him alone. Someone else needs to be there to help me along. I might not remember everything he has to say."

"So take Inspector Grigsby."

He said reproachfully, "Harriet, you're not taking this seriously. Grigsby! If Grigsby feels the necessity to go, which he doesn't seem to, he can make his own arrangements."

"Sorry. Count me out. Why not take Nina with you?"

"What a good idea!" That crooked, beguiling smile lit up his face. "Why didn't I think of that?"

"Why not, indeed?" she'd answered drily.

She had almost begun to believe, by the time they'd reached the coffee stage of their meal last night, that it was only too depressingly probable that the true facts about her mother's murder might never emerge, that they could remain forever silted up in the sands of Egypt. Either that, or the police were on the right track, thinking the murder originated nearer home, something she didn't want to acknowledge and pushed to the back of her mind with an unaccustomed thrill of superstitious fear, as if merely thinking such things would cause them to happen. Despite the euphoria created by suddenly finding she had a new and very agreeable nephew and ally, she'd been tired, and still rather despondent after her meeting with Kit. But this morning, when Tom arrived with his harebrained plan (so cheeky that it might actually work) it had revitalized her, strengthened her determination to go on.

Unlike Harriet, Nina had been game, and had instantly agreed to go. Personally, she said airily, she'd never encountered much difficulty with officialdom when she was serving in Egypt, being safely sheltered under the blanket of His Majesty's government, but added that the little she did know was sufficient for her to see what a tedious task it would be to obtain any useful information from the authorities, much less at long distance. She could visualise the willingness to help: yes effendi, no madame; the smiles, the charm; but also the promises that never came to anything, the lethargy that amounted to indolence. To take care of it yourself, yes, that was the best thing. She'd blithely driven off to London with Tom to pick up what she would need, leaving Harriet to contain her impatience to play her own part.

In the clearer light of another day, Harriet acknowledged that she'd allowed that abortive, wholly unsatisfactory visit to Kit the previous day to sidetrack her, to deflect her from what she instinctively felt to be the root of the matter – or at any rate the branch from which the events that led to the murder had grown. She ought to have trusted her own instincts rather than let her fear for Kit overrule them. Now, she determined to put suspicions that Kit had lied to her to one side and try another tack. Apart from Beatrice herself, and possibly Amory, both of them now dead, there were only three people, as far as she knew – Wycombe, Millie

Glendinning (later Kaplan) and Hallam – who'd been in Luxor and presumably knew what had happened there. (And, of course, Iskander, whom Tom and Nina were going to see.) At least, she could talk to those here. Millie first, she thought. Tomorrow, she would go up to London and find Millie.

Meanwhile, the day outside was bright and blowy, and the little strip of back garden that she called her herbaceous border was crying out for attention. Leaves were blowing in drifts into corners and into the bottoms of the hedges, the clematis had flowered its last and needed to be cut back, and even the indomitable michaelmas daisies were definitely past their best. The opportunity was there, and she was alone. A good day for secateurs and determination, she decided as she went to get her gardening gloves. Then the post arrived with a plop on the doormat and after she'd opened the single letter which lay there, the prospect of gardening faded like the smile on the Cheshire cat.

By now, she'd read it through three times, each time with a mixture of disbelief, pain and shock. Even so, the shadow that had lain over her for most of her life shifted, just a little. It was very nearly, but not quite, as bad as she had feared.

'*You have been gone just over an hour and already I am regretting the things I said, but more importantly did not say, to you,*' Kit wrote. '*Just because a man puts on a dog collar, it doesn't make him a saint – or less of a coward. The police will no doubt be coming to see me, and in view of what has now been discovered at Charnley, I see that I'm no longer justified in keeping to myself what I know about the last night of your mother's life. But before I speak to the police, I have to let you know what I couldn't bring myself to say to you face to face.*'

By now the next page was indelibly committed to Harriet's memory. But as she compulsively turned it over to read it yet again, there came the sound of a car drawing up on the road outside the cottage, beyond the few yards of the tiny front plot and the low stone wall that divided the garden from the footpath outside. She dragged herself away from the letter. She hadn't expected Tom to have brought Nina back so soon, and she wasn't ready to face them. The letter had left her disorientated. She stuffed it into its envelope and then into the pocket of her skirt, before going to let them in. Outside the front door stood her two sisters. Daisy – and Vita.

"We've come to see Tom," announced Daisy, her face alight with anticipation, when they were inside. Harriet sighed inwardly. She might have foreseen this after ringing Daisy with the news this morning. "I could hardly take it in – is it really true he's Marcus's son – and Rose Jessamy's? Yes, of course it is – I knew there was something about him, but I couldn't put my finger on it when he came to see us – why didn't he say who he was then?"

"I expect the opportunity didn't arise." Or perhaps he hadn't been sure how Daisy would take that sort of news. "I'm sorry, but you've missed him. He's gone back up to London with Nina."

Disappointment clouded Daisy's face. "You mean we shan't see him?"

"Depends on how long you can stay. An hour, an hour and a half, they should be back by that time."

"Well, I dare say we can stay until then," Vita said. "That isn't the only reason we've come – why I've come, anyway." She hesitated. Daisy's eyebrows rose. "I had those two policemen interrogating me yesterday and...the truth is, I quite desperately need to talk to someone."

Without thinking, Harriet heard herself say, "And I'm the last resort?"

She refused to meet Daisy's accusing glance, and when she looked towards Vita she found, unexpectedly, no room left in her for more sarcasms. The acid comment, '*What's wrong with your husband or that tame psychiatrist of yours?*' died on her lips. Her predictable responses to Vita were becoming unattractive. This was, after all, her sister. As children, they'd been inseparable, closer together in age to each other than to Daisy, and though they seemed to have lost their way somewhat over the years, she was still Vita, sometimes selfish, frequently neurotic and always obstinate, victim of traumatic events, even if they were often of her own making. At the moment, despite her beautifully cut saxe-blue costume and the little burgundy hat trimmed with a long pheasant's feather, tilted fetchingly over one eye, she looked terrible, so pale and fragile, at the end of her tether. Harriet did something she hadn't done for years. She put her arms around her sister. Vita began to weep and Harriet didn't try to stop her. Daisy said nothing, but went into the kitchen and presently came back with a tray of tea.

Harriet almost thought her own bitten-back words had been spoken, or conveyed by some process of thought transmission, so apt were Vita's next words, her voice muffled against Harriet's shoulder. "Oscar thinks I ought to speak to Myles. But I can't bring myself to salve my conscience at the expense of–" She broke off abruptly and began to dry her eyes. She took off her hat, patted her hair into place, blew her nose and pulled out her compact.

"Say what to Myles?" demanded Daisy, busy with sugar and milk.

Their tea poured, out came the story that Vita had told to the police, all of it news to her two sisters. Committed to being resolutely unshockable, Daisy listened silently, tugging down the sleeves of her faded dusty-pink jumper, which seemed to have shrunk in the wash, but she was obviously shaken: Vita, admitting to lax behaviour not a lot different from that of her own unruly charges at Hope House, and with much less excuse! The revelation came as less of a surprise to Harriet. Bertie Rossiter had never stood high in her estimation. She didn't exonerate Vita entirely from the mad scheme – it had quite possibly been her idea – but Bertie, who should have known better, would have done nothing to dissuade her. In any case, after that letter Harriet had just received, the contents of which came back to her with a jolt, Vita's disclosure about slipping out to meet her young man clandestinely came through as a minor indiscretion, though as for what might have followed had they not been interrupted...Vita had, it seemed, been more their mother's daughter than anyone had realised.

She saw some comment from her was needed. "So, the point of all this is that you saw Hallam coming out of Mama's room at about quarter past two, saying goodnight to her – which means she was alive until that time?"

"Yes. Poor Hallam."

"*Poor* Hallam?" Nobody had detested Clara Hallam as much as Vita, who'd never forgotten an 'accidentally' over-shortened hem on one of her new grown-up dresses – a subtle revenge for some imagined slight received from the young Vita.

"Well, she looked fit to drop – you know how Mama used to keep her up until all hours. She was always a night owl, wasn't she?"

"Mama could afford to be, not having to get up until she pleased the next morning – unlike Hallam or the other servants."

"I suppose that's true. But – there's something else. Something I didn't say to Grigsby. You remember the big looking glass that hung in the angle of the upstairs corridor?"

"The one that was put there so people could see who was coming around the corner?"

"Yes, after Polly Cheevers collided with one of the footmen

coming the other way that time," put in Daisy, emerging from her silence into something she understood better, "when she had an armful of linen up to her chin so that she couldn't see over it? He fell with his face against a doorknob and I remember he had a black eye for weeks."

"What I didn't tell Grigsby – well, how could I? – was that before that, as I was going *out*, I saw – someone, through the glass, going into Mama's bedroom. It – it was Myles. In his dressing gown. A paisley silk he still had when we married," she added irrelevantly.

"Myles? Are you sure it was him and not Papa?" Daisy was incredulous.

"Of course I'm sure! I'd hardly be saying this if not. I saw him quite clearly. And in any case, Papa would have used the connecting door between their rooms."

"But it could have meant mean something quite innocuous!"

"Innocuous, Daisy? At that time in the morning?"

Harriet said carefully, "But you saw Hallam saying goodnight to her, later–"

"I know, that's what's so odd."

"Very odd, if you're implying what I think you are."

There are few secrets between a lady and her maid, and the word that sprang to mind was connivance. Difficult to believe of holier-than-thou Hallam. Besides which, set against any mistaken loyalty she might have had for Beatrice, there was the high regard in which she'd always held their father; indeed, as girls, they'd decided she'd had a crush on him and laughed rather unkindly. It was more likely, Harriet thought now, that she'd simply been grateful to Amory for employing that renegade brother of hers.

The more Harriet thought about it, the more it seemed probable that what Vita had seen was not innocuous at all. She found she was holding her breath as phrases she didn't care to think about came back to her from Kit's letter. Something felt to twist in her heart. She managed to say feebly, "But can you imagine Mama sending for Hallam afterwards, if there'd been anything scandalous going on?"

"If that was all it was – scandal!"

"Vita! What are you saying?" That was Daisy.

"When they were dancing together earlier that evening, they didn't look like lovers to me."

It seemed that Harriet had wrongly thought Vita entirely absorbed by her own concerns that night, though she'd noticed the same thing herself, been oddly disturbed by it; she'd recorded it in her notebook at the time, hadn't she? She hadn't understood then, but she was somewhat wiser now and realised that love – or sexual attraction – could take many forms. "In fact," Vita went on, "they were always cool with one another when you think about it."

"There are two ways of looking at that," Harriet said. In the ensuing silence, one could almost hear the soft fall of flower petals being shed by one of the tawny chrysanthemums.

"Vita, why didn't you mention all this at the time she disappeared?" Daisy asked, at last.

"I suppose then I *did* just think he'd probably had some quite innocent reason for slipping into her room for a moment or two. And anyway, the next day, when we thought she'd gone off with Iskander, whatever the explanation was, it didn't seem to matter. Oh God, I was so ashamed of what she'd done, running off with that man, what it would mean to all of us…"

Harriet looked sharply at her. "Is that why you cut those pages from Mama's journal? To prevent anyone ever reading them?"

"What journal?" Vita looked blank. "I don't remember any journal."

"You must! That grey suede-covered one."

But memory was selective. Vita insisted she certainly hadn't removed pages from anything resembling a journal and moreover didn't remember one of any sort. This was endorsed by Daisy, who was suddenly very critical. "Anyway, what does a thing like that matter? Let's not forget," she said bluntly, "it isn't only Myles we're talking about here. We're talking about Mama as if she were nothing more than a – a tart."

They had strayed into muddy waters. A few days ago Harriet wouldn't have believed all this either, of either her mother or Wycombe, who would never in any circumstances behave dishonourably – and, moreover, with the wife of his best friend. Now, however–

"You don't seem very surprised about all this, Harriet," remarked Vita abruptly.

After reading that letter, how could she be?

'I lied to you, yes,' Kit had gone on, 'but in my own justification, I must make clear that your mother and I did no wrong – at least I was saved from that, which I came to be thankful about later, though emphatically not then. Yes, I was in love with her – as painfully in love as only a young man can be with an older woman. My feelings towards her had always been ambivalent, throughout my childhood and beyond she had been mother and yet no mother. I couldn't – wouldn't – admit that my love for her was hardly that of a son. Until she began to let me know that she felt the same. Every time our eyes met, every teasing word, every light gesture, told me how she felt. I knew it was wrong, incestuous by implication if not in fact, but she must have known that, too, I told myself. Until that night, the night of her birthday, when I found out how wrongly I had read the signals she was sending out – that she had merely been flirting with me, enjoying the admiration and the effect her presence had on me. On reflection, afterwards, I saw that I hadn't, in fact, been mistaken. I don't seek to excuse myself. I wasn't a boy, I was experienced enough to know what was what. I had simply allowed myself to be blind and deaf to reason, to give in to my own desires.

Everyone had either gone home or to bed that night, and I sat on the seat under the deodar, smoking and waiting for her lights to go out, savouring over and over again in my mind the exchanges between us that day. The lights in Amory's study, where he was likely to remain at his desk for hours, stayed on, and so did those in Beatrice's room. Eventually, she came out on to her balcony. I hesitated for a while and then, just when I'd gathered enough courage to go up, someone followed her out there. At first I thought it must be Amory, after all – then I realised that it was not him, but *Wycombe*!

I simply wouldn't, at first, allow myself to believe that of him, but there was no mistaking that embrace, or its fervour. There they were, the two people Amory loved best in the world, deceiving him. I had thought better of Wycombe than that. Moreover, I had always, until then, thought him of a different persuasion. I knew how fond he was of me, as I was of him, too, though not in the way I loved and honoured Amory, Amory who had done so much for me, been my father in all but name. The irony of that did not escape me, it only added to my guilt – that in fact my own situation, my own intended acts, were perhaps even more reprehensible than Wycombe's. As for Beatrice, his wife and the mother of his children, the woman who, until then, I had thought that I truly loved...The scales fell from my eyes. I saw what a fool she'd made of me, I felt like a callow youth, and I could not bear it.

More than that, it would have made you smart, humiliated

you in a way you never could endure, Harriet had immediately thought on reading that...so much that you later killed her, and then, afterwards...?

'You were right, of course. I didn't go home that night with the Lansburys. I went to my room in the guest wing and though I didn't think I could possibly sleep, emotion and the amount I'd had to drink put me out for the count for several hours. I slept like one felled, until I awoke at first light and legged it out cross country for the main line station. And then later, when I heard – about her disappearance and the assumed cause – I simply could not have come back. I could face none of you – you, and Amory who was suffering so much, and Wycombe least of all, though it eventually seemed that he had been deceived as much as I had been. Later, when you and I, Harriet...well, there were many times when I nearly told you, but couldn't. I always put it off until it became impossible to say anything at all.

'That poor devil Iskander, she had him on a string, too. There is no need for the police, or anyone else, to know about her involvement with either him or me, but you must see that I must tell them about seeing Wycombe. If he is innocent, he will have the chance to clear his own name.'

Perhaps, Harriet had at first thought on reading this, grasping at straws, he was mistaken – or lying – about having seen Wycombe, though she couldn't see why – but now, independently of Kit, here was Vita confessing to having seen him going into Beatrice's room too, and she had no reason to lie – quite the contrary. Nor about seeing Hallam bidding Beatrice goodnight afterwards – when Wycombe must already have left her.

There seemed no getting away from the fact that Wycombe was guilty of adultery with Beatrice, but on Vita's evidence he was exonerated from having killed her – unless he had returned, later, which Harriet supposed was possible. Yet there was something almost ludicrous in the thought that he might, actually, have stolen back and strangled her, in the idea of those long, fastidious fingers twisting and tightening that jewelled necklace around her white throat; as if such an act would have offended his stiff sense of propriety and correctness. To kill a lady was not the act of an officer and a gentleman. But neither was betrayal of his friend, and there were many reasons why men lost control and killed the women they loved – Oscar Schulman would know about that – and who knew what had passed between them in that bedroom? Harriet suddenly recalled those telling words Beatrice had recorded: *A fierce excitement beats in me, tinged with shame, when I think what might happen, what I want to happen; then I hear the echo of a still small voice which says this was not precisely the sort of advice that had guided my infant teaching.*

Without doubt, she had been harbouring some very unladylike desires – but it was clear now who she'd been writing about. Not Iskander, but Wycombe. And Harriet reminded herself that she had also written: *'He intrigues, but sometimes frightens me.'*

"What should I do?" Vita asked.

Why should she do anything? Now, after all this time? No doubt Schulman had advised her to speak to Wycombe on the grounds that confession was good for the soul. Or to lance that boil of suspicion before it festered and burst. But what would confrontation, at this stage, do to both of them? Harriet liked Schulman well enough but he was a mind doctor, and after her dealings with them during Kit's mental crisis, she wasn't enamoured of psychiatrists as a race. On the other hand, he was also a professional, no doubt he knew what he was doing "Oscar may be right, but I can't see it. What good is telling Myles what you saw going to do at this stage?"

"You could go to the police, and let them sort it out," Daisy remarked.

"I couldn't do that!" cried Vita, stricken. "Grigsby would immediately assume he'd something to do with the murder!"

"Isn't that what you're afraid of?" her sister said bluntly.

"Of course not!" But Vita's frightened eyes said otherwise.

Harriet felt bound to point out that if Myles was already a police suspect – as anyone there that night was bound to be – then this would be in his favour, but Vita still shook her head.

"Well then, forget it," Daisy averred stoutly. "Better in any case for the lot of us to forget the whole thing, in my opinion. Let sleeping dogs lie."

Was Daisy right? Harriet contemplated the blurred edges of what was right and what was wrong, what should or should not be done. Would it not be better for all concerned to let the truth lie at the bottom of the deep well where it had lain for forty years? No. Emphatically no. Whatever came of it, it was always better to know the truth. For years, Harriet had harboured a nasty, lingering suspicion about Kit and her mother and occasionally, in bleak moments, had been convinced that his avoidance of her meant that he had somehow been involved in Beatrice's death. His letter had at least lifted some of that doubt. Some inner caution, however, warned her to think twice before revealing the letter's contents, even now. Not yet, until she was more sure. They might all, especially Vita, have to face the fact, sooner or later, that Wycombe had had feet of clay, that Beatrice had not been the faithful, loyal wife they had all imagined her to be. That their long-held perceptions of the untroubled, happy life at Charnley were wrong – that it had, in fact, probably been falling apart for a long time. Yet, how could this have justified her murder? "Doing all this for her – you must have loved her very much," Nina had remarked when Harriet had first announced her intentions. But Harriet feared it was because she had not loved her enough – or not enough to recognise how much. For the bottom had fallen out of all their lives when she had disappeared.

It was only a feeling, one that could never be substantiated, but without a shadow of doubt Harriet felt that Amory could not have been unaware that his wife was carrying on an affair beneath his very nose. Which led to the conclusion she had been afraid of from the very instant that she had heard of the discovery of Beatrice's body. Harriet was quite certain the police must have thought of it, too. Grigsby wasn't tripping over his feet in his haste to find the person responsible for their mother's death, but she was sure he had his theories, including this one, the one Harriet feared most of all.

The sun had by now moved away from the front of the house and inside it was growing dark. Harriet switched on a lamp, glanced at the clock. "They should be back any time."

"Perhaps we ought to come back another day," Vita said.

"Well, you'll have to make it soon. He's off to Egypt the day after tomorrow."

Daisy exclaimed, "Egypt? You mean he's going back home?"

"Not permanently, not yet, anyway."

A car drew up behind Daisy's in the lane. There sounded footsteps now on the path outside, voices. With relief, Harriet went to open the door and let the young folk in.

Chapter Seventeen

Nina had been a real sport, Tom considered, as ready as he was to ignore all the negative sides of what Harriet – no chicken-heart, herself – clearly regarded as a disaster-prone undertaking. Nina, however, had agreed on the instant. "Why not?"

But clothes! No time to buy something suitable to the climate, no clothing coupons left, anyway. Panic stations.

"Clothes? Just take your ordinary things," he'd advised carelessly. "It's October, it won't be blazing hot. Anyway, we'd better travel in uniform – if you still have yours?"

Yes, she had, shoved to the back of the wardrobe where she'd thankfully bundled it on her demob. They'd picked it up from her bed-sit on that flying visit the day before. You could always travel anonymously in uniform, he'd told her with conviction, no questions asked if you looked as though you'd every right to be there. Wearing the now unfamiliar tunic and skirt made her feel as though she were in disguise, she said; she felt stealthy, like a female Richard Hannay in a John Buchan novel, and she'd had to resist the inclination to look over her shoulder every five minutes. Not to worry, said Tom – and his confidence was justified. Their arrival on board the York at RAF Lyneham, in Wiltshire, along with assorted civilians and a few army officers, was nonchalantly received by the breezy pilot, who was so used to ferrying odd bods around all over the place that he took it for granted plane-hopping was what everyone would do if they got the chance. Forces personnel, people on unspecified, official business, civvies scrounging lifts – as long as he didn't have to know the details, he took it as much in his stride as Tom had when faced with the bevy of new aunts he hadn't known he possessed.

* * *

Neither the journey nor the overnight stay at the RAF base at Luqa in Malta had been precisely comfortable, and Nina had arrived in Fayed the next day feeling airsick and jaded after the five hour flight from Malta, the drone of the aircraft's engines still in her ears, to find that Tom's estimation of what was boiling hot and hers didn't coincide. After a hitched lift into Ismailia, followed by a hot and sticky train journey into Cairo, encased in thick airforce blue serge, she wanted nothing more than a cool bath or shower.

Tom seemed to feel the need to apologise for a lack of comfort in the Heliopolis flat, but if there had been nothing else but sufficient water and a bed, Nina would have been satisfied. In fact it was a perfectly adequate second-floor apartment in a new block in what had once been a city created for the worship of the Sun-god, and was now a modern suburb of Cairo. It wasn't luxurious but it was spacious, sparely furnished for coolness in the heat of the summer. Faded, silky rugs on marble floors, where the insidious dust gritted under your feet and lay in a light film over everything. Books and artefacts untidily occupying every flat surface, making up for the scarcity of ornament. Clearly, it was the home of two men without female influence, who were rarely there, its only distinction being several paintings on the walls which it was impossible to ignore. "Your mother's?"

Tom nodded. "Pretty good, aren't they?"

"I suppose I shouldn't be surprised at how beautiful they are, after seeing what was left of those frescoes at Charnley," Nina replied, instantly drawn to them.

But these were gentle, exquisite watercolours, as far removed from what it had been possible to see of the decorations in the Jessamy rooms – or for that matter from the brilliant tomb paintings of Ancient Egypt – as it was possible to imagine. Modern paintings in soft muted tones that sought to capture the essence of this sun-baked land: the pale browns, beiges and salmon pinks of the sand and rocks, the soft turquoise and teal colours of sky and water. Reflections in the Nile, the sharp triangular sail of a felucca; an irrigated field, and white egrets following a solitary, Biblically-attired figure leading a buffalo and a plough; a sickle moon in a pale green evening sky; the glittering white domes of a mosque contrasting with the colourful, vibrant crowds in the narrow streets below. Tall stands of feathery palms at a watering place in the desert. The Pyramids at Giza rising from the arid desert sand; a group of racing camels.

Tom's voice broke into her absorption. "Would you like some tea? There's bound to be some, somewhere."

Still awash with the Thermos-tea doled out at regular intervals on the aircraft, full of the last packed meal, she declined the offer in favour of taking a shower, while Tom telephoned Iskander, who was expecting to hear from him. He'd previously made a brief telephone call from England, warning Iskander of their arrival – a difficult connection which Tom had had to book and wait hours for, and the line had been terrible. In the end he'd deemed it better to wait until now to make what was bound to be a complicated explanation of the real reason for this visit, The long conversation, conducted in Arabic, was still continuing when Nina, in a cotton wrap, emerged from the bathroom.

She wandered out on to the balcony until the call ended, leaning on the railing, sharing it with a small bright green lizard, lying motionless in the sun. A brilliant, rampant bougainvillaea twining itself around the rails of the balcony which looked out over the distant prospect of Cairo, several miles away, was luxuriant enough to provide shade as she gazed out over the city's minarets, spiking the sky through the haze. Traffic passed unceasingly below on the road into Cairo – modern cars and bell-ringing bicycles dodging the occasional camel or fodder-laden donkey. The air rising from below was thick with perfumes and the smell of dust and petrol fumes. England seemed very far away. As Tom came out to join her, she moved and the lizard suddenly darted away and disappeared, following its own compulsions.

"Sorry that took so long. I thought I ought to put the old boy in the picture as to how things are before we meet. He swears he knew nothing of what happened after he left Charnley the morning after the party, until Marcus told him about it when he came out here with my mother."

But, thought Nina, if Iskander had anything on his conscience, that would be the line he would take, wouldn't he?

"He seemed quite upset about Beatrice, and he wants us to meet to talk about it. He insists on buying us dinner tonight in the old town. I know the place, and the food will be good. Put your best bib and tucker on."

"What do you suggest I wear?" Every woman's first thought on being invited to any social occasion, and Nina was no exception. "My nice uniform or that silk frock of Harriet's she made me bring despite your advice not to bother about clothes?"

"Is that what I said?" He grinned. "If I did, it must have been because I knew you'd take no notice. Don't women always pack everything but the kitchen sink, regardless? Isn't that why your bag was so heavy?"

"I didn't notice you staggering under it."

A couple of cotton dresses, a light suit and Harriet's frock could hardly be regarded as excess baggage, thought Nina, as she made up her face, brushed her dark hair till it shone and put on Harriet's chestnut silk. Fashions hadn't moved forward much since the war, and it didn't feel dated, with its draped neckline and a sleek fit over the hips before falling into a gentle flare. And oh, what luxury, to feel silk against your skin – the chance to wear such borrowed finery! Especially if it brought to a man's face the sort of look that

Tom gave her as she came out on to the balcony where he was waiting for her.

But all he said was, "Come and watch this."

They leaned on the balcony rail, with the tops of the feathery palms waving below, watching an ineffable, glorious sunset of fiery oranges and rose-gold. He moved nearer and put his arm around her shoulders while the black velvet night dropped with startling rapidity. And there they stayed under the brilliance of the stars until it was time to leave, talking quietly. The bougainvillaea wreathing around them had lost its vividness but the starry blossoms of a creeper glowed white in the dusk. There was a jasmine somewhere whose scent was heavy on the night air. And electricity flashing between them where his hand rested on her flesh.

He said, "My father would love to meet you, I know. But that's for another time, hmm? He's working up-country at the moment. Pity he isn't here now."

But somehow she didn't think he really meant that.

Harriet had found Millie by the simple expedient of looking in the telephone directory. Not dead, after all then, but living in south London. She made a brief call, and arranged a visit for the next afternoon.

A bus took her to the nearest point, after which she found herself walking through ruined, scruffy streets of red brick houses and collapsed buildings, where children, rowdy as packs of stray mongrels, kicked balls and jumped to skipping ropes, and chalked hopscotch squares on the pavements. Buddleia and willow herb and bright yellow ragwort clung to unlikely places on staircases open to the street, on unsupported bedroom floors, sprang from rubble-filled basements. But quite suddenly, rounding the corner, Harriet was immediately into a quieter, more prosperous area, the way it happened in this city, working class streets cheek-by-jowl with those of higher pretensions – no less scarred, but not as dilapidated, and free of the ragamuffin hordes.

And here was where Millie now lived, a short, peaceful, cul-de-sac, miraculously untouched by bomb damage, as if invading aircraft might have been intimidated by its patrician elegance, the only evidence of war being the years of neglect to peeling paint and greying stucco. But the house Harriet sought at least had shining windows, scrubbed steps and a brightly polished bell push with several cards next to it. So, flats now. Millie, unlike Vita, didn't live in solitary splendour in this house. She pressed the bell next to the name Kaplan, Flat 1, and presently the door was opened, not by Millie herself, but by an elderly woman whose face was vaguely familiar. The hallway had a pre-war look and smell. Furniture polish, fresh flowers, old fashioned furniture. The woman nodded to Harriet, saying shortly, "Mrs Kaplan's expecting you." She stood back and indicated an inner door on the right, adding, "She's in the drawing room," at the same moment that Harriet placed her. It was Clara Hallam, her mother's maid. Older by nearly forty years, but not looking much different, hair now iron grey, upright and rigid as a broomstick, still flat as a washboard. Mouth drawn into a familiar purse of disapproval. I am not welcome, thought Harriet. The same aura of self-righteousness hung around the woman as it always had.

They looked at one another, unsmiling. "How are you?" said Harriet at last, recovering from the shock. "I didn't expect to see you here." The last person, actually.

"Didn't she tell you when you rang? I've been Mrs Kaplan's housekeeper for thirty-seven years."

Since she had ceased to be …. since that awful day…since – then. A disconcerting beginning to a meeting Harriet was already half wishing she hadn't instigated.

She collected herself and stepped forward. The door was

held open for her to pass through and closed after her, without a word of announcement. But then Millie, if this small person sitting by the fire was Millie, must have heard the exchange in the hall.

"I somehow expected you might come, even before you rang – one of you, at least, and I thought it would be you, Harriet. Excuse me for not getting up." A small claw-like hand indicated a stick leaning against her chair and was then held out, weighed down with rather grey diamonds. For some reason Harriet remembered that hand better than she remembered the face that went with it. For the woman in the chair seemed no more than middle-aged. And Millie had to be well over eighty.

"Sit over there where I can see you. That's right. Oh yes, I always knew you'd become handsome, Harriet. Good bones, one can always tell. You're wearing well – why have you never married? No, I won't ask. That seems to matter nothing these days." It *was* Millie, irreverent as ever.

"Thank you for agreeing to see me, Mrs Kaplan."

The gamine look that must have been so appealing when she was very young now gave her the appearance of a wise little monkey. And yet to Harriet, still disorientated after having the door opened to her by Clara Hallam, it seemed that Millie looked more attractive than she had in her middle years. Then she smiled, and when she did, the marks of a face-lift showed, one that had possibly taken place some time ago and at closer range could be seen to be in need of repair; there were all the tell-tale signs, the stretched skin at her temples, the lifted wattles and the tiny tucks beside her mouth. She had, however, wisely forsaken the heavy, rather desperate make-up of that time and was painted expertly and with care. Her silvery hair was drawn simply back. She was dressed severely in a black Chanel suit, and though she seemed to have shrunk, her upright posture and her perfectly groomed appearance gave her stature. Millie Kaplan, despite her rather racy past, had also worn well.

Harriet had been waved to a chair on the opposite side of the hearth, where a coal fire burned brightly. The room might have been lifted from her childhood memories of houses exactly like this. A cut-glass bowl of roses, rather too much beeswaxed furniture, tea set out on a lace edged cloth, a silver teapot. There was bread and butter (not marge), scones, real strawberry jam with no need of marrow to eke out the fruit, and a Fuller's walnut cake. Harriet was reminded that Millie Kaplan was very rich.

"Will you pour?"

Harriet dispensed the tea, passed the scones. Having enquired about Vita and Daisy (of course, Daisy was born to espouse causes – hadn't she been a suffragette once? And Vita – clever girl! – had always known which side her bread was buttered. Quite a catch, Wycombe – despite his age, but what did that signify?) Millie came straight to the point. "First let me say again how sorry I am about your mother – what a dreadful thing! Oh, my dear, when I read in the papers that she'd been found! My dearest friend, Bea! I thought my heart might not stand the shock. It isn't often, at my age, that I find I have cause to be ashamed, but I have to confess I was. That my first thought was of myself and my bad heart." Millie heaped jam on to a scone. "Do have some more of this. There's plenty more where it came from. I don't believe in rationing. All very well during the war, but what are they thinking of now? Mr Churchill would never have allowed it to go on. Too many of those dreadful Labourites around – you take my advice and keep your eye on them!" She passed the cut glass jam dish across. "All these years, I've been condemning her – and now!"

The jam was stiff with fruit, rich and red on the silver spoon. Harriet deposited some carefully on her plate and then looked up, to find Millie's bright, intelligent eyes on her face. "My mother? Condemning her? So you too believed that she'd run away with Iskander?"

"Frankly, yes. What else was there to believe? Despite evidence to the contrary. I'm sorry, perhaps you don't think it's proper for me to say that of your mama."

"The time for being proper has long past. But...what do you mean by evidence to the contrary?"

"Ah, well, now–" Millie looked a little put out, as if she'd said more than she meant.

"I *have* read what she wrote in what she called her Egyptian journal," Harriet prompted, unwisely, because it allowed Millie to avoid an answer to her question.

"So that's what you've come to see me about. You want to know about that trip up the Nile."

"Yes. I believe what happened there must have had some bearing on her murder. If you're sure it won't tire you–"

"Tire me? Harriet, I used to be the greatest gossip in London and it isn't often I get the chance nowadays! And I've always thought that was where it all started – your mother and father were never the same afterwards." Millie's hand went to her gold chains. The loose rings on her fingers slipped about and winked in the firelight. "He filled her head with silly nonsense."

"My father did?"

"Amory?" Millie laughed, not quite kindly. "Can you imagine him having the imagination to fill anyone's head with nonsense? Nor the sense of humour, if you'll forgive me. No, I mean the Egyptian, of course. He was besotted with her."

Harriet sipped her tea. "He must have been very young at the time."

"Well, that's hardly anything new, is it? A young man's infatuation for a beautiful, older woman? Especially when she encourages it. Oh, don't look like that ! It was quite the thing, you know, in our day, not frowned upon at all – or not much, in certain circles. Rather romantic – courtly love, and all that, a knight and his lady. And Bea – well, she was never averse to being – admired – by anyone." She cocked a bright eye at Harriet. There was a sense of more being meant than was actually being said.

Harriet was silent. Needing time to absorb and accept this not very acceptable view of her mother, although it merely endorsed what Kit had written, she dived into her bag and brought out some of the photographs taken at the birthday celebrations that she had thought might be needed to jog an old woman's memory. She needn't have been afraid of that, but she handed them over just the same.

"Oh, dear!" exclaimed Millie, immediately diverted by the one of herself. "What a mistake it is to look at oneself forty years ago – how very ageing that outfit was!" She threw a complacent look at Harriet, as if expecting a comment that she now looked younger than ever. And perhaps compliments are due, Harriet thought, if only on the way she was managing to live. Here she was, having survived those terrible wartime years, as surely only someone like Millie could, living on black market food and what must have been hoarded perfume and cosmetics and the clothes her clever, expensive dressmaker had designed for her in better days. Looked after by that dragon. Hallam. But let's not approach the subject of Hallam just yet.

Harriet declined another scone, and obediently poured more tea for both of them.

"That journey up the Nile was a mistake, you know," went on Millie. "Nothing to do, day after day, but watch the scenery – which I must say all looked the same, after a while – unless you took trips to visit those boring ruins. I think Glendinning had it right – use the trip to get in some fishing and shooting. He had a wonderful time at the Turf Club, too. Boring, did I say? Well, not always. Intimidating, sometimes. Some of those places frightened the life out of Bea, and no mistake."

"Like the temple at Luxor?"

"Yes," said Millie shortly, casting her a quick sidelong look. She glanced again at the photos she'd placed on her lap and picked out the one showing Iskander. "He didn't look like that in Egypt. Mostly wore one of those nightshirt things, like a native, though I must admit he was a cut above that. But it wasn't calculated to make one regard him as an equal, though Bea never seemed to see it that way."

Harriet was becoming accustomed to Millie's jumpy, inconsequential conversation and determined not to be thrown off the subject. "When you say she was frightened, you must have been meaning the experience in the temple at Luxor?"

Millie said, after a pause. "Must I? Perhaps. Well, I don't know if I can explain that. You haven't, by any chance, been to Egypt?"

"Regretfully, no."

Millie fell silent again, crumbling a morsel of scone on her plate. "Those old tombs – I'm not a very imaginative person, Harriet, but I have to say there was definitely something creepy about them. It doesn't take much to credit those tales about the curse on the opening of Tutankhamun's tomb – though of course that wasn't discovered then. But those dim torch lights, the silence and the stifling heat...there were bats." She shuddered, remembering. "So many dead people – no matter they'd been dead thousands of years. There was something unnatural, uncanny about those sarcophagi – and those mummies–" She stopped abruptly. "Forgive me. I'm an insensitive old woman."

Perhaps *mummy* had not been a well-chosen word in the

circumstances, but Millie was not as insensitive as all that, thought Harriet, and a good deal sharper than anyone had ever given her credit for. She began to wonder if her mother had not perhaps been quite fair to her friend in that journal of hers. "What *about* the Luxor temple?"

Millie's expression showed she wasn't eager to reopen the subject, but since that was why Harriet was here, she wasn't going to let it go willingly. And after a while, Millie sighed. "Something happened to her there – some weird experience that I, for one, didn't feel, though I was there. She said afterwards she felt some sort of horror that she couldn't explain, someone close behind her who actually touched her intimately. At which point, she turned and ran – bumping her head on the door lintel and passing out for a few minutes. We got her back to the hotel and into bed. She was perfectly all right afterwards."

"She described all that in her journal. Do you think she could have imagined it?"

"Wishful thinking, more like. Oh dear, I'm sorry – whatever it was, it simply terrified her. But it didn't excuse–"

"Go on. Please."

"No, I've said enough." She closed her eyes briefly. "I'm too old for all this."

"You know that's not true! Go on – what happened next?"

Millie continued to be evasive. "Nothing. Amory arrived the next day, then we went on to Assuan, and Abu Simbel, that's all."

"She was well enough to go with you?"

"Oh yes, we all went, then we returned to Luxor. Your father had found he could spend a little more time there than he'd originally thought, so the men spent several days exploring the temples on the west bank. Neither Bea nor I went with them. She'd already been there once, and I'd no desire to go. The crew took the boat back to Cairo, but we'd decided to return by train. We stayed in the hotel meanwhile. Lovely hotel," she added reminiscently, "I believe it's called the Winter Palace now."

"And that's all? That's all that happened? What about Iskander?"

"Oh," Millie said vaguely. "He'd suddenly decided to go back to Cairo. He left us before Amory arrived. They were all like that, you know, the Egyptians. Unpredictable."

Harriet said, with sudden insight, "It wasn't what happened to my mother in the temple that was important, was it? It was what happened afterwards. Was it something to do with Iskander – and why he left so unexpectedly?"

"Your mother always said that you were too sharp for your own good, Harriet!" Relapsing into silence, Millie closed her eyes for so long that Harriet thought she might have dropped off to sleep. But then she opened them and they were sharp and bright as ever. "Let it be," she said, "No good will come of stirring mischief up at this stage."

"It's a little more than mischief! Somebody *killed* my mother, strangled her. It's a matter of trying to find out who did."

"Does it matter now? Iskander's probably dead himself by now. It's only old dinosaurs like me who are still alive. And Myles Randolph, or so I hear."

Harriet said, "Iskander is, too. He's a respected professor of Egyptology at the university in Cairo." There was a silence. A lump of coal fell into the heart of the fire. Ash feathered around it and then the flames burned brighter.

"That cross you're wearing – he gave it to her. An ankh, it's called – supposed to be the symbol of life. Ironic, isn't it?"

Harriet had forgotten she had been wearing it, like a talisman, ever since coming across it. "She was fascinated by him, wasn't she?"

"Iskander? Yes, in a way. He intrigued her. So much so that

I began to think she might do something very silly, that she might have regretted, but we arrived in Luxor quite soon and that put a stop to that."

"My father arriving, you mean?"

"No," Millie said quickly, "I simply meant that we were back with civilised company."

Her tongue still ran away with her as, according to Amory, it always had. A rattle-pate he'd called her, perhaps not without reason. Had she been referring to *Wycombe*? That meeting him again in Luxor had provided opportunity for clandestine meetings with Beatrice? Had the affair started then? Or had it started earlier, in Cairo perhaps? And had Amory found out – either then, or later? Or suspected – and then, on Beatrice's birthday night many years later, found them together – and killed her? Insupportable thought – and in that case...why had he spared Wycombe? Perhaps a more subtle revenge had been exacted in taking his own – to him now worthless – life, and leaving Wycombe with a lifetime of guilt. It was a picture Harriet could all too easily envisage – the nightmare she had been afraid of all along, the alternative to Kit having killed Beatrice. People, perhaps Beatrice most of all, had always underestimated Amory, looked at his surface sobriety and failed to see the underlying depth of feeling and emotion.

Where did Iskander, then, fit into this? "What bothers me," Harriet said, "is why my mother *did* invite Valery Iskander to Charnley. She didn't seem to like him very much, as I remember, whatever she'd once thought of him."

"Unfinished business? To make amends? Who knows? Whatever the reason, she made the biggest mistake of her life."

"You do believe he killed her, don't you?"

But Millie, having planted her barb of suspicion, shrugged and was not to be drawn further. She shook her head and helped herself to another slice of walnut cake, dabbing at the crumbs of coffee icing with her finger.

"You know," she said at last, unexpectedly, "I used to envy Bea her beauty, the way men fell at her feet, but beauty's a burden. Your mother couldn't cope with it."

Thinking of the way Beatrice had always seemed to accept compliments as her due, so graciously, this sounded to Harriet very much like a contradiction. But then Millie added, "She had to live up to it all the time, seeking reassurances, because it was all she had, in the end."

This was shrewd of her. It was the first time anyone else had ventured to remark on it. Harriet herself had always secretly felt that Beatrice might have had few inner resources to fall back on, but recent events had shown that was too easy a judgement, too superficial. Beatrice had been a more complex character than that. She – and Millie – could both have been cruelly underestimating her. "Didn't she ever worry that sort of thing might distress my father, I wonder?"

"I shouldn't think so," said Millie, "Beatrice never thought of anyone but herself, did she?"

Half an hour later, Harriet knew she'd wrung from Millie as much as she was prepared to divulge. Before she left, however, she had to know about Hallam. "She told me she's been here since she left Charnley."

"Yes. My maid at the time had just left me and I hadn't found another. I knew Clara would be looking for another position. She wasn't keen to come and live in London, but she agreed to give me her services until I found someone else. As it happens, she decided to stay. She's been with me getting on for forty years."

What could account for this surprising change of heart on both sides? According to Beatrice's journal, Millie had endured the sour Hallam's ministrations with ill grace after

Millie's own maid had departed in Cairo, leaving her high and dry.

"She's a dismal old thing but we've always managed to rub along," Millie said, reading her thoughts, "in fact, I doubt I should manage at all without her if ever she were to leave. Though of course, she never would." Her tight smile bordered on the secretive, but for a moment there, her face had looked quite bleak at the prospect.

"Come again, Harriet. It's been a long time since I saw anyone from the old days."

"I will." Impulsively, Harriet bent and kissed her. "I'm sorry we lost touch. It's been a pleasure to meet you again." This was true, for Millie, despite age, arthritis and loneliness, had lost none of her vivacity, the sparkle that had been so appealing in her younger days.

Hallam was there at the door the instant she opened it, too quickly for her to have been far away. Closing it firmly behind Harriet, she walked with her down the hall to the front door. There she paused in the act of opening it. "I heard about them – finding your mother," she began stiffly. She hesitated, then plunged her hand into her pocket. "Here, take this!"

Harriet reached out to take the manila envelope but the old woman kept it clutched tightly in her knotted hand, reluctant to let it go. "What is it?"

"Only some old papers she asked me to take care of before she – before she – disappeared."

Harriet was nonplussed. "I don't think I understand."

What was the woman implying? That Beatrice had had some prescience of her death? She refused to believe that of her mother – though maybe she had been afraid of prying eyes seeing what she'd written, and Hallam's next words seemed to confirm this.

"You know what she was like. Secretive."

Clara Hallam was no longer the lady's maid, having to watch her words and her attitudes. After a distance of forty years, bringing altered relationships, the need for pretence had gone and she was able to speak the plain truth without fear or favour – yet the criticism was unconsciously softened by a sigh, and Harriet knew that she was lying. Given that strange, twisted relationship she suspected had existed between them, it was scarcely credible that Beatrice would have entrusted Hallam with an envelope containing private papers, even supposing she'd had any unlikely premonitions of her coming death. If the point of it was secrecy, she would surely have been aware of the possibility that the woman might open it?

"They're pages from her journal, aren't they?"

Harriet had once or twice come across her mother in her bedroom, reading or writing in that mysterious little grey suede book, and at such times it had immediately been slipped into a drawer. Hallam, however, would certainly have known of its existence and although it was furnished with a lock, would have known where the key was hidden – as it undoubtedly would have been. Harriet was convinced that it was Hallam herself who had cut those pages out, and kept them for reasons of her own – but why? Out of misplaced loyalty to her mistress, because they had contained something damaging to Beatrice?

Had Harriet so far misjudged her?

After a moment, Hallam nodded. "Yes, that's what they are."

"Why didn't you hand them over before?"

"That doesn't matter. They weren't important, as it turned out – but they might be now."

She saw that the woman's eyes, like Millie's, had been drawn to the golden ankh on its chain around Harriet's neck, and that she was staring at it, fascinated.

"Do you believe in ghosts?" she asked suddenly, moving to stand too closely for comfort near Harriet. She was not, after all, as unchanged as Harriet had thought. On the contrary, at such close quarters she showed every year of her age in her face, every bitter thought that had dragged it into its harsh lines. "I do, and so should you. Mark my words, you should! They come back to haunt you, when you least expect it. You shouldn't have interfered. But you always were a meddlesome creature!"

"That's rubbish!" Taken aback as she was by the spite, Harriet still noted that Hallam had probably overheard most of her conversation with Millie. Interfere? What had she done that anyone could class as interference? Nothing more than insist that the past events she'd resurrected from Beatrice's journals had some significance, and she was certain this wasn't something she might later come to regret. Wasn't she?

She realised the envelope was at last being thrust into her hands, and only when it was safely stowed in her bag did the maid snatch up her coat that was lying across a chair, almost throwing it at her. "Go now." Her voice was shaking. "And don't come back, bothering her. She can't tell you anything – and never forget, she was a good friend to your mother, despite everything."

Harriet left, closing the door very quietly behind her.

Chapter Eighteen

The restaurant where they had arranged to meet Iskander was a narrow building halfway down a shadowy street situated somewhere in the dun-coloured confusion of the old city, crammed with the sort of shops that might have come straight out of The Arabian Nights. Flaring torches and single electric light bulbs dangling from a flex were the only illumination for the dark interiors of booths piled with splendours like Aladdin's cave. Trading was still being carried on as they made their way to the rendezvous, the whole ceaseless bustling life of the city continuing undiminished by the arrival of darkness.

Iskander was late. "Not to worry, he'll be here" commented Tom, unfazed and clearly not expecting anything else, accustomed to the masterly sense of inactivity and supreme indifference to the clock that was masked by the noise and commotion in which Egyptians existed. Why hurry? Life here was but a footstep in the sands of time. A man who makes haste is a man who has no faith in the eternity of Allah.

Nina herself wasn't unduly impatient for Iskander to arrive. She was quite happy to watch the passing scene while sitting comfortably in a rattan chair in the restaurant window, in front of the velvet curtains behind which the serious business of eating was going on. On a window-seat nearby, a middle-aged Egyptian couple, smartly dressed, she with her plump fingers loaded with diamonds, he with gold, sat blissfully sharing a narghile. As they smoked, the gurgle of the water through the glass pipes provided a gentle accompaniment to the Arab music wailing from within the dim interior of the restaurant. She and Tom sipped scented, syrupy, violet-coloured dinks from tiny glasses, brought to them by the proprietor himself, who had welcomed Tom back like one of the lost sheep of the house of Israel.

At last he arrived. Valery Akhmet Iskander. Despite the photograph taken at the birthday party, when he'd been wearing western dress, Nina had formed in her head a picture of a dark figure in a traditional white galabeya. But here he was, snappily dressed for the occasion in a sand-coloured suit, a dazzling white shirt and a red tie. She knew him to be of mixed race but here, in the flesh, it seemed to her as though the Russian in him had grown predominant as he'd grown older. His hair was no longer dark but grizzled. He was lighter-skinned than she had imagined he would be, stockily built and inclined to a paunch. His smile stretching from ear to ear, he threw his arms around Tom and kissed him on both cheeks. Then he stood back, regarding him intently. Gently, he put up a hand and touched the scar on his face. "A badge of courage, my dear young friend," he said softly. "I am so very sorry."

"Inshallah, Valery. Malish." Nina suspected Tom's tongue was firmly in his cheek. *The will of Allah. It doesn't matter.* Well, maybe it didn't, to Allah.

With an ambiguous wave of his hand and his brilliant smile, Iskander accepted, or brushed aside, this fatalism. "It does my heart good to hear you call me by my name again. No one calls me that any more – Professor, yes. Or just Iskander. The young are too egalitarian, eh? These Nationalists. And this, I take it, is Miss Nina? Enchanté, m'selle."

Her hand was taken in his warm, plump clasp and raised to his lips. Dark spectacles obscured the full impact of those famous light eyes, until he took them off and gave her a very shrewd look. She thought, yes, for all his cordiality, this was a man capable of harbouring deep resentments.

"Come, let's eat, and then you must tell me all that has happened to you since we last met, Tom."

"When we have time – it's not me we came here to talk about."

"Patience, patience! I have known this young man since he was born, Miss Nina, and he was impatient in the cradle. I knew his lovely mother. His father is one of my oldest, closest friends who taught me all I know."

Did he know that Marcus was Tom's father? Almost certainly. He must have been aware of the situation between Rose Jessamy and Marcus when they arrived in Cairo. And it had been he, after all, who had introduced Rose to the man she was eventually to marry.

All affability and charm, he led the way to reserved seats at a small table in the dim, pulsating interior of the restaurant and ordered a meal whose component parts, apart from some tender lamb kebabs, were unfamiliar to Nina, but the total sum of which was light and delicious. Tom advised her on the choice of falafel, tamaiya patties, seared aubergine and hummus. Iskander pressed her to a glass of mint tea. The serving of the meal was conducted in a leisurely manner that suggested tomorrow was another day, but while waiting for the food to be brought to the table, there were diversions in the form of a dervish dancer, who was rewarded with uproarious applause, as was the emotional Egyptian woman singer who replaced her. Everyone was enjoying themselves immensely. The heat grew and the noise level intensified. It was impossible to talk. "Come home with me," Iskander said abruptly, as soon as they had finished eating. "We can talk better there."

They emerged into the heavy dark night, daytime heat held by the buildings, and from somewhere, Iskander summoned a cab. Hooting and nudging its way through the dense traffic, it eventually deposited them outside a tall narrow building near the arch of the old Fatimid Gate, in a thronged street smelling strongly of spices, filled with dark little shops, and stalls selling but one commodity each – garlic, or oranges, or tomatoes – where trade was still vociferously being carried on under the flare of naphtha lights. Watched closely by three swarthy men in striped galabeyas, smoking under the shelter of an awning, they followed where Iskander led, into the dark interior of a shop, where the chief merchandise seemed to be pots, pans and baskets of every kind, through a door in the back and thence up some narrow stairs which led into his quarters above. "Welcome to my home," he said, quietly but not without pride, seeing Nina's eyes widen at the sight of the room which, though narrow, ran back to front of the whole building, making its size considerable. "I'm lucky, am I not, to live in such great comfort here?"

He fussed around, insisting on providing refreshments, though they had just eaten a full meal. It was not until they were settled on low divans with tiny cups of sweet, thick coffee poured from a planished copper pot with a long, curved spout, and small, sticky sweetmeats in filigree silver dishes were placed in front of them that Iskander indicated he was prepared to hear what they had come to say.

"Sorry to have sprung it on you, but we haven't much time before we go back to England," said Tom.

"Always in such a hurry, Tom! All this way, and now you must rush back. Do try one of these, Miss Nina, they are delicious. No?" He chose for himself a tiny pastry, covered in honey and almonds, and popped it into his mouth.

"I wish we didn't have to go back so quickly, I'd have liked Nina to see something of Cairo, but there's no time. We're here unofficially, as it is."

Iskander smiled understandingly at this. That was something he recognised, pulling strings, greasing palms, bargaining. Then his smile faded. "So, to this sad business. You wish me to help. How can I do this? But stay a moment – I think you may find this difficult to believe, but I must repeat it, for it is the absolute truth. When I left Charnley that morning, I knew nothing of the events that had happened there. I went straight to London and took ship for Egypt as soon as I could. In too much of a hurry perhaps, but I had my reasons. I had no idea that Beatrice had disappeared, until I heard it from her son when he came here." His face set in melancholy lines. "And now she has been found. Such a tragedy."

He listened with a grave, then incredulous face to the explanations of where and how Beatrice's body had been discovered. "Bayah-tree-chay. How beautiful she was. A perfect English rose. And her deportment! Not even the women of Nubia, trained from childhood to carry loads upon their heads, could have been more graceful!" He heaved a deep sigh and chose another pastry. "And so – the mystery of her disappearance is now solved – leaving an even greater mystery, eh? I have no doubt the police suspect me."

"The man in charge doesn't appear to think so."

"Nevertheless…"

A small silence ensued. Tom fingered his scar. Uncertain as to how to proceed – or perhaps unwilling. An hour or two earlier, after his call to Iskander, he had surprised Nina by saying, "I fear she's going to be disappointed."

"Who is?"

"Harriet. She's so adamant that Iskander must be involved."

"And you don't want to admit it, if he is?"

"Iskander's my father's friend – and mine. I just don't want to believe he had anything to do with the damned affair."

Nina had realised, of course, that he'd wanted to come here, not to establish Iskander's guilt, but his innocence. And now that the subject of the Nile trip and the reasons why the party had split up in Luxor had to be broached, she could see Tom was hesitant to begin. Well, she was the one, after all, who had read Beatrice's journal in full, whereas Tom had only had time to read it in parts; the rest of what he knew was only what she had been able to tell him. She was duty-bound to help him out.

The large room was cool, and smelled faintly of spices and jasmine. Iskander was evidently a man of taste, and not short of money. Against white walls and a marble floor were dark antiques and ancient rugs, sitting in pools of light cast by hanging lamps of wrought iron and jewel-coloured glass. The sofas on which they sat bore huge cushions of damask and silk in glowing colours. A whole wall was devoted to books. Mushrabiyeh-work tables carved in lacy trellis bore many more. There was again that light, gritty dust over everything, as if the desert sand encroached even this far into the city. Dust that filtered everywhere, impossible to keep out.

Into the silence the noises of the street intruded, just as Nina was about to speak Voices were raised in shouts. The unmistakable roaring groan of a camel was unexpectedly heard among the hooting of motor horns and a policeman's whistle. Iskander showed no surprise or irritation, but rose and pulled the shutters across the two tiny trellised balconies which overlooked the street, and the room was enclosed in its own quietness again.

The small interlude had given Nina time to decide how to begin. She explained about the journal which Beatrice had written, and which Harriet had discovered, and found Iskander responding quite willingly to the prompting.

"Ah, yes, that journal!" He smiled reminiscently. "I remember how she would write in it, each day, on the dahabeah, how she would recall what we had seen and ask me to explain the intricacies and contradictions of this land."

"She did seem to find your country very strange and hard to understand."

"But she was in thrall to it, as many other people have been. It has held – and still does hold – a strange fascination, and no-one can tell who this may fall upon."

"I think she was a little frightened of how it made her feel. One experience in particular seems to have affected her very strangely. Do you recall an incident in the temple at Luxor?"

He shrugged and spread his hands, which could have meant yes or no, and watched her as she went on to recount what Beatrice had written about the episode, aware even as she did that this was perhaps open to interpretation. "Whatever it was, I think it affected her so much because she had just, before starting out on the trip, lost an unborn child."

The light eyes stared at her piercingly. His face was expressionless, but she thought he hadn't known this before. The room had become close since shutting the windows and he rose to switch on an electric ceiling fan. The paddles whirred lazily, stirring the warm air but not bringing much coolness in. The silence went on, during which he absently demolished a couple more of the delicacies in the silver dish and drank some more coffee.

Finally, he said, "I will tell you the story as best I can."

"The English party were staying at the Luxor Hotel – now the Winter Palace. There had been an incident in the temple earlier that day, which was troubling me very much – or rather, my dear lady's reaction to it was. It was fortunate that she had recovered so quickly from the injury to her head, but I could not make out what it was that had made her so afraid that she had turned to flee and thus not taken enough care." He paused. In the effort to find the right words to convey his meaning, the hitherto easy flow of his English was becoming stilted. "She was taken back to the hotel to lie down and recover, and the visit to the temple was abandoned by the rest of the party. Later, in the cool of the evening, I walked up to the hotel from where the dahabeah was moored, to find out how she was. As I entered the gardens of the hotel, I saw a pale glimmer ahead of me in the darkness – and there she was, walking towards me, dressed in a loose white gown. I was overjoyed to find she had recovered and I hurried to meet her, hoping to speak with her and find out what had caused her to become so distressed that she had fled the temple and walked blindly into the stone lintel. When I drew level with her, I could see that she seemed to be weeping bitterly, and hadn't been aware of my approach. It distressed me very much to see her in such condition and I stepped up to her and reached out to take her hand, hoping to comfort her in a way she had always found soothing. To my astonishment, she half-screamed and drew back, crying, 'Don't touch me! Haven't you done enough already?' Her sobs increased and she turned about and ran back the way she had come, straight into the arms of Major Randolph. 'Don't let him touch me! Keep him away from me!' She was quite hysterical. And then I saw that she was holding together the bodice of her gown, as if it had been torn open..."

His affront was palpable. Time had done nothing to soften the impact of his shock, but after a second or two he went on with a tale evidently still crystal clear in his mind.

"Ah well, I forget myself. It is of no matter, now... She began to scream that I had touched her – improperly – that afternoon in the temple, that I had just attempted it again. She was hysterical. As for Major Randolph, that stiff Englishman, he was beside himself with fury. He sheltered her in his arms, while reviling me with all the names under the sun. Imagine my feelings! I had no idea what she meant by those accusations, but she was led away and I was given no chance to defend myself, then or thereafter. My protestations were not listened to and she – she said not a word in my defence. I was struck dumb by her treachery."

He leaned forward and filled their three tiny cups with yet more of the cloying coffee and after sipping, went on: "The sum of it was, I was dismissed, sent back to Cairo like a criminal. I burned with the injustice of it, but I was a young man, only just embarking on my career, with little or no redress against people like that. And it followed me, that incident. I had done nothing wrong, it was blown out of all proportion, but my days of guiding European parties around to earn a little money to help me until I established myself as a teacher were numbered. I had no choice but to try and forget it. I did the best I could for money, plunged deep into my studies and I might say came through with the highest honours, helped and encouraged by your father, Tom – by Professor Verrier. Gradually, of course, as the years went by, the incident was forgotten – by all but me. The unfairness of it still rankled. I determined I would not rest until I had seen Beatrice Jardine once more and forced her to tell me why she had levelled those false accusations against me. Then I would be satisfied. By that time, I had reached a professorship myself. I arranged to take time off, and went over to England. I wrote to her, asking her to see me, though I did not expect her to agree. I would have forced myself into her presence, if necessary. However, there was no need for that. To my amazement, she wrote back in the most pleasant terms, inviting me to stay with her and her family at their country home."

"You didn't go over to England to see her with the idea of revenge?" Tom interrupted the flow gravely. Revenge, to the Arab nature, was a matter of honour, and Iskander was part Russian, as well, not a nation renowned for lying down for ever under injustice.

"No, no. As Allah is my witness, that was not my intention. I would have been satisfied if she had simply given me a reason for doing what she did, had told me in what way I had offended her. At first, I was puzzled as to why she had invited me to Charnley at all, but I soon realised that she feared I would make trouble if the invitation had been withheld, and that she hoped to persuade me that the business in Luxor had all been a big mistake. 'I did not know what I was doing that evening, Valery,' she said, whenever I approached the subject. 'That bump on my head must have made me a lit-tle delirious. Can't you understand?' She begged my forgive-ness for casting suspicion on me, but how could I give it without some more satisfactory explanation? Her conduct had nearly ruined my prospects of a career and I could not easily forgive that. On reflection, I realised she was playing for time, trying to think of a way she might wriggle out of the situation. But I was older and more experienced than I had been in Luxor, and I was on my guard. I had no intention of being caught in the same way twice, for I had begun to see her in a very different light." He shrugged. "Maybe she had changed, or maybe I had previously been simply too naive. What I did see was that she was toying with the young man – Kit – as she had with me all those years ago. He was neither so young or so naive as I had been that time in Luxor, but still, I could see he was dazzled by her. She was playing him off against Lord Wycombe – in the same way she had once played me off against him." Iskander paused dramatically.

"Trying to make Wycombe–"

"Jealous? Exactly, Miss Nina. Well, finally, I lost my patience. I had not come all that way to be fobbed off. I wanted a full admission from her, an apology – and I wanted it then. I told her at her birthday party that I would wait no longer, that if she would not agree to give an explanation that satisfied me, I would go straight to her husband. I could see she was frightened by that. She told me to meet her in the conservatory after the party was over. So, after the last guest had departed, I went there and waited. And waited. I stayed there until the house should grow silent. But there was much noise, which went on for a long time. There were many com-ings and goings, mostly, I think, due to the exuberance of the young people. Because there had been elderly people at the celebration, who left early, the party was over too soon for them, before it came to its natural end and everyone was tired enough to go straight to bed and sleep soundly."

He smiled faintly. "I had heard of what went on at those country house parties, but that night there were no unattached lady guests and the daughters of the house were of unexceptionable character. No, I believed Beatrice was waiting until all had settled before she came down, so I curbed my impatience. I sat and smoked until the butler – what was his name? Ah yes, Mr Albrighton – came in on his rounds, to check that everything was secure for the night. He asked me politely if there was anything I required but I said no, I would finish my cigarette and then go to bed. He turned off all the lamps but one, bade me a civil goodnight, and I was left alone again.

"When it became apparent she was not going to come, I put out my cigarette and sat quietly, thinking about what I should do. I must have fallen into a trance, or I may have dozed. When I came to, I was stiff and cramped. I stood up, ready to retire to my room, when I heard someone come in through the very door that Albrighton had just locked. I drew back a little, into the shadows behind a large plant, but I must have made some sound, for I suddenly felt myself seized roughly by the shoulders and pulled forward into what light there was.

"'Take your hands off me, Copley.' I had recognised my assailant as the chauffeur.

"He gave a curse. 'What were you doing, hiding there in the dark – sir.' The last word was added as an afterthought, servant that he was. The insolence of his tone was not to be believed, but he had never shown me any respect, having all the Englishman's distrust of 'foreigners'. He added, with a little more prudence, but hardly less insolently, that I had startled him, he hadn't seen me sitting there in the shadows. Which was clearly meant to be – and was – taken as a reference to the colour of my skin.

"'What are you doing in here this time of night?' I asked. In the dim lamplight, he looked wild and dangerous – and, I thought, not a little afraid.

"It was then that I saw why he might have reason to be – for he had a companion with him. 'My sister and I wanted to have a private word, sir.'

"His sister, that was a rich invention! The woman who had been standing behind him, and who had said not a word was Beatrice's maid, Clara Hallam. I knew the woman well, but disliked her none the less for all that – we had, after all, spent several weeks together in the close confines of the dahabeah. What the pair of them were doing there was none of my business, or indeed, how they had entered through the conservatory door when I had just seen the butler lock it. I assumed an assignation between the two – and that the chauffeur had no doubt at some time had a key cut for his own purposes. It was apparent they had been up to no good, but that was not my concern, I had other, more important, things to think of.

"'I will not mention this to anyone,' I told them. 'I am leaving' – I glanced at my watch, it was nearly three in the morning – 'by the earliest train.' For this was the decision I had come to. It was a sad end to my bold enterprise, but during my long vigil, I had seen how futile my hopes were. After closely observing her behaviour towards the two men she had been flirting with that evening, under her husband's very nose, seeing how she enjoyed the spice of danger, I had come to the conclusion that I was not going to get the explanation I had come to England for, much less an apology, from Beatrice Jardine. She had merely been putting me off all this time. If necessary, she would have gone to Amory herself, to put him against me before I had the chance to speak. For all his reserve, anyone could see he was besotted with her and would have believed her rather than me. More importantly, I believed that now the explanation for her previous – and her present – conduct, was self-evident. She was in love with Lord Wycombe, and he with her, though I had seen that all was not well between them. I disliked Wycombe as heartily as I believe he disliked me, but I believed him to be a man of honour. I guessed he was guilty about carrying on an affair with his friend's wife, reluctant to continue – or resume – what I believed had begun in Egypt. I saw that she was again trying to make him jealous, this time by using the young fellow Kit as she had once used me. I think, perhaps, until that time in Luxor, Wycombe had resisted her but, recalling vividly how she had run into his arms after pretending I had violated her, how tenderly he had held her...yes, I am certain that was when it had begun."

"'I'll say no more about this,' I repeated to the chauffeur, 'But you will drive me to the station to catch the first train to London in the morning.'

"We looked at each other and he knew that I was capable of carrying out my threat. Which he obviously had every reason to be afraid of. His 'sister' had said not a word throughout.

"'Not in the motorcar,' Copley said, 'The trap will have to do.'

"And with that I had to be content. Thus did I leave Charnley. My hopes dashed..."

Chapter Nineteen

It could only be a good omen, the letter which arrived for Harriet that morning from Tony Bentham's solicitor, lifting some of the gloom occasioned by that encounter with Clara Hallam the previous day. The solicitor informed her that Tony had met and married an Australian woman in South America, would not be returning to England and therefore had no further need of his cottage. Harriet was to be given first refusal to buy it, and whatever of its contents might have taken her fancy.

This was something she hadn't dared to hope for, yet now that the opportunity presented itself it hit her like a blow to the stomach that much as she loved the cottage, buying it would mean commitment to the kind of life she wasn't sure she wanted to be permanent. Finding somewhere like this had filled a need, but was she prepared to spend the rest of her life pottering about in this quiet village where nothing happened? Was that what she really wanted? Unsettled, baffled by her own disconcerting change of heart, she made herself a cup of coffee, putting off a decision for the time being. The travellers – Tom and Nina – were due to land any time now from Egypt and before they arrived, she wanted to get her mind straight about the packet Hallam had thrust into her hands.

It constituted a disjointed collection of small snippets and snatches, written at various times in the weeks just prior to her mother's death, almost as though Beatrice had felt compelled to use her Egyptian journal in an attempt to finish the story begun there, to close the circle.

'*I have had a letter from Valery Iskander,*' the first of the pages began, '*and am at my wits' end to know what to do. It gave me such a shock that I was prostrate for a whole day after* reading it, lying in my darkened bedroom with one of my headaches. Neither smelling salts, eau-de-cologne nor Hallam's tisanes helped in the least. He wants to come and see me here, at Charnley! I had thought that was all behind me, that terrible time in Luxor...'

Then later: 'Nothing must be allowed to disturb the sweet tenor of our lives – so dearly fought for, so hardly won – yet still so precarious! It would kill Amory to find out what started in Egypt, what has continued, albeit only occasionally, but I am afraid that Iskander will betray me to him. The only way is to invite him here, to see what I can to do prevent that happening.'

Later still: 'He is here. He frightens me to the depths of my being. I look at those cold, light eyes and I believe he is quite capable of killing me if I do not do as he wants. But if I do, I shall be held up to ridicule, and as for my husband...

'Amory frightens me, too. For all we have been married these five-and-twenty years I do not believe I truly understand him. Beneath his reserve, I know there is a depth of passion I can no longer arouse. I have tried, God knows I have tried, but all too often he puts me aside when I move towards him, as if I had suggested something shameful. Without physical connection, what is there to hold him to me? It maddens me to distraction, for I am still attractive to other men. I have not yet, like Millie, lost my looks. Yet it is only by the reassurances of men like Kit, like Iskander eleven years ago, and in a sense by Myles, that I am able to keep the fear at bay. There are times when I wonder if Amory suspects, times when I am sure he does, for what else can explain his indifference to me?'

Another entry, different ink: 'Oh, God, what am I to do? If Iskander forces me to tell the truth, Amory will see it as a humiliation to himself, which is the one thing above all others that he cannot stand.'

The next page was written in such haste, or distress, every

stroke of the headlong writing expressing frustration and fear, that it was barely decipherable. *'Valery Iskander is no longer the eager boy who danced attendance on me and stroked my hands and told me foolish, allegorical stories of princesses and crocodiles and how the sand obscures the shape of whatever lies beneath it. Perhaps not so foolish, at that. Perhaps he was saying how lies can obscure the reality. It was pleasant then to encourage his admiration, and rather daring, though of course nothing could have come of an association with him. I wonder that I never saw under that soft exterior and wide smile, a purpose which to me, at least, is terrifying. What madness came over me in Luxor? I can only feel that I was driven to it by that terrifying experience in the temple – whether it was real or whether I did indeed imagine that hand – that flesh and blood hand – cupping my breast. But I cannot excuse what I did later, in the garden of the hotel. I was made mad by Myles' stubborn refusal to admit there was anything more between us than a temporary desire which we should fight. I would have done anything to break his resistance – and at least my histrionics succeeded. His chivalry overcame his scruples when I rushed into his arms. Later, he came to my room for the first time.*

'I know that his regard for Amory has always held him back from committing himself to me wholeheartedly. But it has always been more than that. He never speaks about his ambivalence towards women in general, which I recognise but unlike most women care nothing about, for on the few occasions we are able to be together, his passion for me is as strong as mine for him.'

Several things about Myles that Harriet had begun to consider ever since Kit's letter suddenly seemed to make sense. She wondered how much Vita had ever known.

The last entry merely said *'Iskander. What am I to do?'*

Squeamish as she felt about doing so, having regard to the

intimate nature of the contents, and how it would implicate Wycombe, Harriet knew she must hand the papers over to the police, though she would wait before giving them to Grigsby until Tom came back with Iskander's written testimony of what had happened the night before he left Charnley. In a call from Egypt Tom had confirmed that Iskander had indeed harboured resentments over the Luxor affair, but had not sought revenge. But, she thought–

The shrill sound of the telephone made her jump a mile. When she lifted it, the measured tones of Oscar Schulman came over the line. "Can you come up to London immediately? Your sister needs you – I think you should be with her, Harriet."

"Oscar? What's happened?"

"It's Wycombe," he said.

Oblivion. Oblivion is all that matters now. Then at last it will be finished.

The water feels shockingly cold as you go in, far colder than you'd imagined it would, despite the clothes you're wearing, though why did you take your shoes off, you old fool? Reflex action, probably, but they would have helped, filled with water and dragged you down. Instead, there's this unspeakable slime underfoot, so disgusting it almost makes you turn back, squelching up through your toes, and there's waterweed twisting itself obscenely around your legs, sharp stones that threaten to cut your feet to ribbons, though you can hardly feel that for the cold – and anyway, what does it matter now? The water will soon come to your waist – chest – chin – into your mouth and nose, until your ears are filled with a great, ceaseless roaring. And then – nothing.

Will there be last minute regrets, causing you to panic and fight helplessly, too late, against what you have chosen to do?

It's not too late to turn back, even now.

But that would defeat the object, go against all you decided to do, years ago, if matters reached this point. Yes, there will certainly be a struggle. A few violent moments when that primitive urge to hold on to life causes you to fight, despite yourself. Courage! The moments will pass. Soon, soon, it will be over. Everything. Over. Done with. All that.

And then there will be nothing left except this useless old body that will sink into the stinking mud at the bottom, where it rightly belongs, along with the frogs and toads or whatever other pondlife lives here. Where it ought to be left to rot and disintegrate, though you know that will not happen. You've read about people who drown. Fish will nibble at your flesh and your eyes, the skin on your hands will wrinkle like that of the washerwoman who used to come once a week to boil linen in the copper and scrub shirt-collars and cuffs against the rubbing board in the steaming tubs. Then gases will fill your body and bring it to the surface, where it will float quietly on the still water, bloated and obscene, until, sooner or later, some unfortunate soul finds it.

But you will at last be absolved of guilt. Maybe I shall at last be forgiven.

Linus Grigsby was not a happy man. He sat in the pub, alone, a pile of unread notes in front of him, staring down into his beer, leaving his pork pie lunch as yet untouched, and contemplated choices he wished he didn't have to make, which of several jobs was to be given priority: certain developments that morning concerning a warehouse job in Wapping and a consignment of stolen sugar, or the publican who'd been attacked and robbed late last night, on his way to deposit his day's takings in a safe-deposit. Interesting rumours had also reached Grigsby that one of his old enemies had recently extended his criminal activities by entering the West End pornography business. They were all cases more demanding of his immediate attention – not to say more to his inclination – than the Jardine affair. Yet he was uneasy with leaving that one, unsatisfactory as it continued to be, simmering indefinitely on the back burner. For one thing, the Press had got their teeth into it , and scenting scandal, however old, and there not being much in the way of juicy news at the moment, they were prepared to prod it back into life. Society stories – even minor society – were always newsworthy, and this one had the added fillip of gruesome overtones by way of the corpse being mummified, and a hint of salacious sex – for had not Beatrice Jardine, exemplar of white, upper class xenophobia, been assumed to have run away with *an Egyptian?* The Press were not about to let go this titbit, in fact they were all set to have a field day. And although the investigation was yet in its infancy, several letters to *The Times* had already been brought to Grigsby's attention, pertinently demanding whether justice was not being allowed to lapse, hinting that questions should be asked in high places and alerting the powers that be to the dangers of letting the matter slide into oblivion.

But Grigsby had a nasty feeling that part of the problem lay within himself. However he might hate unfinished business, and however much he might privately think the solution was clear as day, the result of the old eternal triangle, he couldn't rid himself of the feeling that something, somewhere was escaping him. He'd had a clear picture in his own mind from the beginning of what had happened on the night of June 21st 1910: to wit, Amory Jardine surprising his wife in flagrante delicto with her lover, and killing, first her, then, later, himself. Nothing so far had given him cause to think otherwise – except for the question of why Jardine hadn't killed the lover also while he was at it. But there it was, a niggle that remained at the back of his mind.

He sighed and turned to the notes. It was all there, in his

own confident, sprawling handwriting and in Fairchild's neatly typed pages, all of it pointing to the fact that the clue to the murder lay in the nature of the victim herself. On the surface she'd led an apparently blameless life – though not when you came down to it. For one thing – why had everyone been so willing to believe, when she had disappeared, that she had bolted with the Egyptian? It came back, every time, to Valery Akhmet Iskander. Grigsby groaned at the thought of what interviewing him at second hand, through the Cairo police, would entail, because of course he couldn't envisage his superintendent giving sanction to any suggestion that Grigsby should go out there himself. Knowing only too well, from his service days in Italy and various other war zones, the wild and woolly excitability that in his opinion stood for competence in most foreign police forces, Grigsby couldn't imagine faring any better with the Egyptian authorities. He thought, though, that he might have to brace himself for doing battle with them in the end. There was no getting away from the fact that Iskander had left Charnley in suspiciously hasty circumstances and, Grigsby asked himself, what had the fellow been doing, staying there in the first place? The Jardines had been nothing if not conventional in their choice of friends and associates and no satisfactory explanation for such an unusual house guest had yet been put forward.

But as to murdering his hostess...For one thing, the padre, Sacheverell, had seen her in a compromising situation on the balcony of her room with Wycombe at about twelve-thirty, near as dammit, if he was to be believed.

Myles Randolph, Lord Wycombe. He was the wild card, able to be given any value the holder pleases. The family friend, the valued uncle. Grigsby had known other 'uncles' like that. Beatrice Jardine's daughter, Vita, however, had sworn that she and her young man had heard sounds coming from the unoccupied room where the corpse had eventually been found only half an hour later than Sacheverell had seen the lovers together on her balcony. Moreover, Beatrice had been alive at about 2 a.m. when Vita had heard her maid, Hallam, saying goodnight to her. This established parameters for the time of death, but didn't necessarily, in Grigsby's book, exonerate Wycombe. There was nothing to prevent him having gone back after that and killing her.

He pushed the file away impatiently. If Wycombe hadn't killed her, then who else – apart from the husband, still odds-on favourite with Grigsby – was left as a suspect? Out of the people staying there that night were only realistically left Rose Jessamy and Kit Sacheverell himself, and despite the reservations he'd voiced to Tom Verrier, he didn't lay much on the theory of that young woman as murderess.

The interview with Sacheverell, the padre, Father Christopher as he apparently wished to be known, had got them nowhere, apart from establishing that he'd slept at Charnley that night and for some reason left the next morning by the earliest possible train, walking several miles across country to catch a main line train not subject to the vagaries of Sunday timetables as was the branch line that served Charnley. It was not inconceivable. A few miles would have been nothing to him. He had, after all, been a young and presumably fit man. But Grigsby had sensed something behind that abrupt departure that wasn't being revealed. As a suspect, he'd had means and opportunity, but as for motive? He'd been a great favourite of Beatrice Jardine's, apparently. She had been a surrogate mother to him. As likely to suspect the dead son, Marcus. Yet Grigsby had been left wondering.

Were they, after all, left with Rose Jessamy as a suspect? Means and opportunity, yes, but again no motive. Those missing garnets still bothered Grigsby, but he couldn't fairly see her strangling Beatrice for them – and she had, in fact, every reason to wish to keep her employer alive. She had the best means and opportunity of disposing of the body, but anyone reasonably handy and familiar with her techniques could have hit upon that hiding place.

Which brought another niggle: as Harriet Jardine had pointed out, her mother was no light weight, and unless she'd been murdered in situ, it would have needed at least two people to manhandle her body into the west wing.

With a sigh, Grigsby took another swig of beer. He pulled his plate towards him, bit succulently into his pork pie and chewed, staring down at the foam sliding down the sides of his pint glass. He speared a pickled onion and popped it in to join the pie. Half a mo' he thought all at once, galvanised, his masticating halted – how about this, how about the maid, saying goodnight to her mistress –

The pub door burst open and Fairchild hurried in, a look of controlled excitement on his patrician features Grigsby swallowed the onion, whole. "What the hell?"

"Wait for it, Guv. They've found another body at Charnley."

He didn't get the reaction he expected. "Not another mummy?" Grigsby asked flatly, when he could.

"No, this time it's a floater. In the lake."

"She left a letter, Mrs Kaplan," said Fairchild later. "With her handbag and shoes, by the edge of the lake. The missing garnets were in the bag, too."

"Oh, those garnets! I found them in her – I found her gloating over them years and years ago. It was how I got her to stay with me all that time. She called it blackmail, but I preferred to think of it as self-preservation." The old woman suddenly looked a hundred. "Who's going to look after me now?"

"Perhaps you'd like to see the letter."

"I don't know that I would." But all the same, she took it

in trembling fingers and began to read.

"The Bible tells us that God is not mocked: for whatsoever a man soweth, that shall he also reap.

This was one of the first things I learned from my religion. That you must take responsibility for your own actions in life. So I make no claim for anyone's sympathy over what happened to Mrs Beatrice Jardine, except to say that what I did was for the master, Mr Amory Jardine. He had never given me anything much more than a kindly glance, I was simply his wife's maid, always there, but he was a good man and I couldn't stand by any longer and see him deceived. Also, I never forgot how he'd helped Fred after that spot of bother he'd been in. Fred was a handful and no mistake, but I was very fond of him. He'd always stuck up for me against my stepfather, who was a sight too free with his fists when he'd had a drop, and he wouldn't allow his brothers to make me into the family drudge.

Beatrice was four years older than me, but we played together when we were children. Until Miss grew up and went away and became a society lady, I used to go up to the Big House when I was sent for – though only because I was told to go, not because I wanted to. They said she was lonely – but how could I believe that, living in that beautiful house with a nanny and a governess and dozens of servants, whatever she wanted to eat and cupboards full of toys and nice clothes to wear? She was so pretty, too, with golden ringlets and a pink and white complexion. Whereas I – well, I was only eight years old when it all began, and I still believed in magic, that one day I might be transformed from an ugly duckling into a fairy princess. But being with Miss made me aware that I never would be. I soon learned to read in people's faces what they thought when they saw us together – and I knew by the way she smiled that she saw it, too, and liked it. But even if the positions had been reversed, if she'd been the plain one and me the beauty, she would still have had the advantage over me, with her money and her upbringing. And her nature, that took it all for granted.

I never wanted to be a lady's maid, not to anyone, least of all to Miss. My spirit was too independent for that – even my stepfather couldn't beat it out of me – but when she offered me the position when she became Mrs Jardine I knew I'd be a fool not to accept. My mother had died, and the only prospect I could see ahead of me was a lifetime of skivvying for that household of great, hulking, working men – Fred excepted. No one would ever marry me. I'd inherited most of the ugliness of the family (and all its sourness, according to my stepfather). Going into service was the only way I could see out of a life I hated. The difficulty would be in controlling the rebelliousness Nature had endowed me with. But I vowed, with God's help, I would learn.

I knew how lucky I was to have the chance. Pampered and lapped in luxury as Madam was, never lifting a finger to help herself, she was no worse than any other ladies of her class and upbringing, I suppose, most of them having less regard for servants than if they were the carpets they trod on. But the position of lady's maid was easy, compared to that of other servants in the house. One of absolute luxury after what I'd been used to. Washing delicate silk and lace underclothes and blouses by hand, ironing them while they were still damp to bring them back to perfection, was about the most strenuous task I'd be asked to do. There was a lot of sewing, small repairs and alterations and so on. I was even allowed to make some of her simpler clothes, since my mother, who'd been a sewing woman up at the Hall, had taught me from an early age to be handy with a needle. There were plenty of perks, too, especially in the way of cast-offs. Not that I would ever make a fool of myself trying to wear any of Madam's clothes, should she ever see fit to give any to me (which in fact she never did) but she was generous enough in tossing over to me presents she'd been given that hadn't pleased her. And half-read books, stockings which only needed a darn or two, silk underclothes that I could make over, an umbrella or a leather handbag she'd grown tired of. When she went up to Mount Street in London, I went with her of course, and on visits to other country houses, where I thought I might meet other women in similar positions, though I never managed to make friends with any. We visited interesting places, here and abroad – the best of which was Egypt, where it all began. That was where I maided for Mrs Kaplan, Lady Glendinning as she was then.

At least *she* didn't expect you to be at her beck and call, day and night. She was kind to me, in her own fashion. (I know she has always thought I've stayed with her all these years because she found the garnets one day when she was snooping in my room, and blackmailed me into not leaving, but the truth is, after Beatrice Jardine, I liked working for her. She's always talked to me as if I was a human being, and we even had a laugh or two together sometimes.) But the time in Egypt didn't last long. It was soon back to Charnley, and the old routine, the children – and Mr Jardine.

How can I explain what he was like? He was such a nice man, always pleasant, though I guessed he had worries of his own that he didn't share with his wife and family. All the same, he found time and the money to order that grand birthday party for her.

What a party that was! One that I was never likely to forget.

Long after they'd all gone home and I'd been dismissed for the night, Madam decided to send for me again. I was already in bed and fast asleep when the bell woke me. I was bone-weary after dancing attendance for hours, being there ready with pins and needle and thread for ladies who'd had their trains trodden on, or for those who needed hairpins to fix their hair because their maids hadn't done it properly in the first place. A box of headache powders ready to hand, a flask of eau de cologne and another of smelling salts. I'd waited for Madam to come up to her bedroom and then I'd helped her to undress, as far as she wanted me to. But at last I got to my own room, and fell into bed exhausted. When the bell rang I looked at the clock and saw it was twenty to two. I'd only been in bed an hour! What was she doing, still awake at that time?

Well, quite often she was up half the night, playing cards or gossiping and tittle-tattling with her friends. Of course, she could stay in bed all the next day if she wanted to, and I don't suppose it ever occurred to her that I had to be up betimes, just in case she took it into her head to rise early for once and needed me to help her into one of those extravagant outfits of hers. But that night, she'd sent me to bed an hour ago. Well, that was Madam all over. Never thinking of anyone else, exactly as she was when she was a girl. No one else in the world but Beatrice – though what with those sweet smiles and never losing her temper, no one ever suspected how selfish she was. Except her husband. But he loved her in spite of it.

The bell rang again as I was throwing on some clothes. I hurried to her room, by then half expecting some emergency, such as that when she'd lost the child.

I soon found she'd sent for me to do nothing more than undo her necklace, her birthday present from Mr Jardine. A beautiful thing it was, garnets set in marcasite, hanging from a thin silver chain, part of a matching set. There was something wrong with the clasp, it just wouldn't open. I struggled with it but it was stuck, fast. "You'll have to have it cut off tomorrow," I told her.

"Cut off? Well, then, I must sleep with it round my neck all night! Like an odalisque." She smiled and put her hands to where the necklace lay against her white throat and stroked it.

I had no idea – then – what an odalisque was but I had my answer as to why she wasn't yet in bed and asleep, like any other good Christian soul. She was still undressed, with nothing on under the black jap-silk kimono. Her stockings were flung across the room and her silk chemise had slid in a pool to the floor where she'd stepped out of it. Her eyes were brilliant and her cheeks flushed, when she moved she seemed languorous and heavy. The little smile stayed at the corners of her mouth.

He had been to her. She thought no one knew, on those occasions. But I knew, always. I had the sense to keep my mouth shut, but there isn't much a maid doesn't know about her mistress. And the master, her husband, Amory – oh yes. Well, if he didn't know, he must have been blind. About his friend Lord Wycombe – and the shameful way she flirted with young Kit. There had been others, from time to time, as well. I don't think he ever knew about the disgraceful way she'd treated that Iskander, but I'm sure he suspected *something* had gone on that time in Egypt, the way everyone was subdued when he arrived, the way the trip back to Cairo down the Nile was cancelled without any reasonable explanation.

And for some reason, I couldn't stand the thought of all this any longer. I heard myself say, as if we were still girls together, what I'd always wanted to say to her then, but never dared: "You should be ashamed of yourself, Miss." And when she stared at me, all haughty and those blue eyes like chips of ice, I added, for good measure, "A good man like that."

"What? What was that you said?"

It was too late to go back.

* * *

I hadn't hated her, not really. She had her good points, like everyone else, and I don't suppose she could help her nature, any more than I can help mine. I stared down at her, lying on the pretty flowered carpet. She was the ugly one now. Her lovely face was all mottled and swollen, and for a while I couldn't take in what I'd done. How I'd stood behind her and taken up the slack of the necklace and twisted it until it bit into the soft white flesh, and she finally went limp.

And then I heard Mr Jardine in the next room, his hand on the doorknob, the door opening. There hadn't been much of a struggle, but I suppose he must have heard something. I bent down over her with some idea of covering up her body. She was still breathing. Oh, thank God, thank God! My own breath nearly stopped with relief, but I cried out to him and he rushed into the room, pushing me aside. He began to try to revive her and all at once I felt such a desperate urge to vomit I had to turn aside to use the slop pail under the wash-stand. I thought my stomach would never finish heaving, but all the time I could think of nothing else except to thank my maker that she was still alive. But when at last the shaming sickness stopped, and I turned around, expecting her breathing to have come back to normal, I found the master was still kneeling over her, his face as white as chalk.

"It's all over. Go and get Copley. Find your brother, we need his help."

He never gave me a word of blame, or asked me why it had happened. I expect he knew.

It was Fred's suggestion to put her body behind the chimney-breast in the west wing room. He'd helped the young woman painter enough to know what to do. He was handy, and he'd always been quick to learn. As soon they were gone, I did as I'd been told and packed a valise with things, as if she'd suddenly taken it into her head to go away. (We had to leave the fine details of this plan until later, but it turned out to have been a good idea, for afterwards, we came across Iskander in the conservatory and learned he was leaving first thing the next morning, so it looked every bit as though she'd run off with *him*.)

I grabbed a pile of underwear from the drawer and threw it over the valise to cover it, picked the armful up and opened the door. Imagine my shock when I saw Miss Vita coming towards me. Without even thinking about it, I turned and said "Goodnight then, Madam," into the empty room behind me, and with my free hand closed the door. Miss Vita appeared not to notice anything out of the ordinary; I think she was too busy finding some excuse for being out there herself, fully dressed, in the middle of the night. At any rate, she said nothing. She was no doubt as glad to escape as I was.

There was no sleep for me that night. I was worried over what Madam called her Egyptian journal. I had made it my business to see what it was she'd been so busy writing those last few days, so I knew that if anyone else came across it and saw how terrified she'd been of him, they'd never believe she'd left Charnley of her own accord, with him. First thing in the morning, I went back to her room and cut out those last pages. It was then I saw the rest of the garnets, lying on the dressing table.

That was something else: if she *had* run away, as we had to make them believe, she would surely have taken the whole set, so I slipped them into my pocket. The thought of wanting them for myself never entered my head. Me, wearing such things? For a moment, I contemplated taking some of her more valuable jewellery as well, to make it look even better, but I knew if Fred found out I'd done that, he'd want to sell it, and that would ruin all our plans.

As it was, everything went as we hoped.

When the family at last accepted that she really had gone, I left Charnley quietly, without any fuss, before they had the chance to dismiss me. No one tried to stop me, or ever came looking for me. I doubt whether they noticed I'd gone. I couldn't ask for a character reference in the circumstances, and for a while I wondered how I was going to earn my bread. Then I met Mrs Kaplan's ex-maid by chance and heard she was looking for a replacement.

I have been punished. I have prayed for forgiveness, but God hasn't yet forgiven me such a great sin. He has chastised me by giving me a long, weary life in which I have lived that night over and over again. But I can take no more. My greatest remorse is that I caused that good man, Mr Jardine, such sorrow that he was forced to end his own life.

"And there we have it," Grigsby had said heavily, after this had been read out to the assembled family. "A full confession. Backed up by Professor Iskander's testimony, confirmed by what Lady Wycombe said. All the same–"

He broke off as his gaze rested on Harriet Jardine He wasn't a man for sparing people's feelings unduly but sometimes, he thought, there was a case for doing so. When it came to the point where pursuit of non-existent evidence to vindicate his own theories would lead them exactly nowhere, expediency won hands down. He looked Harriet straight in the eye. She didn't flinch. Then he said quietly, "That's how it happened. Apart from one or two loose ends to be tied up, the case is closed."

"But that's not how it happened," Harriet said at last, to the passenger in the seat beside her. "Not really, and Grigsby knows that."

Kit didn't immediately answer. She looked at his strong, beaky profile and also fell silent, miserably aware that perhaps she ought not to have spoken. But she would never be able to unburden herself to either of her sisters, and it had unexpectedly come to her that the one person she might talk to was Kit. It had given her a sharp stab of unbounded joy, like a light illuminating the dark misery of the last days, to feel that perhaps their differences were at last over.

They were now driving back from Wycombe's funeral. She was heading for London, where she had business regarding the purchase of the cottage. Kit had unexpectedly turned up at the funeral with Daisy and Guy, but had begged a lift back to town with Harriet.

The funeral, in accordance with Wycombe's wishes, had been a quiet and simple affair, and he now lay buried at Stoke Wycombe next to his ancestors. There had been few people there apart from the family, for he was so old he had outlived most of his generation.

He had died quietly, although the end had come suddenly The shock of recent events, said Vita, had taken their toll of his energy and possibly the will to continue living. One day after lunch, sitting quietly in front of the fire with the manuscript of a proposed article on pre-war German painters which he was preparing on his knee, he had fallen asleep and simply never woken up.

"We talked before he died, Harriet," Vita had told her. "I did as Oscar had advised – and no, I don't blame myself that it had upset him, just the opposite. He was relieved to have cleared the air, and so was I. He had, you know, been determined to keep me from finding out about any feelings he'd had for Mama, to avoid causing me pain, but in the end...well, the last days were more like the time when we were first married – and after the boys died – when he was so – so kind and loving to me. And I'm so thankful that at least we didn't part with anger and recrimination."

She still looked strained and preoccupied but she seemed to have regained her balance. She was now a very rich woman. Wycombe, having no heirs and there being no entailments on his estate, had left everything to her. She talked of selling Stoke Wycombe, when the endless business of document signing and legal shenanigans was over. Meanwhile, Schulman was taking care of her. The future, for Vita, was not as bleak as it had been. She had found a certain peace at last, which was more than Harriet yet had.Throughout the funeral, she had been frozen into calm but now that the anaesthetic necessary to keep up appearances was wearing off, the pain was well-nigh unbearable.

"Harriet," Kit said at last, "Talk to me if you wish."

She turned towards him a face he thought he would remember for the rest of his life for its mixture of shame and uncertainty, and such grief that he couldn't help sliding his arm along the back of the seat and squeezing her shoulder, the nearest thing to putting comforting arms around her that he could make in the circumstances.

She acknowledged it with a hunch of the shoulder that brought his hand to her cheek.

This was no good. She couldn't drive like this, seeing the road through a lake of tears. She drove on for a few hundred yards until she came to a convenient lay-by where she could pull the car in behind a large white furniture van. There she sat for a while, trying to find a steady voice. He waited until she could speak.

"She was breathing, Kit, when Hallam turned round to be

sick. But she was dead when she turned back."

"Well, yes. Your father tried to revive her but she was too far gone."

She shook her head. "Do you believe all that? Do you really believe it?"

Please don't say we shall never know, she prayed silently. Please don't say that.

He was silent for a very long time. "No, my dear, I don't think I do. But whether we believe it or not, that's the official verdict. We can do nothing but bring more misery by trying to cast doubts on something that can never be proved, one way or the other."

There was a long way to go before she could accept that, but he had sounded so strong and confident that, just a little, she felt a flicker of something that might be hope, and she knew that he was right, and that she'd been right to tell him what was troubling her.

"It all seems to have been so pointless. That business at Luxor, it was all something and nothing, after all, blown up in her mind – and in Iskander's too, I suppose. Though I suppose it all began long before that. They both had such unhappy childhoods – my mother, and Hallam. They both needed so much to be loved."

"Going back to first causes is an unprofitable business, Harriet."

They sat looking at the graffiti scrawled in the grime on the back of the furniture van. Advice to Clean It; a less polite injunction; a heart with an arrow and Ted loves Susan. "At the moment, I cannot imagine how I'm going to live with this for the rest of my life, but somehow I suppose I shall manage."

"Oh yes, Harriet, you will. You've always managed," he said sadly. "You'll start again."

"An old woman like me?"

"Don't say that. But don't bury yourself away from

everyone, Harriet. That's not you." He hesitated. "You and I, Harriet—"

She said, shaking her head, "It won't do, Kit, not after all this time."

She had been expecting this, and perhaps he had, too, for he said immediately, "Then come and work with me. We can still be friends, can't we? We're desperately in need of someone like you in the parish and I have room in my vicarage. What's a woman of your capabilities doing buried in the country, *marking papers*, for heavens' sake?"

Though she was able to smile weakly, he'd made his point. She let him go on. "I know there's a job going in the Diocesan Finance Department. Just the ticket for you."

The idea grew and was suddenly tempting. Not that job, perhaps, but something similar, challenging. She would still buy the cottage, and rent it until such time as she retired. But she was a long way off that yet.

Come on Harriet! Life goes on, after all, as they say. She dried her eyes and blew her nose and turned the key in the ignition, and started off again in the direction of London.